BLYTHE SPIRIT

Judith Miller is half of the duo behind the bestselling *Miller's Price Guides*, including the *Miller's Antiques Price Guide* which now sells 150,000 copies a year. She has written books on interior design and period decorating, including *Victorian Style* and *Period Finishes and Effects*. She makes regular appearances on television and radio and lives in North London.

Also by Judith Miller

How To Make Money Out Of Antiques

Miller's Antiques Price Guide
Miller's Picture Price Guide
Miller's Collectables Price Guide
Miller's Collectors Cars
Miller's Classic Motorcycles

Understanding Antiques
Pocket Dictionary Of Antiques
Pocket Antiques Fact File

Period Details
Period Style
Country Style
Period Finishes and Effects
Victorian Style
Period Fireplaces
Period Kitchens

BLYTHE SPIRIT

Judith Miller

Mandarin

A Mandarin Paperback
BLYTHE SPIRIT

First published in Great Britain 1996
by Mandarin Paperbacks
and William Heinemann Ltd
imprints of Reed International Books Ltd
Michelin House, 81 Fulham Road, London SW3 6RB
and Auckland, Melbourne, Singapore and Toronto

Copyright © Vista 2000 Limited 1996
The author has asserted her moral rights

A CIP catalogue record for this title
is available from the British Library
ISBN 0 7493 1895 3

Phototypeset by Intype, London
Printed and bound in Great Britain
by Cox & Wyman Ltd, Reading, Berks

I

The gavel dropped. 'All done at five thousand five hundred? Your number please, sir? Two Three Eight, thank you. Lot number forty-five, a 1933 Bluthner grand piano in an ebonised case . . .'

Sally Blythe looked at the four sheets of paper in her hand then up at the auctioneer.

'I have numerous commissions on this one and can start the bidding at two thousand pounds. Two thousand? Thank you.' He nodded right and left as the offers continued.

'Two thousand two hundred . . . two thousand four hundred . . . six hundred . . . eight hundred . . .'

She watched intrigued as catalogues or numbered cards flicked discreetly in the direction of the podium, trying not to move in case she somehow became involved in the bidding.

'Three thousand, and a fresh bid . . . three thousand two hundred . . .' The verbal ping-pong went on while Sally peered out from under the brim of the big black hat she'd put on partly because of the weather but mostly to hide the hair she hadn't had time to wash that morning. At the time, she'd thought she'd better look smart, as she'd expected the other auction-goers to be. But to her surprise, they'd turned out to be terribly ordinary-looking – grey baggy jumpers,

1

old checked shirts and Marks & Spencer rain coats. After the first fifteen minutes, she'd realised that you didn't have to look well-heeled to be taken seriously.

'I have three thousand six hundred with me,' the auctioneer was saying. 'All done at three thousand six hundred?' The gavel dropped again.

Sally scribbled the figure on to her catalogue in the way she'd seen everyone else doing, as soon as a sale was closed. She'd been quick to observe and adopt the posture of a seasoned trader, when in actual fact, she'd never been to an auction in her life and was only here now because she thought she ought to get a feel for the thing before she let the one item of any value that she owned in the world go under the hammer.

Her eye moved down to the description of the next lot. 'Teddy bear, c. 1920, sixteen inches high', the catalogue stated. As she looked up, the sad old fellow was being plonked on a chair at the front of the room. Battered and bruised and with one ear slightly adrift, he looked like something out of a children's picture book. Threadbare Fred bear, she thought to herself, remembering the nickname her father had given to the teddy he'd kept, as a kind of mascot, on a shelf in his study. It was funny how he'd had it all those years and she'd just accepted it as a memento of childhood. It had taken until recently to find out that the toy had been given to him when he was no more than a few weeks old by the father he would never quite remember, because the mustard gas that hadn't succeeded in killing him during the Great War, finally did for him three years later. Why hadn't her father ever told her? Why hadn't she ever asked? It seemed a silly detail. But like the other unanswered questions that had been bothering her since he died, suddenly, and to her abject sorrow, they seemed important now.

Sally looked around the large, dingy hall with its cold grey walls and serious marble pillars. She'd been standing there for almost an hour and still hadn't got over how bleak and impersonal it was, how gloomy it felt with its clutter of furniture, pottery, pictures in frames, boxes and bric-à–brac, all of which must once have been someone's prized possessions. She'd imagined that the auction house would be a bright and exciting place, not some cavernous room with the atmosphere of a covered market. She wondered how she would feel when that table her father had left her was just another item set out for sale; one of the many left lumped together in long rows, waiting their turn in the lottery.

But I need the money, she told herself, as she fought the lump that was rising in her throat. Things were too desperate for there to be another way and she knew that sentiment would have to take second place to sense from now on.

The teddy bear was being announced. Sally looked from it to the foot of the podium, where a crystal vase full of daffodils and tulips stood on a table, the one splash of colour in the room. Her spirits lifted a fraction. She began to study the auctioneer. He was a young man of about thirty, tall and thin, with light brown hair that would have looked better for a trim. How odd, she thought, as she watched him turn the gavel in the palm of his hand before opening the bidding, I'd have expected someone older, somehow. More an Arthur Negus type . . .

'Starting at one hundred pounds,' he was off again, 'one hundred and twenty, in the middle.' But before long, interest in the teddy bear seemed to wane. He scanned the room with a modicum of hope. 'All done at one hundred and thirty?' he asked, finally, raising the gavel again.

'And one hundred and forty from a fresh place.'

Sally's attention was taken by the woman who had made the new bid. As she glanced towards her, a ray of sun filtered in from one of the long windows that edged the top of the room and settled on the woman's light red hair, making her stand out from the crowd. Sally looked at the checked sports

3

jacket she was wearing over a dark purple waistcoat and blue denim jeans and wondered why the whole lot didn't clash. Instead, they almost went together naturally in the sort of way clothes did in the fashion shots she saw in women's magazines. It was a look she'd always supposed was terrific if you were a seven-stone super waif who had just turned nineteen. And yet here it was being worn with considerable aplomb by a woman who had to be in her late-forties.

The thought hit Sally like a slap in the face. In the back of her mind, she'd known that she'd been letting her standards slide these last eighteen months. It irritated her every time she looked in the mirror. The same way the sound of her own voice irritated her, badgering her sons to get dressed and ready for school, or to eat their tea, or go to bed. On and on, like a cracked record she'd ask, cajole, then finally give way to raising her voice. It was all so unlike her.

As she stood staring at the red-headed woman Sally remembered how only that morning she'd gone to the wardrobe in search of a decent suit and blouse and found, to her dismay, that most had a button missing, a hem partly down or a mark in an obvious place. The dismay had given way to alarm and then anger. She'd always been such a snappy dresser. Now she was the proud owner of a cupboard full of lovely clothes that were unwearable. And why? Because she never had time for herself, that's why. She never seemed to stop worrying, to stop and consider what was actually happening to her, because she'd got herself into a bind. Problems with the kids, problems with money ... there never seemed to be an end to it. The divorce and its aftermath had dragged her down and she'd let it drag her down, instead of fighting it. She'd let herself get trapped in a vicious circle.

Well enough, now, she promised herself, once and for all. I'm definitely going to get a grip on myself.

4

Her mind went back to the table and the money she might make from it. Although she had no real idea of its value, she'd thought it might fetch a thousand pounds or so. But compared with some of the things she could see around her, she began to think that it might be worth more. She started to take particular note of the price guide given in her catalogue for similar pieces which were up for auction, circling figures and underlining descriptions as she went down the list. But when she'd finished marking out the first two pages of the catalogue in this way, she came to the conclusion that there was no rhyme or reason to any of it. Age seemed to bear some relation to the prices given for the various pieces that were detailed there, but not to the extent that she had expected, and much of the other information given was meaningless to her. The more she tried to make sense of it, the more confused she became. It was obvious that she would have to go much deeper into the whole subject to make the most out of selling her table.

A frisson of excitement went round the room. Sally left her notes and looked back up at the auctioneer.

'Fifteen thousand, gentleman in the middle by the post,' he was saying, above a ripple of whispers.

Sally craned her neck to see who was standing against the pillar a few feet ahead of her, but her view was obscured by the heads of other people taking a similar interest.

'Fifteen thousand five hundred . . .' The auctioneer jabbed the biro in his hand to left and right as he picked out the bidders.

Sally glanced at her catalogue to find out what was causing the stir. It turned out to be a large black settle and six chairs, two of them carvers. They were described as eighteenth-century Flemish pieces and the approximate upper limit of their value was stated as seven thousand pounds. Sally went on tip-toe to see over into the next row, where the furniture in question stood unceremoniously between a bookcase and a large brass bird cage. From where she was, the pieces looked to be in pretty bad shape, fit, she thought, to be thrown away or given to the rag-and-bone man. Chunks of horse hair were sticking out through tears in the upholstery, bits were missing from the white inlay that decorated the chair backs. How on earth could things in that condition be worth more than fifteen thousand pounds?

She could see a man in a red sweater holding his catalogue up to the auctioneer and not moving it a fraction as the bidding went up. For some inexplicable reason, it was obvious that he was determined to have that set of furniture, come what may.

'Fifteen thousand seven hundred . . . eight hundred . . .'

Wow! Sally thought. The auction room had suddenly come to life and she could feel her adrenaline rising. On impulse, she turned her catalogue over and started to sketch out the shape of the chairs, adding notes and arrows to remind herself of the finer details. From what she could see, the inlay seemed to picture a family group of a man, a woman and two teenage boys. They were all in a type of costume familiar to her from school history books. The sort that was worn around the Civil War period. She strained to get a better view but could only see two figures on the back of the settle in any detail. The man, whom she took to be the father, was wearing a large plumed hat and knee-high boots, very much in the cavalier style. The woman's dress, though, was rather less distinct. Sally could just make out the low-cut neckline and three-quarter-length sleeves. The rest was a blur.

'Damn,' she muttered, frustrated that she couldn't see more. She thought of moving round to the next row to take a better look but couldn't quite summon up the nerve. Instead, she went on sketching and jotting, furiously noting down everything that she thought might be of any relevance along the side of her drawing.

'Eight hundred and fifty . . . nine hundred. Anyone make it sixteen thousand? All done at fifteen thousand nine hundred.' A murmur of surprise went up from the crowd as the auctioneer brought the gavel down and the man in the red sweater secured his trophy. Sally watched him give his number and then quietly note the sale figure down on his catalogue with a nonchalance that defied scrutiny. She stared at him, then at the settle and chairs. There seemed no logic at all in what she had just witnessed, yet the bidders must surely have known what they were doing. The thing intrigued her. She conjured up a picture of her table in her mind and weighed it, merit for merit, against the others that were standing about, looking for buyers. It seemed to her that hers was in a different class, though she had no proof of it. And even if there were proof, she had no yard stick by which to measure it against the other lots for sale, in terms of value.

Suddenly, she wanted to know about every item in the room, all the tables and chairs, the cupboards, the wardrobes, all the fixtures, fittings and furniture that had seemed no more than the mundane artefacts of everyday life until that moment, right down to the last silly little nicknack.

Yet how to have it make sense? There had to be some way.

Sally folded her catalogue slowly as she realised that there was a means by which the mystery might yet be solved. There'd been an antiques guide in the window of the book store she'd passed in the High Street. And now seemed like a good time to invest in it.

A squall of fine rain gusted in from the sea front as Sally picked her way across the pavement through a barrage of umbrellas. Clinging on to her hat, she crossed the road and headed for a side street where she knew there was a café that served a half decent meal. Silently cursing the weather, she gripped the paper bag which was in her other hand and hoped that her book wasn't getting ruined. Worthing, she decided, as she neared her destination, was definitely not the place to be on a wet Wednesday in February.

The café on the corner was already crowded with shoppers taking a lunch-time break. Peering in through the steamy window, Sally couldn't tell if there was a seat available or not.

No use standing here like a drowned rat, she thought, as another gust of rain soaked her legs. Might as well go in and take a chance.

The queue shuffled forward, damp and uninterested, as Sally shoved her package under her arm and rearranged her handbag. The trays were all gone and she could already see that it was going to be difficult to juggle a sandwich, plate and can of Coke with her one free hand. She ended up crashing all three down in a heap in front of the woman at the cash register while she rummaged in her bag for her purse.

The checkout woman seemed more than usually out of sorts that particular afternoon.

'Three pounds fifty,' she said, sullenly, putting her hand out under Sally's nose. Sally had been to the place often enough to offer a pleasant smile while she tried to find the change. But the pinched mouth, which was caked with a horrible ice pink lipstick, showed no sign of a response. Sally paid quickly and pushed her way through to a table by the window which had just come free.

She took her seat with some relief and dumped her handbag by her feet and began to organise things so that she could read as well as eat. Settling in a little, she peeled the sodden paper off her newly purchased book and was glad to find that the cover was still intact. She opened it, skipped through the introduction, then started turning the pages. It struck her immediately that, until that second, she'd had no idea that there were so many types and styles of furniture.

Hardly anything answered to a simple description. There was, for instance, no such thing as a cabinet. There were bureau cabinets, display cabinets, cabinets on stands, side cabinets, chiffoniers . . . the list seemed endless. If she hadn't already become so fascinated with it all, she'd have wished she hadn't started.

She took a bite of her sandwich and ploughed on through the arm chairs, dining chairs, chests, commodes, wardrobes, desks, dumb waiters, mirrors and frames, screens, sofas and settees, until she realised that she'd never be able to keep the whole thing in her head. There was just too much to take in, and she hadn't even touched on tables yet.

She carried on turning pages, nevertheless, entranced by the colour photographs of sublimely beautiful things. Half a sandwich later, she was still so engrossed in her book that she didn't bother to look up when a man walked over from the counter, tray in hand.

'Is this seat taken?' said a quiet voice.

'No, help yourself.'

He'd taken off his overcoat and settled himself into the chair, before she noticed that she was sitting opposite a red sweater. Not any old red sweater. *The* red sweater. She looked at it, then at the man wearing it, and slowly began to blush.

'I'm sorry,' he said, 'did I catch you?'

'No, no,' she replied quickly, moving her legs aside under the table anyway. 'It's perfectly all right.'

There was an embarrassing silence as he returned to his Shepherd's Pie. Damn! Sally thought, putting the book with its obvious cover, white with a broad red stripe, face down on the table. She tried flicking through a couple more pages but felt too uncomfortable to get into it. A moment later, she closed the book and started toying with the remains of her sandwich, pushing it around the plate with her forefinger while she tried to gather her wits.

'Not too sparkling?'

'Pardon?'

'The sandwich.'

'Oh, it's okay. I'm . . . er . . . not very hungry.' A few moments passed before she added. 'How's the pie?'

'Not bad.'

'Oh.' Her hand moved to her Coke glass. Soon, she was twiddling with that, too. She was aching to ask about the settle and chairs she'd seen him buy and was casting around for a way to keep the conversation going. She was caught between not wanting to sound nosy and her own pride. It was not until the man began to look as if he was ready to leave that Sally finally threw caution to the wind.

'Excuse my saying,' she started coyly, 'but I couldn't help noticing you at the auction this morning.'

'Really? Must have been the hat.'

Sally was confused for a moment. He hadn't been wearing a hat. But then she looked up, saw his smile and realised that he was teasing her.

'Was my hat so conspicuous?' she asked, feeling rather embarrassed.

'Actually, I thought it looked a treat,' he replied.

'Thank you.'

She grinned and began to relax a little. 'I, er, was rather interested in that set of furniture you bought.'

'I noticed that.'

'Pardon?'

'I noticed you were interested.'

She thought he must have seen her taking notes.

'Not as a purchase, you understand,' she explained, 'more . . . um . . . as a piece.'

'Oh?' A shutter seemed to go down between them as she glanced innocently across the table.

'It looked so very unusual.'

'An unusual set, yes,' he said, in a way that indicated that

10

that was as much as she was about to get out of him on the matter.

'I'm sorry, I didn't mean to pry.' She looked away, uneasily aware that he was studying the book that lay on the table in front of her.

'I'm surprised you need that,' he said, nodding towards it.

'I'm interested in antiques.'

'That's why you were bidding me up on the settle and chairs, I take it?'

Sally's jaw dropped.

'Come on,' he added, 'I saw you. Every time I turned round you were nodding towards the podium.'

'I did no such . . .'

'Did you come for yourself or for your husband?' he asked, brusquely.

'I don't have a husband,' she said, looking angrily down at the wedding ring that she'd been turning around on her finger. 'I'm divorced, if you must know. I keep the ring on because I don't want people to think that I'm an unmarried mother.'

She'd flung the statement out like a challenge and he could see that she was perfectly serious.

'Now it's my turn to apologise,' the man said, realising his mistake. 'It's just – you can't be too careful in this business.'

Sally was still angry. 'I wouldn't mind, but I don't even know what you're talking about.'

'It doesn't matter.'

'I think it does. You obviously thought I was up to something.'

'It was just the way you were scribbling then looking up, scribbling then looking up. I hadn't seen your face before and it made me suspicious.'

'I was *drawing* the chairs, that's all, damn it! What's so suspicious about that?'

11

'Everything. It's not what an ordinary onlooker would do.'

'God, you're exasperating! Look, I couldn't understand why the settle and chairs were worth so much, so I took a few notes. There's nothing more to it than that.'

'I'm sorry,' he said. 'I didn't mean to upset you.'

She looked him square in the face and decided that he was being genuine. 'That's okay,' she said at length. 'I suppose I shouldn't be so prickly.'

'Ah, you're not as rough and tough as all that.' He extended a hand in her direction. 'My name's Ken, by the way, and now that we've had our first row, I think we should agree not to ask each other awkward questions.'

She took the hand and shook it. 'Sally,' she said. 'Sally Blythe.'

'Well, Sally, it's a pleasure to meet you on this fine spring morning.'

A sudden burst of rain rattled on the window as he spoke, making them both laugh.

'So what *can* I ask you then, that's not going to get me into trouble?'

'Oh, anything personal.'

'Really?'

'I'll give you a potted history of my life to make it easier, shall I?'

'If you like.'

His voice took on a serious tone. 'Back in the age of the woolly mammoth and sabre-toothed tiger, when I was just a lad . . .' He paused, gratified that she'd already started to chuckle. 'Think I'm kidding, eh?' He smiled. 'All right, then, let's spool forward a bit. Brrrip! Ah, yes, Eddie Cochrane. Remember him? Buddy Holly, then? Oh, I see the slightest glimmer of recognition flicker across your otherwise glazed eyes.'

'Well, I think everyone's heard of him.'

'Sad, really,' he said, shaking his head. 'Don't know what you missed. I expect all that sort of thing is just so much black-and-white footage to your generation.'

'You're not that old.'

'A hundred and sixty-three at last count.'

'And I'm a Dutchman.'

'Very kind, I'm sure, but I'm sorry to inform you that unlike many of the items you saw on sale this morning, I am a genuine antique.'

Sally watched him push back his shock of steel-grey hair in a gesture of mock narcissism.

'Yet not a line on your face.'

She'd thought out aloud, but it was true. The only thing that might have given his age away was a slight thickening around the waist.

He looked surprised for a second, then recovered himself, although the eyes behind the horn-rimmed spectacles betrayed a certain lack of confidence. Sally noticed and was rather charmed because he hadn't tried to hide it.

'So what brings a poor old codger like you to a place like this?' she said. 'Or does that fall into the Awkward Question category?'

'Hmm, almost. Let's say I'll tell you if you tell me.'

'Oh, mine's easy. I came into town to go to the auction because I'm thinking of putting in a table that I've got and I wanted to get some idea of what it might sell for.'

'That explains the scribbling and the antiques guide.'

'That's what I was trying to tell you before.'

'You came into town especially, you say. Don't you live in Worthing, then?'

'No. Near Brighton. Out in the wilds of Fulking, in fact.'

'Nice bit of countryside – and a decent pub.'

'Shepherd and Dog? Yes. Don't get down there too often, though, and when I do it's full of day trippers. Anyhow, it's a little too far away to call it my local, exactly.'

13

She looked down at her hands for a moment. What she wanted to say was, 'Actually, I live almost three miles from anywhere, in a tiny, rundown cottage with no one to talk to but the kids, the cat, or perhaps the odd passing rabbit.'

He seemed to catch her mood and changed the subject. 'So you've got a table you're thinking of selling, have you?'

'Yes. I don't know much about tables, I'm afraid, but it looks reasonably elegant. There's a rather lovely vase of flowers depicted on the top – oh, and a couple of butterflies.'

'Painted or inlaid?'

'Some sort of inlay, I think. I wish I could sound more informed about it but I never took much interest except to think that it looked like the sort of thing that you shouldn't eat off.'

'More something that should be admired?'

'Yes. It was my father's, you see. He left it to me in his Will.'

'Ah.' He thought for a while and then fumbled in his pocket. 'Look,' he said, 'here's my card. If you like, I could take a look at the table for you.'

'Oh, thanks.' She took the dog-eared offering and squinted at the lettering on it. *Ken Rees*, it read, *Antiques and Fine Art*. 'I would like you to, if it's not too much trouble?'

'No trouble at all.'

'It would be nice to know exactly what it was. I mean, I suppose I might get a clue or two from the antiques guide but it'd be better if someone who knew what they were talking about looked at it.'

'I'm sure I'll be able to help.'

'It's very good of you to offer.'

He shrugged and glanced at his watch. 'Well, I must be going, I'm afraid. Still, it was nice talking to you and I hope you'll give me a ring.'

'I will,' she said, shaking the hand that he offered again as he stood up to leave.

'Hey, just a minute,' she added suddenly. 'You didn't keep your side of the bargain.'

'What bargain?'

'You said that you'd tell me what you were doing here if I told you what I was doing here?'

'Another time, perhaps.' He fastened his raincoat, gave her an impish smile, then turned and walked away.

2

Saturday morning started bright and crisp, though the big pine tree in the garden still hung heavily with the rain that had fallen during the night. Sally stood at the bedroom window, a carrier bag filled with toys in her hand, and tried to decide whether it would stay clear beyond lunchtime. It was hard to tell. There was something about the topography of the Downs which affected the weather, often keeping the Fulking area dry while a bank of cloud stayed suspended over the south coast. On other days, when the wind came in off the sea, Brighton and Worthing could be bathed in sun while the countryside a few miles away languished in the gloom.

Sally finished gathering the bits and pieces that she hoped would keep the boys entertained for the day and packed them into the car, wellies and all, just to be on the safe side. She was part-way down the drive before she realised that the one thing she'd meant to put in for herself was still lying on the kitchen table. She turned back, grabbed her book, locked up and started off again.

The drive to Steyning was made through narrow country lanes where the banks and hedgerows were beginning to come to life. Fragile blossoms clung to the branches of the wild cherry, although the leaves were still in bud, making the bare branches of other trees all the more stark by comparison. To look at them, it seemed as though spring was hesitating a little before really getting started but then, Sally told herself, as she whizzed along in her rose pink Mini, that's what she thought every year, only to find, almost before she could blink, that the whole lot was out in a riot of greens.

Heather was looking out for them from the doorway of her small gallery when the Mini, slowed by the queue of traffic in the High Street, finally nosed its way alongside. Sally wound down the window to find out what she was gesticulating about.

'Quick, round the side,' she called. 'I've saved you a parking space.'

Sally ducked the Mini into the first turning on the right and found a man in a Fiat bang in the middle of the road, angrily surveying the two buckets and brooms that her stepmother had arranged in what was now the one empty spot in the street.

'You've no right to do that,' he shouted as Heather appeared to clear the barrier away. 'This is a public highway, you know. First come, first served.'

'I did come first,' she said acidly. 'At seven-thirty this morning, to be precise. Anyway, I happen to live here, so if you'd kindly move along, my daughter is waiting to park.'

'Cow!' the man yelled as he slammed his foot on the accelerator.

'Charmed, I'm sure.' Heather curtsied lightly, using one broom as a prop, then ushered Sally into the space.

'What a horrible man,' she said as she climbed out of the driving seat.

'World's full of them, dear,' Heather replied, kissing her on both cheeks, in continental fashion. 'Oh, Lord, now Matthew's upset. Come here, darling.' She reached into the

17

Mini to unfasten Sally's three-year-old, whose bottom lip was starting to quiver. 'There, never mind.'

'Why was the man horribubble?' The word had been unfamiliar to him, so he picked the nearest one to it that he knew.

'Because he's ignorant, dear. That means he doesn't know any better. I'm sure you won't grow up to be like that, will you?' She smoothed his hair as he shook his head, very seriously. 'Now come on, I've made your favourite lunch.'

Sally watched her put Matthew down and lead him gently by the hand. It never ceased to amaze her how good Heather was with the children when she'd never had any of her own. She was totally natural with them, although she could hardly be expected to be, considering.

A twinge of guilt troubled Sally as she followed along with Jonathan, who was struggling with the bouquet of daffodils and pussy willow that they'd cut from the garden. For a long time, Sally had been openly hostile to her step-mother, out of jealousy, probably, she thought now. It had been a childhood problem, mostly. As she'd grown up she'd come to understand that Heather was not a threat. But as a girl, Sally had hated the fact that her father so obviously loved her. It seemed to take away some of the affection she had thought was rightly hers. Yet in all the years they'd known each other, Heather had only ever treated her with kindness. With the benefit of hindsight, Sally wondered where she'd found the inner strength to have such patience.

'Righty-ho,' Heather chirped as she shut the front door, turning round the sign that hung in it, so that it read 'Closed' to the outside world. 'Think we'll have some peace over lunch, don't you? But I hope you won't mind if I open up again later, I could do with a few customers.'

'No, not at all.' Sally followed her through to the back of the house where the living room lay next to the artist's studio where Heather worked. It was a fairly large room, bigger

18

than usual for a house that dated back almost to Tudor times, but it had obviously been built that way, for it boasted a fine inglenook fireplace which took up most of the facing wall. Sally found herself looking round the room with fresh eyes. The grandfather clock that stood in one corner came under particular scrutiny. She was peering at the dial and the etched arch above it, where a bland-faced moon was sinking gently behind an astral globe, when Heather reappeared from the kitchen.

'Has it stopped again?' she said, with no apparent concern.

'No. I was just looking at the face. I hadn't noticed that it was so detailed.'

'Yes, it's rather nice, isn't it?' A clang from one of the fire irons made her turn her head away. 'Try not to get so close, Jonathan. You'll get all sooty and then I shall strangle you.'

'Then will I be dead?'

'Very probably.'

'And you'll have to take me to hospital, for the doctor to make me better.'

'Something like that. Now come along, lunch is ready.'

'Can I bring my armour mens?'

'He means his knights,' Sally interjected, then added to her son, 'No. I've told you before, you can't play and eat.'

'Oh, go on, he's only five and it's not exactly The Ritz.' Heather smiled at the child. 'You can bring one. Choose the one you like best and we'll see if we can feed him too.'

'What about his horse?'

'Jonathan!' Sally exploded.

'Oh, he doesn't look very hungry to me,' Heather laughed. 'But bring him along anyway and we might find something for him. You too, Matthew, come on . . . yes, bring your car.'

The party of four made their way into the kitchen where a white linen cloth had been spread over the old oak table.

'Taking a bit of a risk,' Sally commented as bowls of spaghetti bolognese were set down in front of the boys.

'Oh, it doesn't matter. No point in having things if you don't use them.'

'My good cloths never get out of the drawer these days,' Sally said, a little sadly. 'If it can't be hosed down . . .'

'I know, I know. But you've got to attend to your own needs as well as those of the children, otherwise there's no point in being an adult.'

'How do you mean?'

'I mean that as an adult you appreciate the finer things. Like crisp linen cloths, good cutlery, crystal wine glasses. It's not a matter of spoiling yourself, it's a matter of feeling that you are where you ought to be – grown up.'

'Oh?'

'Well, look at it sensibly. What are you going to do, keep the whole lot in mothballs until the children are eighteen? I mean I know people who do, but it's such a waste. Anyhow,' Heather added, reaching for her glass, 'here's to my own very special people and lovely it is to see you. Cheers!'

She leaned over to Sally and chinked her glass, then did the same with the boys' tumblers of orange juice. They caught on to the idea and started bashing their glasses together in a way that threatened to get out of hand.

'Steady on, chaps,' Heather said. 'Let's have some eating too. Now, Sally, what have you been up to this week?'

'Oh, this and that,' she replied, not sure exactly how to get into a conversation which, inevitably, would lead to speaking of her father's death. She was sensitive enough to have taken in the muted tones of the outfit Heather was wearing. It was a grey shirt, striped with black and finishing in a black collar held together with a gold pin. Her skirt was grey too. To anybody else, she would just have looked well turned out. To Sally, who knew how her artist's eye loved a vibrant colour, the ensemble spoke of mourning.

20

'Come on, now, don't disappoint me,' Heather urged. 'I was relying on you for a rattling good natter.'

'I thought you got quite a lot of that in the shop – er, gallery, I mean. Sorry.'

'That's all right. It is a shop of sorts, I suppose, except that what I'm selling is something of myself. People don't think of that. They just float in, airy-fairy, mutter their way round the paintings and then generally disappear without so much as a fond farewell.'

'Business not good, then?' Sally said, but she was thinking that she, too, had never really seen what Heather did that way either. Each painting was part of her personality. To sell one must be bitter-sweet, to say the least.

'That,' replied Heather, cutting across the thought, 'is the understatement of the year. Don't talk to me about an upturn in the recession!'

'Yet they say things are on the move.'

'By the time they move in my direction, I'll be too old to care.'

Sally laughed. 'I'm beginning to feel pretty much the same way myself.'

'More wine?' Heather asked.

'Shouldn't really, I'm driving.'

'You've only been here five minutes. Not rushing off, I hope.'

'Of course not. Anyhow, there's not a lot to rush off for.' The words were out before Sally realised that she could have put it more tactfully. 'I mean, I was hoping to stay for the whole afternoon. If you don't mind, that is?'

Heather couldn't resist arching an eyebrow, although she let the gaffe pass. 'Stay as long as you like. Stay overnight, if you want to, then we can get quietly pickled without worrying about it.'

'But you haven't got room. Anyway . . .'

21

'Anyway what? Give me one good reason why you have to get back to the cottage tonight.'

'I . . . well, what about the boys?'

'Two mattresses on the floor will sort them out. Bet you'd love camping, eh?'

The children cheered enthusiastically.

'There,' Heather said. 'Now what's your excuse?'

'Can't think of one – pass the wine.'

'That's the girl. Oh, how lovely, I'm going to have company!'

Sally took a long look at her stepmother and began to understand how alone she must feel, here in a house where almost every corner held some memory of her husband. Sally had been too busy with her own grieving really to take it on board before, but two months had passed and life had returned to some semblance of normality for her. For Heather, a vacuum had opened up that could not readily be filled.

'Right,' she said, pushing back her chair. 'Who's for pudding?'

'Me!' came two little voices in chorus.

'Well, those plates had better be squeaky clean by the time I come back from the kitchen, otherwise no apple pie and ice cream.'

Sally watched Heather go out of the room. There was an energy in her step, in her whole manner, that was so appealing. As Sally's father had so often said, she was like a breath of fresh whirlwind. Why, then, did Sally find it so hard to relax with her, to accept her as an ally, especially now when they shared a common grief? She thought back to the days of her childhood, to a time she had tried to blank out of her memory because she'd never been entirely able to cope with it. Nevertheless, she remembered, as though it was yesterday, the faces of the policeman and woman who had come to her school to tell her that there'd been a terrible

22

accident. It occurred to her that those faces were all she'd ever been able to recall of that moment. Everything else, the headmaster's office, the day, was black.

'Here we go,' Heather said as she brought the apple pie in with a flourish, 'hope you've left some room for it.' Then she noticed Sally's face. 'Are you all right?'

'Yes, I'm fine,' she lied. It wasn't the first time that she'd tried and failed to remember exactly what her mother had looked like. The effort left her feeling drained.

'Shall we walk down to the meadow afterwards, get some air?' Heather went on.

'That's an idea. I am a bit full.'

'Good. I've got some stale bread that the boys can give the ducks. There might even be a swan down there.'

'But I thought you wanted to open up again after lunch?'

'Well, it won't harm for half an hour. Anyway, our day is more important.'

They finished the meal and headed out down the back streets towards the meadow. The weather held and it was comfortable enough to sit on a bench and watch the children throwing stale bread to the ducks while they sat and talked.

'So,' Heather said, 'now that they're out of ear-shot, are you managing all right?'

'Yes, got the tank replaced in the end – it'd only imploded, that hard frost we had. Now I'm waiting for the living-room ceiling to dry out.'

'I don't mean with the house. I mean you. How's the money situation?'

'Dire.'

Heather nodded. 'That's what I thought.'

'Why?'

'You've gone so thin. Practically nothing left of you.'

'Don't have much of an appetite, to be honest. The boys are happy enough with beefburgers and fish fingers and I

23

can't get into doing much for myself. Cooking for one seems pointless, really.'

'I know.'

'I'm sorry,' Sally said, slowly, 'I'm sure you must do.'

'Oh, I don't just miss him at mealtimes . . .' Heather's pale blue eyes dulled to grey as she spoke. 'Evenings are the worst. Sometimes I'm still sitting in the chair at midnight. Can't face going upstairs.'

'I know it's not a fair comparison, but I felt like that, too, when I was first on my own.'

'Did you?'

'Yes. Then I began to think how nice it was to have the whole bed to myself. You know, not wake up in the middle of the night 'cos he's turned over and taken the duvet with him or because he's snoring like a chain saw.'

Heather smiled. 'Ah, but you're still angry.'

Sally blinked but made no reply. The comment hit home with an accuracy that stung.

'You are angry, aren't you?' Heather persisted. 'With him, I mean, and unless I'm much mistaken, a bit angry with yourself.'

'I am not!'

'Sally, Sally. I've known you since you were ten, remember. Give credit where it's due.'

She shrugged. 'Well, I suppose you're right. But I think I'm justified. I don't think that I deserved – that the children deserved – to be abandoned.'

'That may be so but there's precious little point in being angry about it. Initially, yes, because of course it came as such a shock. But the time comes when you have to put anger aside. It's such a negative emotion and if you're not careful, it'll eat away at you, bit by bit, until you won't be able to recognise a positive thing if it bites you on the ankle.'

Sally knew what Heather was saying was true but she still hadn't ironed out the dent in her self-esteem. She just couldn't understand why Philip had deserted her for *that* woman. She wasn't even particularly pretty.

He had to go and shack up with someone in the same department at work, didn't he? she thought, miserably. How stunningly unoriginal.

The fact that it was all so crass was no salve for Sally's wounded feelings. But she wasn't prepared to admit it, yet. She could sense that Heather was waiting for her to open up, so she played dirty and hijacked the conversation to her own advantage.

'Don't *you* feel a bit abandoned at times?' she said, thinking she'd turned the thing round rather cleverly.

'Of course I do,' Heather replied, 'you always do when you lose someone you love, for whatever reason. And in my case, I didn't just lose a husband, I lost my best friend.'

The simple, forthright way which Heather had when it came to expressing emotions made Sally feel ashamed of pussy-footing around her own. She looked at her stepmother steadily for a moment, then suddenly took her hand. 'He really loved you, you know.'

'I know.' She nodded. 'And he really loved you, too. Never forget that. You were all he had left, after the accident. He poured every emotion he had into you. In a way, you see, he never really forgave himself for being the one to survive.'

'But it wasn't his fault.'

'No. And it wasn't his fault that he died and left me on my own either.'

'Oh, Heather, how can you stand it?' Sally flung her arms around her as the tears welled up.

'It's hard, sweetheart, very hard. But we had many years together and lots of wonderful times. That's what I cling on to.' She hugged Sally against her whilst she struggled against her own tears. 'Anyway, he'd have hated to think he would leave me miserable. And the same goes for you.

25

Come on now, don't let the children see you upset . . . come on, you're making me soggy.'

Sally dried her eyes and tried to smile. 'How did you get to be so strong?'

'Strong? Me? Piffle. I'm at peace with myself, that's all.'

'Well, how did you get to be at peace with yourself then?'

'By accepting that things change, that they will and must change. It's the natural order of things. All the time you're growing, developing, changing, everyone and everything around you is doing the same. Accept it. Let yourself go with it and don't hold back. That's all I'm saying.' She patted Sally's hand. 'Let's get going, shall we? I'm beginning to feel a bit chilly.'

'You know,' Sally said, as they made their way back towards the house, the children trailing sticks behind them, 'I've been meaning to ask you something.'

'What's that?'

'I've been thinking about what I should do with that table Dad wanted me to have.'

'Oh? Did you want to take it?'

'No. Well, not exactly. I was thinking of selling it.'

'Gracious. Were you really?'

'Don't you think I should, then?'

'I think it's yours to do with as you feel fit. It's just that it's been in the family for a long time.' Heather looked at her seriously for a moment. 'Is the money situation really that bad?'

Sally grimaced.

'I see. You know, if it's a question of getting by for a while . . .'

'Don't you dare even think about it,' Sally interrupted. 'You've got enough on your plate without trying to bale me out.'

'There's no need to be proud about it.'

'It's nothing to do with pride, it's to do with being practi-

26

cal. Not only do I not need the table, I've got nowhere to put it. And even if I did, I should always be looking at it, thinking, I could have paid the rent for a year with that.'

'Yes,' Heather nodded, 'I can see your logic. So what will you do, sell it privately?'

'Don't know. To begin with, I thought I might let it go to auction. But then I met this man who's a dealer of some sort, who said he could look at it for me.'

'How did you meet him?'

'In a café, in Worthing.'

'Sally!'

'After an auction, I mean. I went to the auction there this week – he was buying furniture – and I just happened to bump into him again at lunchtime, that's all.'

'Well, honestly, you're a dark horse. Why didn't you tell me before?'

'Didn't have time. And anyway, it didn't seem very appropriate.'

'But how do you know that you can trust him?'

'I don't – except he didn't come across as untrustworthy.'

'Well, there's a lot of rip-off merchants in the antiques business, you know.'

'I'm not completely dim,' Sally retorted. 'I have every intention of checking out what he says. In fact, I brought something along that I was hoping you'd take a look at with me . . .'

'Unbelievable,' Heather said, pushing her half-moon glasses back on her nose, 'look at this, a thousand pounds for a set of Dave Clark Five dolls and a bunch of junk from Herman's Hermits.'

'Told you it was fascinating. Weren't they much good, then?'

'Oh, we thought so at the time, although I wasn't keen on the Hermits. A bit saccharine for my taste.'

Sally giggled. 'Look at the haircuts.'

'Yes. They were all copying the Beatles – see.' Heather pointed to an autographed photograph of the group. 'Ooh, wasn't McCartney dishy?'

'Still looks good today, for a man over fifty.'

'Some of us manage it,' Heather said, saucily.

'I never think of you as fifty – miles too sprightly.'

'Heavens, you're not finished at half a century, you know, although I have to admit that things keep popping up to remind you that you're no spring chicken any more.'

'Rubbish. You're in great shape.'

'Tell that to my knees when the weather's damp. They're like a ruddy barometer.'

Sally laughed. 'Gosh, look at that, up to six thousand pounds for a hat worn by Vivien Leigh in *Gone With The Wind.*'

'You know,' Heather said, turning back to the furniture section, 'I'm beginning to wish you'd never shown me this antiques guide. I feel as though I should double the contents insurance.'

'Makes me feel like poking through every little junk shop I might come across in search of lost treasure.'

'Huh! I should think the dealers round here are well ahead of you.'

'You never know.'

'Speaking of dealers, who is this chap you met the other day?'

'Ken somebody. Hang on.' Sally searched through her handbag and finally found his card, holding it under the table lamp so that she could read it. 'Ah, yes. *Ken Rees – Antiques and Fine Art*, it says here.'

'Fine Art, eh? Well, there's something I can put him to task on.'

'Yes, I suppose you could. Do you really think he might be a villain?'

28

'Guilty until proven innocent, in my view. What's he look like?'

'Oh, he's about five foot eleven, well built . . . hair's completely silver and he's rather tubby round the waist.' She thought for a moment, then added, 'Face is good though – strong features. I had the feeling he'd look better without the glasses.'

'And how old do you think he is?'

'Less than sixty but a bit older than you, I'd say. I mean, he was talking about Buddy Holly and all that.'

'Whatever got him on to that subject?'

'He was telling me his life story.'

'Chatting you up, you mean.'

'No, not at all. In fact, he was very polite – almost to the point of being apologetic.'

'Humm. You've got to watch these older men. They know how to take their time.'

'What do you mean?'

'I mean that they might come across as incredibly avuncular but you've got to watch out for the hidden agenda.'

'Heather! Really.' Sally squirmed. 'Why would he be interested in me?'

Heather shot her a meaningful look.

'Well, I'm certainly not interested in him – from that point of view anyway. I just think it would be a good idea to have him look at the table. After all, he obviously knows about that sort of thing.'

'Have him look at it, by all means.' She got up and stretched. 'Come on, bedtime.'

'It'll mean inviting him here . . .'

'All the better. And I think you should let me deal with him.'

'Why?'

'I have some experience in these matters.'

'Antiques?'

29

'Don't be a twit.'
'Oh, you mean older men?'
'Quite.'

3

It was one of those days when the phone never seemed to stop ringing. Ken Rees made himself another cup of coffee and went back to his work for the umpteenth time. He'd already decided that he would buy the pair of miniatures that Tom Appleton had brought in that morning, but he hadn't yet made his mind up whether to sell them on or keep them for his own private collection. Tom was a collector himself and had a keen eye for a good piece but they didn't call him 'The Laundry Man' for nothing.

Ken turned one of the pictures under the light on his desk and wondered whether Tom was up to his old tricks on this one. It was possible. The two miniatures were very good at first sight. Both were of the English School, but he guessed they'd been painted at least a century apart. Yet there was something about the later piece that was putting him off . . . That and Tom's reputation for passing off fakes. Really clever fakes, mind you, a lot of work obviously went into them, but Ken wasn't about to catch a cold that way. The ploy was to have, and be noted as having, a really solid collection. That way, forgeries could be slipped into deals, having gained credibility by their association with the genuine article. It was a practice well known amongst dealers in works of art, they called it 'washing', and Tom had it down to a degree that had earned him his nickname.

Ken examined the portrait of the young man in military uniform more closely, taking it out of its frame in order to make a better assessment of the art work. It was a delicate operation, for one touch of a damp or greasy finger would bring the water colour clean off the ivory upon which it had been painted. He held it firmly between his thumb and third finger, checking the portrait front and back for signs of ageing. Next, he looked inside the frame that he'd just taken off. As he'd suspected, there was hardly a trace of dust around the edges of the glass. He put the frame down again and considered his findings. It was arguable that the portrait had been recently cleaned; it was hard to tell since the back of the frame was velvet and could be removed and replaced at will. Had it been wood, it would most likely have been sealed with tape, which in itself would indicate how recently the back had been open. Yet the picture had supposedly come in a lot of five family portraits from a private house in Norfolk. It was unlikely that they would have gone to the trouble of having the miniatures cleaned if they'd decided to part with them.

He opened the other frame to make a comparison. This covered a particularly fine portrait of a young girl in a blue Empire-line gown and was painted in a way which allowed the natural translucency of the ivory to enhance both the texture of the dress and the girl's delicate skin tones. It was quite beautiful, and Ken hardly had to glance at it under the light to know that it was original. There was a certain sense of a piece being right that couldn't be expressed in words. It was more a feeling, a kind of instinct, that was enhanced by years of handling antiques of any sort. Something either felt right or it didn't, it was as simple as that. And if it didn't feel right, you walked away.

Ken put the miniatures back into their frames and thought

over what he would do with the portrait of the young man. To sell it on to another dealer might mean tarnishing his own reputation, if he tried to build up its provenance too much. The trouble was, he was not completely certain that the piece was wrong. It was only a matter of opinion. But opinion counted for everything in this trade. No, the better options were either to put in into auction with a healthy reserve, or else in the shop at the price of an original and allow a lot of leeway on negotiation.

The telephone rang at the same moment as the door bell. Ken picked it up in his left hand, putting his right on the buzzer that released the safety latch. He nodded to the middle-aged couple who came in but gestured towards the phone to show that he was temporarily tied up.

'You know that bookcase Jim had the other week?' came the voice on the line. 'The one he swapped for two grand and that Chesterfield?'

'Yeah.'

'Well, it's only turned up in London for ten.'

'You're kidding?' Ken said, but this was Mike Elstein and he didn't joke about anything much.

'No, saw it in Webster's. Walked past it once, then thought I knew it from somewhere. Got a high polish on it now – too much, if you ask me – and that's what threw me. But it's the same one, all right.'

'What did George say, then?'

'He should worry! The Chesterfield was a piece of garbage. Don't know what Jim was thinking about taking it from him. Still, I reckon George didn't get more than five. I could practically hear him going green . . .'

'Hang on.' Ken put his hand over the mouthpiece. His male customer looked ready to poke through the canvas of one of the oil paintings. 'Not too close, sir, you'll set the alarm off.' He was lying about the alarm. That only went on when the shop was closed. The remark was his fail-safe against the type of philistine who thought nothing of touching the goods.

'You busy?'

'A bit.'

'Okay. Look, can you call me back about that sewing table? I think I might be able to do something on it.'

'Yes, all right.' Ken put the phone back on the hook and turned his attention to the middle-aged couple. 'Are you looking for something in particular?'

'No, just browsing,' the woman said, but the fact that he was now watching them closely obviously made them uncomfortable. They moved from the main body of the shop to the raised level at the back then wandered down again.

'Can we look down there?' the woman asked, nodding towards the roped off stairway to the cellar.

'Restoration only,' Ken replied, though he would have opened it up for a likely sale.

'Oh,' the woman said. 'Well, thank you.'

Ken watched them leave with a sour look. He disliked time wasters but they were a common feature of the daily routine in the shop end of things. It could be a real bore. Hours could go by without a potential customer in sight. Still, just one sale could make a week of waiting worthwhile. It was a funny business. Ken took off his glasses and rubbed his eyes which were feeling sore from the after effects of the bottle of red wine he'd killed the night before. The last glass was what had done it. Nearly always was. Yet time and again when he was sitting there around midnight and thinking of turning in, he'd have that last glass, even though he didn't need it. It was one of the sadder aspects of living on your own.

He pondered on the thought for a moment. Drinking at home was considered a bad habit in this country but he'd got into it by association, really, years ago, when he was living in France. There, wine was taken with every meal

34

except breakfast, as a sort of *digestif*. It was the way he'd continued to drink it, never without eating and never without a glass of water to hand. The combination got him nicely mellow but never, ever drunk.

He remembered 1976 with total clarity. It was a milestone year. And not just because it was the last time he'd let himself get stinking, rotten drunk. It was the year of his thirty-fifth birthday, and he'd thrown what he'd jokingly called his 'half-dead' party, on the biblical basis that a man's natural span was three score years and ten. The venue had been the café beneath the apartment he shared with Odile which stood in a prime location on the Rue Emile Grand, straight across from the museum and within sight of the marvellous thirteenth-century cathedral at Albi. There they'd sat with a bunch of friends, mostly students home for the long summer break, arguing late into the night about the relative merits of the current trend in poster art. The subject was debated keenly, not least because they were all aware of committing a kind of sacrilege, comparing work of psychedelic artists like Rick Griffin, Stanley Mouse and Martin Sharp with those of the great originators of the poster form, Cheret, Millais, and of course Henri Marie Raymond de Toulouse-Lautrec, in whose birthplace they happened to be sitting.

Somehow or other, the debate resulted in a challenge and Ken had ended up stripped down to his underpants at the edge of the River Tarn, trading insults with a friend of a few hours before as they prepared to swim in and out of the arches of the Pont Vieux until they reached the other bank. It was an absurd and dangerous proposition but his temper had been hot in those days.

It was only when he reached the third arch that the alcohol and chilly river water conspired to produce a rock-solid cramp in his legs. The suck of the current pulled him under as he fought for a grasp on the ancient stone column ahead. Once, twice, he went down into the relentless black, dimly aware of Odile's piercing screams, her face dwindling into a whirlpool of unrelated visions from the past. He didn't remember what happened next, although someone had obviously pulled him out in time. All he knew was that he woke up two days later with an almighty hangover and his hands scratched to ribbons by the stone. The café owner's wife was sitting at his bedside, shaking her head. Odile was gone.

'If you don't care whether you live or die, why should I?' read the note she'd left. But he knew the rot had set in to the relationship long before his latest act of stupidity. The real problem had been her need to settle down, along with the attendant biological urges. He said he wasn't ready for that type of commitment and, in its way, the statement was true. But he hadn't revealed the whole truth either to her or himself. With the benefit of hindsight, he realised that it was the responsibility of having children that he was trying to avoid.

He released a long breath between his teeth, more a hiss than a sigh. An awful lot of life had gone by between then and now but the memory of Odile, probably more than any other woman he'd felt he'd loved, stayed with him. Perhaps because he'd have been glad of that family now – there was an element of nostalgia in the thought. More definitively, though, it was to do with the relationship itself. There had been something unique about it, a depth of friendship that went beyond mere romance. Whatever that special mix had been, he'd never found it again in quite the same way, although he'd done his fair share of looking.

The sharp crack of keys being knocked against the window pane made Ken start. He reached for his glasses and squinted through them to see Tom Appleton, his hat pulled down over his forehead and his rain coat collar turned up, looking for all the world like a latter-day Harry

Lime. Ken released the safety catch on the door and let him in.

'So what's the story?' Tom said before he'd finished crossing the threshold.

'Now you're beginning to sound like one too.'

'Like what?'

'Like a refugee from some hoary old *film noir.*'

'Huh! Bit of a movie buff, are we?'

'Ought to be, we couldn't afford a television in our house.'

'You're breaking my heart. Look, I'm parked on double yellows round the corner so I can't hang about. Do we have a deal or not?'

'You'll have to bring your price down – don't like the look of your military man.'

'What do you mean?'

'You know.'

'I'd be hurt if I didn't know you better. All right, four hundred the pair.'

'No chance.'

'Three fifty then, and that's my last offer.'

'Call it three and save yourself a parking ticket.'

He hesitated then nodded. 'Okay. Cash though.'

Ken went to the safe, opened it and counted out the price in twenty-pound notes, folding them into his palm before passing them over to Tom. He put the money straight into his pocket. He didn't have to check to know it would all be there.

'You're a hard man to do business with,' he said with a frown.

''Bye, Tom, give my love to the traffic warden.'

Appleton raised his hand to his mouth land smacked it loudly with his lips. It was his way of saying: Kiss my arse. Ken smiled and waved him away. He should be in Brighton New Jersey, not Brighton East Sussex, he thought.

*

There was just enough blue in the sky to tempt Ken away from his usual make-do lunch of instant soup and an uninteresting roll. He locked up and headed off down Ship Street. The wind had picked up, sending long streaks of cloud scudding across the horizon and a mixture of sand, sweet papers and discarded fish and chip papers along the sea front. Ken pulled the lapels of his coat together as he came round the corner of The Old Ship hotel and made his way, head down into the wind, across the road towards the pier.

The fresh air made a pleasant change from the stuffy atmosphere of the shop. Dust had a way of clinging to old furniture; it was almost as if it had a homing instinct for the stuff. The sharp tang of iodine soon cleared away its stale remnants as Ken stood against the railing, watching the colour of the water around the pier change from deep green to sparkling turquoise as shadow and light played on its surface. There was something mesmeric about watching the sea, he thought, rhythmic ebb and flow. For all its calm now, there was always the feeling that its terrible power was only just held in check, brooding on the edge of breaking loose.

His reverie was spoiled by the crackle of a loud speaker and the fatuous tones of the pier's resident DJ who had whacked up the volume to play his favourite 'Golden Oldie'. Ken moved away from it past the amusement arcade and the souvenir shops, where soft toys and sticks of rock dangled garishly in the breeze. He decided to take refuge in the tea room at the end, the one place that managed to retain some of the elegance of the Victorian era.

'Blowing the cobwebs away?' a familiar voice enquired behind him as he skirted the small fun fair towards his destination. He turned to find Tony and Jon, arm in arm in their customary way.

'Oh, hi. Coming in for lunch?'

'Might as well,' said Tony. 'We could do with a sit down after *that* experience.'

'Problems?'

'It's him,' Tony retorted, giving his partner a long-suffering look. 'I keep telling him that it's a load of old nonsense, but will he listen?'

'She's always right, despite what you say,' said Jon, trying to maintain his dignity. 'She predicted Mother's death, remember?'

'How could I forget?' came the waspish reply. 'You were crying for two months before she even showed any signs of going.'

'Come on, you two,' Ken put in, 'let's find a table and you can tell me all about it.'

He didn't usually like gays but Tony and Jon were good friends, more married in every sense than a lot of the heterosexuals that he knew. They'd been together for twenty years and, notwithstanding the bickering, each would have given their life for the other. What was more, Ken remembered how Tony had nursed Jon's mother after her stroke, spending hours teaching her to speak again, even dealing with the incontinence bags. If that wasn't a loving act, he didn't know what was.

'Now,' he said, taking a seat in a quiet corner, 'I'm all ears.'

'Oh, it's Suzanne again,' Tony started. 'She's told him he's going to lose something very close to him.'

'Might be his string vest!'

'It's not a laughing matter,' said Jon, touchily. 'You don't know, she's a real visionary, that woman. You can tell by the way she interprets the cards.'

'Well, I wouldn't mind if she wasn't so gloomy.' Tony reached over and touched Ken on the arm. 'Always reminds me of the soothsayer in *Up Pompei*. You know, "Woe, woe and thrice woe!" The Happy Medium, that's what I call her.'

Jon had the good grace to laugh and the ice was broken.

As the atmosphere between the two thawed, Ken found himself relaxing. He liked being with Tony and Jon. There was some special quality in the intimacy they shared, a homeliness that was missing in his own life. For that reason, he was always pleased to take up the dinner invitation that they'd issue about once a month. There was an added attraction, too. Dinner, for Tony and Jon, meant a very lavish affair. And since the meals that Ken cooked for himself tended to be very much make-do-and-mend affairs, it was something he always looked forward to.

'Have you heard what they're putting on at the festival this year?' asked Tony.

'Tell me the worst.'

'Only *Richard III* in Romanian.'

Ken groaned. 'You ought to offer to do a turn for them.' He was thinking of the 'act' that Tony and Jon would put on whenever they had a dinner party. The couple would camp up well-known bits of old movies, mimicking the over-stated facial expressions and breathless RADA accents of the thirties and forties so well that their guests would soon be crying with laughter. Then, to round the evening off, they'd insist that everyone joined in a sing-song around the piano, when every old music hall number you could think of would be dredged up.

'What? Us?' said Jon, looking rather alarmed.

'Why not? I should think you'd go down a bomb. A damn' sight funnier than some of that alternative comedy they serve up.'

'Yes,' agreed Tony, 'the alternative is it leaves you cold.'

'Not on your Nelly,' said Jon emphatically, his Northern burr suddenly more pronounced. 'I couldn't stand everyone pegging us as a couple of old screamers.'

'Your political correctness is slipping, dear.'

'I wish you wouldn't say things like that, Tony,' he came back. 'You know I'm not afraid of saying what I am. It's just that what we do is – well, private. Nobody's business but ours.'

'Quite right,' said Ken. 'Anyhow, come on, tell me what you've been buying recently.'

'I know what I wish I'd bought,' Tony became more serious, 'and that's that painting by Karl Albert Buehr. You know, *Tea Time*, the one that went for over a hundred thousand at Phillips'.'

Ken nodded. He'd put in a bid for three thousand by telephone himself, but he wasn't going to let on about it. 'Caused a bit of a sensation at the saleroom, by all accounts,' he commented. 'One of his usually makes no more than two and a half.'

'Yes, but it was bought by an American and you know how they are about their own. He seemed to want to make something of a statement, said that Buehr was in the same league as Frieseke and Ritman, according to the press.'

'Not in my book.'

'Mine neither but it probably means that the next one to come out will make two or three times more than it's worth.'

'Well, I don't think I'll be taking the risk, even if I get the chance. Might just be a one-off.'

Tony agreed then added, 'Actually, I did see something the other day that I'd like your opinion on.'

'Oh? What was that.'

'Don't want to go into any detail here,' he said in a conspiratorial way, 'never know whose ears are flapping. Why don't you pop over to The Old Rectory sometime later in the week – whenever you've got a moment? We could discuss it then.'

'Okay.' Ken's tone was casual but he knew that whatever it was, it had to be something special. Tony and Jon had an incredible knack of picking the cream of the crop. They also had great contacts.

'Good. I'll expect you to call.'

When lunch was over, Ken made his way back to the shop and put in a call to Joseph Van Dalen to see how the restoration on the settle and chairs he'd bought at the Worthing auction was coming along. He knew the answer would be 'slowly', because that was the pace of the man. He was, though, a fine craftsman, descended from a family of cabinet makers whose work, back in the seventeenth century, had found favour with William of Orange. Van Dalen himself would have been in the original workshop in The Hague to this day, had it not been smashed up by the Nazis when they found that the family had been sheltering Jews. The episode had caused the young Joseph to flee to England where he settled, showing no inclination to return to his native land.

'You're going to have trouble with that inlay,' he told Ken, in the slightly accented but immaculate English so common of the Dutch. 'Not that I can't get some ivory, although of course it will never rival the quality of the original. But there's the problem of cutting it. The tools no longer exist for such intricate work.'

'Could you make something up?'

'Probably but it'll take time and, needless to say, it will be expensive.'

'That's okay,' Ken said, 'the client has the means.'

The phone was hardly back on the hook before it rang again. Ken viewed it with some irritation before picking it up.

'Hello?'

'Oh,' said a voice, surprised by the curt greeting. 'Is that Mr Rees?'

'Yes.' This wasn't one of his regulars. He cast around for who the woman might be.

'This is Sally Blythe. We met in Worthing, if you remember – the table?'

'Ah, the lady with the hat,' he said, picturing rather the

42

retroussé nose and well-proportioned mouth that had been most of what could be appreciated from under it. 'Yes, how are you?'

'Fine, thanks. I was wondering if you still wanted to look at it . . . the table, I mean?'

'Certainly. When would be a good time?'

'Perhaps you could suggest one? It's over at my step-mother's house, but she's there most of the time. I could make my arrangements to fit.'

He reached for his diary. 'How about Friday, three o'clock?'

'Sorry, that'd clash with picking the children up from school. Could you make it four?'

'Yes, four will be no problem.'

'Let me give you the address . . .'

Ken took the information down, already preoccupied with the thought of what opportunities might lie in store for him at the house in Steyning. Where there was one item of interest, there were certain to be others. His dealer's nose was already twitching in anticipation.

'Friday at four, then,' Sally was saying. 'Oh, and my step-mother's name is Heather, by the way.'

'Heather . . .?'

'Blythe, of course.'

'Oh, I didn't realise you used your maiden name.'

'Why not? I like it. Blythe by name, blithe by nature.'

'Very apt.'

'I'll see you on Friday.'

'Yes. I'll look forward to it.'

4

The appointment with the bank manager was not going very well. Grave and pasty-faced, he handled a bundle of statements, all of which ended with an overdrawn balance and stated, simply, that he could not allow the situation to continue for very much longer.

'I understand your predicament and I sympathise,' he said quietly, 'but from the bank's point of view, we need to see regular amounts being paid into your account.'

Sally felt the familiar tightness in her stomach. This conversation was exactly what she'd feared most and she was at a loss as to how to cope with it. She sat, twisting her hands in her lap, her mind fogged by anxiety, not knowing what to say next.

'Is there anything your solicitor can do?' the bank manager went on.

'I think he's trying his best,' she replied. 'The trouble is, the system itself is incredibly slow. You see, every time there's a problem in getting the maintenance paid, I have first to complain to my solicitor, who's up to his neck in work anyway, then he has to apply for Legal Aid to enforce the court order, which can take a fortnight to come through. Next, I have to swear an affidavit, which has to be lodged with the court, and then the court has to find a date to hear the case which can be anything up to three months from the original application. In the meantime, of course, I'm trying to keep myself and the children going and we can't exactly live on fresh air.'

The bank manager nodded but Sally had the feeling that she wasn't scoring many points.

'What happens virtually every time,' she continued, 'is that the other side wait until the date of the hearing to settle. That means that we've gone to all that trouble and turned up at court just for a cheque, which could perfectly well have been written at any stage before, to be passed between the two solicitors and the hearing to be called off. Not only does that cheque take three or four days to clear through my account, it only wipes out the back debt of maintenance. By then, of course, I have built up a backlog of debt myself, so my account goes back to zero or below for all of five seconds. It's a vicious circle, Mr Fielding, and there is nothing in law to stop the entire process from happening all over again the next time the money falls due.'

'I thought they could put ex-husbands in prison for that sort of thing?'

'Only if they stoically refuse to pay a penny.' Sally sighed. As if the whole situation wasn't depressing enough already without having these financial worries to contend with as well. It wasn't as though she'd exactly *planned* to find herself suddenly divorced and left totally responsible for two children and an endless stream of bills.

The bank manager thought for a moment. 'Is there anything you could do in the way of work? What did you do before you were married, by the way?'

'I worked for a company that sets up conferences – organising meetings, writing scripts for presentations, that sort of thing.'

'Skills that are in some demand, I would have thought.'

'Well, yes, they are, but I simply couldn't put in the hours. I have to get my elder son to school by nine and collect him by three, that cuts the day short, then there's the younger one to cater for. He goes to nursery two days a week. Those two days are effectively all the spare time I have.'

'Isn't there a granny or an aunt who could help you out?'

'No. I have a step mother, but she has a small business to run, I could hardly ask her to take the littlest over. Three-year-olds need a lot of attention.'

'I see.'

There was a worrying pause during which Sally realised that she was probably making her case look worse than even the bank manager had suspected.

'There's a good chance that I could get rid of the overdraft quite soon, though,' she said, trying to strike a note of hope. 'I, er, inherited something from my father, you see.'

'A bequest'

'Yes.' God, she thought, if I tell him it's a table, I'm sunk. 'I'm told it could be as much as five thousand pounds.'

'The Will hasn't been read, yet?'

'No,' she lied, frantically suppressing the blush that went with it, 'but I should know something more concrete in the next couple of weeks.'

'Ah, then there is light on the horizon.' The bank manager seemed to relax marginally. 'Well, under the circumstances I am prepared to bear with you, for say . . . another month. But I'd appreciate it if you'd keep me informed as to what transpires.'

'Yes, yes, of course.'

He stood up and opened the office door.

'Thank you for coming in.'

'Thanks for all your help.' Sally walked away, although she felt more like running. Out on the pavement, she took a series of deep breaths to steady herself before crossing the street and heading towards her favourite sandwich bar. It was only eleven o'clock but the nervous energy that had been driving her for the last half-hour had burnt up the bit of breakfast she'd managed to wolf down, cereal bowl in hand, as she followed the children from room to room making sure they were dressed and generally ready for the off.

Now I'm really flying by the seat of my pants, she thought as she turned past the huge department store that occupied the corner as well as a fair proportion of Brighton's main street, What am I going to do if the table turns out to be worth no more than a few hundred pounds?

The problem hung over her for the length of the narrow cobbled alley in which fishermen's cottages, transformed into a row of lovely little shops and restaurants, leaned comfortably together. The natural charm of The Lanes lay as much in their atmosphere as their meandering passageways. There was a sense of history in that small square of land, all that was left of the heart of a village which owed its survival to the sea. For centuries, fishing had sustained that community but trawling the deeps had not provided the wealth to build the great stone façades which now hemmed it in on every side.

The Prince Regent's passion for leisure had brought first the court and then fashionable society to the south coast, a trend which filtered down to the new but moneyed middle classes in Victorian times. The two eras left their unmistakable stamp on Brighton, though the frivolity of the Regency period, so apparent in the Prince's Oriental pavilion, was tempered by the more solid structures and stern bronze adornments of the later age. The worship of God, empire and, above all, commerce, made their mark on the landscape of the growing town, while the little port of Brighthelmstone shrank to a few back streets.

Soothed slightly by the intimacy of those streets, Sally bought herself a cup of hot chocolate and went to sit down at one of the white plastic tables which stood outside the sandwich bar. Gradually, she began to order her thoughts, picking over the events that had led to her present troubles, searching for a way forward. It was something of a cathartic exercise. She was not the type of person who liked to indulge in self-pity, but even she had to admit that life had not been very kind to her lately. Coping with the legal end of the divorce alone had been virtually a full-time job, never mind having to come to terms with the emotional trauma. Then, to cap it all, just when she was beginning to adjust to her new situation, her father had suddenly died. It was not so much the sequence of these unrelated experiences which had thrown her but the timing. She couldn't help concluding that whatever logic lay behind the ordering of the universe, it had to be pretty perverse.

The double tragedy threatened to weigh her down again. Grasping around for something more cheerful to think about, she suddenly remembered the cartoon that she'd cut from a magazine recently. It was entitled 'God at his computer', and pictured an old gent dressed in a white sheet sitting in front of a computer terminal. The screen showed a man walking down the street, blissfully unaware that a piano hung precariously over his head, suspended from a rope, or that God's finger was poised over a button marked 'SMITE'. The visual joke seemed to sum up perfectly the way she felt about things and she'd added it not only to her collection on the notice board in her kitchen, but also to her vocabulary. 'God's finger's on the SMITE button,' she'd say now, whenever something went wrong. It was her way of trying not to get too gloomy over her circumstances.

The chat with the bank manager had been too worrying for the joke to lift her spirits on this occasion. Anxiety piled upon anxiety and soon she felt completely oppressed by the burden of her responsibilities. For a while, it felt as if she were trapped in a quagmire, unable to move in any direction.

48

But, slowly, she came to realise that there was something she'd overlooked. There was no doubt that she was beset by problems but almost all of these had been produced by external influences. There was something more, something within herself that was wrong. What she needed to do was identify it, pin it down, then find the central cause.

She began to mull over the conversation she'd had with Heather at the week-end. It was true that Sally was still angry, and if the emotion wasn't exactly on the boil any more, it was certainly on a slow simmer. The collapse of her marriage had seemed sudden and brutal. It took some reflection before she was prepared to concede that it had not been going well for some time. In a way, they had both been clinging to the wreckage of a relationship which had been fine and dandy in the first flush of romance but had not been strong enough to weather the more mundane aspects of permanent union. Steady jobs, mortgages and children were a great killer of passion, she thought now. And in their case, the gilt had worn off the gingerbread quite quickly. Neither she nor Philip were great ones for routine and he had gone on avoiding it while she was obliged to keep plugging the gaps. The result bred a two-way resentment; she because she got tired of carrying the can for just about everything, he because he began to see her more as a parent than a partner or lover, and therefore began to rebel.

The explosion, when it came, was not entirely unexpected but the effect was devastating. Much more than the upheaval of leaving home, much more than the hateful tone of the solicitor's letters which followed, more even than the pain and confusion that the children suffered, was the over-whelming sense of loss that Sally felt. It became lodged in her consciousness, opening doors that had been nailed shut on the past. And so the ghosts came dancing out . . .

She shuddered. It was hard to be objective when it seemed that everything you'd ever loved had been snatched away

49

on a whim of fate. Still, there were the children. She was grateful that at least she had them. In many ways, having to be there for them had kept her sane. That and the purity of their affection.

She looked into the bottom of her empty cup. Motherhood was an achievement of sorts but it wasn't the whole picture. Of all the resentments that she'd felt inside her marriage, perhaps the greatest was for the loss of identity that it inevitably involved. That sense of self-worth, that each individual needs in order to fulfil themself, had been sublimated for too long.

Sally stared unseeing across the pretty cobbled street and wondered how she could begin to find herself again. But an hour passed without her resolving the question. As she left the sandwich bar and drifted through The Lanes, she was unable to shake it from her mind. On another day, she would have enjoyed looking at the displays of jewellery and curios which filled the windows of the innumerable shops that she passed. Today, though, they failed to distract her. Impatiently, she waited for her watch to register half-past twelve. When the moment came, she was relieved to turn towards Brown's restaurant where she'd arranged to meet her friend Julia for lunch.

'A table for two, please,' she instructed a waiter as he approached past the long bar which ran down one side of the room. 'By the window, if possible.'

There were large windows to either side of the door and the tables set on the platforms behind them were at something of a premium, since the rest of the room was very dark. Sally was glad that they'd decided to meet early; given fifteen or twenty minutes, the restaurant would be full. Brown's had been fitted out in the style of an old-fashioned French bistro and had quickly found its niche as the 'in' place to be. For that reason Sally always felt rather awkward in the place; it was much more Julia's kind of scene than hers.

'Beat me to it, I see,' her friend called as she came in a few moments later, looking, as usual, as though she'd stepped out of the pages of *Harpers & Queen*.

'Oh, I haven't been here long. How are you?'

'Overworked and underpaid, as usual.'

'I'll believe the first bit but not the second.' Sally smiled as they greeted each other with a kiss on the cheek.

'So, what have you been up to this morning?'

'Gloomy meeting with the bank manager – 'strewth, you look like an overgrown schoolgirl.'

Julia had removed her coat to reveal the latest in fashionable glamour: a tiny, low-cut red dress with delicate straps worn over a sweater of the same red.

'On your bike,' she retorted, taking mock offence. She sat down. 'What's the Chief Head of Paper Clips say, then?'

'Something along the lines of, "I think you should start banking with us for a change, Miss Blythe, instead of us with you." '

'Whoops.'

'Yes, not a very pleasant experience.'

'Anything you can do about it?'

'Not a lot – you know what it's like.'

'Yes, I suppose you're pretty stuck really.'

'That's what I thought up until now, but the question is, am I? I mean, am I really stuck or am I just allowing myself to be stuck?'

'Sounds deeply philosophical. Tell you what, let's order and we'll discuss it.'

They made their choices and settled down for the debate.

'Right,' said Julia, 'you've obviously been brain-storming, which is a good sign. Give me your thoughts – in a nutshell, though, or we'll be here all day.'

'Bugger the logic,' Sally snorted, 'it's the conclusions I've come up with that are bothering me.'

'Like?'

'Like I think I've forgotten who I am.'

'In what respect?'

'Well, to put it another way I think I redesigned my personality to fit in with the marriage and now that the marriage no longer exists, I don't know who I'm meant to be.'

'Hurrah! You've finally woken up.'

'What do you mean?'

'Well, I was beginning to wonder when you'd realise that your brain had turned to tofu.'

'There's nothing wrong with my brain.'

'Not if you use it, there isn't. You'd got so into the habit of being nanny, maid and housekeeper, I frankly despaired of you.'

'Thanks for telling me now.'

'Look, Sal,' Julia said, more seriously, 'what's a person meant to do? Say, "I think you should leave that odious toad of a husband, he's turning you into a vegetable"? You wouldn't have thanked me. In fact, you're such a stubborn devil that I doubt you'd even have listened.'

'The marriage was important to me,' Sally protested. 'Anyway, you're supposed to work at relationships.'

'I entirely agree, except that it was you doing all the work.'

'I realise that in retrospect, not that it helps.'

'Well, never mind. The question is, what are you going to do with yourself now?'

'Don't know, really, that's what I wanted to ask you . . .'

She paused while the waiter brought over their food, not shifting her gaze from her friend's face. Julia seemed to be thinking through what she was going to say next while she unfolded her napkin.

'You want my frank opinion?' she said, at length.

'Yes.'

52

'Okay. First off, there's nothing wrong with your personality – it may have got squashed flat, but it's still there. All
that's happened is that you've lost your sense of direction.'

'Well of course I flaming well have,' Sally cut in. 'Plan A
was: Marry the man you love, have children, live happily
ever after. There wasn't meant to be a Plan B, for heaven's
sake, therefore I don't have one. I was totally unprepared for
what happened.'

'You've got eyes and ears.'

'How about, he was brilliant at covering his tracks?'

'Give me a break, you're an intelligent woman, you must
have noticed something.'

Sally sulked because, of course, there had been clues and
she didn't want to have to admit that she'd ignored them.

'I'm sorry, I didn't mean to hurt you,' Julia said, reaching
across the table to touch her hand. 'It's just, you can't go on
forever wallowing in grief. All the things that happened, no
matter how bad, are over now, it's in the past. What you've
got to do is concentrate on the future. It's a question of
reviving yourself, getting back some of the old spark.'

'It's easy to say.'

'I know, but look at it this way. He's made a new life for
himself, why shouldn't you?'

'I've forgotten how to do it . . . how to be single, I mean. I
haven't been single for over ten years. Anyway, what about
the children?'

'What about them?'

'Well, I can't go gadding around without taking their
feelings into consideration.'

'Don't be such a limp lettuce. You're already giving them
all the things they need: love, food, a nice home. That's
what's important. If they're unhappy it's because they know
you're unhappy. Kids pick these things up.'

'But they haven't got their father.'

'That's his responsibility, not yours. Let him explain that

53

one away when they get older. Make him squirm for a change.'

Sally stiffened. The truth was that she still cared for Philip, despite everything. 'I don't know that I can be that evil.'

'It's not evil, it's perfectly reasonable. Stop giving yourself a hard time.'

'Oh, Julia,' Sally sighed, finally giving way, 'it's not really that I'm such a wimp. I just wish I could think of some way of digging myself out of this hole.'

'You will. You've already taken the first steps by analysing the situation in the way that you have. It's about time you started thinking about yourself for a change, about where you're going, where you want to be. You don't have to feel guilt-ridden or selfish about it. Just get on with it, that's what I say.'

'I wish I had a tenth of the belief you seem to have in me.'

Julia took a deep breath and gave Sally a long, steady look. 'I'll tell you a secret, shall I? One of the reasons that you're still my best friend is because you are utterly guileless. Never mind that you're taller, slimmer and better-looking than I'll ever be . . .'

Sally opened her mouth to protest.

'Just shut up a minute and listen. Not only are you all those things, you are also bright. Now I know that you don't necessarily identify with that description because you're too nice to be that self-possessed. But if I were to say the same to anyone who knows you, they would agree. You're one hell of a box of tricks, Sally Blythe, and don't you forget it.'

Sally sat back, stunned, not just because of the unexpected accolade but because the last piece of the jigsaw had finally clicked into place. Accepting that she'd been floundering around with no great sense of purpose had been something of a hurdle but once it was out of the way, she should have been up and running. The fact that she'd wavered had been

54

entirely due to lack of confidence, she could see that now. What Julia had said proved the spur to action.

'I wonder . . .' she mused, the grain of an idea crystallising in her mind.

'Wonder what?' asked Julia.

'Oh, nothing.'

'I sense the stirrings of some mad scheme.'

'Maybe not so mad.'

'Come on, spit it out.'

'I was thinking about that table Dad left me.'

'And?'

Sally hesitated for a moment. 'I'll tell you when I'm sure.'

'God, you're infuriating.'

'And here's me thinking you're my greatest fan.'

Julia laughed. 'All right, I can wait, but I want to be the first to know what the plot is when you're ready to spill the beans.'

'It's a deal.'

By the time the two women went their separate ways, Sally was beginning to look forward to the next day. Prior to her meeting with the bank manager, she'd been quite convinced that the table was valuable. Faced with what looked like a litany of financial disasters, she'd been scared off from that position, that was all. She started to put her fears into perspective and reconsider the possible outcome of the appointment she'd made with Ken Rees at Heather's house. She was sure that someone like Ken would not go to the trouble of journeying out to Steyning for nothing – the description she'd given him of the table must have whetted his appetite, made him think it was worth his while. That being so, she was probably going to be looking at a tidy sum by the time negotiations were over.

Sally became more focused as she set her mind to the task ahead. Somehow or other, she had to find a way of making a living. Not just because the maintenance money wasn't going to be enough to survive on but because she needed to do so for her own sake, that much was abundantly clear. The original plan had been to get shot of the table as quickly as possible in order to get some capital into her badly blitzed bank account. But now she reasoned that if the table turned out to be quite valuable, selling it might give her just the opportunity she needed to break loose from the inertia she had drifted into.

With some of her old spirit, Sally straightened her shoulders and headed off through the streets of Brighton, a new sense of purpose in her step. That table was going to be her way out, she decided. Whatever she got for it must go into a new venture. Now all she had to do was to dream one up.

5

The Old Rectory was one of the few buildings to have remained intact in the small hamlet of Kingston Bucci. Set back from the main coast road by a scant third of a mile, it was a haven of peace and beauty in an otherwise blighted landscape. From where it stood, overlooking a wide expanse of green, it was hard to believe that an ugly jumbly of industrial warehouses and a half-demolished power station were just a stone's throw away in the featureless hinterland of Shoreham. The two areas were at odds with each other, although they shared a common fate: both had catered for the needs of former times; both had been made redundant by social change. Yet the rectory survived to serve a different purpose where the old industries did not, and its solid stone walls looked set to weather several more centuries in the protective shadow of the church to which it had once belonged.

A flight of white fan-tailed doves scattered over the coach house roof as Ken Rees rounded the corner and knocked on the rectory door. He watched them sweep into the sky in a long, breathtaking arch then return to settle with disgruntled clucks and coos, eyeing him suspiciously until he disappeared over the threshold.

'Fabulous, aren't they?' he commented to Jon, stepping into the kitchen where the smell of fresh ground coffee hung deliciously on the air.

'Bloody nuisance more like,' Jon grumbled, darkly.

'I thought they appealed to your sense of the aesthetic.'

'It's all very well until they start breeding. Every year it's the same thing. I hate taking the chicks away, but if I didn't get rid of them, we'd be inundated with the blighters.'

'Don't tell me you kill them?'

'Good God, no.' Jon shuddered. 'I have tried giving them away, but there aren't many takers, so instead I have to let them free. That, I might add, entails me bundling them into a basket in the boot and driving for hours into the country. If you release them anywhere within a hundred miles they find their way back.'

'Last time he ended up in Wales,' Tony laughed as he came through from the drawing room.

Jon frowned at him. 'Just so long as I keep you amused,' he said, tartly.

'Come on, don't be touchy.' Tony went up and slipped an arm around Jon's waist, giving him an affectionate squeeze.

'You only want me for my carrot cake.' Jon smiled, returning the hug with a kiss on the cheek.

'Quite right. Any chance of a piece?'

'It's still hot.'

'Oh, go on.'

'All right, all right, it's your stomach ache.' He turned to Ken. 'I suppose you won't say no?'

'Thanks, I'd love a piece.'

The three moved towards the long refectory table where Jon cleared a space by pushing the paperwork he had been working on to one side. He was a lecturer at Sussex University and often did his marking at home.

'Exams coming up?' asked Ken.

'No, just the usual essays – part of the continual assessment system. It's a bit of a bind for me but fairer to the students, on the whole.'

'Certainly beats having to retain three years' worth of information and hoping to be able to disgorge it all in the finals.'

'Yes. People used to go down like flies in my day – nervous breakdowns, suicide attempts. The pressure to perform was just too much for many.'

'Oxford man, aren't you?'

Jon nodded. 'Of course, the standards were different then, too. I don't know what they teach them in school these days but if you ask me, it's a miracle that anyone gets to university level. Their spelling is abysmal and their grasp of grammar tenuous, to say the least. And that's just the bright ones. Lord alone knows what happens to the rest. I seem to spend most of the time correcting simple errors when I should really be concentrating on the content.'

'That's what you get in Mr Major's Britain,' Tony jeered. 'Bring back Maggie Thatcher, that's what I say.'

'You must be joking! She may be tough but there's too much of the autocrat about her for my liking.'

'Well, everyone is so spineless these days – I mean, look at this European business. We can't sneeze unless it's been discussed by several committees and then ratified in Brussels. I wouldn't mind but look at the state of the so-called European Union! Germany's economy is in a mess thanks to reunification, and coupled with that the crime rate's gone up, which is all grist to the mill for the Neo-Nazis. The French care about no one but the French and lean ever more alarmingly towards the likes of Monsieur Le Pen. And in Italy, where the word politician is synonymous with corruption, they're about to elect a fascist. I ask you! Are these the people with whom Britannia should be getting into bed?'

'Probably not,' remarked Ken, 'but unfortunately Britannia

doesn't rule the waves these days. We simply can't afford to be isolationist any more. Our neighbours' feelings have to be taken into account.'

'I'll worry about that when they start marching through the Chunnel in goose step,' Tony conceded.

'God, you're a terrible old reactionary,' Jon laughed. 'Come the revolution, they'll be sending the tumbrils round for you.'

'I'll go like a lamb so long as I can wear the breeches and ruffled shirt,' said Tony, archly.

'Fool!'

'Quite fancy myself as Sydney Carton. "...'Tis a far, far better thing that I do now ..." '

' "... than I have ever done," ' the other two chimed in, with loud guffaws.

'I think you missed your vocation there,' said Ken when the laughter died down.

'Huh!' said Jon. 'More ham than a pork butcher.'

He got up and cleared the pots away, a quiet gesture that implied the time had come to get down to business. Ken could always tell when the moment had arrived. Jon would somehow fade into the background, leaving Tony to shine, although of the two, Jon had the better schooling in antiques. It was a question of complimentary types; always rather shy and withdrawn, Jon would keep his counsel while Tony did the sales pitch.

'Come on then,' he said, pushing back his chair, 'let's see what you think.' He led the way through to the drawing room. Ken followed, blinking as he stepped into the half-light. The drawing room was long and low, panelled all round in carved dark oak. At once imposing and severe, Ken couldn't help feeling that, in times gone by, no visitor to the rector's inner sanctum could have been left in any doubt as to who was in charge.

'Over here,' Tony said, motioning Ken towards him. He

bent to lift two wooden panels out from beside a superb japanned bureau bookcase.

'A bit of a new area for you?' Ken commented as one panel was turned towards him, revealing an icon of the Virgin and Child.

'They were too good to miss,' Tony replied, turning the second panel over to show a much simpler picture of a Russian saint.

'Where did you get them?'

'Ask no questions . . .' said Tony, mysteriously, but Ken had already guessed that they must have been smuggled out of one of the newly independent states which had formerly been part of the Soviet Union. It wasn't too difficult a thing to do; the authorities were too busy cobbling together some sort of democracy to bother themselves with keeping tabs on art treasures.

'The Mother of God of Vladimir,' Ken mused as he studied the first icon. 'Very fine work. Seventeenth-century, I'd say – the composition shows quite a lot of Western influence, you can see it in the way the eyes and hands have been done, too . . . beautiful.'

'Mmm, I don't usually go for religious pieces, but this one's a bit special, isn't it?' Tony took a pair of gold-rimmed spectacles out of his pocket and peered at the picture more closely. 'Do you see where the paint's flaked off?' he asked, pointing to a couple of tiny marks. 'Jon reckons there's probably another icon underneath.'

'Oh, definitely,' Ken said, lightly passing a finger over the picture's surface. 'The way the craquelure's crazed gives it away. In fact, there's probably two or three under there – they used to paint over them every so often, usually when they'd become blackened with smut from the oil lamps. The question is, if you were to clean off this image, would the one under it be in any way superior?'

'Too risky, then?'

61

'I think so, in this particular case. What you have here is probably worth about fifty thousand pounds. I don't think you'd do better with whatever you might find.'

A twinkle appeared in Tony's eye. He'd patently picked up the icons at bargain basement prices. He took the Madonna from Ken's hand and looked at it with renewed interest.

'Better leave well enough alone,' he said. Then after a pause, 'You know, I prefer this to the other one, can't really say why. Perhaps because the other's too naive for my taste.'

'Well, you say that,' said Ken, picking up the other icon and holding it to the light, 'but in fact the artist was highly skilled – look at the detail, the balance . . . the painting may be stylised but it certainly isn't naive.'

Tony gave it a second glance. 'Still doesn't do much for me.'

'No?' The icon, an image of Saint Charalambos, his long white beard displayed over a simple blue robe, was certainly plainer, but to Ken it had more depth of feeling. It reflected the true tradition of the Eastern Orthodox Church and there was something genuinely inspiring about it. He was trying to find a way of articulating that thought when he noticed that Tony was watching his face.

'You think it's better than the other one, don't you?'

'It's not a question of better,' he replied. 'In fact, this one would fetch a fraction of the price of the other.'

'What, then?'

'Well, look,' he said, taking back the icon of the Virgin and holding it up for comparison. 'What you have here goes a long way towards being a work of art. This, though,' he nodded towards Saint Charalambos, 'is a statement of faith.'

'Very profound.'

'Not really. I suppose it's a matter of taste. You see, when I look at this icon, I can see that the man who painted it really believed what the church taught. It has a simple, almost

62

child-like quality; unquestioning, unsentimental. That's what I find attractive about it.'

For a moment, Tony was taken aback. He was surprised to find such sensitivity in a man like Ken. Not that he was insensitive in manner, but because he was thick-set he looked more the type who would be happiest on a rugby pitch.

'What are you looking for on this, then?' Ken asked suddenly, putting the conversation back into context.

'About a grand,' Tony said, working on Jon's assessment. 'You interested?'

'Not at that price.'

'Want to make me an offer?'

Ken thought for a while, then shook his head. 'Not right now. Look, I've got some more business coming up this afternoon. Perhaps I could call you about it later?'

'Okay, no rush.'

The two moved out of the room and back into the kitchen where Jon was still busy with his papers.

'You off, then?' he called.

'Yep. Thanks for the coffee and cake.'

'You're welcome. Perhaps you'd like to come to dinner soon?'

'Have you got something planned?'

'I was thinking of having a couples evening, for a change. Could do with a few women around to look pretty and generally liven the place up.'

Ken couldn't help registering surprise.

'Oh, he loves his girls,' said Tony, noticing. 'Practically has a harem full of them flitting around.'

'Seems like a terrible waste.'

'We're not all your way inclined, dear,' Jon replied. 'Some of us appreciate women for their finer points. Anyway, you can't spend your whole life surrounded by a bunch of hairy blokes.'

63

'My sentiments exactly.'

'Then perhaps you'd like to start thinking about who you'd like to bring.'

'Oh, you don't want me as a spare?'

'No. It's bring your own bird or nothing. Bit of fresh blood is what we need.'

'Well, I'll have to put my brains to steep.'

'Go on, a quick riffle through your little black book will sort it out.'

'Nothing much riffles through there these days, except the moths.'

'That's your wallet you're talking about,' said Tony, nudging him.

Ken smiled. *'Touché.'*

The prospect of an invitation to dinner cheered Ken as he headed the car inland towards Steyning. A three-course extravaganza courtesy of Tony and Jon certainly held more promise than his usual diet. Although Ken was a good cook, for convenience sake he'd often make do for days with a large stew which he only had to reheat for a decent meal. There was a limit to the amount of chicken or lamb a person could face repeatedly, though, and by mid-week he'd be tempted to throw what remained away and rustle up something more exciting. It was an urge he rarely allowed himself to succumb to. The guilt that only a true war baby could feel when faced with wilful waste would normally get the better of him and instead of following his instincts, he'd end up ladling out yet another portion of whatever was going and tossing a handful of fresh chilli over the top to enliven the taste.

He smiled to himself as he relished the thought of the evening to come. The only cloud on the horizon was the niggling question of whom he could ask to share it with him. There were a number of women who instantly came to mind, mainly the wives of good friends who wouldn't mind them being borrowed for an evening. It was the kind of inverted compliment he'd grown used to. Yet while it was nice to be thought of as trustworthy, the implication that he was therefore 'safe', irked him. He only remained celibate because the women that he knew were either off limits or, frankly, desperate. The ones in the latter category were generally divorcees in their late-forties and although he, perhaps better than anyone, empathised with their plight, he was not one for filling a gap just because a gap needed filling.

He went over the list of possibles as he drove steadily along the long, straight stretch of road that led away from the coast. There was, of course, always the option of smoothing things over with Valerie, his latest involvement, but that carried with it the risk of getting back, yet again, into the ever-decreasing circle of their fundamentally doomed affair. It was a shame, because he was really fond of her and knew that she cared terribly for him. Yet in the year or so that they'd been seeing each other there'd been perhaps two months of real happiness. After that, it'd been pretty much on-and-off. He thought of all the moments they'd shared and began to feel rather sad. There was part of him that longed for her warmth, yet that on its own had not been enough to make him commit to a longer term arrangement. It all came back to the usual thing: he was looking for more in a relationship than gentle togetherness whereas she was prepared to compromise.

'Such is life,' Ken said to himself, shelving the problem for consideration some other time. For the moment, he was more concerned with his next appointment. He turned off the roundabout that lay at the foot of Steyning village and started fumbling in his jacket pocket for the envelope on which he'd written the address that he was looking for. It was not very illuminating, and he managed to go both ways down the High Street before deciding it would be easier to get out and walk.

The polite tinkle of a bell, reminiscent of an old corner shop, announced Ken's arrival some minutes later in the front of the half-timbered house which doubled as a gallery. He stood for a moment, expecting a response, but when none came, began looking around. There was a range of pictures dotted around the room but his attention was drawn to a collection of water colours which were arranged on one particular wall. Instantly recognisable as local scenes, they were not the sort of thing to which Ken was usually attracted but there was something about them that made him move closer – a vivacity of style that was missing in so much of the genre that could be seen elsewhere. He was admiring one of the group, a powerful study of nearby Bramber Castle, when a woman appeared from the back of the shop.

'Can I help you, or are you just looking?'

He glanced aside into a pair of piercing blue eyes, made all the more striking by the mass of black hair which framed her face.

'Oh!' he said, taken aback. 'I hope I'm in the right place. This is number thirty-two?'

'Yes . . . why, what were you expecting?'

'Well, a private house, to be honest.'

She looked him over for a moment, the flicker of a smile playing at the edges of her mouth and increasing as she realised how well he fitted Sally's description.

'I take it you're Mr Rees?'

'I am.' He looked a little surprised.

'Then you're in the right place.' She offered her hand. 'Heather Blythe.'

'Pleased to meet you.' He used the moment to make a better assessment of her. He'd expected her to be nearer the age he'd imagined Sally's father must have been. A whole range of intriguing questions went through Ken's mind as he shook the offered hand then released it, more slowly then he'd intended.

Heather took the compliment casually. 'You'd better come through,' she said, leading the way into the living room. 'My daughter isn't here yet, but I'm expecting her any minute.'

Ken noted the reference as he followed along behind her. It interested him that she should identify her relationship with Sally in closer terms than Sally did herself.

'Can I get you a cup of tea or something, while we wait?' Heather asked.

'That'd be great – if it's not too much trouble . . .'

'No, no. Just make yourself comfortable.'

But Ken remained standing after she'd left the room. There were, as he'd hoped, a number of things in there that merited closer inspection, the most obvious of which was the grand-father clock which had just begun to strike four. He went over to it and began to examine the dial, checking to see if it belonged inside the flame mahogany case. The detail of the flower motifs in each corner of the dial indicated that it was in its original setting; if they had been partly obscured, he would have been certain that it had come from a different clock.

'Thought you'd come to look at our table,' Heather remarked as she came back in, slightly irritated that the stranger had started checking out the goods before being invited to do so.

'Hum,' he replied, without a flicker of remorse, still gazing at the clock face. 'You know, it's quite rare to find the "Strike/Silent" feature on provincial clocks.'

Heather looked blank.

'The switch here on the left-hand side,' he continued, 'for turning the chimes on and off.'

She put down the tea tray she'd been holding and went over to where Ken was standing.

'I didn't even know they could be turned off.'

'Well, if you think about it, when the clock was new, it would probably have stood in the hallway of a reasonably grand house, and the floor being stone or marble, you would have been able to hear it striking in every room. At night time, when that would have been something of an inconvenience, the butler would switch off the chimes, then in the morning he'd switch them on again.'

'How very practical.'

'Yes,' he said, taking a step backwards to look at the bottom of the wooden case. 'Of course the fact that the clock was standing on that type of floor also meant that it would have been mopped round a couple of times a day. Nobody would have thought twice about it, but in time the water would rot the wood. This plinth is a replacement, see.'

She didn't see, but looked at the plinth anyway. 'Does that detract from its value?'

'Not really, it seems to have been sympathetically restored. What's more important is that the dial and movement are still intact.'

'And how do you know that?'

'Well, the dial is original but I'd have to take the hood off to check the movement.'

'Hood?'

'This bit here, at the top of the case. But it'd have to be done carefully. It'd be a shame to damage the fretwork on the sides – it's rather fragile, you see, and easy to damage if your fingers stick through.'

Heather looked at him with a degree of astonishment. She'd been planning to draw him out on his knowledge of art, give him a mental run around the block to test his integrity, but now it seemed something of a fruitless exercise. This man was obviously in command of his subject.

'I had no idea that clocks could be so interesting,' she said, at last.

'There's a lot to look for, it's true.' He smiled. 'But, you know, every piece has its own peculiarity – or personality, you might say. That's what makes my work fun.'

She smiled in return, beginning to like him better. 'Yes, I suppose it must. Ready for that cup of tea, now?'

'Oh, sorry, forgot all about it,' he said as she moved away towards the long, low table which stood in front of the sofa. He lingered to listen for a moment before turning to join her. 'The movement's a bit out of balance, you know.'

'Is it?'

'Yep, it's not even.'

Heather looked up from pouring the tea. 'So tell me, Mr Holmes,' she said, dryly, 'how do you come to that conclusion?'

'A clock goes *tick*, *tick*, not *tick*, *tock*,' he declared, bending to take a cup from her hand.

She creased up with laughter.

'Honestly – ask any clock maker,' he said, laughing too. There was just enough time to catch the scent of her hair before he stepped away.

The shop bell clattered and hurried footsteps brought two children dashing into the room.

'Hello, my loves,' Heather called, putting down her tea cup to give them a welcoming hug. In seconds they were squirming all over both her and the sofa.

'Don't overdo it, boys,' said Sally as she came through the door. 'Sorry I'm late.'

'No problem,' Heather replied. 'Tea?'

'Yes, please, I'm absolutely gasping . . . Oh, hello, Mr Rees, you found the house okay, then?'

'After a minor detour.' He got up and smiled. 'And please call me Ken.'

She came over and shook his hand, but it seemed to Ken to be rather a perfunctory gesture. She was more brittle today, he thought, probably a bit frantic, what with the school run and the traffic. The tension was apparent on her face; the features looked sharper than they had the last time he'd seen her, but it would probably pass once she'd settled down.

'Have you looked at the table yet?' she asked.

'No, we were waiting for you to arrive.'

'Oh, good. I want to hear everything you've got to say.'

'That could take some time, if his appraisal of the clock's anything to go by,' said Heather, as she returned from the kitchen.

'Oh?'

'Mmm, very instructive, I must say.'

'Really? I take it you've been getting acquainted, then?'

'After a fashion.'

Ken was beginning to feel uncomfortable with this line of conversation when, out of the corner of his eye, he saw a cushion fly up off the sofa. He caught it just before it sent the tea tray flying out of Heather's hand.

'Whoops, nearly scored an own goal,' he said quickly, desperate to defuse the anger that Sally looked ready to unleash on her sons.

'I think we'd better find you two something else to play with,' said Heather, tightly. 'Come on, into the studio, I'll find you something to draw on.'

The children filed after her meekly, aware that they'd missed retribution by the skin of their teeth.

'I could murder them sometimes,' Sally fumed.

'Never mind, no harm done,' said Ken, softly.

She looked at him. 'Are you always this calm?'

He shrugged. 'Try to be. Anything else is a waste of energy.'

She nodded, seeming to relax a little. 'Well, what do you think of the house?'

'Lovely. Can't beat the feel of old wood and stone. It creates an atmosphere all its own.'

'Mmm, that's what I like about it too – makes me feel secure.'

'There is that element to it but the thing that always affects me most about places like this is the thought of how much human life has gone by in them . . . generations of people have called this home, and from the cradle to the grave it has seen them through who knows how many happy or sad hours. In a way, it's as though the walls have absorbed all that, they almost speak of it. There is the most marvellous sense of history and continuity. I think that's why we tend to feel more at ease in or around old things.'

'Is that why you're in antiques?'

'Not entirely, but it's certainly one of the reasons I enjoy it. I love beautiful things, of course, but I get a different kick out of handling the more mundane pieces, tables, chairs, cabinets – things like that. They've been used and touched by hundreds of people before me and they'll go on being used and touched long after I've gone, but I like to think that a little bit of me goes with them just because they've been through my hands.'

'You're giving me the chills,' said Sally, who was thinking how odd it was to have come across someone as enigmatic as Ken in a café in Worthing. It wasn't just that the town, as well as the venue, fitted so badly with her image of a place where one might find such a person, but he himself didn't seem to fit his appearance either. She looked at the clothes he was wearing today: a pair of casual slacks topped off with a rather old-fashioned V-necked sweater over a shirt that was unbuttoned at the collar. It was all so restrained, as if he were purposely trying to look as inconspicuous as possible. Yet for all his efforts, conscious or unconscious, he had an unmistakable presence.

'Right, that's fixed them,' Heather's voice broke in as she came back into the room. 'Thank heavens for a couple of pieces of A4 and a box of poster paints.'

'Well, I hope they aren't going to create even more havoc,' said Sally.

'They'll be all right. I've moved anything that matters out of harm's reach and put them on the floor with masses of newspaper. Now, are we any further forward?'

'With what?'

'The table, of course.'

'Haven't even looked at it yet.'

'Well, don't you think it's about time we did. It's almost five o'clock. The next thing you know the boys will be howling for food.'

'I'm sorry, I didn't realise . . .' said Sally, then to Ken, 'it's this one over here.'

He hardly had to follow her with his eyes to know which side of the room she would go to. It had taken the most cursory glance round to identify the table he'd been invited to see and even at a distance it had the feel of a good piece.

Sally cleared a vase of flowers off the table's highly polished surface then stood back so that Ken could make his judgement. But he approached it with such apparent lack of interest that her heart started to sink. He looked at the marquetry inlay for a long time then passed a hand lightly over the top of it. His face still registered absolutely nothing.

'I'll have to turn it over,' he said, suddenly.

A space was cleared for the inspection to be made. Once the table was upside down, Ken looked more closely at the legs and feet. Sally stood twitching for a few minutes, wishing she knew what he was looking for, and was about to ask when he arrived at an opinion.

'Actually, it's very good,' he said, to her relief. 'Tell me, do you know where it came from?'

Sally turned to Heather.

'It belonged to your grandmother,' she said, adding more quietly, 'She gave it to your mother – as a wedding present.'

There was a pause whilst Sally took the information in, then swallowed hard.

'I still have to sell it.'

'If I were you,' said Ken, sensing she was upset and trying to move beyond it as quickly as possible, 'I wouldn't sell it locally. It needs to go to a major auction house.'

'Oh?'

'One of the London rooms,' he continued. 'I think Sotheby's would be best.'

'Gosh!' Sally livened up. 'Is it really valuable, then?'

'Should get around twelve grand for it. Maybe a bit more.'

She let slip a squeal of excitement. 'Oh, Heather,' she said, hugging her stepmother. 'Isn't it wonderful?'

'Well, it's certainly a bit of a surprise, but how do you suggest we go about getting it to Sotheby's?'

'I'll take it,' said Ken. 'It's no trouble.'

'But I presume you'd be expecting some sort of commission for that service?' observed Heather, sharply.

'Of course,' he replied, in a matter-of-fact way. 'I'd have to have the vendor's commission.'

'Which is?'

'Ten per cent.'

'Ah.'

'But, Heather,' Sally cut in, 'twelve thousand pounds!'

'Minus ten per cent and, no doubt, Sotheby's commission.'

'You're still looking at a much better sale price than you could expect elsewhere.' Ken shrugged. 'Still, it's up to you.'

Sally hesitated for a moment. She looked at the table, then at Heather, and finally at Ken. She took a deep breath.

'I say, go for it.'

6

Sussex Gardens had been closed to traffic, making the old road a pleasant refuge for the shoppers and students who came to browse around the odd, cosmopolitan mix of retail outlets that ran along either side. There were discount stores, book shops, a delicatessen, a hobby shop and a whole range of junk shops selling everything from Victorian lace to copperware and pottery. It was these in particular that took Sally's interest, and she went along making a mental note of everything she saw in a determined effort to learn as much as she could about what was saleable, why and at what price, in the baffling world that called itself the antiques trade.

She smiled a mischievous little smile. So far, she hadn't told anybody what she was up to and she was rather enjoying the element of secrecy. For weeks, now, she'd been shooting around the district in her Mini, checking out the various markets that were to be found. The idea of getting involved in antiques dealing had been growing steadily ever since Ken's visit to Steyning. It was obviously a risky business but it did have huge appeal. It seemed to her that if a person researched the thing carefully enough, they should be able to make a reasonable living at it. But that was before she'd gone into it in any depth. The trouble was knowing what to start with and how. And that, she decided, was going to be a tougher nut to crack than she'd first imagined.

Sally looked around at the tea caddies and cups, the coal scuttles and cast iron pans, the horse brasses, toasting forks and sad little pieces of chipped crockery that once had been 'A present from . . .', with a sense of mounting confusion. Who was to know what value to set on these leftovers from past lives? Certainly, she couldn't gauge it. To her mind, a lot of what was termed 'antique' looked more like terrible old tat, some of it no older that yesterday's papers, yet there was obviously a market for the stuff. The concept intrigued her. At one end of the business, people made thousands on the turn of one deal; at the other, traders were content to take a small profit on a regular basis. She wondered how hard it really was to make a living at the lower end of the scale, the place she would obviously have to start with no introduction and virtually no knowledge.

Maybe it's just a madcap scheme after all, she worried, perhaps I should try something more conventional. But she'd gone over that time and again without finding an acceptable solution. There just weren't the hours in the day for a conventional career, even though she'd taken the first step towards buying herself more freedom by having her youngest son go to nursery school for the whole week instead of just a couple of days. He was coming up to four soon anyway, and needed to get used to the routine. But that still only left six hours, between school runs.

It's not enough, she thought, and what would I do in the holidays, anyway? No. My only chance is to find something that can be done profitably and quickly. And right now, this looks like my best shot.

She thought again of the table, and the twelve thousand pounds that Ken had estimated it should make. It was a relief to know that there was going to be money in the bank at last. There'd be a bit of a wait for it, and it would have to be used cautiously when it came. But at least there would be capital.

Well, why not? she asked herself, as her confidence slowly began to rise again. If you don't gamble, you can't win.

Sally went on down the street in a happier state of mind, aware that she was feeling better about herself than she had for a long time. Her attitude to life had changed radically over the past few weeks. From the moment she'd realised that she was going to be financially secure, at least for the immediate future, a great weight seemed to lift from her shoulders. Organisation on a scale that even she had forgotten she was capable of began to order the little household she had set up with her sons, and the change affected everybody, so that the atmosphere was already calmer and more positive. An equally sudden transformation had brought the countryside to life too. Swathes of blossom hung heavily on the fruit trees and cascades of new leaves shone in countless shades of green wherever she looked. The sight of spring in full tilt, with its promise of the summer to come, matched Sally's new mood and the whole prospect of getting involved in something new thrilled her, not least because it promised to be an adventure. Nevertheless, she was sensible enough to realise that she was going to have to limit her risk-taking.

With that in mind, Sally made her first and most difficult decision. She set herself a deadline, a year at the most. If she wasn't making money from antiques by then, she told herself, she'd have to knock it on the head. Once she'd committed herself to that vow, Sally settled down to make a thorough study of the business. The funny little junk shops of Brighton's back streets took on a different aspect as she searched for clues to the bargains of the future and started to formulate a plan of action that she hoped would set her on the road to success.

Without a word to Heather or any of her friends, she set about her mission. The indoor markets of Brighton and Lewes became regular haunts and any information she could glean from the traders she found there was stored away for future use.

One of the things that struck her as strange was how different the markets were. Brighton, with its silver and jewellery, was definitely up a peg on Lewes, although of the two towns Lewes gave the greater impression of permanence and wealth. She came to the conclusion that Brighton catered more for passing trade. All season, coach loads of Dutch, German and American tourists would arrive, mostly middle-aged or elderly couples, ready primed by thoughtful tour operators to a level of expectation that could only be induced in the hard-working taking a rare chance of relaxation. So, in holiday mood and with wallets bulging, the husbands were willingly persuaded by the wives to part with rather more than they would have done otherwise on some pretty trinket that would, ever after, be called upon to reawaken the memory of that moment of supposed romance.

Lewes was a different matter. Only stragglers, Sunday drivers or those in the know found their way to the indoor markets there. Alongside booths which contained the type of furniture and effects which could be found almost anywhere in the trade warehouses of the Sussex coast, there were others specialising in light fittings. The sheer variety was an attraction in itself and it was well known to enterprising householders as a useful source of lamps and lanterns that would have cost twice as much at Christopher Wray's.

Faced with the sheer diversity of goods on offer at every turn, Sally got into the habit of carrying around a notebook and pen so that she could scribble down thoughts and comments or make little sketches of the things she saw. Then at night, when the children and the chores had been dealt with, she'd sit down with a drink and take time to compare her drawings and notes with the photographs and descriptions to be found in the antiques guide that she'd bought after the Worthing auction. Before long she developed a feel for the type of thing that was likely to be a good investment and at last she thought she was ready to take her first risk. With that aim in mind and the monthly child allowance tucked into her purse, she drifted along Sussex Gardens waiting for something to take her eye, only mildly restrained by a combination of shyness and guilt.

God, I hope that Ken Rees knows what he's talking about, she thought as she rummaged through a boxful of old periodicals which had been dumped amongst the general clutter in the shop she had stopped at. But the worry wasn't bad enough to distract her for long. Beside the box, with its handle sticking out of a brown paper bag, was a parasol which looked as if it had been put down in a hurry and forgotten. She drew it out of the bag to take a better look. The black silk cover was embroidered with yellow rose buds and dazzling russet leaves and the edge was fringed around with fine lace very similar to the strips she'd seen at the antique textiles shop at the other end of the street. She fingered the lace carefully, admiring its intricate rose design. The quality of the work seemed very good. She looked up to where the shop owner was standing in conversation with another customer and decided to make her move.

'Excuse me,' she said, going over to him with the umbrella back in its paper bag, 'what are you asking for this?'

The shopkeeper glanced at the package, taking a greater interest in the handle that was protruding out of it than what was hidden in it.

'Fifty quid,' he answered, without bothering to take the examination further.

'I haven't got that much cash on me,' Sally fibbed.

'What have you got?'

'About forty.'

'Okay.'

Startled at the speed of the deal, she fumbled with her bag and found the money whilst the shopkeeper continued with his conversation.

'Thanks,' she called as she left in some haste, feeling as if she'd done quite well.

Further down the street, Sally wavered outside the shop selling old textiles. The window contained a selection of nightgowns, christening robes and bedlinen as well as some more peculiar items, like a pair of leather riding boots and a pith helmet. She wondered if her parasol would be of any interest. Summoning up her courage, she went inside and waited for the opportunity to talk to the woman behind the till.

'I see you deal in Victoriana,' she said, at last.

The woman nodded.

'I have a parasol to sell, if you'd like to see it?'

'We don't really deal with that sort of thing,' said the woman, bluntly, 'but I'll take a look.'

Sally took the parasol out of the bag and handed it to her. The woman opened and closed it and examined the lace before handing it back.

'It's quite nice. What do you want for it?'

'I'm not really sure, what do you think it's worth?'

The woman gave her a sour look. 'I'm not here to give valuations.'

'Well, I don't know what you might be able to sell it for.'

'Look, dear, I'm busy. You tell me what you want for it and I'll tell you whether I'm interested or not.'

Sally was cowed but not beaten.

'Seventy pounds,' she tried.

'No.'

'Sixty-five?'

'No.'

'Well, I don't think I can let it go for any less.'

'Fine.'

Sally put the parasol back into the brown paper bag and turned away.

'Well, thanks anyway.'

The woman looked at her for a moment and seemed to relent.

'There's a place in North Street that sells a lot of stuff like that, why don't you try them?'

Sally turned round. 'Thanks, I will.'

For the ten minutes it took to drive to North Street, Sally was kicking herself for being so obviously inept. She realised she would have to be a lot more hard-headed if she wasn't going to blow her next chance. As she pushed open the door of the shop, she tried her best to assume a nonchalant look.

'Morning,' she said to the old lady inside, 'I've got a parasol to show you.'

'I think I've got as many as I can take,' the old lady replied, gesturing upwards. An unbelievable array of umbrellas dangled from hooks covering every square inch of the ceiling.

'Gosh, you have got a lot.'

'Yes.'

'They're lovely,' Sally added, admiring one in particular, which was of a delicate lilac shade on a very slim bone handle. The price tag hanging from it read £140.

'Mmm, I like the more unusual ones, like that. The majority of parasols you get are plain black and they don't sell so well!'

'Oh?'

'People buy them for weddings these days, you see. They want white ones or some pastel shade.'

'Oh.' Sally began to feel as though she might have made a bad buy after all.

'Still,' said the old lady, 'let's see what you've got.'

The parasol came out of its paper bag again. There was a pause whilst it was opened, turned and felt.

'It is very striking,' the old lady said. 'In good condition too . . . belonged to your grandma, I expect?'

'Someone in the family although I don't know where it came from originally,' replied Sally, being economic with the truth.

'And what would you like for it?'

'I thought about seventy pounds.'

'Ooh! I can't do it for that.'

'But it's worth about a hundred,' said Sally, picking a figure near to the one on the lilac umbrella.

'To a customer, perhaps, but it wouldn't be worth my while buying it at that price. I have to consider the upkeep of the premises – light, heat, rates, that sort of thing, and it doesn't get any cheaper.'

'How much of a profit do you have to make then . . . if you don't mind me asking, that is?'

'Well, it's not something I'd usually tell someone, but – it varies. Over a year I suppose it averages out at about thirty per cent, but to achieve that, you're marking things up at anywhere between ten and one hundred per cent.'

'Heavens.'

'I know it sounds a lot but there are more expenses than you think involved in running a business.' The old lady sighed then added, 'I can see you're disappointed.'

'I had hoped to get a reasonable price.'

'Well, your parasol is a nice one, I must admit.' She ran her hand over the carved hook handle while she gave it some thought. 'Tell you what, I'll give you fifty-five for it.'

Sally smelt the prospect of a slightly better deal. She made a face as though the haggling process was distasteful to her.

'You couldn't make it sixty, could you?'

The old lady looked pained. 'Oh, I suppose so. Don't know what I'm thinking of, though . . .'

Back in the car, Sally breathed a huge sigh of relief. She was twenty pounds better off than she had been an hour before. The small triumph gave her an appetite for bigger and better things.

I know that setting up a stall is the logical place to start, she thought, but I'd have to spend time finding the right things to put on it, and I might end up taking too long doing that to really justify any money I might make. I wonder if I ought to have another string to my bow?

She'd toyed with the idea of trying to get into house clearances before but had more or less given up on it as she couldn't see herself, at all of nine stone three, wrestling single-handedly with a pile of bulky furniture.

Maybe I should take a closer look at what's involved, she thought now. If the profit element is good enough, it might be worth hiring a man and a van to help me do the heavy work.

Sally sat and pondered for a while. Practically all the shops that she'd been around that morning had been packed with stuff that had obviously come from house clearances. If other small traders could do okay out of it, why shouldn't she? She smiled suddenly and turned the key in the steering block.

'Home, girl,' she said, leaning forward to pat the console of her Mini. 'And don't spare the horse power.'

Early the next Saturday morning, two disgruntled children were packed up and driven off to a field on the side of a wind-swept ridge at the top of the Downs where a collection of cars and vans stood ready for the fray. A sturdy man with a ruddy face stepped forward as they turned through the gate.

'Buying or selling?' he said, pushing his face up to the driver's window.

'Buying.'

'Over there, please.'

Sally manoeuvred the Mini over a series of bumps and pulled up alongside a Land Rover.

'What are the people doing, Mummy?' her three-year-old asked as she lifted him out.

'It's a boot sale.'

'I don't want any boots.'

'Not welly boots, silly, car boots – you know, the bit we put the shopping in.'

'Are they selling their shopping?'

'No, they're selling things they don't need any more.'

'Will there be any toys?' said Jonathan, perking up.

'I expect so. Come on, undo your seat belt.'

'Oh, good.' He scrambled across the back seat and jumped out right on his mother's foot.

'Ow!'

'Sorry.'

'Honest to God, as if I didn't have enough problems,' Sally grumbled, bending to give her foot a rub. 'Here, hold Matthew's hand will you?'

'I'm cold.'

'Well, put your hood up.'

'Will there really be toys?'

'Yes, yes.' She led the two of them towards the lines of bric-à-brac, some arranged neatly in boxes, more heaped together on the grass in an impossible jumble, the whole lot presided over by a range of seemingly proud owners.

'Get your rubbish here!' yelled one, with absolute candour.

'Yeah, dead right,' said his neighbour churlishly. 'Reckon that lot'll end up back on the dump.'

'Got out of bed the wrong side, did we?' returned the first pitch-holder, his fixed smile never wavering. 'Here, this'll cheer you up.'

83

A photograph album was handed across, the contents of which produced a rich oath from the second man.

'Where the hell did you get this?'

'Never you mind . . .'

Sally moved on quickly, picking her way past old clothes, gardening tools, bicycles, electrical appliances, pictures, golf balls, and a whole parade of other battered bits and pieces that seemed to have been plundered from every attic, cellar and garden shed in the county.

'This wind's ruining my cuttings,' a woman selling bedding plants complained to her husband. Then, seeing Sally pause to look, added, 'Here you are, dear, geraniums, fuchsias, busy Lizzies – nothing over 50p.'

'However do you manage to do them for that?'

'Oh, I don't expect to make much, just enough to cover the compost and the cost of heating the green house,' the woman replied, cheerfully. 'We're pensioners, you see.'

Sally bought a mixed tray of plants, thinking to split them with Heather later on.

'Do you do a lot of these boot sales?'

'Loads, it's a nice hobby and you meet some nice people. Mind you,' she added, lowering her voice, 'you've got to watch out for the ones selling dirty videos.'

'Is there much of that about?'

'You get all sorts round here, love, but most of them are harmless.'

Sally passed along a few paces to a pitch offering a weird and wonderful selection of boating paraphernalia. In amongst the widgets and whatsits that obviously had some vital use, if only she'd known anything about the subject, was an incredibly ancient and rather revolting-looking latrine. She couldn't imagine who would covet such a thing and was about to turn away in disgust when she spotted an old typewriter lying on its side at one end of a large cardboard box. She lifted it out and saw that it was an early portable machine, fixed on a rigid base which also served as the bottom of the carrying case. The lid, now minus a handle, was laying nearby and an important-looking notice inside gave the serial number as well as a 'world-wide' guarantee, pledged by the Remington Typewriter Company at an address in Gracechurch Street, London. Sally tried the keys and carriage return. They seemed to work well enough and, although the ribbon was missing, she reckoned the type-writer was in good order.

'How much for this?' she asked the boy who was minding the pitch while his father haggled with another trader close by.

'Oh, that's my one,' he said, with evident pride that at least this sale could be negotiated without reference to an adult. 'A tenner, it is.'

'Ten pounds, eh?'

The boy's eyes lost their sparkle as he began to worry that he'd set his sights too high. Sally saw the crestfallen look and didn't have the heart to press the issue.

'Okay,' she said, handing him a note, and was rewarded by a blissful smile.

'Mummy, Mummy,' a voice called behind her, 'can I have this?'

Sally hadn't noticed the boys wander away from her and over to a car in the opposite row. She looked round to see Jonathan running up clutching something plastic.

'What is it?'

'A Mysteron star ship,' he said, reverently. He was a keen *Captain Scarlet* fan.

'But it's got a bit missing.'

'I don't mind.'

'Where did you get it from?'

'Adam's mum. She's over there.'

Sally tucked her typewriter under her arm and followed him across to the back of a Ford Escort where she just recognised the mother of her son's playmate who was swamped by the out-sized blue anorak she was wearing.

'Sally!' she called. 'What are you doing here?'

'Having a poke around, what about you?'

'Didn't you know. This is my little side line.'

'What, you mean you do it regularly?'

'Yes, every week-end. You'd be surprised how many boot sales there are.'

Sally eyed the collection of toys, baby clothes, books and computer games lying around her friend's feet.

'Is it worth it, then?'

''Course. It only costs four or five pounds a pitch. I soon get that back.'

'Where do you get the stuff from?'

'Oh, all over the place. Relatives, friends – anyone who's got something they don't need. I can always do with more, though.'

Sally thought about the advert she'd put into the local paper two days before. *'Lady buyer wishes to purchase antiques and quality home effects,'* it read. She'd deliberately accented the female element. It made her ad different from the rest and, she hoped, more attractive to the sort of elderly person who might worry about inviting strange men into their homes. However, she had realised that if she got any replies for serious removals, she could end up with quite a few things that she didn't want to sell herself. It occurred to her that someone like Adam's mum might be the perfect outlet.

'Are you looking for anything in particular?' she asked.

'No, I sell everything – I mean, you should see some of the stuff people manage to shift at these things. Half of it you wouldn't have thrown at you.'

'I must say I have been a bit surprised at what people will buy.'

'It's the idea of getting a bargain that does it, you know, a bit of something on the cheap. Nobody minds parting with a couple of quid, and now and then they pick up something worth having.' She nodded towards a man in a beaten up wax jacket who was sifting through the goods on a pitch a couple of cars away. 'See him? I saw him pay fifteen pounds for a doll at a boot sale in Hove a couple of months back. I thought it was a bit steep at the time, but rumour has it that he flogged it at Christie's for over a thousand.'

'He obviously knows what to look for.'

'You do get a lot of dealers, although many people come just for fun.'

'You enjoy it, then?'

'Yes, I think it's great. Gets me out of the house, anyway.'

'And what do you do with the children?'

'Leave them with their father, of course. I told him, unless or until he ups the housekeeping, he won't be having the pleasure of my company at weekends!'

Sally smiled. 'Well, look, I've been thinking about doing something similar myself but I've hit on a bit of a problem.'

'What's that?'

'I've decided to set up a stall on one of the indoor markets, but I only want to sell a limited range of things. I'm bound to pick up other bits and pieces whilst I'm buying and I'd been wondering what I'd do with them.'

'What kind of bits and pieces?'

'Books, records, personal effects.'

'I'd sell them for you.'

'Would you?'

'Absolutely – like I said, I can always do with more.'

'How would we go about it though, money wise, I mean?'

Adam's mum frowned for a moment. 'Tell you what,' she said, 'you show me what you've got and say how much you want for it. We'll agree on a price and then I'll sell it on for whatever I think I can get.'

'Fair enough.' Sally was relieved. It seemed a good way of solving the problem.

'Mummy, *please* can I have this?'

She looked round at Jonathan, who had been clinging hopefully on to his star ship for the length of the conversation.

'I suppose so. How much do you want for this, Jean?'

'You can have it.'

'No, go on, I must give you something.'

'A pound, then.'

'You sure?'

'Yes.'

'What about me?' came a sad little voice at her side.

'Oh, poor Matthew!' Sally said, stroking his head. 'What do you want, darling?'

He held up a Postman Pat puzzle. She took it from him to show her friend.

'What do I owe you now?'

'Make it one pound fifty.'

'Doesn't seem much.'

'Every little helps – I've got my eye on a dress in Hannington's. Hundred and twenty quid it is, but if I have a good day, I should be able to buy it next week.'

'Really?'

'Yeah, but not a word to old tight wad at home.'

Sally laughed. 'Won't he notice?'

'Him? He wouldn't notice if I put on a feather and danced a fandango.'

For the first time since the divorce, Sally felt glad that she didn't have to go through the marital charade any more.

'You serious about doing business, then?' she said, shrugging the thought away.

'You bet. I've got a whole summer wardrobe to stock. Just give me a ring when you're ready.'

7

Sally's grandma was getting to be very useful, despite the fact that she'd been dead for almost twenty years. From her first mention in the umbrella shop, she had embarked upon a posthumous career which would have amused her in life. As convenient excuses went, Grandma's supposedly recent demise was the most credible way of opening a business discussion. So it wasn't as if the old girl's name was being taken entirely in vain. And, Sally thought, she was probably smiling somewhere right now at the idea of being able to help her granddaughter get ahead.

Armed with a boxload of booty, Sally had been beetling from shop to shop along the coast, looking for a good buy. The typewriter she'd picked up for ten pounds had been put back into working order for another ten and then gone on, to her delight, to fetch a hundred. This in its turn had helped pay for a collection of unusual pieces that she'd put out on the stall she'd taken in one of the indoor markets in The Lanes. The market had a strange mix of tenants. There were a couple of small antiques traders in the booths on the lower floor. The upper floor, though, had a watch mender, someone selling old prints, a fortune teller and a small café. Sally found herself sandwiched between these three days a week and actually felt less nervous than she would have done if she'd have been under the continuous gaze of other dealers.

Business had been slower than she'd hoped, but it had led to some useful conversations. One in particular had ended in an invitation to view the contents of a garage in Rottingdean. There, she'd been forced to take a gamble that she'd been hoping to put off until she had real money behind her. The owner, who was impatient to get rid of the last of his mother's possessions, insisted that everything would have to go, if anything was going at all. That put Sally in a quandary. Although there was a very good chest-of-drawers and some boxes of saleable china, there were two dreadful old wardrobes that she couldn't imagine anybody wanting. But the man had stuck to his guns. Praying that she wouldn't be damned for all time for staking two months' child allowance and most of the profits from her stall so far on one deal, she handed over two hundred and thirty pounds. Another forty went to a lad she'd met in the pub one lunch break, who had nothing to his name but a transit van.

God was in his Heaven that day, she thought, thrilled that she'd managed to sell on the chest-of-drawers for two hundred pounds almost immediately. The wardrobes, though, were going to be a problem. Right now, they were languishing at the back of the barn which stood to one side of her cottage in Fulking, draped with tarpaulins.

I suppose I'll find someone to take them, eventually, she told herself, and fell back to worrying over a more pressing issue. The more she went around buying and selling, the more she realised that what she really needed was a bigger car. The rose pink Mini of which she was so fond was simply too small to be of much use. One piece of furniture or two or three boxes, and it was crammed to the roof. Nevertheless, she hung on to it. She couldn't afford an estate car yet anyway, she told herself. But there was another reason, too. The Mini, for all its faults, was a symbol of her freedom; it was the first car that she had ever owned. As such, she had grown attached to it and saw it, in the long-term, as being restored and kept in semi-retirement, until the day that one of the boys got their driving licence.

All this, though, was before the tree incident. It happened on a Friday, at the end of a week when she was feeling pleased with herself for having netted three hundred and fifty pounds on the sale of one cup and saucer alone. The stroke of luck had come directly out of the garage clearance, for in one of the packing cases containing crockery, she'd come across the sole piece to survive from a coffee set made in the eighteenth century. How it had survived and what it was doing wrapped in a piece of yellowing newspaper alongside some other, equally cherished pieces, she didn't know. But the quality of the porcelain and the freshness of the painting had convinced her that it was something special. Going on the markings on the underside, she was able, with a little research, to discover that the cup and saucer had been made at the famous Worcester porcelain factory during what was known as the early 'Dr Wall period'. The statement in itself meant almost nothing to her, but since it placed the piece as having been made between 1751 and 1770, Sally realised she was on to a winner. By mid-week she'd found herself a dealer whose eyes lit up at the prospect of adding this rare hand-painted piece to his collection, and so, after a bit of bargaining, she walked away with seven crisp fifty-pound notes in her purse.

The coup was unexpected enough to get Sally dizzy with excitement and she spent the whole of the next day in the barn, unpacking as many things as possible. As she carefully put the better items to one side and repacked the rest, she couldn't help feeling that there had to be something else in there that was just as great a find. But when she'd finally worn herself out with looking, she began to scale down her expectations. What she had set aside was reasonably good, especially the couple of pieces of silver that she'd come across, and all in all, there was easily going to be enough to keep her stall going for another few weeks.

She turned over the pair of grape scissors that she'd decided was going to be her star exhibit, seeing if she'd learned enough yet to be able to decipher the silver stamp without referring to her handbook, but she was too tired to drag the information from her memory. Slipping the scissors into her pocket, she took them into the cottage for a polish along with the little creamer jug that she'd found. They would have to be valued and properly labelled, she thought, before going out into the world.

When Friday arrived, Sally's confidence in herself was in very good shape. So much so that after dashing the children off to school, she decided to pop over to Steyning to share her secret with Heather at last. As she came to the hill that led up to the village, she had a sudden impulse to buy some warm croissants. There was certain to be coffee percolating in Heather's kitchen, and she felt like a piece of sheer indulgence. Moments later, she was standing inside the baker's shop a few hundred yards further up the High Street.

'Whose is the pink Mini?' said a man in a white overall as she was about to be served.

'Mine.'

'Could you drop it back a couple of feet, my delivery man's here?'

'Of course, sorry.'

'No, it's all right,' the man continued, walking with her out on to the street, 'just his bonnet'll be sticking out beyond the junction if he leaves it where it is.'

Sally was only halfway into the car when it started to move backwards. With her feet still outside the open door, she grabbed hold of the steering wheel in an effort to gain control. There was a shout from the man in the white overall as the Mini gathered speed. All Sally could do was to aim for the brakes as she swung her legs inside, all the time yanking violently at the steering wheel in the hope of avoiding the line of parked cars which she could see in her rearview mirror. In a trice, the Mini shot sideways across the road with Sally certain that something had to be coming the other way. She gave up her struggle, putting her arms up over her head to cushion the impact she was sure must come. There was a terrible crunch and the Mini stopped dead.

Feet were running towards her, voices were calling. As she gradually lowered her arms and looked up, Sally saw that she hadn't been hit by another car at all. Instead, the Mini had slammed into the trunk of a large fir tree. Her relief at being alive, if bruised, mingled quickly with surprise and thankfulness that nothing and no one else had been damaged.

'Oh my God! Are you all right?' The face of the man from the baker's shop had turned as white as his overall. He stooped to help her out of the driving seat.

'Yes, yes, I'm okay . . . I think the hand-brake must have gone.'

'Are you sure you're all right?'

'I'm fine, really. Oh, poor old car!' Sally looked at the crumpled mess that had been the boot and bit her lip. 'Now what am I going to do?'

'You should sit down for a while, you'll be suffering from shock,' said a woman passer by. 'Cup of sweet tea is what you need.'

Sally had already started shaking and was trying hard not to give way to tears.

'Can I phone somebody to come and get you?' asked the man in the overall, clasping her elbow.

'No . . . thanks anyway. My step-mother only lives down the road, I was on my way to see her.'

'Good. I don't think you should drive in that condition.'

'I don't think I'll be able to anyhow. Looks like my car's a write off.'

'Oh, I don't know, pretty robust are Minis. Here, give me the keys.'

Sally handed the man the car keys and watched while he turned them in the steering block. To her amazement, the Mini started, first blast.

'There you are,' he said, grinning widely. 'I used to have one of these back in the sixties – great little motors they are.'

'I can't believe it!'

'Ah, she's not ready for the scrap heap yet. Mind you, it'll probably cost you more to get her straightened out than she's worth.'

'Oh, dear.'

'Never mind. You're still in one piece, that's the main thing. Did you say you were going somewhere close by?'

'Yes, just down there on the left, the art gallery.'

'Oh, Mrs Blythe, is it?'

'That's right.'

'Well, why don't you walk on down and I'll bring the car? She'll be all right to park. So long as she's left in first, she won't roll away.'

Wobbly-legged, Sally started off down the street, the high spirits that she'd felt before the accident, completely evaporated. She watched the crunched up shape of her Mini slide past her down the hill and disappear round the corner where Heather's house stood. The man from the baker's shop appeared as she approached the junction.

'Here's your keys,' he said. 'Now, don't forget, I've left her in first.'

'I won't . . . thank you. Thank you so much, you're very kind.'

'Not at all.'

'Won't you come in for a moment?'

'No, thanks, the delivery man's still waiting for me.'

'Of course. I'm sorry to have caused you such trouble.'

'No trouble. If a man can't help a lady in distress, he's not much use, is he?'

Sally smiled. 'I wish there were more like you.'

Heather was busy taking down a collection of small paintings and replacing them with a new set when Sally walked in. 'Well, hello, stranger,' she called, then noticing Sally's face, 'Gosh, you look pale. Are you sickening for something?'

'Just had an argument with a tree.'

'What?'

'Just crashed into a tree with the Mini.'

'How on earth did that happen?'

'The handbrake went and I went flying across the road.'

'Lord above! Are you hurt?'

'No. Bit shaken up though.'

Heather took her arm. 'Poor darling. You'd better have a cup of something hot and sweet.'

'That's what a woman up the street said.'

'Well, she was right. Come on.'

'I must have given everyone a terrible fright,' Sally murmured as she let Heather lead her through to the kitchen. 'It was awful – one minute there I was sitting outside the baker's, the next I was parked in a pine tree.'

'The big one on the other side?'

'Yes.'

'Well, I don't suppose you did it much harm.'

'No, but you want to see the state of the car. The boot's practically in the back seat.'

'Thank heavens the children weren't with you.'

'Oh!' Sally's bottom lip began to quiver at the thought of what might have happened. Heather quickly put her arms around her.

'There, sweetheart, it's all right. It's only a silly old car.'

'I don't mind so much about that,' Sally sniffed, 'I was just so excited . . . it was such a lovely week until that happened.'

'I was beginning to wonder what had happened to you.'

'I know I should have phoned you before, but I wanted it to be a surprise.'

'I thought you were up to something,' Heather said, going over to switch on the kettle. 'I've had Ken Rees calling me. He's been trying to get hold of you but says he kept getting your answering machine.'

'Well, why didn't he leave a message?'

'I don't know. Some people don't like answering machines. Anyhow, he said he's got the date of an auction and wants to know when he can collect the table.'

'Any time convenient to you, I suppose.'

'He said he needed to discuss it with you first.'

'What is there to say? I've already agreed that he should take it up to Sotheby's.'

'Maybe he wants to go through the figures with you – I mean, we know that he's looking for his ten per cent but we never did find out what the auction house's commission is going to be.'

'Fifteen per cent plus VAT – I checked.'

'Been doing your homework, then.'

'You could say that.' Sally began to cheer up. 'In fact, I think you'll be quite impressed when I tell you what I've been doing.'

Heather gave her a quizzical look. She was thinking how like her father Sally was, not in looks so much, except around the mouth, but almost exactly in temperament; deep, secretive, never prepared to give anything away until she was certain of the outcome.

'You are a blighter,' she said.

A shriek of delighted laughter floated in from the garden where the children were playing. For once, it sounded as if the boys had managed to get a game of football together for more than ten minutes without its leading to tears.

'Go on, Matthew, go on!' came Jonathan's excited voice. 'That's it . . . Goal!'

The window had been opened to disperse the heat of the kitchen into the heat of the day. Sally passed a hand over her forehead and turned down the grill. It had done its usual trick of going from nil reaction to cremate mode whilst she'd popped to the bathroom. She'd been just in time to save the dinosaur shapes from complete extinction but not before the fat collecting in the bottom of the grill pan had filled the room with a blue haze.

'Blasted thing,' she said, going over to fling open the side door. As she did so she saw what had been causing all the merriment. Lying on the grass with his arms and legs in the air, in the attitude of a stunned sheep, was Ken Rees. The boys were rocking him from side to side, trying to get him to stand up.

'Ref! Yellow card!' Ken complained as the children piled on to his chest, giggling. Sally stood in the doorway, tea towel in hand, wondering how he'd got so familiar with them so quickly.

Suddenly, Ken grabbed a boy under each arm and flipped over.

'Grrr!' he said. 'Now I'm going to have you for my supper!'

Two high-pitched screams met the mock threat as they struggled to get free. Then there were more giggles as he ran towards the cottage with them wriggling on either side.

'Here you are, madam,' Ken grinned at Sally's astonished face, 'two sacks of nutty slack.'

'Thanks, but the central heating's oil-fired.'

'Blimey, can't give it away these days.'

'Oh, God! The chip pan!' Sally dashed back into the kitchen to rescue the children's tea. It was a close run thing.

'Mummy, I can dribble,' said the newly released Matthew, panting and hiccuping with the effort.

'There's a surprise.'

'He can too,' Jonathan added, as he followed his brother to his mother's side. '*And* he beat ... er ... what's your name.'

'Ken.'

'And he beat Ken to the goal.'

'Did he now?'

'Pushed me over, the brute, didn't you?' Ken smiled.

Sally brushed past him to put two plates on the table.

'Surprised he didn't bite you, that's his usual line of defence.'

'Must run in the family.'

She shot him a vexed look. 'Come along, children. Oh, hang on, you haven't washed your hands.'

'Oh, Mummy!' cried Jonathan.

'Oh, Mummy!' Matthew mimicked, taking his cue.

'Come on, lads, bit of water won't harm you,' said Ken, lifting first one, then the other so that they could reach under the tap, then added in a loud whisper, 'Anyway, if we don't do as we're told, Mummy won't let us play again.'

The boys settled down to their meal with enthusiasm while Sally continued to watch Ken with a curious air. It intrigued her that there always seemed to be something new to discover about him.

'I don't suppose,' she said, 'you'd be averse to a cup of tea?'

'Not normally,' he replied, 'but since the sun's over the yard arm, I thought you might prefer something a little stronger.'

He disappeared before she could object and came back with a bottle of Rioja.

'Should let it breathe, really, but what the heck?' he said, calmly opening the cutlery drawer and instantly locating the bottle opener.

'Well,' Sally gasped, 'you certainly have style if not . . .'

'Finesse?' he finished. 'Ah, there's the rub.'

'You know, this is rather . . . unexpected.'

'I said I would come today.'

'I know, but, well, you were early, and I didn't have time . . .'

'To tidy up? Stuff and nonsense. Unless the Queen's about to arrive, I should let down your hair and not give a hang.'

Her hair had a particular lustre, he noticed, a tawny brown set off by highlights of red. Her skin tone was pale and fragile, the clear white of egg-shell porcelain. She looked, at that moment, intensely child-like, uncertain, fearful. It was a look that melted away his usual restraint.

'Cheers!' he said, then checked himself, remembering the children.

'Cheers,' she replied, with a smile that lingered around the edge of the glass.

A minute passed with them eyeing each other carefully. It struck them both that they were engaged in some sort of match play, like masters at a game of chess, weighing up the opposition, planning the opening gambit, pondering the next move.

'I was thinking,' he started, 'that perhaps you might like to come with me to the auction.'

'To London? It's a nice idea, but what about the children?'

'They can come too, if you like.'

'I don't know . . . they're not a lot of fun on long journeys.'

'Then perhaps Heather might take them for the day.'

'It's possible, but I don't like to put on her.'

'She didn't seem much put upon the other week. In fact, I thought she handled them very well.'

'Yes, she's extremely good with them. It's just, well,

they're my responsibility, not hers, and she has her own work to do.'

'You know,' he said, patiently, 'there is such a thing as letting other people help you, especially when they actually want to.'

'You think I'm too independent?'

'I think you give yourself a hard time.' It was a natural reaction, he thought, a way of trying to prove to the world that you could manage on your own when the truth was that you were aching all over for someone to hold out their hand.

Sally reconsidered. The idea of going to the auction had gone through her mind several times, only to be put aside because of the logistics involved. Now she thought that Heather might step into the breach, after all. She was always offering to help.

'What date did you say it was again . . . the auction?'

'May the twenty-fourth, just under a month's time.'

'Still in term-time, then,' she mused. 'If Heather only had to do the home run and give the kids some tea, it mightn't be too much to ask.'

'She'll be delighted.'

The subtle shift of grammar, making the statement fact rather than conjecture, gave him away.

'You've already asked her, haven't you?' Sally demanded.

'Well, I did mention it, yes.'

'Cheeky devil! So you've been conniving behind my back.'

'There's no need to get all defensive about it. Actually, it was more her idea than mine in the first place. When I phoned to make arrangements about the table, she said she thought you should go to the auction, if possible, because she imagined you'd want to see the thing through to the end and because she thought it would also be an interesting experience.'

'I still think you've got a nerve.'

'When you've quite finished being so tetchy, young

woman, you might like to say thank you. Whether you come to the auction or not is of no possible consequence to me. Either you want the table sold or not. Either you want to see it sold or not. The choice is up to you.'

Sally saw that he had started to turn pink and decided to back off.

'I'm sorry,' she said, 'you must think me very ungrateful.'

He gave her a glance that acknowledged that to be the case.

'I would love to come to London, really. It's ages since I was there . . . and I very much want to be at the auction, for all the reasons Heather said.'

'Hmm.'

'Honestly.'

'All right then. So the arrangement's firm?'

'Yes.' She noticed that the children had gone very quiet. 'You two finished yet?' she added lightly. 'Come on, it must be freezing by now.'

'Is there any pudding?'

'Yoghurt or fruit, but not unless you eat that first.'

'Of course, you realise that we'll probably have to wait several hours for the table to come up,' Ken cut in. 'There'll be more than a hundred lots for sale.'

'That's not a problem. I'm looking forward to seeing what else will be under the hammer.'

'I think you'll be a bit surprised – Sotheby's is a different kettle of fish altogether from what you saw at Worthing.'

'I expect it'll all be incredibly beautiful furniture.'

'Depends on your taste, as far as that goes, but yes, there'll be a lot of excellent pieces.'

'Hope mine won't be put in the shade.'

'I doubt that very much – it's an unusually good marquetry table, genuine William and Mary with no sign of restoration. The photograph in the catalogue should stimulate some interest, then there'll be the viewing day.'

'You've collected it already?'

'No, I'll be doing that this Saturday. I've got some other business in London that day, so I might as well take it up at the same time – kill two birds with one stone.'

'Have you taken a photograph of it, then?'

'Sotheby's will take their own – but yes, I went over to Steyning on Monday and took one, just to make sure.'

'Heather didn't say.'

Ken shrugged, since he couldn't see a reason why she should, except that he felt she'd known that the photography had been something of an excuse for him to spend some time in her company. It was rare to come across someone he felt attracted to in the course of his business, and typical of fate to present him with two women who fell into that category at the same time. That they were of the same family too put him in rather a quandary. Still, there was plenty of time to see how that one would pan out. If he'd learned anything about women, it was that they would make their interest in him or otherwise plain at their own speed. Only a fool tried to rush the process.

'More wine?'

'Yes, please, it's delicious.'

'Oak aged – can't beat it.'

'So, you're a connoisseur of wines, as well.'

'When it comes to the good things in life, I could easily become a gourmand.'

'Really? And does that epithet apply across the board?'

'Now you're getting cheeky.'

Sally gave him a wicked smile. 'I think I'm going to have to watch you.'

8

'Turned out nice again!'

A relentless drizzle fell from the slate-coloured sky, so that by the time he'd looked round from locking the car door, Ken could hardly make out the face of the speaker. He took off his glasses and squinted into the gloom. The blur in the fawn trench coat slowly took on the shape of Jim Foley.

'You made it then?'

'Not without a good bit of cursing – just how many Eglwys Bachs are there in this part of Wales?'

'Almost as many as there are Llanfairs, if the sign posts are anything to go by.'

'Sign posts? That's a laugh. I reckon I was going round in circles for at least an hour. Really irritating it was. Just when I thought I was getting somewhere, I came to a junction where the so-called sign post had two arms pointing in opposite directions, both marked Eglwys Bach.'

'Yes, I found that one. I suppose the natives must use their Celtic intuition to get around.'

'Huh! Well, I hope it's worth it, now that we're here. By the way, are you with us or against us today?'

'Who's us?'

'Me, George and Derek.'

'Ah, the three stooges. No. I'll plough my own furrow, thanks.'

'It's your loss.'

'That's a matter of opinion. Come on, I'm getting soaked.'

The two men turned to walk up the gravel drive towards the front of a large country house which, at that moment, looked as inviting as a funeral parlour. The grey plain-rendered elevations, at once grand and austere, were made all the more forbidding by the dark clouds that rolled over the roof tops and it struck Ken that there was something horribly final about a contents sale.

'So what have you got your eye on?' Jim asked, as they approached the front door.

'The double oven and grill. You?'

Jim snorted. 'Sarcastic bastard.'

Other dealers were dashing into the house and crowding the corridor beyond. Loud exchanges of conversation gave away a large contingent of Londoners who seemed to be in party mood despite the weather and the long drive. Ken nudged Jim in the ribs and nodded towards them.

'Yeah, yeah,' he said, as he squared his shoulders and pushed past, but he could see that it was going to be tough operating a ring against that type of opposition. The whole point was to arrest the bidding, keep it down so that a piece could be bought at much less than its market value. Later, it would be re-sold at a good price and the profits split between members of the syndicate. Jim began to search the room for familiar faces. It looked like he, George and Derek were going to need some help if they were going to have any kind of success today.

There was an expectant buzz as the auctioneer mounted the podium that Sotheby's had brought up for the occasion.

'Good luck,' Ken said as he moved off, leaving Jim to his own devices.

The florid face of the auctioneer broke into a mischievous grin.

'*Bore da,*' he beamed at the assembly. '*Croeso a Bryn Nant.*'

A peal of appreciative laughter rang out, coupled with applause from one corner of the room.

'Or, to those of you from south of Shepherd's Bush,' he added, to suppressed cheers from another quarter, 'good morning and welcome to Bryn Nant.'

He adjusted his dicky bow and took up his hammer.

'Now I hope that you gentlemen are on form, because I'm pleased to say that every lot on offer has already attracted an order bid.'

Ken watched the eyebrows being raised as dealers turned to each other and exchanged whispered comments. He was mildly amused to see Jim, George and Derek in a huddle, obviously hacking out a new plan of action.

'Right, well, we have a lot of business to get through,' said the auctioneer. 'I'll open the proceedings with lot number one in your catalogues, two late-eighteenth-century white marble Campana urns, starting at seven thousand pounds . . .'

The bidding got underway with a sense of urgency that seemed to take local private buyers by surprise. Ken watched their bewilderment mount as the offers flooded in from the London art trade, pushing the asking price beyond their reach.

'Eighteen thousand, thank you . . . nineteen thousand . . . twenty thousand . . . twenty-five thousand . . .'

The bids were coming thick and fast, taking the price up and up. When it reached thirty thousand, Ken began to wonder if it would ever peak.

'Thirty-three thousand – splendid, sir,' the auctioneer was blustering. 'And one hundred . . . and two hundred? Well done, sir . . . Anyone make it three hundred?'

Across the room, Jim's jaw hung loose. Ken smiled to

himself, glad that the Brighton boys' cartel was getting a thrashing. He thought of the jibes and thinly veiled threats he'd weathered over the years because he'd always refused to get involved in syndicate rings and was glad.

'All done at thirty-three thousand, two hundred pounds,' said the auctioneer, bringing down the gavel with a flourish. 'Lot number two, a set of twenty-four Regency mahogany armchairs . . .'

Ken refocused his attention and prepared to enter the bidding. His customer in Milan had expressed a particular interest in the armchairs and his brief was to get them, at anything up to one hundred thousand pounds. He felt quite confident, considering that Sotheby's was looking for between forty and sixty thousand for them. But again, the bidding took off, racing from fifty to eighty thousand in a matter of minutes. It hit the one hundred thousand mark at speed and continued to spiral upwards. With six contenders in the room and another bidding by telephone, Ken knew he was well out of the race. He decided to make a call himself as soon as the lot was sold so that he could get fresh instructions from his client.

'One hundred and ten thousand . . . and twenty thousand . . .'

A murmur of surprise went up and dealers who were leaning against the walls or larger items of furniture that stood dotted around the edge of the room, craned their necks for a better view of the knot of people seated at their centre. Ten rows of ten chairs had been set out in the middle of the room, and the bidding was now concentrated amongst the buyers occupying them.

'One hundred and thirty thousand . . . and forty . . . and fifty . . .' The auctioneer's eyes were sparkling and he took on the slightly mad look of a greyhound whose prey is within inches of its nose.

'. . . sixty thousand . . . one hundred and seventy thousand . . .'

Someone seated in the centre of the room shook his head.

'. . . eighty thousand . . . ninety . . . two hundred thousand . . .'

Another bidder shook his head.

'Two hundred and five thousand pounds . . . and six thousand . . . and seven . . .' The gavel wavered over the top edge of the podium.

'Two hundred and eight thousand . . . and nine thousand . . .' the auctioneer continued. Only one of his bidders remained in the room. The other, still on the telephone, was going to make it a fight to the finish.

'Two hundred and ten thousand . . .' he looked towards the assistant at his side whose mobile phone was almost welded to his ear. The assistant nodded. '. . . one hundred . . .'

All eyes followed the action from the centre of the room to the side of the podium, back and forth, like a crowd at the Wimbledon finals.

'. . . two hundred . . . three hundred . . . four . . .' The last nod had come from the assistant with the telephone. People held their breath to see if the bidder in the room would follow. He hesitated for a moment, then nodded.

'Two hundred and ten thousand five hundred pounds . . .' The assistant was saying something into his mouthpiece. Finally, he looked up and shook his head.

'All done?' The auctioneer gave a quick glance round the room then brought down the hammer with a crash. 'Sold for two hundred and ten thousand five hundred pounds, and a spirited effort, if I might say so, sir.'

Everyone seemed to be talking at once and Ken used the moment to slip from the room to make his call. It was still raining as he came out of the house and ran over to use his car phone. The line to Milan kept breaking up and, to his irritation, his client decided to be petulant over the loss of the Regency armchairs.

'Look,' Ken said, his exasperation mounting, 'I worked within your figure, there was no way of knowing what would happen. People are hurling money around and, on present form, I'd say that everything is going to make three or four times the estimated price, maybe even more . . . Pardon? Yes . . . No, I guess it'll be about an hour before the engravings come up and probably another hour on top before the statuettes . . . I'm sorry, I didn't catch that . . . Well, it depends how far you want to go . . . Yes . . . yes . . . all right . . . I'll give you a call later.'

He put the phone down and sat motionless for a few moments, watching the rain stream in rivulets down his windscreen. He was still gathering his thoughts when a Daimler came up the drive and pulled up a couple of hundred yards away. He watched the exhaust fumes vaporising in the cold air, masking the registration number. There was something familiar about the car that he couldn't quite put his finger on and he was considering where he might have seen it before when a figure emerged from the house and walked briskly towards it.

The man who had come out of the house got into the back of the car. Ken kept watching, trying to work out what was going on. He glanced at his watch. It was just gone noon. If his gut feeling was anything to go by, he reckoned this was a planned meeting and one that wasn't meant to be observed. Sure enough, within minutes the car door opened and the same man got out. From the way he moved, he'd got something inside his coat.

Ken sank down in his seat and waited for him to pass by, all the time keeping an eye on his side mirror. The Daimler moved off before he could get another good look at it, but he was already pretty certain who the man in the rain coat was: Derek. He saw him open and close the boot of his Toyota,

108

then walk back to the house. He glanced round once from the doorstep then quickly disappeared.

Well, well, Ken thought, I wonder what he's up to? He straightened up in his seat, torn between staying in the car a little longer and going straight back into the house in case anyone had noticed he was missing from the saleroom. He settled for going back in, making a point of hovering around the reception room where the engravings and statuettes he'd been instructed to buy were on view.

'Funny-looking oven,' said a voice behind him, as he examined the three Borghese Graces with an interest that had evidently given away his intentions. Ken just smiled pleasantly.

'I think we can guarantee you a run for your money there,' Jim went on. 'Unless, of course, you're prepared to change your mind about joining us?'

'Stow the arm twisting,' Ken replied with some menace, although the smile never left his lips. 'And, in the words of the prophet, go forth and multiply.'

'You'll be sorry you said that.'

'What? The next time you've got a "strop" to get shot of? Give me a break.'

The practice of completely making up pieces and passing them off as genuine was a method of business fairly customary to Jim. He drew himself up to his full five foot eight and glowered from under his bushy eyebrows.

'If you'll take my advice, you'll let Derek and George do their own dirty work,' Ken added, more moderately, aware that confrontation was not one of Jim's usual tactics. He'd been well wound up, that was all. 'Let's not spoil a good working arrangement, eh?'

Jim grumbled and stomped off, leaving Ken to his examination of the statuettes. He'd been told to get them at any price although he doubted that they were worth much more than the estimated value of four to six thousand pounds.

Clients were funny things, he thought, though the ones with serious money were generally shrewd. That wasn't to say that they always had great taste, but canny they were. Every once in a while they'd get a bee in their bonnet about a particular piece and become wildly extravagant, but not often.

Ken wondered what was so special about the Borghese Graces for his man in Milan. There was no telling. Maybe it was just that the wife's birthday was coming up or an anniversary of some kind. Whatever the reason, they'd soon be back in their native land, dancing in the sunshine, on one of many tables in one of many rooms in one of many mansions.

He turned back towards the saleroom. It was going to be a bit of a game if Jim, George and Derek had their way. Still, he was up for a laugh. He put his head round the door to see which lot was currently under the hammer. It was a painting that he had no interest in. Moving very quickly, he went out to the car and put in a call to his contact in Edinburgh.

'Arlis? It's Ken. I need a favour . ∴. yes . . . look, I'm at the Bryn Nant sale and the Brighton boys are going to bid me up on a piece . . . yes . . . no, it's for a client. You'll come in by telephone, will you? Good . . . What? . . . Lot number sixty, three Graces . . . no, no limits, and I'll cover you if it goes wrong. Fine. I just want to see the look on their faces when they get to the top and I drop out . . . yes, usual old crap. Catch you later.'

So much for the skirmish, he thought as the receiver went down. Now for the coup de grâce.

It had been a good day, all in all. With the statuettes and the engravings in the bag and arrangements in place for their shipment to Milan, Ken turned the car down the gravel drive with a feeling of triumph. Seventy-four grand, it had cost, seventy-four flipping grand! That was six times over estimate. And whilst Jim, George and Derek had certainly done their best to force the price up on his pieces, they could hardly be blamed for what had happened on the other lots. Almost everything had sold at way over estimate. The pictures and furniture alone fetched more than two-and-a-half million – twice the figure Sotheby's had expected. Even the cheaper lots went at ridiculous rates. A set of pewter soup plates, some copper saucepans, a couple of Edwardian single beds and Victorian wash stands made more than five thousand pounds in total. Even a plain white-painted medicine cabinet sold for four hundred and sixty-two pounds. The auctioneer had been worth his salt, there was no doubt of that.

By the time he got to Shrewsbury, the rain had stopped. Ken pulled over into a lay-by to make his call to Scotland.

'Heard the latest?' His contact's voice sounded tense.

'Go on.'

'Wil Browne's been lifted.'

'What?'

'Taken in for questioning.'

'No! Why?'

'Something to do with the stately home robberies.'

'What? Abbotsford House?'

'Not just Abbotsford. Floors Castle and Luton Hoo as well, apparently.'

'Wil would never be involved in something like that. Anyway, they're several hundred miles apart.'

'Maybe, but according to the Detective Sergeant who came round to talk to me today, the robberies were probably carried out by the same gang.'

'Thought they reckoned that whoever turned over Abbotsford had come from the continent? I mean, it was the family heirlooms that went missing, wasn't it? Stuff that was miles too well-known for anyone to risk fencing in this country.'

'Yes, but you and I both know that you don't have to go to

Belgium, France or Holland to find a collector who's hell-bent on having Bonnie Prince Charlie's whisky quaich or Napoleon's cloak clasp, even if they never come out of the safe.'

'True . . . but I can't believe it. What would they want with Wil Browne? He's as straight as they come.'

'I know that and you know that, but as far as the police are concerned, he's got some of the best contacts in Europe *and* he's a Fabergé expert.'

'What's that got to do with it?'

'It was mostly Fabergé jewellery and other trinkets that went from Floors Castle and Luton Hoo – very selectively chosen, by all accounts, things that were easy to transport.'

An image of the clandestine meeting he'd witnessed at Bryn Nant went through Ken's mind.

'Know anyone with a Daimler Sovereign?' he said, suddenly.

'What registration?'

'Don't know, didn't catch it.'

'Not much use, then. Why?'

'Bit of shenanigans I saw earlier, that's all. Probably no connection.'

'Oh?'

'Might have been out of the ordinary, might not . . . tell you about it another time. Anyhow, you okay?'

'Fine, thanks. Could have done without a visit from the CID though.'

'What did they want with you?'

'My connection with Wil plus a couple of other people they've got their eye on. Wanted to know if I'd been offered certain things.'

'Blimey. Must've given you a turn.'

'Not really. How do any of us know what other dealers are up to on the side? You could trade with someone for twenty years and not know all their business – you know how it is.'

'Yes. Still, the police could take some convincing of that.'

'That aspect bothers me less than the thought of unwittingly handling stuff that later turns out to have been stolen. Ignorance is not yet an excuse, under the law.'

'Now you're getting me worried. What else went in these robberies?'

'All sorts: clocks, snuff boxes, ornaments. List as long as your arm. Best I can say is that if you see anything you're not certain of, give Scotland Yard's arts and antiques squad a quick bell.'

'You bet. Listen, thanks for today, by the way. I'll return the favour sometime.'

'My pleasure. Talk to you soon.'

Ken started the car up and made for the M24, still turning the conversation over in his head. He'd heard about the burglary at Abbotsford House, the Borders mansion of Sir Walter Scott. Seemed like a real professional job. Of course, the thieves had been helped by the fact that the property was open to the public. It would have been easy to make a note of the lay-out and security system whilst walking round posing as a tourist. In all probability, they'd have had buyers already lined up for the pieces they intended to take. Stealing to order was not unknown on the shady side of the antiques business.

The robberies at Floors Castle and Luton Hoo seemed to fall into the same category, inasmuch as they too were open to the public. On the other hand, if most of what was taken was smaller items, as his contact had said, it was unlikely that they had all been on display. On that basis, it was reasonable to suppose that someone with inside information had been chattering. Perhaps someone in the trade who had sold the very same pieces to the owners of the stately homes, or their agents, some time before.

The names of some likely candidates for that type of roguery came readily to mind, although he was certain that any of them would have put enough people between themselves and subsequent events to appear unimpeachable. He leaned forward and clicked on the radio. No point in worrying about it now, he thought, though he meant to keep his eyes and ears open in future. God, what on earth is that racket?

The pained screeching of dissonant violins assaulted his senses. Radio Three had evidently found some new 'modern classic' with which to offend its listeners. He flipped through the programmes until he found something less irritating and settled back for the long haul down the M1. The events of the day unspooled in his mind as he drove along, mingling with thoughts of other sales that were coming up in the next few weeks. Christie's had a couple of interesting ones, both in private houses. The first of these, at Mere Hall, in Cheshire, promised to arouse the interest of his Italian collectors as almost every lot had been acquired by relatives of the present owners during the late-eighteenth and early-nineteenth centuries when taking the Grand Tour of Europe, then very much *de rigueur* for the social elite. Going by the feverish bidding that he'd witnessed at Bryn Nant, Ken felt sure that most of the pieces on offer would attract two or three times the estimates given in the catalogue. Not that that would worry the majority of his clients. It would inhibit his private buying, but in the end it was all swings and roundabouts. What he lost on private deals, he could make up in commissions. Nevertheless, the mood of the market was so volatile that it would have to be watched.

An even more exciting prospect was the sale a month later at The Mill House, Sonning on Thames, which promised to lure the heavyweights in the industry. This one was a real curiosity as house sales went, as the owners were antique dealers themselves and everything in the house had always been for sale. Now, though, it seemed they wanted to get rid of the lot in one fell swoop. He wondered why. A couple of minutes' musing offered no concrete reason, though that was not really important. It must always have been something of an odd arrangement, he thought, to be living in a place where whole rooms were likely to be snapped up by clients at a moment's notice. Yet it didn't seem to bother the owners, who had only ever bought the goods to sell them on. He shook his head. What it must be to have the great and the good jet in to Heathrow with their decorators and literally buy up whole collections. That's what he called a cool operation.

Making a mental note to give The Mill House a look in on one of the viewing days, Ken started to focus on the London end of his own activities. There was quite a bit of business in hand for the next few weeks. The settle and chairs he'd bought at the Worthing auction were ready for delivery to his client in Cheyne Walk, negotiations were nearing a close on a couple of pictures that his eccentric art collector wanted for his barge in Little Venice, then there was Sally's table coming up at Sotheby's . . .

'Oh, bugger!' he exclaimed, realising that he'd meant to phone her to finalise arrangements for the day of the sale. And there wasn't long to go now. He moved the car over to the slow lane and dialled her number.

'Yes!'

'Hi, it's Ken. Have I caught you at a bad moment?'

'Matthew's screaming the place down, my hair's in curlers and I'm due out in five minutes' time, does that sound bad enough?'

'Sorry . . . going anywhere nice?'

'I will be when I can get off the phone. Damn' thing's never stopped ringing.'

'Guess I'd better let you go.'

'Look, I'm here now, at least tell me what it is.'

'Just wanted to settle the arrangements for next week.'

'Can't we talk about it tomorrow?'

'Sure. When's a good time?'

'Oh, I don't know ... for heaven's sake, stop *whingeing*, Matthew ... how about the morning? Actually, I've just thought, perhaps you could drop by? There's something I want to ask you about.'

'What's that?'

'Piece of furniture I've picked up – could do with an opinion.'

'Something for the house?'

'No, something I'm selling.'

'Selling?'

'Yes.'

'From the house?'

'No. I bought it privately. Oh, does it matter?'

'What? You mean, you're dealing?'

'In a small way.'

'I had no idea.'

'Well, you don't know everything about me, do you?'

'Why are you so abrasive?'

'I'm not being abrasive, I'm being frantic ... Stop it, Matthew ... God! I'm going to throttle that child in a minute.'

'Okay, calm down. Look, I'll come over around ten, all right?'

'Fine.'

The phone went down with a crash, leaving him startled at the other end.

Saints preserve us, she's started dealing, he thought. And I suppose she thinks she knows something about antiques on the basis of one auction and a decent table. Triumph of enthusiasm over experience, as usual. Probably landed herself right in it ...

The motorway slid by and his initial indignation gave

way to concern. Whatever was she thinking of, getting involved in a business she knew nothing about? She had no idea of the pitfalls, of the barriers that would be put in her way. She couldn't afford to make mistakes, didn't she realise that?

He envisioned the road to ruin she had set herself on and began to feel annoyed again. If she'd had some money behind her, that might have been one thing, but to go galloping off on her own like that . . . absolutely bonkers.

Why couldn't she wait? he asked himself. But then, of course, she was hardly the most patient person on the planet.

9

'Well?'

'Hmm.'

'Oh, come on . . . what do you think?'

'What did you pay for it?'

'Never mind, just tell me what you think, for heaven's sake.'

'Not more than five hundred, I hope?'

'Ken!'

He shrugged. 'Proportions aren't right.'

'How do you mean?'

'Cabinet's set a bit too far in from the top of the bureau.'

Sally had a closer look. There was a slight recess between the two that she hadn't noticed before. She passed a finger along it.

'Is that a problem?'

'Not necessarily. If it is a "marriage", it's quite an interesting one.'

'Don't get technical on me.'

'Two separate pieces that have been put together to make one,' he explained. 'It was quite common in the 1920s, although it started well before then. Once antique furniture became fashionable, you see, they'd try to restore large pieces that had been sold off and split up in the late-eighteenth and early-nineteenth centuries.'

'Why? I mean, why were they split up in the first place?'

'To fit into smaller houses. You can't get something that was made for a rather grand house into a cottage, so they'd take bureau bookcases or bureau cabinets apart, stick feet on the cabinet and veneer on the top of the bureau and finish up with two pieces of furniture they could both use and accommodate.'

'And in the 1920s they tried to reverse the process?'

Exactly. Except inevitably, they'd be marrying up two pieces of furniture that had never belonged to each other in the first place. As you can imagine, the result was not always a great success.'

Sally stroked the front of the bureau, enjoying the feel of the wood.

'But how do you know for sure that it wasn't always like this?'

'I don't. You can tell something from looking at the back. Otherwise, though, it's just instinct – what my eye tells me is the case. I could only be certain if I took off that moulding at the base of the cabinet.'

'Don't like the sound of that.'

'It'd be okay. Anyway it's the only way of knowing. If there's veneer under it, then it's a "marriage". It was pretty rare for them to remove it when they joined two pieces.

'Otherwise?'

'Otherwise you'll see carcase timber.'

She hesitated for a second. 'Go on, then.'

'Eh?'

'Take off the moulding. You've got me itching to find out if you're right now.'

'I'm right.' He grinned. 'Want a little bet on it?'

'What sort of bet?'

'The sort that costs time rather than money.'

119

'I beg your . . .'

'Oh, nothing onerous. Unless, of course, the idea of spending an evening in my company fills you with horror?'

'Not entirely.'

He saw her teasing smile and bent closer to it.

'I hope you know,' he said, 'that you're playing with fire.'

'Oh?'

'Oh.' His intonation emphasised the point. He put his head back and looked at her. It was hard to judge what she wanted. He could have made the first move right then, all the signals were there, but he felt he should play his hand cautiously.

'So what's the deal?' she said, still smiling.

'If I'm right, you come to a dinner party with me. If I'm wrong, I retire bruised and try to think of somebody else to take.'

'What sort of dinner party?'

'One to remember, if past examples are anything to go by.'

'Not alone, then?'

'No, there'll probably be at least twelve of us. It's a couple of friends of mine. They like to have a crowd.'

'Sounds fun.'

'I think I can guarantee that. Willing to risk it?'

'Positively worried I might miss it.'

'You won't.'

'Arrogance, Mr Rees?'

'Experience, Miss Blythe,' he said, reaching into his back pocket. 'You are speaking to the man whose penknife has revealed richer treasures.'

She watched while he carefully prised the moulding away, holding her breath in case the knife might slip, but the delicacy with which he worked soon put her at ease. It was quite remarkable to see the large fingers moving along the wood, keeping an exact yet light pressure, like a doctor taking a pulse. And again, it seemed to her to show a side of

120

him that wasn't readily apparent. One that she'd decided it would be interesting to explore.

'QED,' he said, standing aside to show her the result.

'I don't know whether to be pleased or not – I was sure I had my dates right on this one.'

'Which were?'

'Between about 1770 and 1790.'

'I'd say that was correct – what's the problem?'

'I thought it was original.'

' "Marriages", my dear, are the bane of the furniture collector's life. Still, both pieces are of the same period, so it's not the disaster it might have been.'

'What do you think it's worth, then?'

'About two, two-and-a-half grand. Where did you get it from?'

'House clearance in Bexhill.'

'You have been getting about.'

'Well, I was until this morning. The Mini conked out at the end of the drive.'

'Wondered what it was doing there. What happened, by the way? You seem to have taken a hell of a bash.'

'The handbrake went when I was parked in Steyning High Street a couple of weeks back. Went whizzing into a tree and stoved the boot in.'

'It kept running, though?'

'Yes, much to my surprise. Anyhow, it looks like she's had it now. She'd been smelling of petrol and I think the tank must've sprung a leak.'

'And you still drove it like that?'

'What else was I going to do? I still had to get the children to school.'

'You're mad – the lot of you could have been blown up.'

'I had no choice.'

'You could have told somebody.'

'Like who? I didn't want to frighten Heather, and anyway

121

I can't keep running to her every time something goes wrong.'

'Might I make a suggestion?'

'Suggest away.'

'Next time you're in trouble, give me a ring.'

'I'm sure you've got better things to do than run round looking after me.'

'Maybe. But if I can help, I will. And,' he added, carefully, 'no strings attached.'

She was tempted to remark that there was no such thing as a free lunch but thought better of it, replying instead with another smile.

'You'd better tell me about this dinner party, then.'

'Seven thirty, Thursday. Dress: smart-casual. I'll come and pick you up.'

'Is that it?'

'Why? What else do you need to know?'

'Well, things like, who are your friends for a start?'

'They're a couple I've known for a long time. Nice people. One's a dealer, mostly in art, and the other lectures in philosophy at the University.'

'Interesting. Been together long?'

'Ages.'

'And they're happy?'

'Very.'

'That's good. Can't stand the pained atmosphere of married couples whom you can tell are really just putting up with each other.'

'They're not married, they live together, but it comes to much the same thing.'

'Oh. There are no children then, I take it?'

'No. Although I think Jon would've liked to adopt, if he could.'

'Poor thing. Something wrong with the mechanics?'

'More the biology.'

'Eh?'

'He's a man.'

'Obviously.'

'And so's his partner.'

Sally gasped. 'What? You mean they're gay?'

'As a ribboned Maypole.'

'You bugger!'

'Your charge is false in the extreme, madam, and I have the scars to prove it,' he mocked, flourishing an imaginary cap.

'Why didn't you say so at the start instead of stringing me along?'

'I wasn't stringing you along, I was answering your questions precisely, that's all. My friends' sexuality isn't what's important, it's what they're like as human beings. And as far as that's concerned, they rate pretty highly in my book.'

He had a superior look on his face and she knew he'd got her.

'You are infuriating,' she said.

'No more so than you at your best, my dear.'

'Ooh! Take off those glasses so I can hit you.'

He removed them at once and levelled an intentionally provocative gaze on her.

'Well?'

There was no response.

'Perhaps I should put the light on so that you can take a better aim?'

'Don't be daft.' She studied him hard. 'You know, you should get different glasses, those hide your face.'

'A good idea, some would say.'

'Seriously, though . . . they spoil your features. Tell me, was your hair very black?'

'I was born grey.'

'How sad. And you're wrong, it's silver.' She tilted her

123

head to one side and eyed him curiously. 'Do you really feel so old?'

'Of course not. I'm aware of my age, that's all.'

'You could knock ten years off it and no one would know.'

'Flattery will get you everywhere.'

'Will it, indeed?' She moved closer. 'Like where?'

He took a breath.

'That question is rather unwise in a darkened barn in the middle of nowhere.'

'Let me be the judge of that.'

Her mouth was raised towards him, the lips slightly parted as though there was something more to say. He bent and closed his own mouth over them, gently drawing her towards him, holding her in the embrace. At first it seemed to him there was a certain resistance in the way her mouth moved with the kiss, a holding back that argued against her former boldness. When the barrier dropped, though, it went at remarkable speed, her mouth suddenly pliant, her body almost collapsing against his. He felt the rush of emotion sweep over her and savoured it for a moment, but none of that prevented him from reading it for what it was.

'It's okay . . .' he whispered. 'Let it go.' Now he stroked the hair back from her face, knowing before he looked that her eyes would be shut fast. He stroked her hair, finding something in the texture, not looking at her any more but at some point in the darkness, clasping her against him, waiting for the shaking to subside. He held her like that for a long time, knowing that what she was going through was only the beginning, that there'd be so much more to unlock before she was free of the past.

Ken stood staring into the shadows as the minutes went by. Of all the ways he had thought of their relationship going, the one that had seemed the most likely was this: that he would care for her more than she would ever know and that she'd come to rely on him precisely because of that.

He'd been over it again and again and every time he'd come to the same conclusion. It was a Catch-22 situation. He couldn't not feel the way he felt about her. On the other hand, he didn't want to run the risk of her trying to reciprocate those feelings in her still-damaged state. It would be a complete disaster, he thought, if she were to start to love him now. A year or two down the line, she'd wake up and realise that it had been less to do with him as a person than it had been to do with feeling obliged or simply loving the way that he loved her. And when she woke up to either of those facts, she'd see that she'd shackled herself to a man she could never really belong to.

Her body began to relax against his and he knew that, given her present state of confusion, it would be so easy for him to tip the balance in his favour. But whilst it was difficult to hold a woman so close and remain altruistic, Ken fought back his own desires. Perhaps, in time, he thought, she would come to him of her own volition. Perhaps. It was too soon to guess exactly how it would play out. In the meantime, the thought at least left him the comfort of being able to hold on to some kind of hope. Yet, in the back of his mind, the persistent niggle hadn't entirely gone away. Something told him that at some stage in the future there'd be a moment of truth, one that would remind him of this first embrace. A point would come when she'd find herself, when she'd relax and he'd feel her recover. That would be the moment for which he'd have to steel himself. The moment when he'd know that he'd have to let go.

It was almost as though nothing had happened. With a lightness that was a thin glaze over her embarrassment, Sally locked the barn door and led the way to the house. She felt strangely caught between two conflicting emotions. She had wanted Ken to kiss her. Suddenly being so close to him had stirred up all sorts of repressed longings. But she'd led him on more by way of a test than an invitation and now she was annoyed with herself for losing control.

I don't know about worrying about keeping an eye on him, she thought, it's me I'm going to have to watch . . . oh, God, what if he'd taken it seriously?

She agonised over what she'd really intended. She wasn't sure whether she was ready to get involved with a man again or not. Yet the thrill she'd felt when he held her, the sense of being scared but somehow secure . . . She was tempted to explore further, although she knew she should hold back.

'I suppose that's it for a while,' she said, in an easy way that was meant to cover her bewilderment, and nodded towards the defunct Mini. 'Stopped my gallop for a while to come.'

Ken followed her gaze. 'Maybe you needed to slow down a bit, anyway.'

'What do you mean?' She felt hot. It was as if he'd read her mind.

'I mean, you need time to work out exactly what you're looking to achieve.'

'In what way?'

'With the antiques – presumably you've gone into house clearances with some aim in view?'

She shrugged, relieved. 'It's a way of making money.'

'I think it's more than that.'

'Oh?'

'You've obviously gone into it in some depth.'

There was a pause while she decided whether to open up or not. What she didn't want was for him or anyone else to tell her that she had ambitions beyond her abilities.

'I think it's fair to say that I've got the bug,' she replied, carefully.

'And?'

'Don't know. It's too early to say where I'll go from here.'

126

'Well, you can't afford to sit on the stock.'

'I know that.'

'So how are you going to get rid of the stuff in the barn?'

'Piecemeal, I suppose, at least the larger items. The smaller things I can put on my stall.'

His look of surprise earned one of ill-concealed triumph from her.

'Seem to be making a success of it, in a modest sort of way,' she said with a crafty smile.

'Doing the markets then?'

'Yes.'

He thought for a while.

'You know, if you mean to deal on any real level, you'll have to move up.'

'Why?'

'Because no one will take you seriously otherwise. Market trading . . . well, it's dabbling in it.'

'Says who?'

'It's the way it's seen and, unfortunately, opinions matter. Rightly or wrongly, most of the better dealers are men. They're going to make it as difficult as they can for you as it is – no point in handing them fuel for the fire.'

'You trying to put me off?'

'Not at all. You should know your enemy, that's all.'

She opened the kitchen door and walked pensively over to the sink, automatically reaching for the kettle and filling it. Breakfast pots were piled haphazard on the drainer, still waiting to be washed, and she began to shuffle them aimlessly.

'Is it really going to be that tough?' she said at last.

'Depends.'

'On?'

'Your attitude of mind. I don't doubt your determination but others will. You've got to prove you mean business.'

'Oh, I mean business, all right.' Her face set and he had

127

the impression that she was ready to bulldoze anyone who got in her way. The tea pot came in for some rough handling as if to reinforce the point. He watched her for a moment or two and then asked the question that he'd been wanting to ask for some time.

'Was it very bad?' he said, suddenly.

'What?'

'The divorce.'

She stopped, startled.

'I'm sorry, perhaps . . .'

'Why do you ask?'

He hesitated before answering. 'Because every so often it seems like you want to take the world by the throat and strangle it.'

'Doesn't everyone?'

'Not in the same way.'

'What's different about my way?'

'The hurt shows.'

'I don't see how you reach that conclusion.'

'There you go.'

'There I go what?'

'On the defensive again.'

'Why are you goading me?'

'Sally . . .'

'Well, why? One minute you're telling me how hard it's going to be for me because of all these bloody men. The next you're saying I should roll over and take it like a pussy cat.'

'No, I'm not.'

'You *are*.'

'You're over-reacting.'

'I'm getting damned cross, if that's what you mean.'

'Well, stop being cross. Not everyone's trying to kick you in the gut, especially not me.'

'Just what are you trying to do, then?'

'I'm trying to get you to see that there's a difference between aggression and tenacity.'

'What are you, my therapist?'

'I'm your friend, I hope.'

'Don't insult me with platitudes.'

'Will you calm down? What I'm saying is, be forceful by all means, but let it be a show of strength, not weakness. If what drives you is basically a deep-seated desire to get back at the world for some suffering you've been through in the past, you may well succeed in getting where you want to be but you won't have solved anything. In the end, you won't be able to look around and enjoy what you've built up. There'll always be that pang of insecurity because you've lost something important to you before and you're afraid you may lose it all again. People like that are ten a penny – you meet them all the time in every walk of life. And what are they? I'll tell you. Sad little soldiers who've made it by some people's standards but never quite by their own. There's acres of difference between them and you because you have the ability to face what's happened, understand it, learn from it and move on. That's what I'm getting at, ultimately. I'm saying, don't fall into the trap. Be determined, be persistent, get out there and carve the bastards up if you want, but do it for the right reasons.'

He'd taken the wind out of her sails and she gulped a couple of times to straighten up.

'You amaze me.'

'Likewise.'

'Honestly?'

'Why the surprise?'

'Don't know really. Sometimes it's difficult to know how people assess me. You in particular.'

'Because you're attractive?'

She looked at him cautiously.

129

'No need to be coy – you are very attractive and I can imagine that it has as many down sides as up.'

'I don't want to sound big-headed but it does make you wonder what people are really interested in you for.'

'Is it you or is it the scenery, you mean?'

'Exactly. How are you meant to tell? How are *they* meant to tell, for that matter?'

'It's a thorny question. But in my experience no matter how beautiful the woman, interest wanes after a few months have gone by and you've found there's nothing you feel about her that isn't physical.'

'And another thing that's awkward about it,' Sally went on, not pausing to take in what he'd said, 'is why is it that people always react so violently to what they see?'

'Write you off with a knowing glance, do they? Don't give you a chance?'

'Not all the time but quite often, and it's that that really hacks me off. It's like they make their minds up about you the minute you come in the room. Half the time they don't even bother to talk to you. You know, scratch the surface, see if there's anything worth finding under the gift wrap . . .'

'I'm afraid you'll find plenty of that kind of thing in this industry. In common with other masculine enclaves, the antiques business is rampant with misogynists.'

'That's what you meant by . . .'

'Yes. I wasn't trying to warn you off. Just preparing you for the worst, that's all.'

She continued making the tea. He watched her for a few moments then began to worry that he'd set her back by putting things so brutally.

'Sally?' She looked up. 'You shouldn't take what I've said too seriously. If you're determined enough to make a go of it, it doesn't matter what or who stands in your way, you'll make it.'

I wish I was so sure, she thought, but forced a smile. She'd met with enough disdainful looks in the past month or so to have doubts about whether she'd really be able to win through.

'It'd be nice to think that the odds weren't so heavily stacked against me,' she said, at last.

'The most important thing's in your favour, though. You've got a good eye.'

'Do you think so?' A flash of delight appeared in her face.

'It wasn't so dark in the barn that I couldn't see a few things worth having,' he said, pleased that she'd perked up.

'So you don't think I'm a complete idiot?'

'I don't think you're any type of idiot.'

She brought two mugs over to the table and sat down next to him.

'You know what you were saying . . . about moving up?'

'Mmm.'

'What did you have in mind, exactly?'

'Getting premises.'

'But I couldn't afford it.'

'You could at the right rent.'

'What, in Brighton?'

'Don't see why not.'

'How do I go about it?'

'Well, first, if you're very nice indeed to a certain gentleman of your acquaintance . . .' he dodged the mock swipe that she took at his head '. . . only joking. I could keep my ear to the ground,' he continued. 'There must be someone who needs a tenant. A few months from now, who knows?'

'But really, isn't the price going to be extortionate?'

'Trust me. Anyhow, in just over a week, you'll be a woman of substance.'

'Oh . . . the table! Gosh, I'd forgotten it was so soon.'

'Yes, indeed. And if you don't come out of Sotheby's with a big smile on your face, I'll want to know why.'

'It's so exciting!'

'Enjoy it while you can.'

'Sourpuss.'

'Practical puss. You'll probably have to part with a fair chunk of the proceeds in up-front rental.'

'How much?'

'Depends on the contract. Anyhow, you let me sort that bit out – and don't look at me like that. I just mean it'd be better for you financially, at the outset at least, if my presence were felt.'

'Because they know you?'

'Exactly.'

'Won't they all think there's something going on? You know, between us.'

'Rumours will be cooked up however you play it.'

'But what about your reputation?' She grinned.

'My dear, it is so beyond redemption in that respect, that I shouldn't worry yourself about it.'

'Ah, now it's coming out. Go on, give us a treat. Open up the cupboard and give the skeletons a rattle.'

'Not a chance,' he replied, rather too quickly. 'Anyhow, I recommend that you take my advice for now. Down the line, you'll be in a better position to fend for yourself.'

She was suddenly serious. 'You really do believe I can make it on my own, don't you?'

'Absolutely.'

'Why?'

'Why not?'

'Come on, tell me.'

'I recognise talent and true grit when I see them.'

'Thank you.'

'Don't thank me. You'll make it on your own merits.'

'I mean, thanks for your help with . . . well, everything really.'

'It's a pleasure.'

She hesitated. 'Ken, can I ask you something?'

132

'Sure.'

'About Thursday. Are there really no strings attached?'

'Of course not.'

'Even after . . .'

'None. I mean it.'

'Then why . . .?'

'Ours is not to reason why,' he said, gently. 'Let's just say that there's no fool like an old fool.'

10

'Thanks for running me around like this.' Sally heaved three carrier bags from the footwell of the passenger seat then opened the rear door of Heather's car for the children. 'Come on then, you two.'

'It's not a problem, really,' Heather said, getting out herself. 'Anyway, you'll be mobile again soon.'

'Yes, I've been wondering what to get.'

'Something with a bit more room in it, I should think.'

'Could do with an estate car for ferrying stuff around,' Sally shouted over the noise of the children haring around. 'In fact, I'd been thinking about it before the Mini gave up the ghost.'

'See you've got rid of her?'

'The scrap man gave me fifty quid and took her away. Sad, really.'

'Never mind. End of an era but the start of another, eh?'

'Mmm, in more ways than one.'

Heather stopped lifting shopping out of the boot for a second. 'Sounds like there's mischief afoot,' she said, giving Sally a knowing look.

'Maybe.'

'Sally . . .'

'Don't worry, I was going to tell you all about it. In actual fact, I could do with your advice.'

'Oh?'

'Well, it's only the nugget of a plan, you understand, nothing definite, yet.' She started off, heavily laden, towards the house.

'What are you up to now?' asked Heather as she followed.

'It was Ken's idea, really.'

'Was it, indeed?' Heather's voice had a disapproving ring. 'You've been seeing a bit of him, then?'

'I asked him to come over to look at a piece of furniture, that's all. What's the problem?'

'He'll have his feet under the table before you know where you are.'

'Don't be ridiculous. He's just helping me.'

'How incredibly philanthropic of him.'

'Heather!'

'Well, stop being so naive. Nobody does anything for nothing.'

'I've never heard you be so cynical.'

'Call it justifiable concern.'

'On what basis? The man seems genuine enough.'

'Perfectly likeable, yes, but ask yourself what his motivation is.'

'The ten per cent he's going to get out of the sale of the table, I should think.'

'That's a part of it, I grant you, but what's the other?'

'I can't imagine,' Sally retorted sharply.

'Well, it's not the first time he's been over here, is it?' Heather continued, not seeming to notice.

'No, but the time before he came to talk about going to the auction. And as it happens, he said that'd been your idea.'

'True enough.'

'Well, then?'

'It's just a feeling I've got . . . you shouldn't encourage him to hang around.'

'Why not? He could be very useful.'

'I'm sure. But watch it.'

'Anyone would think he had "Casanova" tattooed on his chest, the way you're carrying on,' Sally laughed as she unlocked the back door.

'A woman on her own needs to be careful.'

'And I'm not?'

'I'm saying you're vulnerable. I mean, how many men have you been out with since you broke up with Philip?'

'None.'

'Precisely.'

'Precisely what?'

'You're not used to being back on the market.'

'Oh, really!'

'Seriously. It's all too easy to fall into a new relationship when a marriage ends, and all too difficult to see that it's not really right for you – that you might be on the rebound.'

'I take it you speak from experience.'

The remark was heavy with sarcasm and Sally regretted it instantly. Heather thumped down the shopping bags and gave her a long, sober stare.

'There was life before your father, you know.'

'I'm sorry.'

'You may think that I'm flapping around like an old hen but I do know a few things.'

'I know you do. I'm sorry. I didn't mean it the way it sounded.' Sally plonked her own bags on the kitchen table and turned to give Heather an affectionate squeeze.

'Put me down and get that kettle on,' she said, smiling at last. 'I'm beginning to feel like I've been on safari.'

'It is a bit hot, isn't it?'

'Let's hope it stays that way for a while, then I can get on with some painting.'

The children came running in begging for orange juice which they gulped down in one before dashing off to play again. Sally glanced after them, shaking her head.

'Got a venue in mind?'

'I was thinking of doing the harbour at Portslade again.'

'Looking away from the factory, I hope.'

'Of course, it's the best angle anyway.'

'Those awful warehouses and that dreadful chimney, I don't understand why they don't blow it up like they did the other one.' Sally sorted two china cups from a collection in a cupboard to one side of the sink. 'Just as well that the postcards always show the harbour.'

'Why not? If you were going to have your photograph taken, you'd want it to show your best profile.'

'Yes, but it must be a surprise for the tourists.'

'It's the same wherever you go. I remember once making a special trip to a little village in the Alps. Everywhere you went you saw pictures of this place, the church with its lovely *zwiebelturm* set off perfectly against these huge, icy white mountains in the distance.' Heather waved a hand, expressively. 'When I got there, I found that there was a busy main road running right alongside it. And the day I got there, it was thick with traffic. So much for the idyll.'

'Where was that, then?' said Sally, suddenly curious.

'Bavaria.'

'Oh, on holiday, then?'

'No. I lived there.'

'Really? For how long.'

'Eighteen months or so.'

'I didn't know that.'

'It was a long time ago.' Heather was feeling suddenly weary from the heat. 'So what's this idea of yours, then?'

'Idea? Oh, yes,' said Sally, absently giving the tea a stir, 'I'm thinking of opening a shop.'

'Are you doing well enough?'

'It's hard to tell but I've been pretty lucky so far and it has to be said that I could do with some way of clearing the things from the barn, it's getting a bit crowded in there.'

'That's the trouble with doing house clearances, I suppose.'

'Mmm. There's plenty of places around to take the junk off my hands but I'd like to hold on to the better pieces. Can't help feeling that I'd make more on them if they were properly displayed.'

'That's probably true but the extra would soon disappear in overheads.'

'Is that what you find?'

'Well, the gallery's freehold, so my running costs are smaller than most, but I'd say it could be quite a big problem.'

'Ken seemed to think he could find me somewhere with an affordable rent.'

'I expect he could – being in the trade and all.'

'There you are, told you he'd be useful.'

'Fine, just so long as your involvement with him stays at that level.'

'Why are you so down on him?'

'I just wonder what his intentions are.'

'Well, I don't think he's about to propose, if that's what you mean.'

'Why should he if he's got this far through life without making that kind of commitment?'

'What's that supposed to mean?'

'He's never been married.'

'How do you know?'

'Let it slip when he came to photograph the table – accidentally-on-purpose, if you ask me.'

'Oh?'

'Made some comment about how lucky I was to have had someone to share so much with.'

'Sounds innocuous enough.'

'Perhaps, but I had the feeling that it was a prelude to something else.'

'Like what?'

'Don't know – something in the way he looked at me.'

'Maybe he fancies you.'

Heather laughed. 'I must have put his nose out of joint then. I told him I thought that there must be something very strange about a man who had never had the urge to settle down.'

'That's a bit unfair. I mean, maybe he never met the right person.'

'Oh, go on. You meet enough people in the course of a lifetime to find a few who you think are right.'

'A few? One or at most two, surely? I mean, there's a limit to the number of people you can come across who are really special – well, special enough to want to spend the rest of your life with.'

'If you're born and brought up in a small community where you stay for the rest of your life, maybe. Not if you get around.' Heather's thoughtful look made Sally inquisitive.

'Do you have many regrets?'

'Me?' She sighed. 'Oh, yes, but mostly ones connected with youth and inexperience.'

'Looking back, you'd have done things differently, you mean?'

'Everyone thinks that, with the benefit of hindsight, but it's a bit pointless. In the end, how you felt at a particular time was how you felt, for good or ill. Whatever reaction you had as a result was probably right too, in its own strange way.'

'But you react to such silly things, especially when you're younger. I mean, I remember finishing with one bloke because he wanted to go on holiday with his mates. I was absolutely incensed that he didn't want me to go too, and yet no one else was taking their girlfriend.'

'Probably thought his mates were more important to him than you were.'

'Yes, I did, but afterwards I thought I'd been a bit hasty.'

'Oh, we all think that sometimes.'

'Isn't it funny how one minute you can be really in love with someone and the next it's all off, especially when you're teenagers?'

'They don't have the monopoly on that. More often than not it's injured pride that's the problem, and in some ways I think it actually gets worse as you grow older.'

'Why's that?'

'Because you've got less patience. If you're a woman, anyway. For men it's more because they tend to take themselves so seriously. There was one chap I went with for a while after my first marriage split up . . .'

'You were married before?'

'For all of five minutes, yes.'

'What happened?'

'It's a long story. Anyway I was talking about this man. Richard, his name was. Turned out to be just as possessive as my ex, in the end. There I was, languishing away, feeling all wronged and discarded, when he turned up at a drinks party given by some friends of mine. We chatted away and got on well enough, then we started going out – usual thing. I had this flat on the front at King's Gardens in those days, although I could hardly afford the rent. Anyway, within a month he'd practically moved in. I didn't exactly object because he was very considerate and extremely well house-trained – quite the opposite to my ex. He was another artist, you know, and rather pretentious with it. At times you'd have thought that being either practical or supportive was against his religion.' Heather gave a loud tut at the memory. 'God, he was a pain, that man! If he wasn't yelling the place down over some imagined slight he'd be lying prone on the bed doing his "misunderstood genius" bit.

140

'By comparison Richard seemed heaven-sent, I can tell you. Well, at least until it became clear that he thought he owned me. A couple of months went by happily enough but then my lawyer warned me that I was risking losing my right to maintenance by having him there more than two or three nights a week. That put the fat in the fire. Richard got very miffed and started saying that I was throwing him out. I mean, what a twit! He wasn't offering to support me, so I didn't see what his argument was.

'Anyway, by then it was beginning to get rather claustrophobic. He wanted to spend every available moment with me whereas I wanted space. The next thing he was talking about marriage when it was miles too soon even to consider and I wouldn't have minded except he always made it sound like he was doing me a huge favour by "taking me on". Given I had virtually no income and he had a nice, regular job, I suppose from his point of view that's how it seemed. But I ask you, what unbelievable arrogance! I was getting by okay and didn't feel like compromising my freedom. He didn't appreciate that and before I knew it was putting the emotional screws on, talking about how much he'd done for me, how much he'd cared for me in my hour of need, and all that.

'Now, I'm a pretty decent person and I did feel rather beholden to him, I have to admit. On the other hand, I had to ask myself why he was trying to make me feel guilty and miserable when he swore he loved me more than anything in the world. I mean, if someone really loves you, the last thing they want is to make you feel bad. Unless, that is, there's something that matters more to them at stake, viz their pride, and in his case, that's certainly what it boiled down to. I wasn't willing to let him sweep me up on his white charger and carry me off into some fate that fitted with his idea of bliss, so he got all hurt and vengeful.'

'I can't imagine you putting up with that sort of treatment for long.'

'Oh, we put up with all sorts for what seem like good reasons at the time, don't we? I suppose I was still reeling with shock from the divorce and, it has to be said, I was rather flattered to have someone fall heavily in love with me so quickly.'

Sally was beginning to get the message. She thought about Ken, about how the kiss had made her want to go much further. She wondered whether the feeling had really been about him, or whether it had been more about wanting to be loved. What Heather had said made a great deal of sense in that context. She made a mental note to keep a grip on herself in future.

'You okay?'

'Yes, I was just thinking.'

'About what?'

'I was wondering how long it takes . . . how long you should give yourself to recover from a relationship that goes wrong. I can see that getting involved with someone too soon could end up being a disaster, but how do you know when you're ready? How do you know that what you're feeling is genuine and not just something that you're telling yourself is right because you're lonely?'

'There's no answer to that.' Heather sighed. 'All I can say is, give it time. Don't rush headlong into anything. Wait and watch.'

'But . . .' Sally started. She was going to say, 'But I've been on my own for almost two years now, surely that's enough?' Instead, she turned the question so that the onus fell on Heather. 'How long was it before you met Dad?'

The roar of a plane swooping low over the house drowned out the reply and Sally found herself looking up at the ceiling, expecting to see a pair of wheels and a chunk of undercarriage. Suddenly, the children came dashing in

142

through the back door, Jonathan wild-eyed with fear and Matthew gasping, half crushed in the armlock that his brother had seen fit to rescue him with.

'What in heaven's name . . .' Heather gasped.

'Mummy, Mummy,' yelled Jonathan, 'someone's crashed into that field.'

'Put him down,' Sally yelled back, seeing Matthew's bright red face turning puce. 'Jonathan, put him down!'

The child released his brother, who started wailing angrily, then burst into tears himself.

'There, darling,' said Sally, scooping the littlest up from the floor whilst trying to comfort the eldest with her other arm. 'There, it's all right, it's all right . . .'

The children continued howling whilst Heather leapt up from her chair and rushed out to see what was happening. She returned within minutes looking ready to start World War Three.

'Of all the stupid, inconsiderate idiots!' She glowered.

'Whatever . . .?'

'There's a group of them, all men by the sounds of things, laughing like hyenas if you don't mind. Well, I'm going to give them a piece of my mind.'

'Heather?'

'It's all right, nobody's crashed, but by golly they'll wish they had when they feel the length of my tongue.'

The children were shocked into silence by the sight of the normally good-natured Heather building up to a proper head of steam.

'Don't worry, my sweethearts,' she said, giving them both a kiss. 'I'll only beat them within an inch of their lives.' And with that, she disappeared.

By the time the boys had settled down enough to follow Sally out to see what was going on, there was an ominous silence from the field where the plane had landed. She craned her neck to see over the hedgerow that lined the lane but it had grown too high. She quickened her pace until she rounded the corner where a five-bar gate opened out on to a large expanse of grass. Close by, four men stood shuffling uncomfortably under the gaze of one visibly angry female.

'Wow, look at that!' cried Jonathan pointing to the yellow and black biplane that stood some distance off. Sally looked, slightly surprised to see a design she associated with something more out of old film footage than modern day flight.

The sight of the plane quickly dispersed any fright that the boys had been feeling and they eyed it longingly from the safety of the folds of Sally's skirt. Heather moved towards them.

'Hedge-hopping indeed,' she muttered under her breath, 'like a bunch of schoolboys.'

Sally glanced from Heather towards the group of men. One, dressed in jeans and a white T-shirt which made the deep tan on his face and arms more noticeable, had his eyes fixed on her.

'Who are they?' she said, quietly.

'Didn't bother to ask,' came the huffy reply, 'but two of them sound like City types. Whoever they are, I've put a flea in their ear, anyhow.'

They certainly looked sheepish enough, Sally thought, wondering just what Heather had said. And still the eyes of the tanned man were trained in her direction.

'I'll go and get the Daimler, then,' she heard one of them say. 'You coming, Steve?'

Two of the group broke off and walked towards the gate, edging round it to give Heather a wide berth.

'Afternoon,' one tried, in an embarrassed sort of way, as he passed by.

'Goodbye,' said Heather, firmly.

Sally was still watching the other two, who seemed to be agreeing something in conspiratorial undertones.

'Can I look at it, Mummy?'

'Sorry?'

'The plane.'

'Not now, Jonathan.'

'Why?'

'Because it belongs to the men,' she said, ineptly. 'Come on, let's go.'

She'd turned at the moment that the man who'd been looking at her decided to come across. She half saw him move towards her, in a last sideways glance.

'Hello,' he said, when her back was already turned. 'Look, I'm sorry we gave you a scare. Didn't see your cottage 'til the last moment . . .'

Heather swung round immediately and gave him a look that would have frozen the Thames. Sally began to feel awkward. At closer range, he was even more disturbing. Those dark eyes held a glint of devilment that was horribly attractive. She was caught between how she thought she should act and a rather more instinctive wish to hear what he had to say.

'Daniel Wiseman,' he went on earnestly, thrusting a hand into hers. 'If there's some way of making it up to you . . . perhaps your kids'd like to look her over?'

At that moment the boys were clinging to the back of her legs as though the giant had just climbed down the beanstalk. Sally tottered backwards under the weight and found herself clinging to his hand in order to steady herself.

'Thank you, but I think we've seen quite enough of aeroplanes for one day,' said Heather, acidly. But Jonathan had poked his head out from behind his mother and was looking at the stranger with renewed interest. He started tugging at the fold of skirt he'd had scrunched up in his hand.

'What?' said Sally, turning. The child's face was exquisitely appealing. 'Oh, for heaven's sake.'

'Come on, I won't bite.' The man beckoned. He could tell

145

that both the boys and Sally were wavering on the edge of being won over.

'Well, it's time I was going,' said Heather, assessing the situation and feeling somewhat put out.

'Oh, do you have to?'

'I'll be up at eight-thirty, as usual.'

The strained quality of her voice put Sally in a spot.

'Can I see it, Mummy? Please?'

Now she was doubly stuck.

'I suppose so,' she said, finally giving way. 'Sorry,' she added towards Heather, who had already begun to walk away. 'See you in the morning.'

The man gave an utterly charming smile and gestured towards the plane in the slightly showy way that a head waiter might use to point out what he considered a prime table. Sally looked from him to his friend, who was watching from a distance, and back again.

'Who's the culprit?'

He shrugged. 'Both of us, I suppose, although James had the controls when we came over your place. He wasn't expecting obstacles – not so experienced as me, you see.'

She eyed him for a moment. 'I take it you've got a licence for the thing then?'

'Of course.'

'What was it, a flying lesson?'

'More a demonstration. He's a client of mine.'

'You sell planes?'

'That's part of my business.' His attention was taken by the sound of a car pulling up at the gate. 'Excuse me a minute.'

Sally watched him go over to say something to the driver, then call his friend who got into the back of the car. It moved off, almost silently.

'Right,' he said, coming back over, 'all set for the magical mystery tour?'

She nodded, letting him lead the way.

'Didn't catch your name?'

'That's because I didn't tell you it yet.'

'Ah.' He smiled slyly. 'And am I to have the pleasure of knowing, or haven't you forgiven me?'

'I might, if you promise to do your hedge-hopping elsewhere in future.'

'Okay, no more hedge-hopping, but you will hear me dropping in to land here from time to time.'

'Oh?'

'It's an arrangement I have with old Wentworth up at the Manor.'

'Looks like I won't be able to object, then.'

'Why?'

'He's my landlord.'

'Suppose he must be . . . owns everything for miles around here.'

'You'd never guess it to look at him though.'

'Know what you mean, he is a bit wild and eccentric. But awfully nice in that very, very English way.'

They'd got as far as the plane and the children were staring awestruck at the monster propeller and great, graceful wings.

'Do you want to go in the cockpit?' Daniel said to Jonathan. But the child shook his head, firmly.

'I think he's a bit scared.'

'Pity, she's a lovely machine. Let's just walk round her then, shall we?'

'So long as it's quick. I've got tea to make and a pile of shopping to unpack.'

'Something good on the menu?'

'Probably fish fingers and chips.'

'That'll please the old man.'

'I don't have to please anyone except myself and the

children,' she said, tartly, noting the look of surprise with satisfaction.

'I . . . er . . .' He seemed to think better of what he was about to say. 'What is your name, by the way?'

'Sally.'

'Just Sally?'

'No.'

'Do you always keep people in suspense?'

'If it amuses me.'

'*La Belle Dame Sans Merci.*'

'I believe you have to be a knight palely loitering for the full treatment.'

He lifted a sun-tanned arm and laughed. 'Not quite the right shade, am I?'

She smiled.

'Interesting lady.'

'You think so?'

'I do.' He lingered, about to say more, then suddenly added, 'Can we meet again?'

'If you're going to keep dropping into this field, we won't be able to avoid it, will we?'

'You don't object, then?'

Sally hesitated. She didn't want to sound too encouraging, but she didn't want to put him off either. 'Not so long as you stay off my roof,' she said, trying to avoid his eyes.

'No problem. Next time I'll try to drop by in more conventional transport.'

11

'Anybody home?'

The house was strangely silent as Ken let himself in through the back door, having knocked on it for several minutes without getting a reply. Somewhere upstairs a hair drier was humming.

'Sally?'

The drier clicked off.

'Is that you?'

'Was the last time I looked.'

'Down in a minute.'

He pulled a chair out but didn't sit on it, leaning forward over the table instead to check his appearance in the mirror that hung on the wall behind. He turned his head from side to side, wondering if she'd notice. The face in the mirror seemed different to him, in a subtle sort of way, and he hadn't quite got used to it yet.

Not bad, he thought, brushing a couple of stray hairs off his jacket, maybe I should have worn a tie after all. The gesture was more for her than the company they were joining. He felt that women preferred formal dressing, but then, he'd never been out with one so much younger than him before. Twelve or thirteen years was the usual limit. Twenty was pushing it a bit.

The glimmer of a memory from a summer long before crept into his mind. He'd been harder, more selfish then, he thought, the girl so very innocent. Not of life so much as of consequences. He'd been careless of the consequences of his actions himself, in those days. They'd both paid, in different ways.

'Will I do?'

He caught her first in the reflection in the mirror.

'Well?'

'You look stunning.'

She pulled the tight black dress an inch further down her thighs in a gesture of mild embarrassment.

'It's not too much? I mean, perhaps the neckline's too low.'

There was a lot of cleavage showing and he was having problems keeping his glance from obviously lingering over it as he turned.

'It's terrific, really.'

'Good. I'm all set, then.'

'Where are the kids?'

'Heather's keeping them over. She said she'd rather, in case we're out late. Didn't fancy driving home after midnight.'

He nodded. An awkward feeling was spreading up his shoulders to his neck and he realised that he minded what Heather might be thinking.

'Right,' he said, quickly, 'let's get going.'

The awkward feeling stayed with him until they were in the car and out on the main road. From the corner of his eye, he could see that Sally was wriggling in her seat.

'Uncomfortable?'

'Nervous.'

'Really?'

'Well, you know . . .'

150

He was concentrating on the driving. There was an old Morris Minor in front, hogging most of the road.

'Why doesn't he make his mind up?' Ken muttered as the car wandered gently across his path and back again. He slammed into second gear and prepared to overtake. 'Bloody idiot.'

Sally turned to look as they passed.

'Not surprised he was all over the place. Didn't come any higher than the steering wheel, poor old devil. Funny, but you know, until I left school, I never seemed to notice how many elderly people there were around here.'

'Most of them going at dot miles an hour in Hove Church Street.'

She laughed. 'You should have more patience, I suppose, but they will do the most hair-raising things. I had an old couple swing right across me there the other day. You could almost hear *her* going: "Ooh, whole roast chicken, two ninety-nine at Cullen's. Albert, quick, pull in ... ALBERT, I said pull in, dear!" And he does, zonk, just like that. No signal. Nothing.'

'You learn to jump when you've been taking orders for the last forty years.'

'What a charming indictment of the married state.'

'And you have evidence to the contrary?'

'It works for some people.' Sally was thinking of how happy her parents had been. At least, she always remembered them as being happy. Perhaps the sadness that had permeated the house in Roedean after her mother's death had made a starker contrast than she'd imagined. There'd certainly been a long, grey time before Heather came on the scene.

'Ken?'

'Yes.'

'Why didn't you ever marry?'

'How do you know?'

151

'News travels fast in these parts.'

'Heather told you,' he said, beginning to feel awkward again.

'True. But, funnily enough, I hadn't given it a thought until she mentioned it. I mean, well, it seemed obvious that you'd be single.'

'How so?'

'Something about you.'

'You can tell a married man by the harrowed look in his eye?'

'More than you can tell one who isn't by the frayed collar on his shirt.'

His hand flew up to his collar.

'Not that one,' she added, 'the one you were wearing when you called round the first time. The one you were wearing the second time looked like it wanted chucking out too.'

'Thanks.'

'Well, it did. No self-respecting woman would let her husband out like that, even if she openly despised him.'

'Ah, back to the element of control.'

'Looking after someone or wanting them to look nice isn't about control, it's about wanting them to feel comfortable. To feel good, if you like. Though I suppose there's an element of wanting to feel proud of them that's about yourself too.'

He thought for a moment. 'Point taken.'

'Heavens, don't tell me you agree?'

'I don't disagree.'

'There's a first.'

'Get you!' he laughed. 'Not a touch of the old pot calling the kettle black here, is there?'

'All right, smart arse.' She flicked him on the leg with the back of her hand. 'Anyway, you still didn't tell me.'

'What?'

'Oh, don't be obtuse.'

152

'The marriage thing . . .' He shrugged. 'Don't know, really. Got close to it once or twice but somehow . . . hard to say . . . I couldn't be certain enough. How can you look that far ahead? How can you be absolutely positive that a promise made today will still be water-tight at some future date, maybe thirty, forty years on? It's a decision that's too import-ant to take an intuitive guess at. And someone's life may be ruined. Perhaps more than one person's.'

She saw from his face that the statement had been some-thing of a struggle. It was honest and open, but she had the feeling that there was more that he wasn't yet ready to say.

'You care about keeping promises?'

'Very much so.' He remembered promises too easily made in the past and the thought shamed him.

'But you can't not make them for fear of breaking them.'

He shook his head.

'You can't. Of course you've got to believe utterly in what you're saying when you give a promise but no one expects . . . well, the impossible.'

'You're saying it's okay to change your mind?'

'No, not exactly. But people change. And often circum-stances can change to the point at which people lose sight of themselves, of each other.'

'That's the tragedy.'

'If you've given it your best shot, where's the blame?'

'In believing in the first place.'

'You can't mean that.'

'Perhaps not quite how it sounded.'

'Well, what then?'

'You've been let down. You know how soul-destroying that is. Why would anyone want to risk doing that to any human being, let alone someone whom they cared about deeply?'

'You don't *know* you're going to do it in advance, do you? You don't wake up one morning and say: "Today, I'm going

153

to go out of my way to let Fred or Mabel down." If you ask me, you've got yourself bogged down with some sort of ridiculous inverse logic. It may make you feel better about what you say, but it doesn't make it true.'

The car screeched to a halt.

'We're here.'

'So I gather.' She turned in her seat, surprised to see him so flustered. 'What's the problem?'

'Nothing.'

'Don't get ice-bound on me.'

He stayed with his hands on the wheel, just staring ahead.

'Shall I tell you something?'

'Why not? You seem to have plenty to say.'

'Look, you've picked apart my motivations often enough, you've had me air emotions that were still raw at the edges, put me on the spot, made me really think things through. What makes you so special and private? Or is it okay to pass comment on other people's lives so long as they don't pass comment on yours?'

'There's a lot you don't know.'

Sally could see that she'd hit a nerve and felt bad about hurting him. She'd felt remarkably affectionate towards him from the start but had let it get out of hand that time in the barn and realised now that she was being too hard on him because of it.

'Of course there is,' she tried, more gently. 'There's probably acres of stuff I'll never know but I doubt it'd alter my opinion of you if I did.'

'What makes you think your opinion of me matters?'

'That,' she said, taking his hand and holding it in her own, 'is the silliest thing I've ever heard you say.'

'You can't have been listening very hard,' he replied, but his face had relaxed and she could tell he wasn't serious.

'You are lovely.' She gave the captive hand a squeeze. 'Not only are you lovely, you're warm, caring and considerate.'

'I wish my mother were here to hear this.'

'Oh, shut up, you prune. I mean it. Seriously.' He turned to her, and she smiled. 'By the way, I love the new glasses.'

He recoiled.

'You thought I hadn't noticed.'

'Well . . .'

'So my opinion does matter?'

'I refuse to be drawn.'

'You're going to tell me that you went out and bought new glasses because of somebody else?'

'No.'

'There you are, then.' She looked at him closely. 'They're good, you know? Makes your eyes look . . . well, almost like they do naturally.'

'Which is?'

'You know.'

'Do I?'

'I'd hazard a guess that more than one lamb went to the slaughter that way.' She caught the twinkle in his eye, and added teasingly, 'Bet you're a hot little number on the sly.'

'Now if I'd said that . . .'

'You'd have got your face slapped. But who said anything about playing fair?'

The door of the Old Rectory opened, sending a rectangle of light on to the gravel.

'We'd better go in, the others are arriving.'

Sally turned to look.

'Who's that?' She nodded towards the tall, slim figure in the doorway.

'It's Jon . . . oh, good, Paul and Lynn Ryan are here. You'll like them.'

'What's the other one's name?'

'Eh?'

'Our hosts.'

'Oh, Tony.'

'And which one's which?'

'Does it matter?'

'Well, I don't know what gays are like. In private, I mean.'

'I think you'll find that they're surprisingly like any other two blokes. Except that they don't fancy women, of course.'

She paused a moment. 'Strange.'

'Well, it is to you and me.'

'I don't mean that . . . I mean, this is strange.'

'Being with me?'

She looked down.

'Does it worry you?'

'Not worry exactly. I just feel a bit . . . odd.'

'In what way?'

'Don't know. Suppose I'm not sure how to act. I mean, it's not as though we're really a couple, is it?'

'We don't have to be, do we?'

'Guess not.'

'Well then.' He smiled, aware that, for once, she was letting her defences drop. 'Come on, it'll be fine. Just act naturally, the rest will follow.'

He got out of the car and went round to open her door.

'Allow me.'

Sally took his hand and swung out of the seat, thinking what a change it made to be treated with some manners. As he turned from locking the car, she quietly slipped an arm into his. They walked down the path and knocked on the heavy wooden door.

'Ken! Lovely to see you.' John shook his hand, then looked towards Sally. 'I say . . .'

'Sally Blythe – Jon Bradshaw.'

'Hello,' Sally said, noticing the look that Jon shot Ken. He covered it quickly.

'Come on in, things are just warming up.'

They followed him into the kitchen where a variety of appetising smells wafted up from the range at the far end.

'Sorry about this,' Jon said to Sally, 'it's a bit of a daft arrangement having people come straight into the kitchen, but it's the way the house is laid out, you see.' He glanced nervously at the range. 'And it can't be changed . . . listed building.'

'Oh,' she replied, wondering why it bothered him so much. The room, with its low, oak-beamed ceiling, looked perfect to her. She paused to gaze at the huge vase of flowers that had been set out on the refectory table.

'You go on up,' Jon said, suddenly moving off at speed, 'I've got to watch my pots.'

Ken took Sally up a short flight of steps which opened on to the most impressive living room she'd ever seen. The panelled walls were hung with pictures of obvious value, carefully arranged and tastefully lit, each begging the eye to look closer. Beautiful china and silver was displayed on console tables at either side of the room, with more set out on the marble chimneypiece around which a knot of guests were gathered.

'There you are,' called Tony, leaving the group to welcome them. 'Hope you're in good voice, young man, we'll be needing you for the sing-song. Are you musical at all?'

The question was aimed at Sally, who at that moment had become uncomfortably aware that her dress was causing a slight stir among the other guests.

'Used to sing in the school choir, but . . .'

'Good. You can give us a turn later.'

'But I haven't . . . I mean, it's years since . . .'

'Never mind. Rule of the house: everyone has to do something. Buck's Fizz?' He waved towards a tray of drinks.

'Thanks.'

He turned to pick up two glasses, handing one to each of them.

'Come and be introduced.'

157

Sally moved slowly forward, giving Ken an anxious look. He smiled and took her elbow.

'Suzanne, Sandy,' Tony flourished, 'do drag yourselves away from the vol-au-vents, dears.'

The couple glanced round.

'Ken I think you already know,' he continued, 'and this is . . .?'

'Sally.'

'Oh, dear, another "S", how very confusing. Well, I'll leave you to mingle.'

Ken was about to say something when a shrill voice cut in from behind.

'Ken, darling,' it warbled, 'where *have* you been hiding?'

An elderly woman in pink chiffon grabbed his arm and dragged him away before Sally had a chance to settle. She grinned weakly at the couple who were standing in front of her.

'Marvellous hair,' said the man, disconcertingly, 'is it natural?'

'Of course.'

'Yes, yes,' he nodded. 'The green eyes . . . got any Irish blood?'

'My maternal grandparents.'

'Fresh, fair skin.'

She was beginning to squirm.

'You should paint her, Sandy,' the woman said, adding, unnecessarily, 'he's an artist, you know.'

'I see her draped in white, something simple and chaste, with lots of soft folds,' he gushed. 'Yes, a lovely nymph at the water's edge . . . no, Ophelia. Ophelia!'

'Such *vision*,' the woman said dreamily.

Sally hated being talked about as though she wasn't there. It reminded her of being small, of being perched in a seat on the back of her mother's bicycle while she exchanged

158

embarrassing details of Sally's behaviour with the mother of a child the same age.

'Having fun?' Ken had extricated himself from the clutches of the elderly woman.

'Think I need another drink.'

He got her one while the artist continued to run his eye over her in the most disturbing way.

'So what's in the stars, Suzanne?' Ken asked, seeing Sally's discomfort.

'You're Virgo, aren't you?'

'Not *intacto*, though, eh?' nudged Tony, deciding to rejoin them. 'Don't tell him too much, Suzanne, save some for later.'

'I'll only have time for three or four people, you know.'

'That's all right, I've already chosen my victims.'

'Victims?'

'Just joking.'

'I'm not doing anything unless you take it seriously.' She tossed back her long brown hair, moodily.

'You *know* I absolutely *hang* on every word.'

'Not according to Jon.'

'Why? What's he been saying?'

But just then a handbell was rung and Jon appeared in the doorway, a white cloth neatly folded over his arm, in the manner of a grand maître d'.

'Ladies and gentlemen,' he announced, with great formality, 'dinner is served.'

'Right, come on, everybody,' said Tony, ushering people out. 'Come on, come on. There'll be hell to pay if the starters get ruined.'

The group began to move out of the room, still hanging on to snatches of conversation that had been interrupted.

'Thank God for that,' Sally hissed in Ken's ear, 'that guy was giving me the creeps.'

'Sandy? He's harmless.'

159

'Did you see the way he was looking at me?'

'Fancied you as a model, did he?'

'That's not all, if you ask me.'

'You're wrong there.'

'You mean he's . . .'

'Ssh.' He led her out of the living room, through into the drawing room. Again, she was struck by the blend of beautiful furnishings.

'I don't know where to look first,' Sally gasped.

A pair of double doors that had been carefully stained to look as if they were original to the house had been opened into the conservatory. The others were edging around the potted palms, looking for their seats at a table which had been pulled out at its centre, where a fantastic display of crystal and Crown Derby glinted by the light of two Georgian candelabra.

'Sit, sit!' Jon waved frantically. 'Look, can't you read. That's Marjorie not Michael.'

Michael mumbled an apology and shuffled two places to the left.

'Not *there*, Lynn . . . oh, Tony, you sort them out, will you?'

He flew off to the kitchen, leaving his partner to cope.

'Take no notice,' Tony said. 'A dinner party simply isn't worth the effort unless Jon can have a good flap and panic.'

They settled themselves down opposite their place cards in time for the presentation of steaming hot *Coquilles Saint-Jacques*.

'How do you manage it, darling?' cooed the elderly woman, as Jon took a seat next to her at the head of the table. 'Ten at the same time!'

'Blood, sweat and tears, love. Blood, sweat and tears.'

'Nonsense, you enjoy every moment,' Tony called above the chatter.

'Only 'cos it keeps me fit.'

Sally was amused by the role play. The idea of a full-grown

man doing the long suffering bit seemed faintly bizarre, yet it had its context. What was an unconventional arrangement in general terms had become almost stereotypical, over time. She watched Tony raise his glass to Jon and mouth 'Love you.' It was meant to be a private moment and she looked away, feeling that she had somehow intruded.

'Hello, "Guest of Mr Rees".' The man to her right had snatched up and replaced her place card in an instant. 'However did the old goat inveigle you into his sweaty grasp?'

'He won a bet.' She smiled across the table at Ken, who looked startled.

'Must've been a good one.'

'Oh, it was.'

'Come on, Ken, get your hand off my wife's knee and confess all.'

'My lips are sealed.'

'He's such a secretive devil.'

'Just as well for you,' put in the wife. 'I'd still like to know what you were up to that time you were both out until two in the morning.'

'Trying to find my way out of his living room. You should see the junk.'

'They *say* they were watching "B" movies.' She winked at Sally.

'That's because we were.'

'Sure they weren't "X" rated?'

'Too old for that now, Lynn,' said Ken.

She put a make-believe violin under her chin and started to whistle 'Hearts and Flowers'.

'Cruel woman, your wife,' he added.

'Nobody knows the pain I endure . . . ouch!'

'You look well enough on it,' said Sally, laughing as he rubbed his shin.

'Wouldn't swap her for a gold clock, really.'

161

'You'd have plenty of takers if you did,' Tony suddenly joined in. 'Which is more than we can say for you, Paul.'

'That's what I like about my friends . . .'

'Oh, I don't know,' Lynn cut across, 'now that he's reached the big Five-O I could cash him in for two twenty-five-year-olds.'

'You could get four thirteen-year-olds for me,' said Ken, 'but I don't suppose that's what you had in mind.'

'No, thanks, I've got enough problems with the two I've got at home. Should have christened them Feckless and Reckless.'

'Shame on you. My godsons are beyond reproach.'

'Take after you, do they?'

'Not unless he's about to get spotty and hormonal,' said Paul. 'The level of lassitude is quite astonishing.'

'Shouldn't be too tough on them, adolescence is a horrible stage.'

'For who? The kids or the parents?'

'Both.'

'Thanks for the advice.'

'Well, I reckon a good old 'un will beat a good young 'un any day of the week,' said Suzanne, as if she had just woken up. Until then, she had been sitting between Paul and Tony, completely ignoring the conversation.

'What is she on about?' asked Tony.

'Sex, of course.'

'Trust Sandy to lower the tone,' Jon butted in as he cleared their plates away.

'She likes a mature man, does Suze.'

'What's she doing with you then?' quipped Tony.

'Just watch it, I haven't finished that portrait of you yet.'

'He's doing me *au naturel*,' beamed Tony, towards the other five.

'What? Warts and all?' asked Ken.

'I don't have warts.'

162

'No, but he's got a mole in an interesting place,' said Sandy, wickedly.

'Well, I hope this picture's for private viewing only.'

'There's nothing I would be ashamed of showing in front of a wider audience.'

'You old tart!'

'Oldish tart,' Tony corrected. 'And you, Ken Rees, are a fine one to talk.'

'There may be snow on the roof, but there's fire in the boiler, eh, Ken?' Paul teased, with a knowing look towards Sally. He was about to add something when Jon reappeared with a silver salver, on which the most perfect Beef Wellington rested. A spontaneous burst of applause went up from the guests.

'*Et voilà!*' Jon boomed above the noise, setting the dish down in the centre of the table with some panache. He turned to Tony.

'You carve, I'll serve.'

'If I must.'

As plates were filled and handed round from their end of the table, Paul saw his opportunity to button-hole Sally.

'So where did you two meet?' he asked.

'At an auction.'

'You're in the trade, then?'

'In a minor way.'

'Meaning?'

'I buy and sell privately but I'm hoping to have premises soon.'

He'd started eating. 'Tricky business, antiques.'

'What makes you say that?'

'I've seen a few people come unstuck.'

'By overstretching themselves?'

'Mostly by not looking after their books.'

'The accounts can't be that difficult.'

'It's not that they're difficult, more that people don't

bother to keep them up to date. Then there's all the cash deals.'

'You seem to know a lot about it.'

'That's because I've had to deal with the aftermath.'

'You're an accountant?'

'No, I'm a doctor, Lynn's the accountant,' he said, nodding towards his wife. 'They don't know which of us to call out first when the Revenue catches up with them.'

Sally looked nonplussed.

'Had a chap only last week,' he went on, 'keeled over with a minor heart attack. He'd been served with a noticed for twenty-five grand in back tax.'Course the silly bugger hadn't put in any accounts for three years.'

'Surely he must have known they'd get on to him sooner or later?'

'This one'd been dealing out of his garage and thought he'd just get away with it. But you'd be surprised where Her Majesty's inspectors have eyes and ears.'

'Sounds positively Byzantine.' Sally shuddered, thinking that she should start doing some serious bookkeeping herself.

'Mind you, the tax men are only doing their jobs, you know. We expect free hospitals, free schools, free policing, etcetera, but the money to fund them all has got to come from somewhere. Why should honest tax payers be left to support the Welfare State whilst the tax dodgers get off Scot free?'

'On his hobby horse, is he?' said Ken, cheerfully.

'It's a moral issue too frequently ignored, in my view.'

'Let's not have morality over the dinner table. And no religion or politics.'

'You're right,' Lynn put in, 'too serious by half. Come on, Ken, liven us up with a couple of jokes.'

'Haven't heard any good ones lately. Well, not that I can repeat.'

164

'Go on, we're not prudish.'

He thought for a while, then launched into one.

'Little girl goes to her mother looking very serious. "Mummy," ' he affected a girlish lisp, making them all giggle, ' "I've seen Daddy's whizzywoo." So the mother, who's quite trendy, says, "Really, darling? And what are whizzywoos for?" "Whizzywoos are for two things," comes the little voice. "Yes?" "One's for doing whizzwoos . . ." "Yes. And what's the other one?" "Cleaning the au pair's teeth." '

The explosion of laughter shook the crockery, turning a few heads.

'Come on, share it,' shouted Tony.

And so the joke was passed up and down the table, starting a competition to beat it that kept everyone on the go until coffee was served.

'Now,' said Jon, when they'd all finished, 'for the highlight of the evening. If you'd all like to join us upstairs . . .'

It was only when she stood up that Sally realised she'd had rather a lot to drink. She steadied herself on Ken's arm.

'You okay?' he asked.

'Fine.'

'Enjoying yourself?'

'Very much. What's happening now?'

'We're going to have a sing-song.'

'Oh, gawd.'

'Don't worry, it's great fun.'

When they got to the living room, Jon was already at the piano, playing a piece in march tempo that was distinctly funereal.

'Any offers?' he called out. 'No? You'll be kicking yourselves in a minute.'

He played it over again.

'Come on somebody. Anybody. At least have a guess.'

' "After the Ball Is Over",' someone tried.

165

'You've got to sing it.'

' "After the ball is over . . ." How's it go? "Just at the break of day . . ." '

Jon began to play a florid accompaniment then stopped short.

'No, it's not that.'

They all laughed.

'I'll do it again.'

' "The volunteer organist",' said Lynn, as Sally sat down on the sofa next to her.

'I don't hear you singing.'

'I'm not sure of the tune.'

'Hopeless,' muttered Jon, rattling over the keys.

'I know,' said Ken, suddenly.

'Right, let's hear it.'

He cleared his throat and began to sing in a rich baritone that took Sally by surprise.

' "Just a song at twilight . . ." '

'Yes!' Jon cried, picking up the bass harmony. ' "When the lights are low . . ." '

' "And the whispering shadows," ' came Tony's tenor, ' "softly come and go." '

People started to hum along as the trio sang on in perfect barber shop style. Sally began to feel a lump in her throat.

'Hasn't he got a lovely voice?' whispered Lynn, smiling.

'I had no idea.'

'He's a man of many parts, is our Ken.'

12

His nerves were jangling at a pitch that made him sick to the stomach. Still half-asleep, he jerked himself out of the chair and threw a hand towards the 'phone. His eyes began to focus on a pine dresser that bore no relation to what they expected to see. With an odd sensation of fear that momentarily threw him, he realised that he had no idea where he was.

'Hello? Hello?' an anxious voice said at the other end of the 'phone. 'Sally? Are you all right?'

'Who is this?'

Silence, and then, indignantly, 'Who's *that*?'

'What number are you calling?'

'Two-six-one, five-four-eight.'

'Heather?'

'Yes.'

'Sorry . . . look . . . God, it's nine o'clock!'

'What's going on?'

'Don't worry, it's Ken,' he said, suddenly coming to. 'Sally's still asleep.'

There was a pronounced silence.

'She's . . . er . . . well, a little the worse for wear, so I thought I ought to stay over.'

'I see.'

He knew precisely what she saw and cringed internally.

'Bit too much exuberance,' he added, lamely, 'nothing a couple of aspirins won't cure.'

'Well, tell her I've taken the children to school, will you?' came the crisp response. 'And get her to ring me.'

The 'phone went down and he let out a groan. No amount of explaining was going to set this one right. He stumbled away from the dresser and knocked a coffee cup off the table.

'Shit!' he cursed, bending to look at the damage. His back felt as if it had been welded to every joint.

'It's no use, Rees,' he muttered to himself, 'you're too old for this game.'

He had meant to spend the night on the sofa but had dropped off instead on one of the kitchen chairs. It had not been very comfortable. Cold and stiff and with his clothes feeling horribly tacky, he began to wonder whether he shouldn't just write off the rest of the day and go home to bed.

Suppose I should check on Madam, he thought, making his way over to the sink. She'd passed out in the car and he hadn't been able to wake her. In the end, he'd resorted to his best improvisation of a fireman's lift to get her upstairs.

He smiled gently and shook his head then started searching the cupboards for painkillers. After a few minutes it was obvious that there weren't any. He put on the kettle and went out to the car to fetch the emergency supply he kept in the First Aid Kit. It was then that a small white delivery van turned up the drive.

'This Jacob's Cottage?' a cheery voice called as it drew up outside.

'Yes.'

'Thank God for that, had the devil of a job finding you.'

The driver got out and opened the back of his van.

'Delivery for the lady of the house,' he said, thrusting a bouquet of flowers into Ken's hands, 'least that's what the boss said. Tag's got something written on it in French. Don't understand it myself, like.'

Ken looked at the envelope that had been clipped to the top of the transparent wrapping. On it was the inscription: *La Belle Dame Sans Merci*.

'Thanks,' he said, uncertainly.

'You're welcome.'

The van rumbled off down the drive, leaving Ken to stare after it. Of the emotions that he could positively identify in those few moments, dismay and resentment had the upper hand. For a while he didn't know which was the sillier, his immediate feelings or the fact that he'd somehow assumed that he was the only man in her life. He went back into the house and plonked the bouquet on the drainer where he stood toying with the idea of taking it up with the tea to see if she'd say anything to satisfy his curiosity about the sender. On the whole, he decided at length, it would be unfair. But in the back of his mind, the Keats he'd learned by rote as a boy still taunted:

> *I saw pale kings and princes too,*
> *Pale warriors – death-pale were they all;*
> *They cried, 'La Belle Dame Sans Merci*
> *Hath thee in thrall!'*

He clicked the kettle back on, irritated by the general state of things. As if having Heather disgusted with him wasn't bad enough for one morning.

'Well, that'll teach you,' he told himself. 'The pathway to hell is paved with good intentions, as my mother used to say.'

He looked around for a breakfast tray and found, instead, a dustpan and brush with which to clear up the shattered coffee cup. He thought of Sally, lying comatose upstairs, of her head on his shoulder on the drive home, of her flinging her arms around him as they left the party and asking for 'another one of those kisses'. There'd been real affection in what he'd felt then.

The danger of strings being attached where he'd promised there wouldn't be offended his principles. But there was no avoiding the fact that he'd grown attached to her. That it was so much in such a short time came as a surprise. Yet there was something about her, something that had struck him straight away, not because of the way she looked, although that was a natural attraction, but more because she was possessed of an inner strength that he admired. So many of the women he'd known had lacked that quality. There'd been a few who'd been capable of being brave in bursts but, generally, they'd really been looking for someone to cling to. If anything, it had been the clinging element that had put him off getting in too deep.

He pondered the thought, remembering the disappointment on a range of pretty faces over the years. In many ways, it had been inevitable. His was a searching mind and for all the solid aspects of his nature, he could not be pinned down in the fixed and narrow way that most women expected. What he needed was someone with a freedom of spirit to match his own. Someone like Sally, if only she hadn't taken until now to come along.

The dishevelled form that looked back at him from the mirror seemed to drive home the pointlessness of nurturing any expectations.

Not exactly love's young dream.

He turned away and went to throw the shards of broken coffee cup into the bin.

Still, I have my uses.

With toast and jam for instant fortification and a glass of water for the tablets she was bound to need for the hangover,

he quietly mounted the stairs, lingering for a moment outside the bedroom door to make sure she wasn't up and
about. When he crept inside he could see that she was still
out cold, an arm stretched over the coverlet, white and
appealing in the thin light from the window.

'Sally,' he whispered. 'Sally . . .'

He bent and shook her gently.

'Uuh?' Her eyes blinked open, focused briefly, then shut
again. 'Oh, God.'

'No, just room service.'

'Very funny . . . ooh, my head!'

'I've got something for that. Come on, the tea'll revive
you.'

She was about to sit up when he remembered.

'Hang on a tick,' he said, grabbing a dressing gown from
the back of the door, 'here.'

She looked puzzled for a second then felt herself under
the sheets. Slowly, she realised that she had no recollection
of getting undressed.

'I'll open the curtains a crack,' he said, calmly walking
across to the window, where he paused long enough for her
to cover her embarrassment. 'Heather 'phoned, by the way.'

There was another groan from the bed.

'She's taken the kids to school and she asked you to ring
back.'

'What did she say when you answered the 'phone?'

'No more than that.'

'She didn't want to know what you were doing here?'

'I had the impression that she'd reached her own conclusions.'

'Oh bugger, bugger, blast and damn!'

'Language!' he said. 'And from such a lovely mouth.'

'Well, she'll think . . .'

'I'm afraid so.'

'Oh, no.'

171

'Never mind. You know and I know that your honour is intact.'

'Is it?'

'Certainly.' He held out the glass of water. 'How would you like your aspirins, fried or boiled?'

She stuck out her tongue, rudely, then took it.

'Tut, tut. Feeling a bit fragile, are we?'

'Fragile's putting it mildly.'

'Here, have some toast, get some blood sugar back into your alcohol.'

'Don't be rotten,' she said, grimacing. 'Was I very drunk?'

'Not really. More – how shall I say? – merry.'

'How merry?'

'Just enough to have a good time before collapsing in a gentle heap.'

'Not at the party?'

'No, in the car.'

'Thank heavens for that.'

'Though in one of your finer moments, I thought you gave a splendid rendition on Jon's flute.'

'I remember that bit. Did it sound okay?'

'Extremely pleasant. You should play more often.'

'Must've been the brandy,' she said, rubbing her forehead. 'I was all right until I got out into the air. What happened after I fell asleep?'

'I brought you home and put you to bed.'

'I didn't wake up again?'

He shook his head. 'Out like a light.'

'So you . . .?'

He nodded.

'And you didn't?'

'I averted my gaze.'

'Wasn't your gaze I was worried about!'

'I assure you that no unclean thought went through my mind,' he said, looking mildly insulted, though the idea of

172

undressing her when she wasn't inert had more than tempted him. 'Eat your toast.'

Sally pushed herself further up the pillows and took the plate from him.

'What time is it?'

'Ten o'clock.'

'Suppose I should be getting up.'

'I'd take your time, if I were you.'

'Feeling a little better now.'

'Good.'

She started nibbling the toast. 'Where did you sleep?'

'Downstairs,' he said, stretching. 'On a chair made out of cast iron, by the feel of things.'

'Achy?'

'Stiff as a board.'

'I'm sorry. You should have gone home.'

'I was too tired. Anyway, I didn't want to leave you in case you were ill or something.'

She was touched that he'd been so worried about her. 'It's very sweet of you, looking after me like this.'

'If I ask you out, I'm responsible for getting you back in one piece.'

'How very old-fashioned.'

'Some old-fashioned ideas are worth hanging on to.'

'You are funny.'

'Am I?'

'I mean, you're such an unusual mix. Not entirely modern, not exactly dated, somewhere in between.'

'I'm from the in between generation.'

He was turning the winder on his watch as if he was thinking that he should be elsewhere.

'Go, if you need to, I'll be okay.'

'Well, there are a couple of things I should really be doing.'

'Go on, I'm all right, honestly.'

'Don't need anything?'

173

'Only a bath.'

'Could do with a wash and shave myself,' he said, feeling his chin. Then, standing, he added as an afterthought, 'Oh, something arrived for you this morning.'

'What was that?'

'A token of someone's affection, at a guess.'

'What's that?' She sat up eagerly.

'A romantic gift and a cryptic message.'

She thought for a second then smiled.

'Is it from someone I know?'

'I should think so.'

'Someone I see quite a lot of?'

'Maybe.'

'You!'

'Not me.'

'You're winding me up.'

'No.'

'Yes, you are.'

He shook his head, emphatically.

Sally was confused. 'Then who?'

'That, no doubt, will become clear in its own good time.'

She wondered how he must have felt. Racing downstairs as soon as the back door closed, she'd only had to see the envelope pinned to the flowers to know who they were from. By then, Ken's car was turning out of the gate and she looked after it, guiltily, thinking how stung she'd have been in his place.

Why today? she asked herself. Then, still feeling sorry for Ken, Why does it always have to be so bloody awkward?

She looked down at the flowers and sighed. Well, it's not entirely my fault. I didn't ask him to get involved. But she remembered the way she'd kissed him the night before and knew she'd been leading him on.

She fingered the envelope absentmindedly. It was hard to

work out exactly what she felt for Ken. More fondness than anything else, she thought now, a kind of warmth that went beyond friendship, but she wasn't sure that there would ever be more to it than that. So what was she playing at? She wasn't sure about that either. He was so easy to like, to be around. That counted for a few points. And he treated her with respect. That mattered as much if not more so. But what did it all add up to, at the end of the day?

Not enough, she decided, tearing open the envelope. Anyway, I've only just started being me. Who knows where it will lead?

The note inside had been written in a beautiful copperplate hand that seemed especially devised to make an impression.

Care for lunch to make up for Wednesday? I'll be round at 12.30 to collect you – Daniel W.

'What?' she gasped, glancing at the clock. 'Oh my God!'

For a moment she was completely flummoxed. There she was mooning around in a threadbare old dressing gown, hung over, hair all over the place, and he'd be at the door in two hours' time. Worse than that, there was no way of stopping him coming.

'What an infernal cheek,' she said, crossly. 'If I still had the car I'd . . .'

But then she remembered the liquid brown eyes and started to smile. Maybe I wouldn't.

She looked at the flowers again and began to think it was quite pleasant to be pursued.

'Why not?' she said, taking the flowers and putting them into the sink. 'Why not? Could do with a bit of excitement.'

She went back upstairs and started to dig through the wardrobe.

'Too formal . . . too casual. Oh, what can I wear?'

The exercise was rather fun, despite the fact that she couldn't make her mind up. With half-an-hour to go, she was still rushing around in her bra and pants though at least she'd managed to have a bath and do her make-up.

'That's it!' she resolved at last, picking a neat little Kookai number. She wondered if it was still fashionable as she wriggled into the short grey skirt.

What the hell? I like it.

One of the big brass buttons was dangling from the double-breasted jacket. She went in search of a needle and thread and was just in the process of ransacking the pine dresser in the kitchen when the telephone rang.

'Hello!' she shouted, without meaning to.

'Oh, we're up, are we?'

'Heather! Sorry, I meant to 'phone you before.'

'What's the panic?'

'Panic? Oh, I . . . I'd forgotten that I'd arranged to meet someone for lunch.'

'Not a late one, I hope. I can pick the children up from school but I'll have to bring them straight over to you.'

'That's okay. I shouldn't be more than a couple of hours.'

There was an awkward silence.

'They were all right last night, were they . . . the kids?' Sally asked, quickly.

'Fine. How was your evening?'

'Very nice.' She was aware that a fuller account was expected.

'Glad you enjoyed yourself.'

'A bit too much, I think.' She laughed, nervously. 'Anyway, Ken looked after me.'

'So I heard.'

Clang! Sally thought. What did I have to say that for?

'Don't know why he stayed, really. I was perfectly all right.'

'Rather the worse for wear was his description.'

'I was a bit merry, I suppose.'

'Well, I hope you didn't do anything you might regret.'

176

'If you must know, he spent the night in a chair. *Downstairs*, actually.'

'It's okay, you can spare me the details.'

'Look, I'm thirty-three, not . . .'

'All right, okay, don't get in a huff.'

'Sorry.' But she wasn't sorry at all. She hated constantly having to justify herself. On the other hand, Heather had been a good surrogate mother and she owed her some regard.

'What time should I be back by?' she said, more calmly.

'Half-three, quarter-to-four.'

'All right.' She thought she could hear a car coming up the drive. 'Look, must go, see you later.'

She'd put down the 'phone before she realised that she should have said thank you.

'Can't get anything right today,' she moaned. 'Blast, where's my shoes?'

She galloped upstairs and shoved on the stilettos she'd been wearing the night before, almost tripping over herself in the effort to do that and get over to the window at the same time. As she looked out, a black Porsche Targa drew up outside.

Wow! That's a bit flash, she thought, watching him climb out of the driver's seat and shut the door. Then, Oh, please don't let him be just all show.

He stood momentarily, looking at the cottage, seeming to be assessing it in a curious sort of way. On impulse, she moved behind the curtain so that he wouldn't see she was waiting, letting him knock twice before she sauntered down with completely contrived nonchalance.

He was wearing a smile that was a picture of audacity.

'Hello, again.'

'Hello,' she said, as coolly as she could manage.

'Ready to go?'

She wanted to say something smart and sharp to deflate

177

his ego but her brain wouldn't move fast enough to come up with anything good.

'I'll just get my handbag.' Damn this hangover!

She crossed the room reasonably elegantly, conscious that he would be following every step.

'It's rather charming,' he said, poking his head into the kitchen, 'like something out of Hansel and Gretel.'

'Yes, and it feels like it's made out of gingerbread in the winter.'

'Drafty?'

'And damp.'

'That's the trouble with old properties. Still, you can't beat them for character.'

'Oh, it's got character all right. Wet rot, dry rot, hardly any putty in the windows, but *bags* of character.'

'What happened to the ceiling?'

'Cistern burst in the big freeze up.'

'Should get it seen to.'

'I would if the landlord'd cough up for it.'

'I can imagine that that could be difficult.'

'But the man's got pots of money. Couple of hundred quid here or there wouldn't hurt him.'

'Have you seen how he lives?'

'The Manor House? Dreadful decrepit place. Only thing keeping it up is the Death Watch beetles holding hands.'

He laughed. 'Like your sense of humour.'

She swung her bag over her shoulder and grinned.

'If I couldn't see the funny side of things I'd be dead with worry.'

He waited while she locked up then walked her to the car.

'Do you like Mexican food?'

'Don't know, never tried it.'

'Here, the seats are a bit deep.' He offered a hand so that she could lower herself in without too much effort.

'Thanks.'

178

'Just stay off the Salsa if you don't like it hot.'

'What?'

'The tomato dip. They serve it with everything.'

The engine gave a throaty roar and they were off.

'Lived out here long?' he asked.

'Two years. Why?'

'Looked like you were still unpacking.'

Sally wondered what he meant for a second.

'Oh, the tea chests. I was sorting through them ready for Saturday.'

'What's special about Saturday?'

'I've got a market stall.'

'Selling?'

'Bits of jewellery, small antiques.'

'Oh. I've got a couple of friends in the antiques trade.'

'Have you?'

'Deal in furniture, mostly.'

'I do furniture but I've got problems with it at the moment.'

'Business slow?'

'It'd be faster if I was mobile.'

'You mean you're stuck out here without transport?'

'Didn't used to be but my car died in an accident.'

'Why don't you get another?'

'I will, when I've got the money.'

He glanced sideways at her.

'Things that bad?'

'They're improving but . . . well, I've got to wait to sell something before I can afford to splash out.'

'But how do you manage? The children and everything?'

'My step-mother's helping me out at the moment. Anyway, it won't be for too much longer.'

'How long?'

'Five days.'

'You seem very certain.'

179

'That's because my best piece is up for auction at Sotheby's next Wednesday.'

'Hoping to make a lot on it?'

'Enough to get by.'

He thought for a minute.

'What sort of car do you need?'

'I was thinking of an estate. You know, so that I could ferry things around.'

'Old one? New one?'

'Whatever's half decent at an economical price.'

'How much?'

'Haven't got a clue until I see what's on offer. A car, to me, is something with four wheels and an engine that hopefully gets you from A to B. The rest is a mystery.'

'Not to me, though.'

'Thought 'planes were your forte?'

'And classic cars.'

'I'm not quite ready for the Rolls Corniche, unfortunately.'

'Could find you a nice Volvo.'

'Could you?'

'I'm off to a car auction in the Midlands tomorrow, anyway. Why don't I look around?'

'Would you?'

'Of course.' He turned the Porsche out of the traffic that was clogging Hove Church Street and headed towards the sea front. 'Hope you don't mind a short walk. There's never anywhere to park around here.'

At the end of the block there was a slip road which ran parallel to the main coastal route. Separated from the fast-flowing traffic by a low brick wall, it provided useful extra parking space, and as luck would have it, someone was just pulling out.

'That's handy,' said Sally, turning in her seat to look at the row of tall terraced houses that ran alongside, 'Isn't this King's Gardens?'

'Mmm. There are some fantastic flats here.'

'My step-mother lived here once.'

'See that one there?' he said, pointing towards a first-floor balcony. 'Belongs to the manager of the casino. It's beautiful inside – all the original cornices and a huge marble fireplace carved with bullrushes. Apparently that's meant to mean something. You know, it's meant to allude to the name of whoever lived there when the houses were first built. Probably one of the royal entourage, back in Edwardian times. Or one of the King's mistresses. Lily Langtry used to live round here somewhere. Her house has a fireplace carved with lilies – and a tunnel that runs from here to the Pavilion, or so they say, so that she could go off to her assignations without being seen.'

'Long way to walk.'

'I don't know if that part's true but she definitely lived in one of these and, of course, Brighton is a maze of tunnels.'

'Is it?'

'Yes, didn't you read about that one they found in the basement of some office that was being extended recently? Estate agents or something.'

'I never look at the local rag, except for the adverts. These tunnels, they can't all go to the Pavilion?'

'No one knows where most of them begin and end. A lot just lead to the beach.'

'Whatever for?'

'So that one could get down to one's private strip without mingling with the hoi polloi, don'tcha know?' He got out of the car and went round to help her out.

'Thanks for the flowers, by the way.' Sally smiled.

'The first of many, I hope.'

'You're presuming a lot.'

'You're here, aren't you?'

'You didn't give me a chance to say no.'

181

'And I won't, if I can help it.' He held on to her hand and raised it to his lips.

'Now you're going over the top.'

'You think so?'

'I think you could be a dangerous man, Mr . . .' she laughed. 'Sorry, I've forgotten your name.'

'Daniel.'

'No, the other one.'

'Wiseman.'

'Oh, yes.'

He took her arm.

'And perhaps now you'll tell me yours?'

'Blythe.'

'Sally Blythe . . . mmm, it suits you.'

'I always thought so.'

They walked back towards the High Street, Sally's heels clicking loudly on the pavement.

'Don't know how you girls manage in those things,' he said, looking down. 'Still, I'm glad they've made a comeback. I like my women feminine.'

'Thinking of adding me to your collection, are you?'

'There isn't a collection,' he said, but she didn't believe him.

It was obvious that he was a regular the moment they walked through the restaurant door. Heads nodded at several tables and Sally got the feeling that she was being given the once-over. One of the watchers was important enough for Daniel to make a point of going over.

'Good to see you,' he said, as the big, hard-faced man raised himself slightly from his chair, apparently for Sally's benefit. 'Down for long?'

'Just a few days,' the man replied. 'I'm at The Grand. You should give me a call.'

They moved away to a table at the back of the restaurant.

'One of your clients?' Sally asked as she sat down.

'One of my contacts,' he said, picking up a menu. 'What would you like to drink?'

'Something inoffensive. Lime juice and soda, I think.'

'No wine?'

'No, thanks. I was out on the tiles last night and I'm still suffering for it.'

'You should have one glass, at least. Hair of the dog and all that.'

'I'll stick to watering down what's already in there, thanks.'

'Okay. Any particular fancy in the food line, or shall I just order?'

'Go ahead and choose. My knowledge of Mexican cooking stops at Guacamole.' She was looking at the hard-faced man who seemed to be viewing them with particular interest.

'Wish people wouldn't do that.'

'What?'

'Stare at you.'

'They don't, unless there's something worth staring at.'

It was supposed to be a compliment, but Sally was still uncomfortable.

'Who is he . . . the man you were talking to?'

'I told you, a contact.'

'What's that mean?'

A waiter came over and Daniel took the opportunity to evade the question.

'Sure you won't have a real drink?'

'No, thanks.' She watched him give the order, studying his movements, trying to pick up clues to his personality. There was a great deal of sophistication about Daniel Wiseman on the surface, she thought, but it seemed to be masking rougher edges. It was the sort of sophistication that was learned rather than natural, and that made her wonder about his background.

'You know, I find all this rather puzzling,' she tried.

'In what way?'

'Well, in the first place I'm not sure why you invited me out. And in the second, I'm not sure I know why I accepted.'

'I should have thought that the answer was obvious in both cases.'

'Mutual attraction, you mean? Well, that's part of it.'

'What else do you need?'

'It's just that I don't usually go out with complete strangers.'

'Do I make you nervous.'

'Not nervous, exactly. I'm just wary, I suppose.'

'What of? I'm not some moustachio-twirling villain, you know.'

Sally laughed. 'I'm not implying that you are but I would like to know more about you.'

'Well, I'll tell you, what you see isn't necessarily what you get.'

'How do you mean?'

'Appearances aren't everything. I may live well now, but it's taken a lot of hard graft to get where I am. I'm just an ordinary guy who happens to have taken a few risks and made something of his life.' He seemed quite serious for a moment. 'I started with nothing but I was determined that it wouldn't stay that way for long. It wasn't easy to get the breaks either, but what I lacked in knowledge I made up for in wit.' He smiled suddenly. 'A bit like you, really.'

'I don't see the parallel.'

'Of course you do, don't try to be too clever.'

She blushed, feeling rather abashed at the way he'd got the measure of her so soon.

'It's okay, I understand,' he went on. 'None of us likes to be thought of as a complete novice. But I'll tell you something important, shall I? You can bluff your way around for a certain amount of time, and you might even have some luck, but it's a very hit-and-miss way of going about things. If

184

you're going to survive in any type of trade, you've got to know your stuff and that applies particularly to specialist fields like antiques.'

'I suppose it is a bit obvious that I've just started out,' Sally said, getting over her embarrassment, 'but I'm doing my best to learn as fast as I can. If only there wasn't so much. I mean, the word "antique" covers an impossibly huge range of goods. No one can be expected to know about everything from hat pins to harmoniums.'

'You shouldn't even try. In fact, it's a dead give away to other dealers if you do pretend that you know a little bit about everything. You may get a bland face staring at you in the pub as you hold forth about one piece or another but word'll go round the industry like wild fire if you slip up.'

'How do you do it, then? How do you get credibility? You'd have thought people would understand that everyone has to start somewhere.'

'Many dealers will have had the advantage of being brought up in the trade. They'll have had a father or uncle or someone to show them the ropes.'

'There must be a few outsiders.'

'Nowhere near as many as there are insiders.'

'But it's still possible to get on the inside. You say that you started with nothing, how did you go about it?'

'Well, one of the first things I did was to set a limit on the types of cars and planes that I was going to buy and sell. As you say, you can't know about everything, so you have to decide what's likely to make a decent profit for you out of the things that interest you most. Both elements are important because although it's pretty obvious that you want to make money, you won't do as well if you're not all that keen on what you're trying to trade. Your enthusiasm's got to be real, otherwise the customer won't bite.'

'Seems like sensible advice,' Sally said, wondering which antiques fascinated her the most. 'Got any more?'

'Just one thing: listen. Listen, listen, and keep listening. Pay attention to what other dealers say and treat them with respect. You'll learn more that way than probably any other.'

She was looking at him carefully as he spoke, surprised and pleased that he was turning out to be so different from the image she'd had of him.

He was right, she thought, what you see isn't necessarily what you get.

13

'Excited?'

'Beside myself. Couldn't even manage breakfast.'

'We'll stop for coffee and rolls part-way, shall we? Can't have you fading away on your big day.'

Sally blinked at the bright skyline where streaks of blue cloud edged with sunlight hovered above the trees.

'It always seems so peaceful at this time of day,' she said, dreamily, 'as if the world hasn't quite woken up.'

'It'll be awake soon enough and clogging up the M25,' Ken replied. 'That's why I wanted to get away on time.'

'How long will it take to get there.'

'About an hour and fifteen, depending on what the traffic's like when we hit London.'

'Bad, I should think.'

'I won't go to the city centre, that'll be hopeless. What I usually do is park in Hammersmith and tube in, it's much quicker. And we'll be able to get away more easily, if we leave before rush hour.'

An early-morning plane was swooping in to land at Gatwick airport as they drove past.

How do they stay up? Sally mused. It's just a big metal tube with engines.

She was thinking about the biplane that Daniel had almost landed on her roof and how it had looked as if it belonged in the sky when she'd watched it fly away. The thought brought an image of him to mind and she smiled, gently.

'Warm enough?'

'Yes, thanks.'

'Want the radio on?'

'No, it's fine like this.'

'I prefer it quiet when I'm driving,' Ken said, settling back against the headrest, 'unless I'm too exhausted to think.'

The miles slipped by and the countryside melted away beneath rows of red-brick suburban houses. After so long in the backwoods of Brighton, Sally thought it looked cramped and crowded, though she'd always fancied life in the city before she was married.

Wonder what that job would've been like? she reflected, remembering the offer she'd turned down years before. It'd come from one of their main rivals in the conferencing business, a company with some major accounts. She'd have been able to move a couple of rungs up the ladder really quickly, if she'd taken them up on it. She'd have been able to afford a mortgage on her own flat, too, on the salary they were talking. The timing would have been perfect just then, in the early-eighties. The property boom had only just taken off.

Ah, well, you can't miss what you never had, she told herself, though when she'd been in the depths of divorce proceedings, she had often regretted that she'd held back her own career so that she could stay near Philip. She remembered, with sudden clarity, that he'd proposed not long after she'd told him about the London job. Maybe it had been something he'd done on the spur of the moment because he'd been afraid he'd lose her otherwise. She'd never know for sure, now.

'Penny for them,' Ken's voice broke in.

'They're worth at least threepence.'

'Not worried about today, I hope?'

'I am a bit nervous, I have to admit.'

'Just relax. You'll enjoy it.' He drew the car in alongside a small cafe. 'Thought we'd stop here, we're about halfway now.'

'Where are we?'

'Hook.'

She shook her head.

'A couple of miles from Chessington. I cut through this way for the A3.'

'Near where the theme park is?'

'That's right,' he said, getting out. 'You should remember this route, you might be wanting to use it yourself soon.'

'The day I start trading in the great metropolis, I shall know that I've arrived.'

The cafe was no more than an outsized wooden hut, the sort of thing that looked as if it had been put up in the thirties. Inside, it was painted a uniform murky cream, a colour that had not been improved by years of cigarette smoke. Still, someone had tried to cheer the place up by putting bright plastic chequered cloths on the tables.

'Good morning,' sang a voice behind the counter. It belonged to a short, stocky man with a strong Greek accent. 'Full breakfast today only two pound fifty.'

'Just coffee and a croissant, for me, please,' said Ken. 'What would you like, Sally?'

'Hot chocolate.'

'Is all right if you've got the figure, eh?' The little man smiled and patted his paunch.

'Are you sure you won't have something else,' Ken badgered. 'Biscuits? It's a long time 'til lunch.'

'Don't feel like biscuits.' She frowned, then the smell of bacon seduced her. 'How about a bacon sandwich?'

'Coming right up,' said their host. 'You sit down, I'm bringing it over.'

189

They chose a table by the window although there was nothing to look out at but the road. Sally glanced at the single carnation that stood forlornly in a small glass vase at the centre of the table then back into the room at the odd assortment of people who had also stopped there for a break. They looked to be workmen mostly, or lorry drivers, dressed almost uniformly in T-shirts and greasy jeans. The slim black skirt and canary yellow jacket she'd put on to match her mood that morning was conspicuous by comparison, and had already caused a few pairs of eyes to linger over the tops of tabloid newspapers. She smoothed down her skirt, self-consciously.

Ken was fidgeting in his seat, searching his pockets for something that he obviously thought he needed.

'Here,' he said, finally locating it, 'I've got a surprise for you.'

He took out a tatty brown envelope and pushed it across the table towards her.

'What's this?'

'Open it and see.'

Sally felt at the envelope, puzzled for a second, then tore it open. Inside was a set of keys. She looked up to see a big grin spreading over Ken's face.

'Well?'

'Congratulations.'

'I don't understand.'

'The keys to your own castle.'

'What . . .?'

'You're in business. I've found you a shop.'

'Ken!' She leapt up and threw her arms around him.

'Steady on,' he laughed, 'people are staring.'

'But it's wonderful!' she cried, taking no notice. 'How on earth . . . but I haven't even sold the table yet.'

'You will have by this evening.'

'What if no one wants it? What if we can't get the price?'

'Stop worrying, will you? It's my risk.'

She hugged him again.

'You must be mad.'

'Perhaps it's catching.'

'Oh, I can't believe it.' She dangled the keys in front of her nose with sheer delight then grasped them tightly back into her palm again. 'What's it like?'

'A bit grubby and unloved at the moment, but we'll soon sort that out.'

'How did you manage it? What about the contract?'

'Sit down,' he said, guiding her back round the table, 'and I'll tell you about it.'

She glanced at the other diners who had all stopped mid-mouthful to watch the side show, and sat down. All at once, her head seemed crowded with questions and she hardly knew which one to ask first.

'It's the ground floor of a place in Middle Street,' he said, keeping his voice low. 'A year's lease extendable by negotiation.'

'In your name?'

'For now, yes.'

'Can you get away with sub-letting it? To me, I mean.'

'As long as you don't want your name emblazoned over the doorway. If you just call it something-or-other antiques, no one will know the difference.'

'What about the owners?'

'As far as they're concerned, it's an extra arm to my business. You'll be minding the shop, so to speak.'

She thought about it for a moment, rather disappointed that she wouldn't be going it alone in the way she'd imagined. But when the idea sank in, she began to see that the arrangement could present bigger problems.

'Gosh, I hope nothing goes wrong.'

'What could go wrong?'

'I might make a mess of it.'

'You won't.'

'What if I do? I wouldn't want you to lose out because of my mistakes.'

'I'll be there to help you, if you want me to.'

'And what about the money end of things?' she gabbled, not really listening. 'I mean, I'll obviously have to pay the rent.'

'I've thought of a way round that,' he replied. 'What we do is open a joint bank account, a business account for which either of us can sign. We use a company name, that's perfectly legitimate, and as long as you pay enough in each month to keep the rent going out on standing order, plus the usual running costs, of course, it'll all be tickety-boo.'

'What about you?'

'I don't touch it after it's set up.'

'But you must have paid a deposit.'

'You can pay it back to me when today's cheque clears.'

'How much was it?'

'I'll tell you when the table's gone.'

'Tell me now.'

'I want you to have the fun bit first.'

She smiled at him, although she couldn't entirely disregard the tinge of doubt that she had about the arrangement.

'You're such a love.'

The breakfast arrived and she took up her sandwich hungrily.

'Given you an appetite, the good news, has it?' Ken said, looking pleased with himself.

'I still haven't got used to it yet. My own shop . . .'

'You'd better start planning what stock you're going to put in it. Have you got very much worthwhile in the barn?'

'A couple of things, but I'll probably have to buy some more.'

'That bureau cabinet I came over to see the other day would look attractive. That's the sort of quality you need.'

192

'How much room is there in the shop?'

'About forty square feet – enough for four or five large pieces and a smattering of smaller ones. Of course, the mix is up to you but it's important to make sure that everything can be properly displayed. There should be enough on show to draw people into the shop but not so much that the place looks cluttered. With furniture, buyers like to stand back and get the feel of a thing, imagine how it's going to look in the place they've got in mind for it.'

'There's a tilt-top tripod table I picked up that could be useful,' Sally said. 'I could put it out flat or upright, depending on the available space.'

'What date?'

'Early-nineteenth century, I think, going on the lion's paw coasters. The top's mahogany with a black line running around the edge that might be ebony inlay.'

'Any sign of restoration?'

'One of the legs looks as if it's been broken at some stage. There's a piece grafted on to the end of it, but it seems to have been carefully done. I think the plinth could be an addition too, but it's hard to tell.' She drew a circle in the air with her finger. 'There's a little round mark on the underside of the table that matches the place where the tripod joins the plinth. The joint must have rubbed against it at some point in its life. You know, it must have stood proud. But when I passed a hand over it, it felt flush with the top of the plinth.'

Ken frowned. 'Sounds like a replacement. Are there any markings on the legs?'

'There's black lines down both sides that match with the one on the table top.'

'That's a relief. It's the best indication that the tripod belongs to the top.'

'You think it might be another "marriage"?'

'It's a possibility. The best thing would be to screw the

193

top down permanently to the plinth. It'd stop people from taking too much interest in it.'

'But then it wouldn't be a tilt-top table and I thought that was a good sales point,' Sally protested. 'I mean, most people don't have enough room to keep a dining table out all the time. A tilt-top can be flipped up and kept in a corner when it's not being used.'

Ken shrugged. 'It's up to you but if a dealer starts looking at it too closely he'll use the fact that the plinth isn't original to bargain you down.'

'Well, I'm not parting with it for under twelve hundred.'

'You might have to settle for more like eight, unless you can find a private buyer.'

'But it's in pretty good nick otherwise, apart from a couple of bad scratches on the surface. I was wondering how you'd get them out, by the way? Polishing, I suppose.'

'Scratches are easy enough to get out but you've got to be careful with polishing, not get carried away. Repolishing spoils a good piece. Part of the beauty of an antique is that it shows signs of age.' He mulled the statement over for a moment, then added, 'Mind you, people can be funny. They take a liking to something then say, "Nice that, but look. It's got a knock on it." Or, "Pity about the ring mark." They don't seem to realise that furniture does get knocked and marked if it's been around for a couple of hundred years. In fact, I'd be very wary of anything that didn't show signs of use.'

'What sorts of signs, apart from knocks and scratches, I mean?' said Sally, hoping to pick his brains.

'Well, when you're assessing something, it's always worth thinking about how you'd handle it naturally. You know, how you'd sit at it, on it or generally use it. Where you hands fall, if you like. If a piece is genuine, generations of hands will have touched it in the same places as you do and each touch will have left a minute trace of oil from the skin. Over time, dark patches build up in those places and it's vital, if you're going to buy well, to look for them because if you don't see any, there's something wrong.'

'So if there's lots of dark patches, it's an okay piece?'

'Only if they're in the right places, that's what I'm trying to explain. There should only be wear on the parts of a piece that would have become worn naturally in its lifetime. You see, it's fairly simple for a faker to simulate areas of wear but more often than not, he'll do it evenly. Now, no piece of furniture gets evenly worn. And if you think about it a bit, you'll see that that must be the case. So that's why, when you're weighing something up, you've always got to bear in mind how it would have been used in the past.' Ken was warming to his subject now.

'Take the inside of a drawer, for instance,' he went on. 'That's one place that should never look stained or greasy. In fact, it's unlikely that anything could have happened to a drawer to make it look that way, given ordinary use. Most of the time, a drawer will have been kept shut, it won't have been exposed to the air so much as other parts of the same piece of furniture. So when you look inside a drawer, even on a desk or a bureau that's three hundred years old, it should look almost as if it were made yesterday.'

'Oh,' Sally groaned, 'there's so much to learn.'

'That's true,' Ken said, 'but you seem to be doing okay. After all, you noticed that the plinth on that table had been replaced.'

'It was more good luck than good management. I was just curious to know how the top had got rubbed underneath.'

'That's exactly the type of curiosity that you have to develop,' he returned, emphatically. 'Every time you're thinking of buying something you should approach it with a sceptical eye, actually looking for faults, hoping they'll be there. With a little knowledge and a lot of detective work,

195

you'll soon figure out whether it's worth the money being asked.'

'It must take ages to get really expert,' she sighed.

'Shall I let you into a secret?' Ken smiled. 'There's no such thing. Not in this business. You lie once, you lie twice, the third time you're an expert.'

Sotheby's. The name stood out proudly in great gold letters on a long blue banner that was visible almost as soon as they turned into New Bond Street. Sally felt a queer thrill bubble inside her. Whether it was from delight or fear she couldn't tell, but the smart stores and shop fronts went almost unnoticed as she passed. Her attention was fixed on that flag and the word 'Sotheby's'; it was as though her whole future was hanging there by an uncertain thread and the prospect of failure terrified her.

Make or break, she thought, clutching on to Ken's arm, for moral support, and all at the drop of a hammer.

Faces drifted by in soft focus as she walked along. All the doubts that had been buried for the past few weeks, under a flurry of activity, surfaced again. Could it really happen? Could it really happen for her, just because she'd decided that it must? The risk, no matter how great, could be no worse than the alternative. She had to push forward. Staying still was not in her nature anyway. But it was really the thought that she might turn into the archetypical 'wronged woman' that horrified her most. Playing the divorce victim might be a way of justifying being stuck in a rut for some people, but not for anyone with gumption.

I'm better than that, she told herself, better than the 'poor little me's, the martyrs to dead marriages. I know it means sticking my neck out, taking one hell of gamble, but I can't see another choice worthy of the name. Anyway, if I sink without trace at least it won't be without having had a bloody good go.

She squared her shoulders and prepared to walk into the auction house with her head held high. I'm going to make it, she repeated. I'm going to make it if it damned well kills me.

They went through the door and into the front lobby where a few casual visitors stood browsing amongst the books and catalogues that were laid out on tables or in racks along the walls. Sally glimpsed them briefly as they passed on into the reception hall where a collection of architectural antiques had been set out for another sale. A number of corridors and staircases led off from the large vestibule at the end of the hall and, for a moment, she wondered if she hadn't just stepped into an up-market version of the Tardis.

'It's much bigger than I thought,' she said to Ken, who had stopped to pick up a sales diary from the reception desk.

'Eleven galleries in all, twelve if you count the book gallery across the street.'

She looked round at the vast pieces of stone and marble displayed against the walls, some of which were still on the wooden pallets used to transport them. There was a curious air about them, as though they knew they were out of place, but they seemed by no means diminished in their new setting.

'Doesn't it look sad?' she said, pausing to admire a substantial stone urn which was standing cheerlessly on a blood-red marble plinth. 'Imagine the garden where this once belonged.'

'Some arcadian idyll devised by Capability Brown, no doubt,' Ken replied. 'Wonder whether it was death duties or a failure at Lloyd's.'

'Eh?'

'Somebody's obviously had to break up the happy stately home to offset their losses.'

'How awful.'

He shrugged. 'It's the way of the world ... come on, they'll have started.'

Sally couldn't help lingering a moment longer. There was a certain poignancy about the urn, about all of the things in the hall, really. Like tired old aristocrats sitting in a consultant's waiting room, they looked awkward, ashamed almost of their fall from grace. Yet there was something in the feel of the auction house, something about its quiet, dignified air, that softened the blow. In that rarefied atmosphere, the pieces seemed to retain some of their stature.

She followed Ken through to the vestibule where two security men were standing chatting.

'Fine furnishings in the large gallery?' he asked one of them.

'Yes, sir.' The man pointed to a staircase on his right.

At the top of the stairs there was another reception room which opened out on to the gallery where the auction was in progress. Sally stood watching for a moment, while Ken went to the desk to sign the register. He returned with a green plastic paddle, the shape of a table-tennis bat, which was numbered 606.

'Are you going to bid?' Sally whispered, self-consciously.

'You never know.'

A knot of people were blocking the doorway. He guided her past them and into the back of the room where he took up a position close to a partner's desk that was one of a number of lots lining the wall. Sally immediately spotted her table in a row to her left-hand side. She nudged Ken and nodded towards it.

'Keep your head still,' he hissed jokingly, as the auctioneer started the bidding, 'you'll have us bankrupt.'

'Lot number eleven, a breakfront mahogany bookcase, George IV . . .'

A young man wearing a long blue overall held up a hand to indicate the location of the piece.

'Thank you,' the auctioneer said, towards the porter.

'Starting at two thousand pounds . . . two hundred . . . four hundred . . .'

The black display board above the podium clicked up the changing figures, translating them in short order from Sterling to Dollars, then on to Francs, Marks, Swiss Francs, Italian Lira and Japanese Yen. Sally held her breath as she stared dead ahead.

'. . . six hundred . . . eight hundred . . .'

The untroubled voice of the auctioneer made the whole process seem no more than polite conversation.

'. . . two thousand eight hundred to me . . . nine hundred . . . three thousand . . . do I have three thousand two hundred?' He looked to the bank of chairs in the centre of the room but there were no further offers. 'Selling at three thousand pounds . . .' The gavel dropped.

'What did he mean?' Sally asked Ken.

'Mmm?'

'What did he mean, two thousand eight hundred "to me"?'

'He had a commission for that price.'

'Why did he start at two thousand, then?'

'To hook other bidders in. They never start at what they know they can get.'

A single chair was being lifted on to the stand at the side of the podium.

'Lot twelve, a set of sixteen Regency chairs . . .'

'What are they doing?' Sally had glanced from the stand towards a row of half-a-dozen young men and women sitting in a sort of pew which had been draped with a red velvet cloth.

'Telephone bids. Ssh.'

The people manning the telephones seemed to be relaxing on this lot. Sally moved her head slowly round to see what was going on on the other side of the room. A group of four men, obviously all dealers, were standing between the rows

199

of bureaux and bookcases. One gave her a disinterested stare. She stared back, then shifted her gaze.

'. . . an inlaid walnut secretaire cabinet, circa 1900,' the auctioneer announced.

'What's that?'

Ken shoved his catalogue under her nose and pointed to the photograph.

'Where is it?'

'Up the top, there.'

Another blue-aproned porter waved an arm in the air but the piece he was showing was obscured by other furniture.

'It seems to be going very quickly,' Sally remarked.

'He's got two hundred lots to sell by lunchtime.'

'Starting at two thousand pounds . . . five hundred . . . three thousand . . . five hundred . . .'

Someone at the centre of the room shook their head.

'. . . not five hundred, madam? Sorry, one hundred . . . I'm bid three thousand one hundred pounds . . . five hundred . . .'

A yellow biro flashed from the telephone bank.

'. . . six hundred . . . seven . . .'

'What happened then?' Sally asked.

'He was trying to lead too high.'

'Pardon?'

'Trying to push the bidding. He wants to get as much as possible, so he takes the price up at whatever rate he thinks he can get away with. Sometimes that doesn't fit with what people want to offer.'

'That's why he starts some things in five hundreds, other times only in one or two hundreds?'

'Yes, the whole game is to pitch at the highest level you think the buyers will go for and keep it running at that level until it's close to whatever price you think the sellers are going to be happy to settle for.'

'Then what?'

'You lower the margin and keep on trying to inch the bidding up, fifty pounds at a time, if necessary.'

Sally kept watching and listening, fascinated by the detail she realised she'd missed at the Worthing auction. If she was to be a serious contender in future sales, she thought, she was going to have to get a grasp of the subtleties.

'. . . sold on commission at four thousand three hundred pounds.'

'So he had that in hand all along.'

'Yes, but he didn't get more than the commission bid, which'll irritate him a bit.'

'Too much play on the castors.' Two of the dealers Sally had noticed before had moved forward to look at a table a few feet away.

'Skin's good.'

'Yes.'

'Is it right, though?'

Their voices became indistinct as the auctioneer announced the next lot but she kept on straining to catch any snippet that might come her way. She watched how they handled the table, trying to learn by example, but then she realised that almost anything that she could pick up from that sort of observation would only help her to bluff her way around. At the end of the day, she would either have to research her subject or rely on someone like Ken for an expert opinion.

'. . . Irish late-nineteenth-century with a leaf-carved frieze centred by a large carved "jack-in-the-green" mask . . .'

The porter at their end of the room pointed out a dark wood side table that, to Sally, looked uglier than sin.

'. . . starting at one thousand five hundred pounds . . . two thousand . . .'

'Ah ha!' Ken had spotted a man sitting near the front of the room who looked very familiar.

201

'. . . six in the back row . . . seven hundred . . . eight on the door . . .'

Sally thought that she'd seen Ken raise the green plastic paddle a fraction, but couldn't be sure.

'. . . eight hundred . . . eight hundred against you . . .' The auctioneer was looking at the man that Ken had his eye on. '. . . nine hundred . . . three thousand on the door . . .'

'What are you doing?' She had definitely seen the paddle move that time.

'Having a little game.'

'. . . three thousand one hundred . . . two . . . three . . . four anywhere?'

Ken shook his head.

'Selling at three thousand three hundred pounds, thank you. Your number, sir?'

'Did you mean to buy that table?'

'No.'

'Then why . . .?'

'Wanted to make sure that was Eddie Paisley. There's nobody like him for sticking in there if he's made his mind up to get something.'

'I still don't see the point.'

'You will.'

Sally tutted at him. 'Can I see the catalogue a moment?'

He handed it to her and she started turning the pages.

'Checking something out?'

'Just wondering when the table's going to come up,' she replied. 'We've been standing here for nearly an hour.'

'Patience, patience, only another six lots to go.'

The next few pieces were sold without incident and Sally's attention wandered for a while. But she watched again with special interest when the table that had provoked comment from the group of dealers was announced. The bidding built slowly from four thousand pounds until, at five thousand, another bidder joined in from the reception room. Suddenly the thing seemed to become an anxious flurry. Sally watched, intrigued, as the figure was rapidly taken up above six thousand pounds, and felt rather pleased when the table finally went to one of 'her' dealers.

'Selling at six thousand nine hundred pounds ... thank you.'

The dealer raised his paddle so that the number could be taken.

'Lot number fifty-nine has been withdrawn,' the auctioneer continued swiftly. 'The next is sixty, a William and Mary table, walnut and marquetry, starting at ten thousand pounds.'

'We're on,' said Ken.

Sally saw her table being pointed out and began to feel nervous again.

'Look, you stay here,' he told her. 'I'll just be round the corner.'

'But ...'

'Back soon.'

The bidding had started with some lively action from the centre of the room. The figures on the display board clicked over and over in seven currencies while the auctioneer coaxed the buyers on in his accustomed gentle tone. Sally looked up towards the top of the gallery and said a quiet prayer. Somewhere in the blue above the big apex of glass that lit the room, God had to be listening.

I know I shouldn't ask, but please be with me on this one ... please!

'... eleven thousand five hundred. ... twelve thousand five hundred ... thirteen thousand on the door ...'

They'd already passed Ken's estimated best price by a thousand pounds and the offers were still coming in in increments of five hundred. Sally felt the adrenaline rise, making her heart beat faster and her breathing tight.

'... fourteen thousand ... five hundred ...' The

203

auctioneer was looking at a man leaning on the opposite door post to Sally. He shook his head. 'Fourteen thousand five hundred . . . and six, sir? Six in the next room . . .'

Someone near the front glanced round then turned back again.

'. . . seven hundred . . . eight . . . nine hundred . . . fifteen thousand . . . fifteen thousand against you . . .'

The man at the front wavered then nodded.

'Fifteen thousand one hundred pounds . . . and one more? I will sell at fifteen thousand one hundred, then.' The auctioneer's hand hesitated for a moment then dropped: 'Sold at fifteen thousand one hundred pounds.'

'Well done.'

Sally hadn't seen Ken come up.

'Oh, you gave me a fright.'

'Happy?'

'Where did you disappear off to?'

'Are you happy?'

'Yes . . . yes. Least I think so. Hasn't sunk in yet.'

'Come on, you can buy me a drink.'

She was still in a daze at the top of the stairs.

'What happens now?'

'We have lunch and head for the hills.'

'You mean we're not coming back?'

'What for? The auction'll be over in around half-an-hour.'

'But the table . . .'

'The table belongs to my good friend Eddie Paisley, now.'

'The one you were playing games with before?'

'Yep.'

'Ken?'

He was smiling.

'Don't tell me it was you bidding at the back?'

The smile gave way to a grin.

'You didn't!'

'Got you another few hundred quid, didn't I?'

'You devil.' She planted a kiss on his cheek. 'Thank you.'

'Mine's a large gin and tonic.'

They were out on the street before the full impact of the day hit her. In the auction room, it had all seemed like a terrific coup, but the adrenaline burst that had stimulated her before seemed to be making her senses do an about turn as it slowly wore off.

'It's a funny thing,' Sally started, 'but I can't quite believe that I'll never see that table again. I mean, it's been around for as long as I can remember, it was in my parent's house before I was even born . . .'

Ken heard the catch in her voice, stopped where he was and took her by the tops of her arms.

'Look at me, Sally. Don't you dare get upset.'

'I'm sorry, it brought everything back. My dad . . . you know. It was their wedding gift, my heirloom.'

'Listen, I know you were attached to it emotionally, but you've got to let go of all that here and now.'

'Maybe I shouldn't have sold it.'

'Of course you should. It was left to you to do with as you wished. You wanted to sell it so that you could get on with your life, make progress. How can that be wrong?'

She didn't answer.

'Look, you want to be a dealer, right?'

Sally nodded.

'Well, if you're going to be a dealer, you've got to be dealer minded. Or to put it another way, you've got to have no more feeling for what you sell than you would for a can of beans. I'm not saying don't admire things for their workmanship or beauty, by all means do that, in fact it's necessary that you should, but you've got to be able to be detached. Nothing is so precious that it can't be sold, nothing has any more value than the price that someone else is willing to pay for it. Sell, sell and keep selling. Sell the shirt off your back if someone takes a fancy to it. It's a deal for the sake of a deal

205

in this business. The sooner you get used to that idea the better.'

She was still looking sad and he wondered what he could say to lighten her mood as they moved off again.

'One time, you know,' he began, 'when my mother was still alive, she sent me out to do some Christmas shopping. Of all the things on her list, the one she wanted most was a home-made Christmas pudding. She was too old to make her own any more, and I knew that it meant a lot to her. Anyhow, there was a lady a few villages away who made a cracking pudding so I went over there and ended up buying five off her. Might make a couple of quid on these in the pub, I thought, and that's exactly what I did. There was just one problem.'

'What was that?'

'Well, they were going so well that I sold them all.'

'And went back empty-handed?'

''Fraid so.'

'Wasn't she mad at you?'

'My mum? No. Just shook her head and said, "You'd be shot of me if anyone would give you a fiver." '

Sally laughed. 'Sounds like she might have been right.'

'A deal for a deal's sake. Don't forget it.'

'I won't. What about our deal, by the way?'

'Humm?'

'The shop, silly. You know, the deposit?'

'I think we've done enough business for one day, don't you?'

'Guess so.'

She was still feeling betwixt and between, glad that she'd come through but sorry that it had had to be this way. She hadn't expected her triumph to be tinged with melancholy and the sensation troubled her.

Ah, well, you can't make an omelette without breaking

eggs, she thought, and the pang of sorrow slowly melted away.

14

'This place,' said Heather, pushing her hair back under the scarf she'd put on to protect it, 'needs a flame-thrower taking to it, not a mop and broom.'

Sally looked up from her scrubbing. 'How long have we been at it now?'

'Two-and-a-half hours.'

'Fancy a break?'

'I could do with a drink, that's for sure.' Heather propped the brush she was holding against the wall and went over to the big raffia shopping bag that she'd brought with her. 'Glad I packed a thermos.'

Sally left her work and wandered towards the plate glass window at the front of the shop.

'It's quite sunny now,' she said, rubbing away a little circle in the layer of polish that had been left caked on the inside of the glass, so that she could see out. 'Looks like it might get hot.'

'That'll make a change for June.'

'Go on, the weather's been pretty good so far, for the time of year, anyway. Maybe we're going to get a proper summer.'

'I wouldn't count on it. The weather in this country is about as reliable as a Latin lover.'

Sally was only half listening. As she peered out of her circle on the world at large and started to see the passers by as potential customers, her enthusiasm finally got the better of her. With bold sweeps, she traced a large and flamboyant S. B. in the window polish with her finger.

'There,' she said, stepping back to admire her handiwork.

'Daft devil,' Heather remarked as she brought up the flask and two mugs, but then she drew a smiley face alongside the initials and they both laughed.

'Feeling good?'

'Terrific.'

'It's a big step forward, isn't it?'

'The biggest and the best yet.' Sally could have hugged herself with glee. 'Who'd have thought it, eh?'

'Mmm,' Heather brushed a layer of dust off the window ledge, grimaced and wiped her hand on her jeans. 'Well, you've certainly got a challenge on your hands now.'

'The main problem is going to be finding the right things to put out on display . . .' Sally was wondering whether the appointments she'd set up for the next week would yield anything of the calibre she needed to add to her stockpile. 'I'm not really sure whether I should go for a mix of styles or whether I should aim at building up a collection of pieces from a certain period? You now, specialise in one era. The trouble is, there's so much Victorian and Edwardian stuff about and, to be honest, I don't find it as interesting as some of the earlier furniture.'

'I think I would concentrate on selling whatever seems to be popular,' said Heather. 'There's no point in being surrounded by things of great beauty which at the end of the day just end up sitting there, taking up valuable room.'

'It's hard to know exactly what's going to take somebody's fancy and why,' Sally brooded. 'I don't find the market that easy to judge. So far, apart from the things that I've kept from the house clearances, I've just been buying pieces that

I happen to like, but it's all rather random. It's true that a lot of the time I've been going on semi-educated guesswork, using my antiques guide and trying to find things that have a similar look. But the rest of the time . . . well, I've had to rely on my own sense of what I think is likely to appeal.'

'I expect that's good enough as long as it keeps working.'

'Yes, but it bothers me. I keep wondering how long it'll be before I make an expensive mistake.'

'The answer to that, I suppose,' said Heather, looking around, 'is not to commit too much of your capital to any one piece. Especially not to something you're uncertain of. Where are we going to sit by the way?'

'On the floor, I guess.'

'Ah, well, it's good for the back.' Heather plonked herself down where she was then pulled her legs up under herself in the Lotus position.

'God, you're supple,' Sally remarked. 'If I did that my hips would start yelling.'

'You should try some yoga yourself sometime, it's good for the nerves.'

'Don't see how twisting your limbs into funny shapes helps your nerves.'

'It's not in that, it's in the breathing. Once you learn how to control your breath there's no pain. I'm surprised they didn't teach you that when you were having the children.'

'They didn't teach us anything much that I remember being useful in ante-natal. It's one thing talking about levels of breathing when you're lying on your back feeling comfortable. It's another trying to keep your mind on it when you're in the middle of a contraction.'

'A friend of mine managed it. Eighteen hours in labour and not so much as an aspirin. Mind you, she'd been practising special yoga since about month three of the pregnancy.'

'Well, I wish I'd known about it when I was expecting my

two. All I could think about when I was giving birth was getting the epidural stuck into my spine as fast as possible.'

'Pity. A natural birth is such a wonderful thing . . . and the baby's so awake when it arrives.'

Sally looked at her quizzically. 'But you've never had children.'

'You don't have to have had them yourself to know what it's like.'

'Rubbish. How can you know about something you've never tried? A bystander's view on childbirth is about as relevant as a celibate's view on contraception.'

'Not necessarily.' Heather had stretched her hands out, palm up, on her knees. She looked at them carefully for a moment. 'I helped deliver a baby once, you know. It was an experience that changed my life.'

Sally was temporarily stunned.

'Must be nearly thirty years ago now, perhaps more,' Heather went on. ''Sixty something – when the student riots were on in Paris. Anyway, I remember that I couldn't get through the barricades to fetch a doctor, so that left me and my poor flatmate to get on with it on our own. Actually, it was probably the best thing that could have happened, as it turned out. I'm sure that anyone who'd known what they were supposed to do would just have interfered. Up until then I'd always thought that childbirth was like how they do it in the movies. You know, the woman screaming the place down, people shouting for bowls of hot water, that sort of thing. But it wasn't like that at all. She was so calm and serene, just wandering about the room, leaning on things, breathing, stretching. It wasn't until the baby was on its way out that she started to look anxious at all.'

'Amazing.'

'Yes, it was. I couldn't believe that the whole thing could be so peaceful. And do you know? The baby didn't even cry when it arrived. Just mewed like a kitten and splutted a bit.

I'll never forget the look on her face when I lifted him up and put him on her chest . . .'

The memory seemed to hold Heather in a kind of a trance and Sally imagined that she was seeing herself back then, seeing again the new mother and her child as they lay together in breathless silence, and some dingy little room with canvases stacked in one corner and bare floorboards, like the ones she was sitting on now.

'And afterwards,' she went on suddenly, 'when I asked her if it'd been painful, she looked at me completely wide-eyed. "Is it meant to be?" she said. It was so touching. Apparently, nobody had ever told her what to expect, so she hadn't expected anything. She'd just gone with it, done what felt right . . . that's what got me interested in things natural in the first place. The yoga was kind of an extension of the idea, later on.'

There was a matter-of-factness in the way Heather had delivered the last sentence, and, watching her face, Sally had the feeling that she was keeping something more important to herself.

'You would have liked your own, wouldn't you?' she asked, gently.

'My own baby? Oh, yes, very much so. But it wasn't to be.' Heather sighed. 'My first husband – well, it would have been pointless with him. He was such a child himself that it didn't leave room for anyone else.'

'What about Dad, though? He was a brilliant father.'

'Yes, but . . .' She seemed to be considering how she ought to explain. 'You see, he was fifty-one when we met. He didn't feel like starting again with nappies and midnight feeds.'

'But you were only in your twenties.'

'Yes. And rather naive. At first, like a lot of other women, I thought he might change his mind. Then . . . well, it was the sacrifice that I made in marrying someone so much older than myself, I suppose.'

212

Sally felt the sadness rise as she pondered on how great a sacrifice that had been. All at once she began to see how easy it would have been for Heather to have been bitter, for her to have rejected the rebellious step-child she'd inherited and just done the minimum expected. Instead, she'd poured all the loving that should rightly have gone into a child of her own into one who'd openly resented her. The thought filled Sally with shame.

'I'm sorry,' she said, taking Heather's arm, 'there's so much I didn't know.'

'You weren't expected to.'

'Not when I was a kid but later . . . later I should have realised.'

'How could you?'

'I could have been less selfish.'

'Oh, darling, you'd lost your mother. It's hardly surprising that you found it difficult to respond to me.'

'I think I felt that by showing you affection, I was some-how cheating on her. I know that sounds stupid, but I think it's the truth.' Sally was struggling to articulate her feelings, to remember exactly how it had been. 'If my parents had divorced and then Dad'd married you, I could maybe excuse it. But it's not as though you were some sort of usurper. You hadn't stolen him away.'

'Nevertheless, that's how it must have seemed.'

'But it's so unfair!'

'Maybe, but it was part and parcel and I can't say I have many regrets.'

'Thank you,' Sally said, hugging her fondly. 'Thanks for looking after me, for loving me all this time.'

'I loved your dad, sweetheart, how could I have not loved you?'

'I can think of plenty of reasons.'

'Well, don't. Don't let's think about the past at all. It's over.

213

It's done. And there's so much to look forward to in the future.'

Sally looked around the empty room and started to visualise how it would shape up in a couple of weeks. The thought of being in control of her own fate, win or lose, appealed to her spirit of adventure.

'A new beginning,' she said. 'Another chance. God, am I going to make the most of this one!'

'Here,' said Heather, putting a mug into her hand, 'let's drink to it. To the good ship Sally Blythe, God bless her and all who sail in her.'

'Could have done with something stronger than tea to celebrate,' Sally commented as their mugs clinked together. 'Perhaps we should have a launching party when it's all spick and span.'

'You'd be better spending the money on something you can sell.'

'Guess you're right. But it'd be nice to give Ken a little thankyou.'

Heather was thoughtful. 'Are you sure it's a good idea his being so involved?'

'I don't think I can do it any other way. Without his name and reputation . . . well, it wouldn't have been easy. Certainly not in this part of town.'

'It's an added responsibility for you, though,' said Heather, 'and mixing business with pleasure is never very advisable.'

'What pleasure?'

'Going out with him.'

'I've only been out with him once and then only because . . . well, it's not going to become a regular thing.'

Heather looked sceptical.

'It's not, really. Anyway, there's someone else on the scene that I'm more interested in.'

'Oh?'

214

'Promise you won't be cross if I tell you who?'

'Why? Don't tell me it's someone else I'm going to disapprove of?'

'Well, you did when you first met him. For very good reasons at the time.'

'What's coming now?' Heather groaned.

'Don't yell,' Sally pleaded. 'It's that man with the 'plane. You know, the one with the dark curly hair and the expensive-looking sun tan.'

'The one that almost scared the wits out of us, you mean? Typical!' Heather didn't try to conceal her exasperation. 'Really, Sally, sometimes you're enough to make a saint swear.'

'He's okay, honestly. Quite gentlemanly, in his way.'

'In the way that leads swiftly to the bedroom,' Heather retorted. 'Too oily by half.'

'Well, I like him. And at least he's young and good-looking. Anyhow, I could do with a fling.'

'A fling?'

'Yes, why not? Why shouldn't I have a good time? I've been on my knees struggling for long enough.'

Heather could see her point but couldn't help feeling apprehensive.

'It's been hard, I know, and you do need to get out and feel part of the waking world. Of course you should enjoy yourself . . .' She hesitated long enough for Sally to guess what was coming next.

'But?'

'But just be careful.'

'You worry too much. I know Daniel's a bit of a playboy but I reckon I can handle him.'

'You do?' Heather had her doubts.

'Ooh, I can't wait,' Sally trilled, bouncing up on her heels. 'I can't wait to get going.' She danced across the empty floor with a wanton air. 'I could put the bureau bookcase there, the table there. Where do you think I should sit, front or back of shop?'

She was off and Heather could see that there was going to be no stopping her.

'How about somewhere in the middle,' Sally went on, mostly to herself. 'With a really impressive piece on either side?'

'Have you got them?'

'No, but . . . gosh, look at the time and I'm meant to be in Rye at four-thirty!'

'Ken taking you?'

'No, he had to go off to Jersey for some reason. Urgent business, he said.'

'You weren't expecting me to . . .'

'Heavens, no.' Then Sally started to look sheepish. 'But I was hoping you wouldn't mind hanging on to the children.'

'I don't mind but sooner or later I'm going to have to do some work of my own.'

'How's it going?'

'Slow, as usual.'

'You could do with getting more exposure, you know, unleashing your talents on a wider audience. Steyning is such a backwater that it's a miracle anyone comes into the gallery at all. You'd never know it was there unless you just happened to be passing by.'

'I've started opening on Sundays for that very reason. I get the odd sale to people who are out for a stroll.'

Sally was staring at the four blank walls she'd just acquired.

'I've just had a thought.'

'Mmm?'

'Well, I could put some of your paintings in here. I mean, there's plenty of space and I'm not going to be able to afford to fill it all straight away. It'd warm the place up, anyway, make it look more homely. No one has a whole room full of

216

antiques after all, unless they happen to be stinking rich. It'd seem more attractive to ordinary buyers, more intimate, perhaps if I laid things out as though they were in somebody's drawing room . . . that's it! I'm sure that buying an antique would be less intimidating to your average Joe in the street if at least some of the surroundings seemed familiar.'

'Does your average Joe have the money to spend on antiques in the first place?'

'I think he does, especially around here. Think of all those people who come to the south coast to retire. There they are, kids off their hands at last, so there's more available cash. They'll have sold the family home and bought a smaller one just for themselves, probably made a little stack from that, too, to put away. And now they're going to furnish their new house, or more likely bungalow or flat. Oh, they'll keep a lot of the old stuff, that's for sure, but they'll want other things, nicer things to put in the rooms now. Things that won't have to stand the daily bashing of little hands and feet any more, things that are lovely to look at, that they can be proud to show their friends. "See how well we've done for ourselves," those things will say. And they'll feel nice and comfy and pleased with life.'

Heather smiled. 'The psychology's nice.'

'It's true, though, isn't it?'

'It's plausible, I agree.'

'What do you say, then? How about sorting out some of your favourite pictures and letting me hang them here? Might even find place for the odd sculpture, too.'

'You'll be coming round and robbing my studio next!' Heather said, amused by the speed at which Sally was forging ahead. 'Come to think of it, it might not be such a bad idea if you did. Then you could choose whatever you thought would fit with the general look.'

'Great. It's a deal.'

'Sal?'

217

'Mmm?'

'You don't think you're going too big, too soon?'

'Oh, don't spoil it by saying that.'

'Well, it is quite an undertaking, running a business, especially when you're still trying to learn the tricks of the trade.'

'I'll be okay, you'll see. Anyway, you know me. Unless I'm balancing fourteen plates on sticks all at the same time, I'm not happy.'

A single note rang out from the clock tower of the old church, marking the quarter hour. Sally checked her watch as a kind of reflex and decided to spend the last minutes before her appointment sitting on a bench in the sunlight, letting her mind wander. She tilted back her head and closed her eyes, enjoying the fresh smell that rose up from the grass around her feet. It was a moment of perfect peace in an otherwise hectic day and one she was determined to relish.

Fragments of unrelated thoughts teased her but she felt too tired to pay them much attention. Instead, she let them shift and fade as they would, allowing the images they brought in mind to tumble together, like so many snapshots, and find an order of their own.

The boys had squabbled this morning, before Heather called to take them to school. Sally had tried to dream up a scheme that would enable her to fit both buying trips and running the shop around an organised home life, but before long she'd pushed that worry aside. It would all fall into place somehow, she convinced herself. Anyway, no niggle was going to be allowed to intrude on the pleasure she felt she had a right to enjoy on this, her first real day in business.

She smiled to herself and settled further back in the seat, preferring to think of the soft upholstery that she'd just left behind in Daniel's Porsche than the hard wooden slats that were actually under her legs. Of the faces that spiralled into her mind, before she slipped into sleep, the last she saw was his. With it, came a glow that had less to do with the heat of the afternoon than she supposed.

She was still sitting completely motionless, hair spilling over the back of the bench, face turned skyward, when he came back across the churchyard carrying two cream cakes in a paper bag. It seemed a shame to disturb her and, for a while, he stood a little way off, just watching. As she started to stir, he finally approached, bending quickly to steal a kiss before she had a chance to move away.

Sally smiled and opened her eyes.

'Ah, Prince Charming.'

'That's *Cinderella* not *Sleeping Beauty*,' he said. 'Still, at least I didn't have to hack my way through a thicket to get to you.'

'Or wait a hundred years before you could wake me with a kiss.'

'Just as well, the cakes would have gone off by then.'

He opened the bag and offered her a chocolate éclair.

'My favourite. Thanks.'

'How did I guess?'

'Yes, how did you?'

'The wicked combination of chocolate and cream seemed to suit your style.'

'I see you're getting to know me rather well.' She turned the éclair from side to side, wondering how she could manage to eat it without looking gross.

'Go on, go for it,' he laughed. 'I'll look the other way, if you like.'

She giggled. 'It's hard to be ladylike with one of these.'

'Think I'll have a snoop around the junk shops whilst you're doing your thing,' he said. 'Unless you want me to come with you, of course?'

'No, I'd better go in on my own. The woman sounded a bit suspicious on the 'phone.'

'I suppose you have to be these days, if you live on your own. Shame, really. Especially for older people.'

'I often think that. It must be awful to feel so threatened by the world.'

'Still, I can't imagine that Rye is exactly seething with potential thieves and rapists.'

'Not like it used to be in the old days, eh?'

'Mmm, extraordinary, isn't it? To look at the place now, you'd never think it had such a violent history.' He glanced across the square of grass where they were sitting towards the solid stone houses around the edges. The steadfast walls had mellowed with age, been softened by the vines and creepers that clung there, but they were still imposing for all that.

'It is rather unreal,' Sally replied, 'more like a film set than a town that's actually lived in.'

'I don't know. You can sort of see pirates and smugglers stomping up the cobbled streets. Wonder what it would have been like to have lived then?'

'Uncomfortable and dangerous, I should think.'

'Exciting,' he said, as though the idea appealed to him. 'This was the heart of rum-smuggling territory. There was a famous vicar who ran the whole thing. Can't remember his name now. Anyhow, he had three henchmen who used to patrol the marshes out there while barrels of hootch were brought in from the smuggler's coves. They wore these incredible disguises: a skull mask and some sort of black cape with a skeleton painted on it, back and front. Must have put the fear of God up anyone who saw them.'

'You're making it up,' Sally laughed.

'I'm not, honestly. It really happened,' he protested. 'Mainly, of course, they were hoping to scare off the excise men. And it worked, too, until the day they got a tip off and broke into the vicar's church. They found the crypt stacked to the rafters with barrels of rum .'

220

'Very *Treasure Island*.'

'Truth is stranger than fiction, you know.'

'So they say.'

A loud whir sounded from the clock tower as the mechanism moved into place to strike the half-hour bell.

'Gosh,' Sally said. checking her watch again, 'better get going.'

'Right. Where shall I meet you?'

'How about the pub at the far end of the street, the one that looks out over the marshes?'

'Okay. In an hour, say?'

'Yes. I think that'll be long enough.'

Sally gave him a wave and hurried off down the lane, trying to frame, over and again, what she was going to say when she got to her destination. She thought about the new advert she'd put into the local papers in the hope of catching the eye of exactly this kind of client: the frail and solitary widow who'd once known better days, the type that she'd noticed so many times in the supermarkets, loading meals for one into a shopping basket that contained little else except for cat food.

'*Lady buyer wishes to purchase fine furniture and other antiques in strictest confidence*,' it had read. And the response to it so far had been pretty good.

She turned the corner still deep in thought. There, in front of a row of pretty cottages where a mass of bright flowers spilled out on to the walkway, was the black-and-white cat of her fancy, preening itself in the afternoon sun.

'Ho, puss,' she murmured as she went up the path, pausing a while to tickle its lazy head. 'What it is to be so relaxed, eh?'

When the door of the cottage opened, the picture that she'd had in mind, ever since the appointment had been made, came even more to life. A trim woman who looked to be in her seventies stood leaning on a silver-topped cane.

'Miss Blythe?' she asked, holding out a hand that evidently expected a calling card to be placed into it.

'Yes,' said Sally, nervously. 'I'm sorry I'm late.'

'Do come in.'

The dark, cramped passage that served as a hall had a musty smell after the clear air outside. Sally followed the old woman blindly into the back of the house where a parlour that looked as if it were kept holy to the memory of a love long dead was illuminated by a pair of Tiffany table lamps.

'This is the one.' The woman pointed out a substantial-looking commode with a marble top and nicely detailed front panel. 'I believe it's French.'

'Yes, I'd say it was.' Sally moved across the room. 'Do you mind removing the photo frames?' she asked. 'I'd like to pull it out.'

'Is that really necessary?'

'I'm afraid so.' She waited for the top to be cleared then tried to lift the commode forward. It was too heavy to bring it very far out. 'Is there anything in the drawers?'

'Well, of course.'

'Perhaps we could just take them out rather than empty them.'

The woman began to look put out.

'I'm sorry, Mrs Johnson, but I'll want to turn it over in a minute. It's the standard practice, I assure you.'

Sally helped to slide the drawers out of the body of the piece, thinking that she really ought to check the interiors, as Ken had advised, but the feeling that she was becoming unduly intrusive held her back. She squatted down in front of the commode, passing hand over the gilt mouldings that decorated the tops of the legs. So far as she could tell, the piece was late-eighteenth-century, an opinion supported by the fact that the marble that had been used to make the top was of the pure white variety so fashionable at the time.

She slid an arm inside the frame and tipped the commode

carefully on its back to look at the underside. Given the lack of light in the room, the colour of the wood seemed to be even, except where the drawer bottoms had rubbed against the frame. All in all, she decided at last, the piece was giving off good signals.

'We can put the drawers back now,' said Sally, setting the commode back on its feet and manoeuvring it into its original position.

'What do you think?' asked the old woman. 'Is it worth very much?'

'I can only tell you what it's worth to me,' Sally replied. 'What price did you have in mind?'

'It's hard to say.'

Sally had a second look at the patterned inlay that decorated the drawer fronts. It was a very fine and elaborate design, featuring a wine ewer surrounded by fruits and flowers.

'Well,' she said, 'I can give you two thousand five hundred for it.'

'Oh, I'd expected rather more.'

'How much more.'

'I have a friend in the trade who said it should fetch about five thousand pounds.'

Sally had the feeling that somebody was playing games. A moment before the woman hadn't wanted to name a price. She was irritated, but unruffled. 'And is your friend going to buy it?'

'It was just his opinion.'

'I'm afraid two-and-a-half is the best I can do.'

A certain sadness crossed the old woman's face and she turned to look at the photograph in a silver frame that stood on a table near by.

'I'd rather not part with it at all, really,' she said, lingering on the picture of a young man whose innocent eyes smiled out from under a naval officer's cap. 'If it wasn't for . . . well, the hospital waiting lists are so long.'

'You're going in for an operation?'

'Nothing major. At least, that's what my doctor tells me.'

By the time she left the cottage, Sally had endured what felt like the whole of her client's medical history, in all its gory detail. It was hardly surprising, she thought, given the difficulty she obviously had getting around, that the old girl needed a hip replacement. But the list of other ailments that seemed to trouble her, which covered everything from angina to bunions, was something quite remarkable, even for a geriatric. Exhausted by the ordeal and feeling very short on sympathy, Sally tottered back down the narrow lane, glad to have got away. When she finally reached the pub, she could see Daniel sitting outside, nursing a bottle of Grolsch.

'How did it go?' he said, springing up to greet her.

'Don't ask. What have you got there?'

'A little present. Thought it'd look good in your new shop.' He lifted up the large carrier bag that was at his feet and placed it between them on the table.

'Can I peek?'

'Yes, but don't rattle it about too much.'

She peeled a layer of newspaper away to reveal the top of a light fitting and a length of flex.

'Oh, just what I needed!' Pushing more layers aside, she gradually uncovered a gleaming brass lantern, its three supporting arms fashioned in delightful filigree scrolls.

'Like it?'

'It's beautiful,' Sally gasped, 'but really, you shouldn't have . . .'

'It was too good to miss. Want a drink?'

'Yes, please.' She was too absorbed with the lamp to notice that he was standing there with an inquiring look on his face.

'Lime and soda?' he ventured at last.

'Good God, no,' Sally exclaimed. 'Whisky, a straight double. I've just blown three grand.'

15

'Bloody hell!' Daniel staggered out from the cubby-hole at the back of the shop clutching his arm.

'What happened?'

'Electric shock.'

'God, are you okay?'

'I'll live.' He flexed his hand. 'If you ask me the place wants re-wiring.'

'Haven't the time – or the money either.'

'Well, you want to watch yourself. Whatever you do, don't go near the main board.'

'What if a fuse goes?'

'You'll have to sit in the dark until I can get here.'

Sally smiled. It was nice to think of his being around on a regular basis.

'Damned dangerous arrangement that, you know,' he continued, 'having a sink so near to the mains. Illegal, I should think, too.'

'It's obviously been there for years without any problems. Anyway, I don't see how I can change it. There's nowhere else for a sink to go and I've got to have the facilities to make the odd cup of tea.'

He was still rubbing his hand. 'I think I could do with one right now.'

'Of course, why don't you sit down for a minute?' Sally picked up the kettle that she'd brought with her that morning and took it into the back. 'Milk and sugar?

'Just milk, thanks.'

'Sweet enough as you are, eh?'

'So they tell me.'

'Oh, and who are they?' She left the kettle to heat up and went back to where he was sitting.

'Just a figure of speech.'

'Really?' She tousled his hair, playfully.

'Come here a minute.'

'I am here.'

'Here on my knee.'

'People might see.'

'Not through the gunk on that window. Anyway, who cares?'

Sally settled on his lap and let him put his arms around her waist.

'You are utterly delicious, do you know that?' He gave her a squeeze.

'You're not too bad yourself.'

'Don't mind if I kiss you, then?'

'Do you need my permission?'

'I don't take my pleasure by force.' He put a hand to her chin and turned her face towards his own. The kiss, long and gentle, made Sally's head swim.

'The kettle's boiled,' she whispered.

'Sod the kettle.' He moved his hand behind her back and kissed her again.

A feeling of complete abandon washed over her in a way that she hadn't known for years. All the tension in her body ebbed away and, caught up in that sensation of release, it was as if nothing existed except the kiss, going on and on until she felt she had no substance of her own, a glorious weakness that ached to be prey to his strength.

'Oh, I could get carried away like this.' He held her close for a moment longer then let her go.

'I'd . . . er . . . better make the tea.'

'Never mind that, I want to talk to you.'

'What about?'

'Us.'

'In what way?'

'I'd like to spend more time with you.'

'You're wasting enough time doing the unpaid chauffeur routine as it is.'

'It isn't a waste of time and I've found the answer to the transport problem.'

'You have?'

'Yes. Nice clean Volvo estate, never been raced, rallied or rolled, only fifty thousand on the clock and an snip at two grand.'

'Fantastic!'

'Lucky to find such a low mileage on a car like that, but then, I can never resist a bargain.'

'What? You've already bought it?'

'That's what you needed, isn't it?'

'Well, yes, but . . .'

'What's the worry?'

'I'll have to go to the bank.'

'There's no rush for the money.'

'I'll have to pay you back sometime, might as well be sooner rather than later.'

'Relax, we'll sort it at some point. Anyway, it's a good excuse for my sticking around.'

'As if you needed one,' Sally laughed. 'Where is the car?'

'Over at my place. What do you say we go down there and get it?'

'Right now?'

'Why not? I've got the light up for you, despite the risk to life and limb, and there's nothing else you have to be here for, is there?'

'Suppose not.'

Sally disentangled herself from his embrace and went to pick up her handbag. She stopped before she reached it, pausing to survey the empty room.

'It's a worry, this stocking up,' she said.

'Why's that?'

'I want to be sure of having the right pieces.'

'They're building, gradually.'

'It's not the furniture, entirely. I think I'm doing okay on that. What I'd like ideally, is to have some decorative pieces, some figures and things to scatter around. I don't want the place to look like a warehouse.'

He frowned for a moment. 'How about putting some pictures in? That'd warm it up.'

'I've got my step-mother working on that, although it would be a good idea to have some old paintings to put up too.'

'I've got a pair at the house that are doing nothing.'

'Oh?'

'Dutch floral, very elaborate.'

'Why don't you hang them there?'

'They wouldn't look right. I like modern furniture myself, you can't mix old and new.'

'What was the point of buying them, then?'

'They were just something I came across whilst I was doing another deal.'

'I don't understand.'

'Well, quite often when you go to somebody's house to talk about one thing, others get mentioned.'

'How do cars and planes fit with paintings?'

'The people who have the money to buy such luxuries are, more often than not, the same ones who like to collect other valuables. To hear about this or that antique is pretty much par for the course.'

'But I still don't see why you would want to buy an antique if you weren't involved in the business.'

'There's always some cross-over. Anyway, I have friends in the trade, so I'm never short of an outlet.'

Sally turned the thought over. 'These paintings, what period are they?'

'Late-seventeenth-century.'

'Worth rather a lot, then?'

'About fifty grand.'

'Christ! That's well out of my league.'

'I know, but we could come to some arrangement.'

'Like what?'

'Well, they're not going to get sold propped up against my living-room wall. If you put them in the shop, they'd at least get seen. It'd kill two birds with one stone, after a fashion. You'd have your space usefully occupied, I'd have somewhere sensible to store them whilst I find someone who might be interested.'

'What if somebody wants to buy them?'

'Then we sell them, if they're talking the right price.'

'And?'

'Split the profit, of course.'

'It sounds a rather generous offer. On your part, I mean.'

Daniel shrugged. 'No more than normal business practice.'

'I don't know . . .'

'Well, think it over. I'll show them to you anyway, whilst we're at the house.'

Sally picked up her handbag at last. 'Got everything?'

'Think so.'

They went out on to the pavement where Sally started fussing with the keys. 'Funny feeling, doing this.'

'Mmm?'

'Locking up. Still doesn't feel like my shop.'

'It will when you've got more than two chairs and a lantern in it.'

'What do you think I should call it?' She stepped back and looked up at the battered paint work above the window.

'Blythe Antiques, I suppose.'

'No, it can't be that.' It had slipped out before she could stop it and her mind sped to think of a way of getting out of telling him about her involvement with Ken. 'I was thinking of something more descriptive,' she added, trying not to sound too hasty. 'Something that gives you the feel of a place where you'd expect to find really good quality things without actually using the word "antique".'

He shrugged. 'Search me, I'm lousy with names.'

'Sally?'

They both turned round.

'It *is* you. Thought it had to be.'

'Julia! Hi!' Sally have her a spontaneous hug.

'Do I get an introduction?'

'Of course. Julia Brown, Daniel Wiseman.'

'Hello,' said Julia, shaking his hand.

'What are you doing here?'

'I was about to ask you the same.'

'This is my new shop.'

'So that's what's been keeping you from 'phoning me.'

'I'm sorry, I've just been too busy. Anyway I thought you were on holiday?'

'I've been back for two weeks.'

'We must get together soon. I've got so much to tell you.'

'I'm sure.' A wicked look crossed Julia's face as she ran an eye over Daniel.

'Why don't you ring me tonight?'

'Out tonight, how about tomorrow?'

'Fine. We can catch up on a few things and maybe make an arrangement then.'

'Okay. Well, I've got to get back to the office, just popped out for some chocolate to relieve the tedium. Looks like you're in a dash, anyhow.'

'Yes. Great to see you, though.'

''Bye.'

Sally turned to check that she'd locked the shop door properly. 'That's my best friend.'

'Smart woman.'

There was an edge to the remark that made Sally's scalp tingle. For a second she worried that his interest in Julia was more than superficial.

What's wrong with me? she thought, as she turned towards him. Finding other women attractive isn't a crime.

Sally slipped her hand into his to restore her confidence as they set off through the Lanes.

'Where is this place of yours?'

'Just outside Henfield.'

'You're quite close to me.'

'That's right.' He smiled. 'And I aim to stay that way.'

'Better behave yourself, then.'

'I'm trying my best, but it's difficult.'

Sally shot him a sideways glance. 'Daniel?'

'Mm?'

'You know what you were saying back in the shop, about us. What did you mean, exactly?'

'Just that I'd like us to spend time together, time for you and me that doesn't involve business.'

'I'm sorry, it must seem rather as if I'm using you.'

'Not at all. I don't do anything unless I absolutely want to. No, what I meant was that I'd like us to spend some time relaxing together, not just the odd evening or lunch, but maybe the occasional week-end. You could bring the kids over to the house, if you liked. Now that the summer's coming they'd enjoy the pool.'

'I'm sure they would . . .'

'You sound a bit hesitant about it.'

'Well, it's just . . . it's difficult, you know. I feel I should be careful with the children – don't want them to get the wrong impression.'

'Nobody's suggesting we do anything more than sit around the poolside with as many long drinks as it takes to keep us cool. That way, we could sit and laze, or read or chat or whatever, whilst keeping an eye on the children. They'd love to splash around. Maybe we could even get the barbecue going.'

Sally was thinking of all the week-ends when the children had begged to be taken out but she'd fobbed them off with a trip to the park because she'd been either too broke or too tired to do anything else with them.

'It would make a nice change,' she said.

'Good, how about we do it next Saturday?'

'This one coming?'

'No, not this Saturday, the one after. I have to go away this week-end.'

'Pity. It's their father's turn to have them that week.'

'There's always another time. We could still make it a twosome, though, couldn't we?'

She considered the proposition for a moment. 'Okay. I don't much like being in the cottage on my own anyway.'

'Good, then it's a date.'

The drive to Henfield, out over the Downs, was especially pleasant. The fields were full of contented cattle and the trees, heavy with leaf, dipped low over the road, dappling light onto the tarmac. Others made dark tunnels where they met at the top.

'Isn't it gorgeous?' said Sally, taken by the way the sun filtered through the branches in hazy stripes. The shafts of light reminded her, curiously, of the religious pictures that you might see on an ancient triptych, the sort where beams

233

shine out from the hands of Christ, in kindly benediction. 'Absolutely gorgeous,' she said again.

'Heavenly,' Daniel agreed, as if he'd picked up her mental image by telepathy. 'It's going to be great summer, you wait and see.'

He started to hum a snatch of a song as he manoeuvred the Porsche along the country lanes. Sally looked at him and smiled.

'You're very cheerful.'

'I've got good reason to be. It's a beautiful day, I'm with a beautiful woman and there's something just as beautiful, in a completely different way, of course, sitting in my garage.'

'Obviously not the Volvo!'

He laughed. 'No. Something very special indeed.'

A mile or so later, he turned the Porsche off the main road and down a long gravel drive. The manicured gardens and impressive white-painted house that appeared at the end of it looked, to Sally, like an estate agent's picture in *Country Life*. She was awestruck.

'What do you think?'

'Very grand,' she said, trying not to sound affected.

'Not too ostentatious, I hope?'

'And you live here all on your own?'

'Not entirely. I have Nero for company.' He pulled the car into the courtyard behind the house where a sleek, muscle-bound Rottweiler had set up a furious racket.

'God almighty!' Sally gasped, watching the dog bound from side to side, flashing its teeth.

'It's okay, he's as soft as putty.' Daniel got out of the car and the dog leapt up to greet him. There was much slapping of its black and tan hide before it seemed satisfied to let him move round to Sally's door.

'Come on,' he said, opening it.

'You sure? Don't fancy having my leg off without anaes-thetic.'

'He wouldn't harm a flea, honestly.'

Sally stepped gingerly out of her seat while the dog snuffled around her calves.

'There, see,' said Daniel, 'he'll be all right now he's got the scent of you.'

'Still don't like the look on his face.'

'He's smiling.'

'Could have fooled me. Isn't it dangerous having an animal like that loose?'

'Not at all. I told you, he's harmless.'

'What do you keep him for, then?'

'He puts people off, don't you, boy?' He stroked the evil-looking head. 'Although he'd never stop anybody from getting into the house if they wanted to.'

'Sounds like a pretty useless guard dog.'

'Oh, he is, in his way. That's how I got him. He'd been dumped at Battersea Dogs' Home by some builders who'd had him on one of their sites. They're the clowns who christened him Nero.'

'Looking at him, I'd say the name was highly appropriate.'

'Not as appropriate as they'd hoped. The site was burgled several times.'

'Oh, hence the banishment to Battersea.'

'Yes, except there was one thing about him that they didn't know.'

'Which was?'

'He likes buildings better than building sites. He might let you get in, but he'll never let you get out again.'

Sally shuddered. 'Can you stop him from licking my ankles? I'm afraid he might get to attached to the flavour.'

'Back!' Daniel commanded, and the dog snapped to attention. 'Car or coffee first?' he asked.

'Car, I think.'

'It's in here.' He crossed the courtyard and released the combination lock that held the hasp of the stable door shut.

The door swung wide to reveal a large space where stalls had once stood. In it was the Volvo, surrounded by neat stacks of boxes that seemed to be used for filing car spares.

'Oh, that's marvellous – exactly what I needed. Thank you. Thank you so much.' Sally edged round the boxes. 'I can hardly believe it. It's just ideal. In really good shape, too.'

'Should do you okay for a few years, unless you do well enough to upgrade sooner.'

'I'll be quite happy to stick with this even if I do start making good money. There'd be no point in anything better. A car's just four wheels and an engine to me.'

'You won't say that when you've seen what's in the garage.' He took her hand and led her to the next stable. It was twice the size of the first and had been turned into a double garage.

'Tell me you don't love the look of this!' He pulled back the door and presented what looked like an old racing car, resplendent in a livery of dazzling light blue.

'Oh!' Sally was completely stunned. She went forward reverently, and fondled one of the big chrome headlights in her palm. 'Isn't she sensational?'

'Coachwork by Vanden Plas and every inch a lady.'

'A Bentley, isn't it?'

Daniel nodded. 'Three-and-a-half litre, made to order in 1934.'

'But what an unusual colour.'

'It was picked to match the evening dress of a girl who took the eye of the Prince of Siam.'

'Really?'

'It was his car and he took it to race meetings all over Europe. In the end, the car became so well known that people started calling this colour Bira blue – the prince himself was called something long and complicated but Bira was his nickname, you see. Anyway, later on they added a

236

yellow stripe to the blue and the two together became the official Siamese racing colours.'

'You don't think of the Siamese driving racing cars,' Sally puzzled. 'The kind of image you get is of a primitive but beautiful culture . . . and a magnificent palace with Yul Brynner stomping around in baggy trousers.'

'*The King and I* was based on a story about this chap's grandfather.'

'I didn't know it was meant to be true?'

'I think its true that there was an English governess in the royal household, but as for the rest, who knows?'

Sally thought about the old film; the pomp and finery it mimicked couldn't have been too far from reality. 'He must have been fabulously rich, this prince.'

'I should say so, but he didn't just buy cars for the fun of it. He was a very good driver, in his day. Won the British Drivers' Club gold star three years in a row.'

'I can just imagine him belting round Le Mans in this.'

'Oh, he didn't race this car. This was the car he kept for everyday use.'

'Imagine.' Sally ran a hand over the trim. 'So it's been hidden away somewhere in Siam until now?'

'Don't know where it's been. Probably in and out of private collections, in between winkling its way round the trade.'

'Are you going to keep it?'

'Just for a short while. If I can't get the price I want for it after a couple of months, I'll let it go to auction.'

'Excuse my asking, but what's it worth, a car like this?'

'About a hundred thousand.'

Sally gasped.

'That's nothing, some classic cars go for several million.'

'You're making me giddy.'

'Better get you that cup of coffee then, hadn't I?'

They wandered back across the courtyard, the dog fretting

and jumping up at them as they walked. Daniel let him in through the back door then showed Sally into the kitchen.

'You could put the whole of my downstairs into this one room, I think,' she said, admiring the light oak cabinets that formed a rectangle, more or less partitioning the kitchen. A single dark-stained beam had been slung low from the ceiling and two others rose up to from the floor to meet it, making a tasteful rustic arch. The building was not old enough for the beams to have been original, but the feeling of age had been successfully recreated, giving an overall impression of authenticity.

Daniel clicked a switch. 'It's always so dark in here, had to wire up spotlights to make the most of it.'

The ceiling, bright with white paint, had been fitted with more dark beams which were picked out now by lights that had been cleverly concealed.

'What it must be to have so much space to work in!' said Sally.

'Yes, I should use it more often but it's a question of time and motivation.'

'You like to cook?'

'I find it relaxing but, you know, there's this thing about just catering for yourself . . .'

'Yes, it seems like too much effort for too little reward.'

'It's well equipped, though,' he said, patting the wooden butcher's table that stood in the centre of the floor. 'You could cater for a siege without a problem here.'

'Certainly got all the mod cons,' said Sally, looking up at the pan rack suspended above it, 'I do envy you.'

'Would you like to see the rest of the place?'

'Love to.'

He led the way through to the living room. In stark comparison, it was completely modern in design, save for an open hearth with black Victorian back plates. The logs in the grate looked to be for decorative purposes only.

'Here are those two paintings I told you about,' said Daniel, pointing out two framed canvases that were leaning against one wall.

'They're superb.' Sally bent closer to them. 'So vivid.'

'Not really my taste but very fine examples of the style.'

'You would swear the flowers were real, extraordinary brush work . . . where ever did you find them?'

'Got them in Belgium, the last time I was over. I have to go back there again this week-end.'

'You travel a lot?'

'I pop over to the Continent every ten days or so.'

'Must like driving.'

'I fly, usually.'

'Yourself?'

'Of course.'

'Not in that biplane, surely?'

'No. I've got a Piper Aztec at Shoreham. You know the little airport there?'

'I've passed it but never thought of it as a serious airport.'

'There's quite a few light aircraft there. I keep three or four out on the grass myself.'

'I wondered where you put them. The stables are big but not that big.'

He smiled. 'You'll have to come over one day and look around. By the way, have you thought over my other offer yet?'

'Mmm?'

'About the paintings.'

'I'd love to have them in the shop, but I'm still a bit nervous about it.'

'I'll put in an alarm, if you like. You ought to have one anyway.'

'Can you do that?'

'Easily. I'm a trained electrician, you know.'

'I didn't know, but I can believe it.'

239

'Come on, we haven't finished the grand tour yet.' He took her arm and wheeled her out into the hall. 'Dining room,' he said, opening and closing the door. Then across the corridor, 'Study.' Another few paces. 'Gym.'

'You've got your own gym?'

'How else would I stay fit?' He shut the door and walked back towards the foot of the stairs. 'Utility room's down there,' he added, pointing, 'but I'm sure you don't want to see that. And up here . . .'

Sally watched him mount the stairs, half wondering whether she was meant to follow him.

'Where've you gone?' He'd reached the top and was peering over the banister.

'Just here.' She went up cautiously.

'This is bathroom one,' he continued, 'bedrooms two, three and four with another bathroom ensuite.'

'It's like a hotel.'

'I think the people before me had a lot of friends.'

'Or children.'

'No, there weren't any children. Odd that.'

'How do you mean?'

'Well, I could never see the point in getting married unless you wanted children.'

'I presume that's why you're still single.'

'Oh, I like kids, but as for having them myself – well, it's different for men, you don't think about having children in the way that a woman does, although I'm sure I'd be thrilled with them once they arrived.'

'You'd make nice-looking children.'

He looked surprised, then recovered. 'Can't imagine what it must be like to see your own features recreated in miniature.'

'It's not just the features, you see your own mannerisms too. It's an embarrassment at times.'

'Guess that must be true. My mum used to say that I walked just like my father, though I never knew him.'

Sally would have liked to have heard the whole story, but thought it better not to ask.

'This is the final stop on our tour,' he said, opening the last door. This time he didn't close it quickly, as he had with the others, but went on into the room. Sally followed.

'I always think that this is the best room in the house, it's got the best views, anyway.' He lingered at the window, looking out over the fields towards a wood in the distance.

'Does all the land belong to this house?'

'No. Just those two paddocks. I'd love to have that wood, though. I go trespassing up there if I'm here in the evening. There's a pair of badgers who have a family every year, I like to watch them.' He'd put an arm around her shoulders and now drew her nearer. 'There's something almost mystical about sitting out in the woods at night. You know, some strange feeling that you get, alone and quite still, with no noise but the stirrings of leaves and grass. It's a feeling that must be as old as the human race, a kind of complete feeling, like that's where you're meant to be, that's your real environment, not towns or cities, bricks and stone. The darkness closes round you like a cloak and for a while you're part of it, part of the great mystery of nature, free just to breathe the cold air and be nothing more than a fragment of life, of no consequence except just you exist in that moment.'

Sally thought the idea quite beautiful. The idyll he'd conjured impressed itself on her and she wondered at his sensitivity.

'I've been doing that since I was a kid,' he went on, 'hiding myself in a corner of some wood, waiting, watching. It was my form of escape . . .'

She leaned against him easily, soothed by the warmth of his body against hers. Instinctively, she snuggled slightly

241

into the hollow of his chest and he bent and kissed her forehead.

'It's so peaceful.' Her voice was a whisper almost lost in the folds of his shirt.

He kissed her forehead again, then her eyes, which closed readily, her nose, her mouth. The sensation of fire rising came over her again and she realised that she was trembling. He held her fast, his hands stroking her back, her thighs, and her body melted to his touch. The minutes passed, and she was wilting against him, his hands, unrelenting, impelling her to weaken further.

'Do you want me?' His breath was hot, so that her ear blazed with the same fire that seemed to consume the rest of her. She could only nod. There were no words. Just sensations, most irresistible of all the low ache that gripped her belly, a leaden, yearning ache that could know only one satisfaction.

He picked her up and stepped the few paces to the bed. Sally felt the softness beneath her but lay unmoving, her eyes shut fast against the fear she felt must come if she dared to watch him undressing. He was beside her in a moment, his mouth moving gently over her face and throat. Still she lay immobile, the leaden ache spreading over all her limbs.

There was no sound, save for his breathing, and hers, quickening as his lips touched her stomach. His hands had released the confining bands of clothes, stroking, always stroking, as they moved and soon she was as naked as he and she felt the glow of his flesh against her.

Gently, so gently, his fingers traced a path along her hip bone, spreading down along her inner thigh. His lips followed, gentler still, caressing, persuading, so that she sighed for the moment that seemed so close, yet he held back, as if waiting for some secret signal. He brought his mouth back up to hers, moving his chest over her as he did so. The kisses, more sensual now, made the low ache in her unbearable. She

242

found the strength at last to move her arms, winding them slowly round his back, her hands coming to rest below his shoulders. The legs that had lain so dull allowed his to find the access they'd been seeking and finally, he was there, the burning pleasure of his entry apparent in her gasp.

He moved slowly at first, still keeping her mouth under his, pushing her lips wider and wider with his own until the desire to open flamed in her hips, too, and her only thought was to give way to the power inside her. Soon, she could not help but give way. His movement, becoming stronger, made her own rise and she clutched to him in little rippling spasms, like a well-spring bubbling from the earth.

The motion intensified, the new rhythm between them a voluptuous urge to take and be taken. And all her body seemed to belong to him, she wanted to be his, all passion and longing, and cried out for him, needing to drown in the flood tide. A moment more and the cries were deep-throated sobs, wanting, wanting until the rage of desire sent flickering tongues like flame to her finger tips and feet. She was peaking now, the edge in her voice betrayed it. Still, he didn't stop, determined to push her to the brink of endurance. The fight was all but lost when she felt him release, and the surge carried her with it, bringing her own conclusion.

Tears welled up in her eyes as she clung to the body that lay, wet and heavy, on her own. The tears were part of another emotion, a sorrow that she'd kept hidden in the depths of her heart. Suddenly it seemed too much, the pain and the sorrow, the struggle always to seem in charge of the helpless self so close to the surface. The relief that this man had given her was a kind of sorrow too. The grief of love lost mixed with new sensations. And suddenly she needed him to love her, to keep her safe, there, enveloped in his warmth.

He stirred and saw that she was crying, silently, though her breast was tight with the effort. He kissed the tears away but more came and his soft entreaties were for nothing. She

243

let the racking pain do its worst, clinging to him all the time, her tears soaking his shoulder. When it had passed, she thought she should try to explain, but somehow he seemed to understand.

'Don't worry, I'll look after you,' he whispered and held her tight. And she believed him.

16

'It's a copy.'

'What?'

'It's a copy.'

'A fake, you mean?'

'No.' Ken looked calmly round from his examination of the commode and pointed to a chest-of-drawers on the opposite wall. 'That's a fake.'

A noise that was somewhere between a squeal and a sob escaped from Sally's mouth.

'Well, what did you expect? You can't know the trade in five minutes flat.'

She felt as though her legs were not going to carry her across the room.

'I don't believe it.'

'I do. You couldn't wait, could you? Get a bit of money in the bank and it's through your fingers like water, isn't it? Really, Sally, it's about time you stopped living in cloud cuckooland. You know nothing about this business, nothing at all. It takes years, not months. But we can't tell you that, can we? Oh, no, not Miss "I'm-going-to-show-the-bastards" Blythe. One sniff of a half-baked deal and you're off like a rat up a drain pipe. Just how long do you think you'll last

245

like this, eh? How long before there's nothing in the house to eat besides fish fingers and beans again? You've got to get a grip on yourself, for the children's sake if not your own.'

Tears started to slide down her face and she turned away so that he shouldn't see. That she'd made a fool of herself was bad enough without his being horrible to her.

'And I suppose I'm meant to dig you out of this mess?' he went on, relentlessly. 'Wonderful. Well, I've got better things to do than keep playing nanny.'

The fit of weeping overcame her and he realised that he'd gone too far. He went up and put an arm around her shoulders.

'Go away,' Sally sniffed, 'just go away and leave me to it, if that's what you feel.'

'I'm sorry. I didn't really mean it.'

'Yes, you did. And I agree. There's no reason why you should have to pick up after me.'

He stroked her head fondly, thinking of all the reasons why he would, anyway.

'Come on, it's not a complete disaster.'

'That's not how it sounded to me.'

'I just worry that you're going to get your fingers burnt, that's all.' He'd heard the rumours the minute he got back to Brighton. The Lanes were practically twittering with chauvinist comments and some kind soul had already started taking bets on her being out of business within six months.

'Well, you'd better tell me the worst,' Sally said, pulling herself together.

'There is some good news, so long as you didn't give too much for the commode.'

'What's too much?'

'Any more than fifteen hundred.'

'Oh dear.'

'You'll be lucky to get more than two or, the best way, two-and-a-quarter grand for it.'

'What's wrong with it?'

'It's not so much that it's wrong, it's just that it isn't right. Not for Louis XV, anyway. See the design is eighteenth-century, in principle, but the proportions and lines are of a much younger piece.'

'But it's exactly how you'd expect it to be, the mouldings, the marble . . .'

'Not if you look more closely. Come and see what I mean.' He took her across to the commode. Now, I can tell quite a lot about this piece before I even touch it. The first point to note is that it's not wide enough, only about fifty-three inches at a guess. An original would be more like sixty-eight and that's quite a big difference. And even though the maker has stuck to the authentic forms of design, the effect of trying to make them work on something this size has been to make it look squashed up and boxy by comparison.

'You mention the mouldings and the marble,' he went on, 'but neither are quite as they should be. The mouldings are too fine and elaborate, for a start, and as to the marble . . . well, ideally I would be looking for a moulded edge. This hasn't got one. In any case the whole slab is thinner than it should be. That would suggest that it was cut with a power saw, something that wouldn't have happened in the eighteenth century, and anyway marble wasn't so hard to come by then, so you could afford to use a hefty slice.

'The definitive test, though,' he said, stooping down and pushing at a piece of the inlay on the front of the drawers, 'is this. There's a little bubble in the veneer here, do you see?'

Sally bent to look at it.

'I can depress it quite easily with my finger. That would tend to suggest that it's modern. Oh, yes, see that chip near the edge of the drawer? That proves it for sure.'

'How?'

'The veneer's not thick enough. Look, it's almost wafer thin. There's no way that that could have been cut by hand.' He stood up and dusted off his trousers. 'No, what you've got here was probably made around 1920. It's a good quality copy, but it's a copy nevertheless.'

Sally was crestfallen. 'I feel like such a twit.'

'It's a mistake lots of people would have made. Where did you get it, anyway?'

'I bought it from an old lady in Rye.'

'Didn't walk with a stick, did she.'

'Yes, actually.'

'Name of Johnson, by any chance?'

'You know her?'

'We all know Dorothy. I suppose she did the impoverished war widow routine on you?'

'She said she was going in for an operation. Hip replacement, that was it.'

'Oh, that's a new story. So what did she make from you?'

'Three thousand pounds.'

'The crafty old devil! Well, you've caught a cold, girl, but you've not come a complete cropper. At least, not with the commode. That chest of drawers, though, is a big, big problem.'

'It looked right to me.'

'Which proves the point that a fake is only as good as the eye that judges it.'

'Thanks.'

'Well, look at the veneer,' he said, going to the other side of the room. 'You thought it was walnut, I suppose?'

'Yes.'

'Well, it's not, just been polished up to look that way.'

'How can you tell?'

'It's too sharp, there's no depth to the colour. Apart from that, the grain of the wood is too straight and uninteresting.'

248

Ken pulled out a drawer. 'And as for this . . . well, I hardly know where to start.'

'I know it's lined with pine, but I thought that was fairly standard on a country piece?'

'It's not the lining that's so wrong, it's the dovetails. Look at them. Appalling!' He turned the drawer sideways. 'Hand-made dovetails have a narrower tail attached to the drawer facing than the receiving joint at the other side; machine dovetails are even-sized. These are machined but whoever did them was a butcher with a Black and Decker. See the gaps in the joints? Bet they're packed with sawdust.'

Sally watched as he took out his penknife and whittled away at the dirt in one of the seams. A piece broke sharply out.

'Glue,' said Ken, performing the same operation on the other joints. 'Yes, too much of it for an honest repair job.'

He put the penknife away and turned the drawer through ninety degrees, so that he could look inside the facing. 'Two sets of bore holes.'

'Yes, the handles have been replaced.'

'But the outer set don't line up with any marks on the front of the drawer.' He held it up to the light, 'Look, the inner ones match with this handle but there's no repair in the surrounding veneer.'

'What's that mean?'

'That the veneer was added after the chest had been knocking about for some time.'

'The carcass is all of a piece, then?'

'All of a piece concocted about ten minutes ago.' Ken tapped the plinth at the bottom with his toe. 'And there's another thing to look out for next time. This chest is trying to look as if it was early-eighteenth-century, right? But if it had been made then, it wouldn't have been given bracket feet. In any case, you can see straight away that the bracket doesn't go with the moulding dividing the drawer fronts.'

'Well, I didn't see it straight away,' said Sally, gloomily. 'So the long and the short of it is that I've been done.'

'Well and truly, I'm sorry to say. What did you give for this excuse for a piece of furniture, anyway?'

'Twelve hundred.'

'I wouldn't take it for fifty quid.'

'But if it fooled me, it'll fool somebody else.'

'Not in this district it won't. Anyway, you'll get a name for passing off strops if you try.'

'What's a strop?'

'What you're looking at now, a made-up piece.'

'I must be able to get rid of it somehow.'

'Best thing you can do with that is set fire to it.'

'I should take it out of the shop, then?'

'If you don't, you'll be more of a laughing stock than you already are.'

Sally blushed violently. 'Why? Who's doing the laughing?'

'Most of your neighbours. But I wouldn't take too much notice, it's more to do with having a woman on the patch than anything else.'

'Miserable sods.'

'One of whom sold you this turkey, no doubt.'

'No. It came out of a garage near Lancing.'

'A garage belonging to one Jim Foley, at a guess.'

Sally's mouth opened and closed, but she didn't say anything.

'That's twice you've been stitched up by the opposition. Well, you'll learn.'

'How was I meant to know? Both times I thought I was dealing with ordinary householders.'

'That's the way to catch a newcomer. Answered one of your adverts, did they?'

'Yes.'

Ken nodded. 'Thought so. Look, Sal, you're going about it the wrong way. Putting adverts in local papers is all very well and good but that's for the small fry. And not only that, it's going to turn out to be one hell of a time waster. Quite apart from the likelihood of getting screwed by the likes of Dot Johnson and Jim Foley, unless you can get an accurate description of what you're going to be shown before you turn out, it's not worth the petrol money driving over to take a look. Very few people can give an accurate description over the 'phone, unless they're another dealer. And even then, you'd have to know you could trust your man's eye.'

'But how else am I meant to go about it? There's a limit to what I can buy at a viable price from other dealers.'

'What you need is contacts, good contacts. That's how you make a business like this work.'

'Where do you get these contacts from?' There's that word again, Sally thought, remembering how cagey Daniel had been about whatever he meant by it.

'By keeping your ear to the ground. If you listen to other dealers talking, you'll find they're swapping stories about what they've seen where,' Ken said. 'Let's say, for instance, that one chap knows someone who's got a watch to sell. He may not deal in watches himself, but he'll know another man who might be interested. If that man buys the watch, he'll be grateful for the tip and the next time he comes across something that his friend might want, he'll pass a tip back.'

'So basically, you've got to get in with the other dealers.'

'That's right.'

'And how do I manage that when they're dead set against me in the first place?'

'Make it worth their while. Once you get to know the sorts of things people like to deal in, you can look out for good examples.'

'It's all a bit chicken-and-eggish though, isn't it? I mean, you can't get in with the dealers 'cos you don't know where

251

the interesting stuff is, and you don't know where the interesting stuff is because you can't get in with the dealers.'

'Well, as it happens, you have an advantage that others lack when it comes to trying to break in to the trade.'

'Which is?'

'Femininity, of course.'

'What? You mean I should use my fatal charms?'

'Only up to the point you're comfortable with.'

'Oh, honestly! So now I've got to flirt with a bunch of Neanderthal-brained creeps to get a whiff of business. God, how banal!'

'What's wrong with you? It doesn't cost anything to flutter your eyelashes.'

'You're the one who keeps telling me that I should do this, that or the other so that I'll get taken seriously. If I go around acting the vamp with these geeks I should think my fate will be sealed for all time.'

'Come on, Sally, there isn't a woman alive who can't walk into a pub and get a few drinks bought for her, and there's nothing wrong in that. Of course, a man will have his eye on the main chance all the time he's buying those drinks, but whether he succeeds in getting where he'd like to get or not depends entirely on the woman.'

'Ugh, it's so tacky.'

'It's human nature, tacky or no.' Ken shrugged. 'I hate to admit it, but we men are as much driven by our biology as women are. We like to think that we're somehow superior because we're less emotional and don't suffer from PMT, but it's all garbage really. Show us a pretty face or a shapely figure, and wham! The old IQ's out of the window and we're after it like a shot. That's not to say we're not interested in what a woman's got in her head, just that the sap rises quicker than the intellect. You could have the brain of Albert Einstein and it wouldn't stop the baser instincts surfacing. Interaction between men and women is mostly motivated by sex. It might not be "modern" or popular to say so, but that's the fact.'

Sally started giggling.

'What's so funny?'

'You talking about sex.'

'What am I, an android? I have natural urges, too, you know.'

'Yes, I know.'

'And you can take that smile off your face.'

She didn't.

'You trying to embarrass me?'

'No. It's just amusing trying to work you out.'

'Well, let's all share the joke.'

'No joke involved.'

'What, then?'

'I don't know. You're one of the warmest, kindest people I've ever met and I absolutely love you, but it's hard to think of you in . . . well . . . to think of you as having sexual urges and all that.'

'I knew I'd wish I hadn't asked.' He made it sound frivolous but he was smarting inside.'

'I don't mean you're abnormal or anything, just I don't see you as predatory. At least not so far as I'm concerned. That's a compliment, you know.'

'Yes. Well . . .' He looked down at his hands. 'Anyway, the point of the conversation wasn't to talk about me or us. What I was trying to get across to you was that you should use everything you've got, every tool in the armoury, to get yourself ahead.'

'Including moral compromise.'

'Which one of us doesn't compromise our morals from time to time if we want to succeed badly enough?'

'None, I suppose.'

'There you are. No one's asking you to do anything corrupt. Some will lie and cheat, like Jim Foley, others will up

253

the ante by playing on your sympathies, like Dot Johnson. All you've got to do is turn on a bit of charm, something that comes naturally anyway, and you'll bag more game than the lot of them.'

'You really think so?'

'I know so.'

'Oh, dear.' Sally sighed. She'd thought that she'd been doing really well in setting up the shop but her zest for the trade had been left a bit flattened by the morning's events. 'What am I going to do?'

'Well, that can stay in place for the moment,' Ken said, nodding towards the commode. 'I'll see what I can come up with for it.'

'What about the chest-of-drawers, though?'

'You're on your own there. But you should get it out of here as fast as possible.'

The thought of Sally getting caught out so soon, especially by somebody like Jim Foley, irritated Ken all the way back to his shop. The chest-of-drawers had been so obviously faked up that he still couldn't believe she could make such a stupid mistake. It was the type of thing that he might have expected from a rank amateur, but not someone with her perception. The incident had put a dent in his confidence that would take some time to fix.

There was a bundle of letters behind the door as he pushed it open. He stooped to pick them up.

Bills, bills and more bills . . . what's this?

He shoved the door shut with his heel and went over to his desk, tearing open the ominous-looking brown envelope as he did so.

'Bloody VAT,' he said, unfolding the contents. ' "Dear Mr Rees . . ." '

He read the rest of the letter in silence, put it aside, then picked up the 'phone.

254

'Can you put me through to Lynn Ryan, please? Lynn?'

'Yes?'

'It's Ken. I've just had a love note from the VAT office.'

'Saying what?'

'They want to pay me a visit.'

'When was the last time they came?'

'I don't know. Three, maybe four years ago.'

'Can't be that worried about you, then.'

'Well, it makes me nervous.'

'You've been keeping your stockbook up-to-date, I hope.'

'Pretty much.'

'Done the last quarter's returns yet?'

'Oh, blast!'

'What?'

'I forgot to send them in, what with the work and then having to go to Jersey in a rush.'

'You are a nit. They should have been in by the end of May.'

'I know.'

'You don't want to be giving the VAT people reasons to be getting too interested in you.'

'I realise that. Do you think it'll be okay if I stick it in the post straight away with a covering note?'

'Maybe. How was your trip?'

'Fine. I'm glad I went, they seemed to appreciate it.'

'I'm sure. How is Jules, now?'

'Okay, basically, but they gave him a nasty bash on the head. I was more concerned about my daughter-in-law to be honest.'

'The baby's going to be all right, isn't it?'

'Yes, I should be a grandfather in just over two months, though it grieves me to admit it.'

'You should be jolly pleased. The shock of that break-in might have sent her into premature labour.'

'I know. Thankfully, she didn't get involved. The burglars

had gone by the time she went downstairs to see where Jules had got to.'

'Must have given her the shock of her life. Did they take much?'

'Not in terms of quantity, but unfortunately the pieces that went were real goodies. They seemed to know what they were after, according to Jules. Once they'd bashed him, they got on with it at an amazing speed.'

'What an awful business.'

'One of the risks. Although I wouldn't be surprised if it was an inside job.'

'How do you mean?'

'Not so much a robbery, more of a reprisal. Jules said he'd been getting trouble from one of the big French rings but he just kept telling them to get stuffed.'

'Like father, like son, eh?'

'He's his own man, if that's what you mean.'

'Well, I'm glad it wasn't worse.'

'So am I. You don't realise how much you care for them until something like this happens.'

'Children?'

'Yes.'

'I think you do, if you're around them from the word go.'

Ken sighed. 'Well, I wasn't and it was my loss. Still, it's a bit late to worry about that now.'

'You've made up for it since, I'm sure. Oh, hang on a minute . . .'

He could hear snatches of muffled conversation as he waited, though his mind had flipped back in time, bringing a vision of a slight but dauntless brunette who'd passed for twenty-three but, he'd found later, had only been seventeen. He wondered if it would have made any difference if he had known at the time. Perhaps, but probably not. He should have known better than to allow the mistake to happen in the first place. But it did and then he'd let her down. The guilt still plagued him, though she'd forgiven him a long time ago.

'You still there?'

'Yes.'

'Sorry, a client's just come in wanting instant attention, so I'll have to go.'

'Okay.'

'Look, don't worry about the VAT thing, we can talk about it when the date for the inspection's fixed.'

Ken put down the 'phone and pushed the letters into a heap. Catching up with bills was never his favourite task and he could feel a mood coming on that was likely to ruin the whole day if it was provoked any further. The bad temper that had been festering since he'd left Sally's shop had been made worse by the reminder of his own past inadequacies. And the fact that his own were personal, not professional, didn't improve things either. He left his desk and wandered into the back of the shop, where he stood staring into the darkness at the bottom of the stairs, wondering if he shouldn't just go and bang a few nails into something to make himself feel better.

Once down in the basement, he gave up the idea of hammering, deciding instead to have another go at a large chest that he'd picked up at a house in Bradford. It was as black as coal and he'd spent every spare hour over a number of weeks working on it, hoping that a hint of something special would appear.

Now that's what you call a good chest-of-drawers, he thought, passing his hand over its surface, then he rolled up his sleeves, took up some fine grade wire wool and a bottle of reviver and started gently rubbing. He rubbed a little harder today, working off his annoyance, thinking all the while of what he'd like to do to Jim Foley the next time he was unfortunate enough to cross Ken's path. After half-an-hour or so, he got his reward. A rich, oyster-shaped piece of olive wood veneer appeared, followed quickly by another and another.

He felt a tingle of pleasure run up his spine. He'd known from the start that there was something unusual about the piece. Ken left the top of the chest and rubbed at one of the sides. Fine marquetry scrolling became clearer and clearer as he worked, finishing in what seemed to be caricatured heads. He put the wire wool down for a second.

Looks as if it might be English, though I'd like to be sure.

He gingerly rubbed another section of the scrolling clean. The more he looked at the flourishes at the ends of each of them, the more he was certain of his hunch.

'Jesters' heads,' he exclaimed, suddenly. 'Must be English.'

He peered closely at each of the scrolls. As he'd hoped, they were all slightly different. The marquetry had been cut a piece at a time, the only known method before the Dutch invented a technique for cutting four or five pieces in one go. The chest-of-drawers had to be pre-1685, he concluded; after William and Mary came to the throne, all marquetry had been cut in the Dutch way.

Ken stepped back and wiped his hands on his trousers. One of the greatest thrills of the business was to make a discovery like this and he was feeling pretty pleased with himself. He went back up the stairs humming, wondering if he should celebrate by buying himself lunch for a change.

Why not? he thought. Could do with a breath of fresh air.

He was about to lock up when the 'phone rang.

'Mr Rees?' The well-bred accent was unfamiliar.

'Yes.'

'Kirkby Mote, the butler speaking.'

Ken suddenly remembered the conversation he'd had with his contact in Cheshire.

'Oh, good of you to call.'

'Mrs Lyall-Bourke has agreed to meet you. She suggests September the fourteenth.'

He wrote the date down on the back of one of the envelopes on his desk.

'Excellent. Perhaps I can 'phone you nearer the day to arrange a time.'

'It will have to be ten-thirty. I take it you will require at least two hours?'

'If I'm to make a proper view.'

'Yes, well, luncheon is always served at one o'clock sharp.'

'I'm sure I'll have finished by then.'

'Good. Goodbye.'

Ken lowered the 'phone, then re-dialled quickly.

'Frank? It's Ken. How did you manage it?'

'How did I manage what?'

'Kirkby Mote.'

'They rang you?'

'Just now. Thanks, by the way, must've been quite a job.'

'Not the easiest, it's true,' Ken's contact sounded smug, 'but the family solicitor happens to be a chap that I knew in prep school.'

'Shows you how important it is to have had the correct training.'

'Quite.'

'Thought the butler had a suitably imperious air.'

'Doesn't he just? I think he sees himself as the old girl's sole protector. Been with her for forty years, you know. Good man but inclined to be frosty. As I understand it, Mrs Lyall-Bourke values his opinion as a judge of character, so you'd better mind your Ps and Qs when you get there.'

'Will I see you at the Mere Hall sale?'

'Yes. You're not after the Nathaniel Dance, I hope.'

'Which Nathaniel Dance?'

'There's only one up, as far as I know, and that's *Venus Appearing to Aeneas*. One of his best pieces.'

'Mythological painting in the Grand Manner is not something I'm often asked to buy.'

'You should start buying for yourself, it's becoming popular again.'

'Not with me. Oh, by the way, are there any local furniture auctions coming up.'

'There's one at Mold in a few weeks, why?'

'I've got a commode that needs selling. It's a copy, but a very good one.'

'One of those nasty little traps that we all fall into from time to time, is it?'

Ken felt annoyed and drew in a breath. 'Something like that. Anyhow, it won't make its price around here.'

'Well, the market's quite perky here, so you should be able to cover yourself.'

'Anything else in the offing?'

'Not unless you've got something for me.'

'Not at the moment.'

'Well, keep your eyes open.'

'I will.'

Ken decided to take a long route through The Lanes. It had turned into another lovely day and he lingered in the sunshine, looking into the windows of the shops he passed, seeing what had changed since he'd been away. As he turned the corner of Meeting House Lane, a familiar figure emerged from a jewellery trader's door, wearing a sneaky grin.

'Scored again, have we?'

Tom Appleton's weasel face creased into what passed for a smile. 'I hear that you're scoring pretty well yourself, these days.'

'Don't know what you mean.'

'A certain little lady in Middle Street.'

Ken blanched. The word was bound to get around sometime, though he'd hoped it would take longer.

'Very nice, too,' Appleton continued, 'wouldn't say no myself.'

'My connection with Middle Street is purely professional.'

'Of course. That's why your name's on the lease.'

'Perfectly legitimate.'

'Most men would just set her up in a nice flat. You have to set her up in business.'

'I've told you, the arrangement is above board. Not that it's any of your concern.'

Appleton shrugged. 'Which way are you walking?'

'Down towards Foundry Street. I need to put my head in at Van Dalen's.'

'I'm going that way myself.'

The two men moved off together through the lunchtime bustle.

'Season's in full swing. The weather must be bringing them out.'

Ken nodded. His mind was on the Coxed and Woster lady's dressing bureau that he hoped Van Dalen could restore. It was golden mulberry, a difficult wood to match.

'He doing much for you these days, Van Dalen?'

'I keep him reasonably busy.'

'Fine craftsman. You don't get work like his these days.'

'No.'

'Here,' said Appleton, suddenly, 'heard about Murray Walker?'

'What's that?'

'Having kittens, he is. Worried stiff about his Wedgwood. Says the market's been killed.'

'Oh?'

'Came back from the ceramics fair at the Park Lane Hotel with a very long face. There's this display there – *The Art of Deception*, I think it's called. Anyway, it's all Wedgwood fakes, about fifty pieces in all.'

'I though that Wedgwood forgeries were few and far between?'

'So did everyone else, until now. One of the London dealers raised the alarm. He sent a plaque that he'd got to the Wedgwood Museum for verification and it turned out to be wrong, going on the original moulds. Now they've turned up a whole mountain of stuff. Seems like one of the company's potters started up a factory producing his own ceramics back in the forties and his side line, unbeknowst to the firm, was reproducing Wedgwood, mostly for the American market, though I suppose quite a bit of it was sold here too.'

'Poor old Murray.'

'You have to feel sorry for him, don't you? They don't know if it's one per cent, fifty per cent or ninety per cent of what's on the market that's wrong.'

'Bad as that?'

'Looks like it.'

They had walked the length of Bond Street and Gardner Street and were heading up North Street. As they neared the Foundry Street junction, Appleton paused to say goodbye.

'Where are you off to, then?' asked Ken.

'Just following a lead.'

'Oh, yeah?'

Appleton tapped the side of his nose, as much as to say. Ask no questions.

'You want to watch it, your reputation'll be getting worse than it already is.'

'I don't touch anything unless I know where it's come from.'

I wouldn't be so sure, thought Ken, but he just nodded and said, 'Glad to hear it.'

They parted company after crossing North Road and Ken walked on a few yards down Foundry Street before turning back. There'd been something in Appleton's manner that had disconcerted him: the way he'd come out of the shop in Meeting House Lane, the look in his eye as he'd gone on his way. If Ken knew anything about Tom Appleton at all, it meant that he was on to too much of a good thing. Ken went back to the top of the street and peered after him. The pace that Appleton was walking at seemed more urgent than it had before. He started to follow, staying as far behind his friend as possible.

This is crazy, he told himself, but the feeling that there was something going on that he ought to know about wouldn't leave him alone. Several minutes later, he saw Appleton disappear into a warehouse in Frederick Street. It was the one that Derek Jones traded out of.

Now what's that connection about? he wondered. Derek doesn't trade in jewellery and silverware.

He was still standing in a doorway puzzling when a large Daimler slid by. He watched it glide down the street and come to a halt outside the same warehouse.

I've seen that car somewhere before, he thought, taking a chance and walking on down the road. As he drew level, he noticed it was a Daimler Sovereign, judging by the registration, one that had come from the Midlands. A square-set man got out and gave him a hard stare.

The house sale at Bryn Nant, Ken remembered, suddenly, but managed to walk by without flinching. In the long detour that he took before heading back to Foundry Street, all he could think about was what might have been in the package he'd seen Derek Jones leave the Daimler with that day.

17

The whole of Brighton's smart set seemed to have descended on Brown's for an extended lunch. The week-end spirit was well in evidence as Sally pushed her way through the crowd that was blocking the doorway to the restaurant and looked around to see if Julia had already arrived. She was standing at the end of the bar with a group of colleagues from another firm of solicitors.

'Can we eat straight away? I'm starving.' Julia left her friends to their drinks and moved through the crush to greet her.

'Glad we booked,' said Sally,

'Fridays are always impossible. You're looking chic.'

'Thank you.'

'Nice to see you're looking after yourself again. Last time we had lunch I thought you were beginning to go a bit scraggy.'

Sally felt put out by the sharpness of the remark, but Julia was often abrupt. 'Well, I was pretty much on the floor then, what with the bank manager giving me a hard time and not knowing how I would ever get beyond pinching and scraping to stay alive,' she said in mitigation. 'If I'd have had any idea that things were about to change in quite so spectacular a way, I wouldn't have been anything like as miserable.'

'It's funny that, isn't it? When you're right in the middle of something that's gone badly wrong, you think you're going to be stuck in that situation for ever.'

'Yes, and it's that feeling of being trapped that stops you from seeing a way forward.'

'Well, I'm really pleased that you've made it,' said Julia, as their waiter pointed out the table that had been reserved for them. 'It was about time you had some luck.'

Sally settled herself in and unfolded her napkin. 'It's a little soon to say that I've made it yet, but I think I'm on the way.' She smiled. 'Mind you, I gave myself a nasty turn a couple of weeks back.'

'Oh?'

'You know me when I get the bit between my teeth. I was so intent on getting the shop stocked up that I let myself get taken in on a piece that was a complete no-no. Looks like I'm going to lose a lot of money on it.'

'Not too much, I hope?'

'Enough to teach me a lesson. Then there was another piece that I misjudged and almost came unstuck with. That wasn't such a bad mistake, more a case of not paying enough attention to detail. Anyway, Ken says he might be able to help me out on that one, so it hasn't turned out too badly.'

'He sounds really nice, this Ken.'

'Oh, he's a sweetheart. In fact, if it wasn't for him I'd still be messing around with house clearances.'

'Can't imagine what that must be like.'

'Not terribly nice. More often than not some poor old biddy's just popped off and the relatives just want to get rid of her gear as fast as possible so that they can get on with selling the house.'

'God, how ghoulish.' Julia pulled a face. 'The thought of

picking through somebody else's private possessions when they've hardly gone cold . . .'

'I know, but you get used to it in the end. The saddest thing is when somebody dies and there's no one – you know, not a single relative or friend – to deal with the estate. That's when you really get the feel of how little one less life bothers the world. All the photographs, the trinkets and souvenirs, all the things that were treasured for some happy memory so long ago . . . box after box of the stuff and there's not one soul on the planet left to care.'

'Awful.'

'Yes. But it comes to us all in the end, I suppose. We none of us know what'll happen to our things once we're gone. Just think of how much you accumulate in a lifetime. Tons of rubbish, when it comes down to it.'

'I know what you mean. I had to go over to my mum's the other day to clear my stuff out of her loft. It was mostly old toys and things that never made it into my flat after I came back from my year in Australia.'

'Lofts are great for treasure hunts. If there's something worth having in a house, nine times out of ten, it'll be in the loft.'

'Thought that was just in the stories?'

'No, I've found some really interesting stuff that way. There was this place in Hastings that had belonged to a man who had been in the merchant navy. Apparently he'd never married and seemed to live pretty reclusively in one of those gorgeous Tudor cottages not far from the harbour. Anyway, you should have seen the state of his loft. I think he must have brought something back from every port he'd ever sailed into.'

'What kind of thing?'

'Oh, Oriental pottery. African carvings, a collection of horrible masks from somewhere like New Guinea.' Sally sipped her drink. 'And, of course, there were loads of ships' instruments – compasses, clocks, that type of thing. I did rather well out of those, actually. There's a dealer in Hove who specialises in marine memorabilia so I sold most of them to him. I'm sure he'll sell a lot on to the London trade at inflated prices but I haven't got the right contacts yet to do it myself. Anyway, I was glad to have covered my losses on the furniture that I cocked up on.'

'It sounds incredibly risky, this antiques lark. One minute you're in the money, the next you're broke. Makes me glad that I've got a nice steady job.'

'You know, I don't think I could work in an office any more. I love the freedom this business gives me. I can do what I like when I like, and just so long as I make more good buys than bad, I can stay ahead of the game.'

'I envy you your freedom, I must admit,' Julia agreed, 'but I don't think the risk factor would do for me.'

'Go on, you're a girl who likes a bit of a gamble.'

'I used to, it's true, but I'm getting fed up with it now.'

'Why's that?'

'Fed up with going from one dead-end relationship to another. I think I need to settle down.'

'But you were always the one who was completely against settling down. I can't remember a time when you didn't have a string of men at your beck and call. Seemed to me you were having the time of your life.'

'Well, I did have a lot of fun, but, you know, you can't go on like that for ever. It's fine in your teens and twenties, but once you reach thirty . . .'

'You're not exactly an old maid at thirty.'

'It's not that. Just I need different things, now. I feel like I want some security, to know where I'm going in life.'

'A house and children, you mean?'

'That's part of it. All my friends are married or about to be. They're getting on with things, and here's me still poncing about with the dinners and the discos, acting like I'll

267

never get wrinkles. What I want, even more than the two-point-four children and point five of a dog, is a man I can rely on, someone who loves me the way I love him. Someone who wants more than a couple of evenings out a week followed by a quick bonk.'

'What about Ashley?'

'Junked him ages ago.'

'You didn't say.'

'Well, I haven't seen you since February, have I? It's almost July now.'

'You poor old thing.' Sally touched her hand. 'What happened?'

'Nothing outrageous. I just got sick of him 'phoning up and going through his entire diary of work to prove how difficult it was for him to fit me into his schedule.'

'You will go for these high fliers.'

'I don't care how high somebody flies, they can still make time if they want to. Oh, I understand how it is with careers, God knows I ought to, I've been wedded to mine for long enough.' Julia sighed. 'It's not that I object so much to a man devoting himself to his job, just that I want him to devote himself to me too, at least for a fair chunk of the time.'

'It's an impossible balance, though, isn't it?'

'I don't think so. Women have to divide themselves between their work and their families, if they want to have both.'

'Yes, but women expect to have to, don't they? We're meant to be super-human overachievers, capable of balancing the baby on one arm whilst conducting a board meeting with the other. That's what we think we ought to be able to do, or at least that's what we've conned ourselves into doing. Talk about women's lib! All we've done is land ourselves with a longer list of responsibilities than we had before.'

'Nevertheless, a lot of women make a success out of juggling career and family. At least two of the partners in my firm are doing it. You're doing it. Why shouldn't I be able to?'

Sally shrugged. 'No reason. I suppose a lot depends on your job. I don't know what it's like for a solicitor. What would you do if you suddenly had children? Try to cut down the workload, I suppose.'

'Hopefully, I'd be in a position to take on only the sort of work I wanted, by then. But that means working my way up to partner status.'

'How long before you can do that?'

'Another three or four years, I should think.'

Sally picked at her food, wondering whether Julia was really serious about settling down. She seemed to be sincere about it, but there was still a chance that it was a whim brought on by the latest romance going kaput.

'So, anything new on the horizon? Men, I mean.'

Julia gave a furtive smile. 'A couple of interesting opportunities have come my way.'

'Opportunities for what?'

'Don't know, yet, but I'm hopeful . . . there's one man I've started dating, a merchant banker, *very* well off.'

'Here we go,' Sally cut in, annoyed because she'd been feeling sorry for her friend a few moments before. 'Honestly, what do you do? Check out their credit rating before you accept an invitation to dinner?'

'I can't help if it I move in those sorts of circles,' retorted her friend, defensively. 'Anyway, it's not entirely like it sounds.'

'You obviously don't realise that every time you talk about someone new, it's swiftly followed up by a comment about how much they're worth.'

Julia looked surprised. 'Is that what I do?'

Sally nodded.

'More than other people?'

'I'm just saying it's noticeable, that's all.'

269

'Maybe it's something to do with being a lawyer. You know, dealing with the facts and figures of people's lives all day.'

'Maybe,' said Sally, but she wasn't convinced. Prestige had always been important to Julia. 'So what's he like, your banker?'

'Big and broad, the way I like them. Nice personality, too.'

'Where did you meet him?'

'At a conference in the City, one of those all-day jobs. He made a point of following me into the bar.'

'Lust at first sight, then?'

'On both sides. I'm keeping him waiting for the Main Event, though. I want him to have to work for it. That way, he'll be even more pleased when I graciously concede.'

'You make it sound like a game.'

'But it is a game, isn't it?' Julia turned her glass around thoughtfully. 'I've never understood why it's okay for a man to fall straight into bed with someone, but not okay for a woman. There's still that stigma attached. You know, that a man who does it as often as possible is the envy of his mates; the woman who does it is just a tart.' She picked up the glass and took a long gulp of wine. 'I tell you, I hope there is such a thing as reincarnation, 'cos next time I'm coming back as a bloke.'

Sally smiled. So even someone as provocatively modern as Julia had old-fashioned feminine doubts. 'Wouldn't get to wear the sexy gear then, though, would you?'

'You never know, dearie.'

'Oh, did I tell you about these gays I met?' It came out all of a sudden, prompted by Julia's camp mime.

'What gays?'

'Friends of Ken's.'

'Like that, is it?'

'Don't be silly, there's nothing wrong with Ken's hormones.'

270

'Got good reason to know, have we?'

Sally flushed. 'Stop it! What's between Ken and me is . . . well . . . platonic.'

'How ghastly.'

'Anyway, he took me to this fabulous house in Kingston Bucci.'

'Where's that?'

'It's the old name for Kingston-by-Sea. You know the place – between Shoreham and Southwick.'

'No.'

'Well, there's only about three streets of the original village left, so it's easy to miss. But this house, the rectory as was, was unbelievable. You couldn't turn round for antiques. These friends of Ken's were having a party. Rather a good one, as it turned out. Well, I ended up drinking too much, so it must have been pretty enjoyable.'

'You don't remember much of it, then?'

'I wasn't *that* drunk. Oh! And there was this weird woman there, Suzanne something-or-other, fancied herself as a mystic. She was with this awful nerd who kept saying he wanted to paint me.'

'What colour?'

'He was an artist, you twit! Suzanne was doing readings for people, you know, tarot cards and palmistry, so I thought I'd let her do mine . . .'

'So that's how you came across the tall, dark stranger.' Julia saw Sally's quizzical look. 'The dish you were with when I bumped into you the other day, silly.'

'Oh, Daniel? No, I'd already met him by then. I told you, didn't I?'

'You said something about him almost crashing a 'plane into the cottage.'

'Yes, that's right. But after that, actually, the very day after this party I'm talking about, he sent me some flowers and invited me out to lunch.'

271

'You're not telling me your mystic predicted that?'

'Not exactly . . . but she did say I was going to have a serious involvement with someone I already knew. For one awful moment, I thought she meant Ken.'

'Maybe she did.'

'I've told you, it's not like that. Anyway, he's over fifty.'

'So?'

'Oh, I think a lot of him, but he just doesn't ring my bells.'

'Whereas Daniel does?'

'Quite.'

'What's he like?'

Sally glanced away, but Julia had already seen the look in her eyes.

'Ah, so you've already . . .?'

'Well, yes.'

'And?'

'Julia!'

'Was he any good or not?'

'I'm not going to give you a blow-by-blow account, but it was pretty terrific, especially for a first time.' She thought for a moment, then added, 'It's a funny thing, though, I felt dreadfully self-conscious. I mean, it's odd going to bed with someone new. I kept wondering what he thought of me . . . it was just so different to how it used to be with Philip. I mean, I reacted more and in a strange sort of way I think that that was as much to do with me as it was to do with him.'

'That's because you're feeling like your old self again. You've got your confidence back.'

'Do you think so?'

'Absolutely. Nothing worse than feeling stuck in a relationship for buggering up your libido.'

'Do you think that's what happened with Philip? I never did figure out exactly why he left. Clare . . . well, she's not what you'd call an oil painting is she?'

272

'Oh! That's what I meant to tell you. The latest is that she's gone off with somebody else.'

'You're kidding?'

'That's what I heard. I thought the news would give you a laugh.'

'Do you know, I *thought* he was being unbelievably nice to me that last time he had the kids for the week-end.'

'He'd probably ask you to feel sorry for him if he had the nerve.'

'I do a bit.'

'God, you're exasperating! How can you possibly feel sorry for a rat like that?'

'He's the father of my children. I guess I'll always feel something for him.'

'Well, don't you dare let him wheedle his way back.'

'No danger of that. There was a time when I might have considered having him back, but I've got my own life now, and I like it that way.'

'What,' said Ken, poking the box with the edge of his foot, 'is this?'

'A job lot of plates, what's it look like?'

'I thought you went to the auction to buy a mirror.'

'I did buy a mirror, but I bought these too.'

'Why?'

'Because this was in with them.' Sally held a finely printed jug with gilt decoration under his nose.

'It's slightly damaged.'

'Yes, but look at the pattern.' She traced the Oriental picture of a fisherman and boat with her finger. 'Irresistible, isn't it?'

'I think I could have passed on it.'

'Well, you'd have missed a bargain.'

'Oh?'

'It's Caughley, I've checked.'

'Meaning?'

'It's worth about three hundred pounds and I only paid fifteen for it. Plus the plates, of course.'

'So you're going to start dealing in ceramics, too?'

'Might as well have a second string to my bow. I need to have some smaller pieces dotted around the shop anyway and things like this are ideal, though I think I'll keep this little fellow for myself.'

Ken shook his head in a gesture of resignation. 'What did I tell you about not getting attached to things?'

'I know, but one little jug won't harm.'

'You'll be saying that about a whole collection of stuff soon.'

'No, I won't. I can be strong minded when I have to be.'

'What are you going to do with the plates?'

'I'll probably put them on the dresser at home. Blue and white looks nice in a kitchen.'

'I suppose you haven't done badly for fifteen quid, then. Any other little indulgences to report?'

Sally grinned. 'I did buy a box of walking sticks, but I sold them on in my lunch break.'

'Good girl, that's more like it.'

'A bunch of us went over to that pub across from the auction room . . .'

'So you're getting along with the crowd?'

'It would seem so.' The pub was called The Whippet Inn, and she'd had to put up with some pretty puerile remarks from the men, but she hadn't let that spoil her day.

'So what did you give for the mirror, in the end?'

'Fifteen hundred.'

'Not bad.'

'Fortunately for me, no one else was particularly interested in it.'

'What were they interested in?'

'A very nice George III breakfront sideboard, for one

thing. A group of the Brighton boys were putting pressure on me to lay off it.'

'And did you?'

'I put in a couple of bids just to hack them off, but didn't push it too far. They were pretty threatening and a lot bigger than me.'

'Sods,' Ken frowned. 'Well, don't let them get you involved in a ring, whatever happens.'

'I've been meaning to ask you about this ring business. What's the point, exactly?'

'Oh, it's a mug's game, but basically it works in one of two ways. Sometimes there's one dealer who's desperate to buy a certain piece, so he pays the rest to stay clear. But more often than not, what'll happen is that a group of dealers get together to buy something at a reduced rate. Either way, everyone in the ring gets a cut of money, either for sitting around and doing nothing, or by dividing up the profit they make on whatever it is they've bought when the piece is sold on.'

'I can understand how the first bit works, but not the second. I don't see how you can be certain of buying something at a reduced rate at an auction.'

'It's fairly easy if you're working as a team. All the dealers in the ring have to do is decide what price they're willing to pay for such-and-such and then pick their man to do the bidding. Since the rest show little or no interest in whatever the piece is, when it comes up, the auctioneer can't get any competition going on the floor. He'll get whatever price he can, usually a lot less than he'd hoped for, and the people in the ring end up with a bargain.'

'Oh, that's how it works.'

'Yes, all very neat. But I tell you, stay away from rings. For one thing they're illegal, even though no one bothers much about them, and for another thing you won't come out any better off for joining one. If you take it on percentage profits, you'll find that the single dealer does just as well in a year, overall, as the man who works with a ring.'

Sally thought for a while, 'There's one thing I saw today that I still don't understand. The same thing happened a couple of months ago, but I forgot to ask you about it.'

'Oh? What was that?'

'Well, the first time it was to do with a table, and at today's sale it was a screen, but in both cases I overheard two dealers discussing the piece concerned and then when it came up for sale, one started bidding. Now, that might have been something to do with these rings, from your description, but one part of it doesn't fit what you were saying. The one man bidding went so far and then dropped out when somebody else entered from the floor. Next thing, the dealer he'd been talking the piece over with previously entered the bidding and ended up buying it. And yet, and this is the curious bit, when I heard them chatting about the sale later, the second dealer was talking to his mate as if it was *him* who had bought the goods.'

Ken smiled. 'I can tell you what happened there. Your first man was obviously the one picked by the ring to do the bidding, but what they weren't expecting was for some other buyer to materialise on the floor. It happens from time to time when a private buyer is interested in a piece. He'll suddenly put his hand up and throw a spanner in the works as far as the ring's concerned.'

'I still don't . . .'

'Hang on, I haven't finished yet. You know how I said that the ring fixes a price that they're willing to pay for a piece before the bidding starts?'

'Yes.'

'Well, the price they pick will be the one that will give them a good profit on resale, right?'

'Yes.'

'So if a stranger enters the bidding and takes the price up further than they wanted, the profit is diminished.'

'Yes, but it doesn't explain what the second dealer was doing.'

'The second dealer isn't in the ring but he has made a private arrangement with the first. You see, whoever gets picked to do the bidding for the ring is the one who carries the can if anything goes wrong. Let's say the ring's decided that the screen you were talking about can be bought for around two thousand pounds but they know it'll sell on for more like three thousand. They agree a profit margin of a thousand pounds, which, if it's split say five ways, gives them each two hundred pounds. Now once that profit is agreed, the man who's picked to do the bidding *must* give the others two hundred pounds each, whether he's able to get the screen for the notional two thousand or not.'

'So once the bidding goes above two thousand, he's operating at a loss?'

'Precisely. Every fifty or a hundred quid it goes over, is fifty or a hundred he either has to make up on resale or dip into his own pocket for. And this is where his friend the second dealer comes into things. The only way the man doing the ring's bidding can get out of his obligation to the others is by losing the piece to another buyer. He makes a deal with his mate on the side to be that other buyer and in so doing, ends up splitting his profit with one man at a reasonable rate instead of five at a punitive rate.'

'God, what a business! I had no idea it was so complex.'

'Ah, there's all sorts of wrinkles in this trade. If you stick around long enough, you'll come across stranger ones than that.'

'Go on, tell me some more.'

'Only if you swear never to try them.'

Sally held up her right hand. 'Guides' honour.'

'Well, one of the favourites around here is faking up bills of lading.'

'What for?'

'Sending things abroad. See, there's no VAT on exports, because antiques count as second-hand goods. Ideally, you get your invoice – manufactured, if need be, by photocopying a real one – make out a nice list of items you want to send – to America, let's say – then you pass it to the agent who's arranging the shipping and he gets it stamped up by customs. Now, the customs men are pushed to their limits most of the time, so on the day your box of itemised things arrives, they just scan the stamped-up invoice and pass the box straight through.'

'What, without checking it?'

'Of course. They haven't got the time or the manpower to check every single box that comes their way. So unless they've had a tip off, they're very unlikely to open yours in order to verify the contents.'

'So you could be exporting more than was on the list?'

'Or less, or nothing at all. The box could be full of sand and nobody would notice. I've known people pull that trick and get away with it.'

'But why would you want to send an empty box abroad?'

'Because you really want to sell the goods here. If you make a sale inside the UK, you have to keep a record of the sale and cough up the VAT when the time comes. The more valuable something is, the more VAT there is to pay. So what you do is make it look like your piece has gone abroad – in which case, as I say, there's no VAT to pay and then the day of reckoning comes, your books are ostensibly up to date and as clean as a whistle. On the quiet, though, you'll have sold this piece back into the trade and thus netted all of the profits.'

'It sounds a terribly risky thing to do.'

'Only if your VAT man gets wind of it, and again, he's

highly unlikely to do so. As in the case of the customs man and the box, your average VAT man has not got the time to poke his nose into everything. What's more, if he wants to look into something, he has to justify the expense of manning up to do so to his boss. These people are public servants, remember, and departmental heads have to keep a keen eye on what's being spent. So unless there's very good evidence that a dealer's up to no good, he won't get his collar felt by the powers that be.'

'God, it's the first time that I've been tempted to feel sorry for the VAT man. I mean, there he is trying to do his job and not only does he get nicely thwarted by the limitations of the system but he gets disliked for what he's doing by the general public to boot.'

'It's not a job that many people would like to admit they had, it's true.' Ken shrugged. 'Still, the best thing is to make sure you've got a clean bill of health to put in front of any of these people, and that means dealing honestly. It may be boring and old-fashioned, it may mean you have to sit and grind your teeth when you see somebody making money hand over fist by using tricks that would be all too easy to copy, but on the whole, it's the best thing.'

'You know, that's one of the things I like about you best.' Sally smiled. 'You have principles. High standards and principles. You're a breath of fresh air compared with the oiks I've been around today.'

'They have their code of practice, I have mine. We're none of us angels in this business but I like my conscience clear enough to sleep abed at nights.'

'Ken, have you always been so upright and moral?'

'I've done my best, in professional terms.'

'What about privately?'

'What sort of a question is that?'

'A nosy one. You don't have to tell me.'

He looked at her for a moment, wondering how it was

that she had the uncanny knack of putting him on the spot and how, instead of avoiding giving away personal details, as he would have done with almost anyone else, he always felt inclined to answer her questions candidly.

'I've behaved badly enough in my time,' he said at last, 'why do you ask?'

'Don't know, really. I suppose in some ways I still haven't got the measure of you.'

'You mean you haven't worked out why I keep hanging around.'

'I don't know why you would want to keep helping me for no particular reward,' she replied, though she had more than an inkling as to what he felt for her.

'Does there have to be a reward involved?'

'It's what most people expect.'

'You just build your business and make it prosper. That'll be good enough for me.'

'Still no strings, then?'

'Still no strings.'

Sally gave him a hug. 'I love you, do you know that?'

'I love you too,' he said. Only he meant it.

18

'Well, how did it go?' Heather glanced up over the rim of her spectacles. From the look on Sally's face, it was pretty obvious what the answer was. She watched her slump, frustrated, into a chair and put her head in her hands.

'Do you know what I don't understand?' said Sally, slowly surfacing. 'How it is these people can let you turn out and go all that way on a wild goose chase? You'd think they'd 'phone you and let you know.'

'Don't tell me it's happened again?'

'Yes. That's the third time now, and it's getting really stupid. Maybe Ken was right. Following up answers to adverts is just a waste of time.'

'So you didn't get anything?'

'Pipped to the post by the knocker boys again. Anyone would think they were following me around.'

'Maybe they are.'

'Oh, come on, even I can't get that paranoid.'

'It does seem strange that they seem to arrive five minutes before you do.'

Sally sighed. 'Luck of the draw, I guess. From what I've heard from the general chit-chat, they target a district and then just go from house to house on the basis that in any given street, at least one person's got something worth having.'

'It's an odd way to work.'

'Pays off, though, doesn't it? In this case they landed a Hepplewhite card table and a Victorian chaise longue for a measley five hundred quid.'

'You'd think that people would know that those sorts of things were valuable.'

'Most people don't have a clue, do they? I mean, look at me. I wouldn't have known that Dad's table was worth as much as it was, if it hadn't been for meeting Ken. If somebody had knocked on the door a week previously and offered me a thousand pounds for it, I'd have taken it like a shot and probably felt well pleased.'

'I suppose that you are going to get ripped off if you let a total stranger into the house.'

Sally leaned forward. 'That's another thing that surprises me. You'd think people would be more cautious. It's one thing being ripped off but much worse things happen. There've been two or three cases recently where women have been murdered in their own homes, apparently in cold blood – or at least for no good reason that the police can ascertain. Someone must have threatened them or persuaded their way into their houses some other way. It never ceases to amaze me how trusting people are. All they need is someone in a uniform or with a half likely-looking calling card and in through the front door they go.'

'There does seem to be a lot of violence these days,' Heather nodded, 'though it's hard to tell whether things have actually got worse or whether it's just that there's more press coverage.'

'Well, I wish someone would do an article on the knocker boys, and not just for my sake. It's dreadful what they get up to. Fancy softening people up by telling them that some terrible old bit of furniture is worth a lot of money and then picking up the really worthwhile pieces for next to nothing on the back of that excitement. And what narks me, even more than the duplicity involved in making the deal, is that the "knockers" act as if they were doing these people a great favour by taking whatever it is off their hands. Bloody disgraceful it is.'

'I still find it difficult to believe that people are taken in by these shysters.'

'It's the usual thing. Once you start talking money, people's eyes light up. From that point on, they'll sell you almost anything.' Sally got up and walked aimlessly down the room. 'Oh, well, I suppose that I'll just have to concentrate more on auctions. Trouble is I don't like the idea of leaving the shop closed too often, but I can't be in two places at once.'

'I've been thinking about that.'

'Have you?'

'Well, I've had a pleasant enough time minding the shop today. Wouldn't mind helping you out as and when you needed.'

'Oh, Heather, it's very good of you, but . . . well, you've done so much for me already and you have got your own place to run.'

'I know, but it's not as if I'm overwhelmed with prospective customers. I actually find it quite relaxing to sit here and sketch and it does have the advantage of getting me into a different environment, which is good for the creative juices.'

'You mean it?'

'Of course I do. I might as well sit here as in Steyning. Anyhow, once we get those pictures up, it'll almost be like being in the gallery.'

'Did you bring them with you?'

'Yes, they're behind the desk here,' Heather bent and lifted up a couple of framed water colours. 'There's the four from

283

that set you liked and I brought a pair of portraits too. Thought they'd make a change from the pastoral scenes.'

Sally went to take a look. 'I haven't seen this before,' she said, as Heather unwrapped one of the portraits.

'It's been gathering dust for years. In actual fact, I'd almost forgotten about it but then I was reminded – you know, when we were doing the cleaning and we were talking about Paris?'

'Yes.'

'Well, I did this then. It's that girl I told you about. The one with the baby.'

Sally saw the pale features, turned in profile, and thought how good and wistful she looked. 'It's lovely,' she said, 'so delicate and fresh. It's almost as if she belongs in another era, the age of Renoir or Degas.'

'I was experimenting with Impressionism at the time. I loved the effect of light and movement that you could create. I did go on to Pointillism afterwards, but didn't like it as much. You have to try out many styles of painting before you're ready to develop a method of your own.' She picked up the second package. 'This other portrait I've brought was done about ten years after this one. You'll see straight away that I'd started to get my own style by then.'

'It's my father!' Sally was genuinely surprised. She'd recognised the face instantly, though it was much more round than she'd remembered it and, of course, he'd had more hair in those days.

'I thought you should have him around to keep an eye on you.' Heather smiled. 'I think he'll bring you luck.'

'We'll give him pride of place,' said Sally, 'right in the centre, over the trestle table, how about that?'

'Yes, I think he'd go well there.'

'I'll get the hammer and picture hooks.'

'And the stepladders.'

Sally went to the cubby-hole at the back of the shop and fished out the necessary equipment.

'Might as well put them all up while we're at it,' she said. 'Where do you think we should put the water colours?'

'Somewhere where it's light. Behind the desk here would be all right.'

'I'd like to have them more prominent than that.'

'The opposite wall, then. They could go two and two either side of the bureau bookcase.'

'That's a good idea.' Sally pulled the trestle table out and manoeuvred the stepladders behind it. 'Pass Dad up, will you? I'll hold him up and you tell me when the positioning's okay.'

They juggled the picture about until it seemed to be in the right spot.

'Hammer and nails,' Sally called, holding out a hand.

'You sure there aren't any wires in that wall?'

'No, but there isn't a power point in the skirting board down there, is there?'

'No.'

'Should be fine, then,' she placed the picture hook and drove the nail home, 'there.'

'Don't let the whole weight go on it at first,' said Heather, handing the portrait back to Sally. 'You can never trust old buildings, the fixing might come straight out of the wall.'

'It felt pretty solid as it went in.'

'I'd still test it.'

Sally held the picture tentatively for a moment, then took her hands away.

'Whoopee!' she said, thrilled with herself. 'How about that? Looks great, doesn't it?'

'Just right.'

'Now for the other one. What's it called, by the way?'

'Claudine.'

'Claudine,' Sally repeated. 'Perfect.' She came back down

the stepladder. 'Do you know, I think I'm going to have to invest in some picture lights. The lantern doesn't do them justice.'

'It's very pretty, though.'

'Isn't it? Daniel bought it for me, wasn't that sweet of him?'

'I'm glad to see he's got some taste.'

'Rather a lot of it, actually. You should see his house, fantastic place.'

'So I hear.'

'You do?'

'The children told me.'

'Oh.' Sally was slightly embarrassed. 'Yes, well, they certainly enjoy his swimming pool.'

'Hmm.'

'Oh, come on, it's nice for them to have something different to do. Nice for me, too. Makes a change to be pampered all week-end.'

'Just so long as you know what you're getting into.'

'I'm not getting into anything, I'm just having a good time. Wish you didn't make it sound like such a problem.'

'I'm just a bit worried that you could get struck on him too fast.'

'I'm not struck on him,' Sally fibbed. 'Anyhow, I can't exactly present the children with a string of men. Imagine what they would think – what their father would think, for that matter.'

'He's hardly in a position to cast stones.'

'Nevertheless.'

'I suppose you're right. Perhaps I judged Daniel too hastily. In any case, just so long as he treats you well.'

'Couldn't be better. It's rather wonderful to have some romance in my life again, makes me feel that life's worth living.'

'You've got plenty of reasons to feel that way, now.'

'Yes, but you know what I mean.'

'Yes, I do.' Heather looked up towards the picture of Sally's father. 'What would you think if I told you that I'd found someone myself?'

'You've got a boyfriend?'

'You can hardly call a man of fifty-six a boy.'

'Heather!'

'Do you think it's too soon?'

'Not at all, I think it's terrific.'

'Honestly?'

'Of course. Why, were you worried?'

'In a strange sort of way.'

'Well, you're not exactly ready for your bath chair yet, are you? I didn't expect you to stay on your own for ever, just because of Dad.'

'You don't disapprove, then?'

'Don't be daft.' Sally gave her a kiss. 'Oh, good, we can swap notes, now.'

Heather laughed. 'I'm sure mine will be very staid by comparison to yours.'

'Who is he, this man? And where did you meet him, anyway?'

'He's an old friend of Jean's. You know our monthly luncheon outings? Well, there was the usual gang of us and we decided to go to the oyster bar. He happened to be there with a colleague, and so we were introduced.'

'Are you seeing much of him?'

'We go out about once a week, Fridays or Saturdays usually. The rest of the time he's knee-deep in work.'

'What does he do?'

'He's a solicitor.'

'Might know Julia, then.'

'Could do. His practice is somewhere in central Brighton, the Old Steine, I think.'

'Julia's lot are just round the corner from there, in Duke's Court.'

'Do you see her very often?'

'More than I used to. She pops in from time to time when she's going out for a sandwich at lunchtimes.'

'That's good.'

'Yes, I certainly feel more part of things now. I think my brain had started to atrophy before I went into business. It was being stuck out in the cottage all day with nil stimulation that was doing it.'

'I was beginning to go a bit stale myself. Still, meeting Jack's been a great boost.'

'I'm so glad.' Sally smiled. 'So now we've both got someone to spoil us.'

'For the time being, anyway.'

'You never know, great oaks from little acorns grow.'

'Gosh, I'm not up for anything very serious yet.'

'Neither am I, but a person can speculate.'

'You really must learn to take your time, you know. And I still think that Daniel's, well . . .'

'Too flashy? I know.'

'I don't mean to be unkind.'

'Don't worry, I understand. But appearances aren't everything.'

'I suppose it's natural to be suspicious of car dealers.'

'Well, he's not your average car dealer, is he? Classic cars are highly specialised. Then there's the 'planes, too.'

'Don't remind me. He's not got you up in one of those things yet, I hope?'

'No, but I wouldn't mind a hop over to the Continent if it was an offer.'

'He flies abroad too?'

'Every couple of weeks or so, if there's the business. And just occasionally, he brings back more than a box of spares for some vehicle that I've never heard of.' Sally went to the back of the shop and brought out the two Dutch paintings that Daniel had given her. 'What do you think of these?'

Heather blinked. 'Oh, Sally!'

'Gorgeous, aren't they?'

'Stunning. But you're not going to put them in here, are you?'

'Why not? They're antiques.'

'I know, but . . .'

'I bet Ken'll be green with envy when he sees them.'

'Why, have you fallen out?'

'No, but he gave me a drubbing over a chest-of-drawers that I bought and even though he was right, it'd be nice to prove that I know what I'm looking at at least some of the time.'

'They're too valuable to keep in a place like this,' said Heather, looking from canvas to canvas. 'Aren't you worried that someone might be tempted to steal them?'

'Daniel's going to put in a burglar alarm for me. I won't hang them until he's done it.'

'I should worry, burglar alarm or no.'

'That's all anyone else has got around here. There must be hundreds of thousands of pounds worth of valuables worth robbing in The Lanes, if you felt so inclined. I don't see why my pictures should be picked on any more than anything else.'

'I think I'd be taking them down and putting them in a safe every night, nonetheless.'

'I haven't got a safe yet. Anyhow, they'll be kept out of sight for the present.'

'Well, I hope you've got them well insured.'

'A man's coming over to talk about it next week.'

'I'd get him round sooner if I were you. And don't forget, list every single item and make sure you get each covered for the replacement value.'

'I will, I will.'

'Just be sure you do. You'll be sunk without trace if anything happens to your stock.'

'Hold out your hands and close your eyes.'

'I'm not sure I trust you.'

'Think I'm going to take advantage of you, do you?'

'It is your favourite time of day for things nefarious,' Sally giggled as Daniel made a move to grab her by the waist.

'I'll get round to the afternoon delight in a minute.'

'Not today you won't, I've got places to be.'

'Oh, go on, just a quick one to send you off with a smile.'

'Since when were you ever quick?'

'You complaining?'

'No,' Sally laughed, and let him gather her into his arms.

'Come. Let me ravish you,' he said, pulling her into a passionate kiss. Sally began to relent.

'Put me down,' she said, half-heartedly.

'Not until you promise to come to bed.'

'Oh, don't be rotten. I've got to be in Arundel by two and I won't get back in time to pick up the children if I make myself late.'

'What about tonight, then?'

'Too late to organise a baby-sitter for that now.'

'I could just come over to the cottage. Tell you what, why don't I bring over a take-away, to save the worry of cooking, and a bottle of wine? That way we can make a long and cosy evening of it without anything to think about but what to have for afters.' He nibbled her neck to reinforce the intentional tease.

'You know how I feel about playing on home territory,' she said, trying to pull herself away.

'I'll wait until the kids have gone to bed.'

'What about in the morning?'

'I'll slip out before they're up. I've got a seven o'clock start, anyway.' He kissed her again. 'Say yes.'

'All right, but what if they hear?'

'We'll stay downstairs. I've been fantasising about you and that hearth rug.'

'Daniel!'

'What's wrong with that?'

'It's wicked.'

'No more so than doing the same thing in a bed. Anyway, it's nice to ring the changes a bit. You might get bored with me otherwise.'

'Don't think there's any chance of that.' She smiled. The idea of making love with an element of risk had its appeal.

'It's a deal, then?'

'Yes.'

'Good. Can I give you your surprise now?'

'If you get much closer you might without meaning to.'

He spanked her on the rear. 'Don't tempt me. Now hold out your hands and close your eyes like I asked.'

She did. There was the familiar rustle of money as she waited.

'You can open them now.'

She looked down to see a bundle of twenty-pound notes.

'What's this?'

'It's your chest-of-drawers.'

'You got rid of it?'

'Said I would, didn't I?'

'Yes, but . . .'

'It's only two hundred quid but better than nothing, eh?'

'Why, it's wonderful. I thought I'd end up putting it on the tip.'

'You don't put anything on the tip whilst I'm around. Could sell sand to the Saudis, I could.'

'But where did you sell it?'

'Up North. I took it in the trailer when I went to deliver the Zita spares.'

'Eh?'

'The ones I went to Belgium for, remember.'

'Oh, yes. I'd forgotten the name of the car. Never heard of it before.'

'Well, there's only two in the world.'

'Difficult to get parts, then?'

'You find them, if you ask enough people. Oh, I've found something else that you might like.' He took her hand and led her out of the kitchen, down the hall and into his office.

'I don't know how you can find anything in here,' said Sally, glancing at the papers that seemed to be strewn everywhere, including the floor.

'I have a filing system of sorts.'

'Glad I don't have to use it.' She watched as he rummaged through some boxes that were lined up by his desk.

'Here they are,' he said, pulling out two bunches of screwed up newspaper. Sally took one and unwrapped it.

'A harlequin,' she said, turning the highly coloured piece in her hand. 'What's the other?'

'Open it and see.'

'Oh, isn't she pretty?' The partner piece, also in yellow, black and turquoise garb, had been damaged but restored.

'Columbine, I think they call her, don't they?' Daniel asked.

'I'm not sure.'

'You'll have to look it up.'

'They're very good.'

'I thought so, not that I know much about porcelain.'

'Where did they come from.'

'Private house.'

'Oh?'

He shrugged. 'Just one of those things you pick up along the way.'

She had a feeling that there was something more to it than that, but didn't like to press.

'You could put them in that display cabinet,' he continued, 'if you decide to buy it, that is.'

'The one I'm going to see today? Yes, I probably will buy it if he'll come down a bit on the price.'

'What's he want for it again?'

'Thirteen hundred.'

'Take a grand in notes and offer him seven hundred for starters.'

'That's not much more than half of what he's asking.'

'Look, you wave seven hundred under his nose and let him negotiate you up. If you make it slow and painful enough, you'll probably get it for eight or eight and a half.'

'You reckon?'

'Sure. The trick is to look as if you're in agony, take it as far as eight hundred and then say that that's all you've got. If he's not happy, make as if to leave. I'll make a small bet that he won't let you go without money changing hands.'

'Well, thirteen hundred is a bit much for a trade price.'

'He knows that. He also knows that it could be a long time before some punter comes along to give him the price as stated. Turnover is the name of the game. What he actually wants is to get rid of the cabinet as fast as he can.'

'I'll have to remember that piece of psychology so that I'm armed and ready when someone uses it on me.' She turned the two porcelain figurines in her hands thoughtfully. 'What do I owe you for these, by the way?'

'Forget it.'

'You can't just give them to me.'

'Why not?'

'It doesn't seem right. I mean, you bought me the lantern when I first started up, then you found me the car and I still haven't paid you for that yet . . .'

'You don't like feeling indebted to me, is that it?'

'It's not that,' she denied, although there was a large element of truth in what he'd said, 'it's just, well, if you're

293

going to give me things that I'm going to sell on, we should have a more business-like arrangement – like we have on the paintings, that sort of thing.'

'All right.' He could sense that the issue was important to her, as a matter of pride. 'Why don't you find out what they are and how much they're worth and then, when you sell them, give me whatever seems appropriate?'

'But you must have some idea what they're worth otherwise you wouldn't have bought them.'

'It was pure guesswork. They had the right look, so I took them.'

'But what did you pay, for heaven's sake?'

'There's no accurate answer to that,' he fumbled. 'They were part of another deal, so it's hard to say.'

The way that Daniel avoided her gaze made Sally slightly uneasy, but the explanation seemed plausible on the face of it. Plenty of other traders swapped goods for goods, or even cash and goods, part and part, although there was an element at the lower end of the market who'd trade in virtually anything, including stuff that had fallen off the back of a lorry.

'Okay, then,' she said, although she didn't entirely like the idea. 'I'll check them out and price them and give you a cut of the proceeds when they're sold.'

'Fine.'

Sally carefully rewrapped the figures while her mind moved on to the display cabinet she was hoping to buy.

'You up to much this afternoon?'

'Going over to Shoreham. Someone wants to try out the Aztec.'

'Thinking of selling it?'

'No, but the chap's looking for a light aircraft. He was talking a single-engine affair, but I thought I could probably inch him up to a twin, once he'd flown one.'

'I take it that the difference in price is worth the effort?'

'Naturally. But more to the point, I know where there's a Piper Comanche that needs a buyer.'

'Nice one.'

'If I pull it off. Anyhow, I thought I'd take him out Kent way, probably drop in at Rochester. He lives near there somewhere.'

Sally's attention had wandered while he was talking. There was a desk diary on the table, lying open at the day's date. At the bottom of the page, where space was left open for evening appointments, there was a curious note. From where she was standing, it looked like the letter 'J' with a question mark after it.

'. . . anyhow, I'll be back in time for supper,' Daniel continued, 'probably come over between nine and nine-thirty, if that's okay?'

'Yes,' she said, rather hastily, 'the children should be well settled by then.'

The incident bothered her all the way over to Arundel, though she tried to think of any other reason for the cryptic note than the one that had immediately sprung to mind. Another woman. The spectre of suspicion followed her through the rest of the day, despite every effort to shake it off. By evening, she was still unhappy, reliving, detail for detail, the events that had led up to her discovering her husband's betrayal.

You're over-sensitive, she told herself, just looking for problems because of past experience. But somehow she failed to convince herself that her fears were unreasonable. She sighed over the washing up, swore at the cat when it mistakenly got under her feet, and generally banged things about in an irritated fashion.

'What's wrong, Mummy?' Jonathan had noticed his mother's discontent and left his knights in armour mid-battle to come to her side.

'Who's winning today?' she asked, deflecting the question. 'The goodies or the baddies?'

'The baddies,' he replied, but went on gazing earnestly at her face. 'Why are you sad?'

'I'm not sad.'

'Are you angry because I didn't finish my pizza?'

She stopped feeling sorry for herself and bent to give him a kiss. 'No, I'm not angry with you, darling. I'm just a bit tired, that's all.'

'Why are you tired?'

'Because I've been working.'

He looked at her, curiously. 'When will you stop buying things?'

Sally smiled. 'I don't just buy things, you know, I sell them too.'

'So that you can have enough money to buy us some toys?'

'That's right.' She hugged him, remembering all the times past that she'd had to tell the children that she couldn't afford toys any more; it was clothes and food, nothing else. 'It's your birthday soon, then you'll have lots of toys.'

'Can I have a Lego castle? It's got five armour mens.'

'Men, not mens,' she corrected. 'Yes, if it's not too expensive.'

'Daddy says he'll buy me a Mighty Max shark.'

'Does he? That's nice.'

'How many days 'til I'm going to his house again?'

'Three.'

'Goody!'

'Do you have a good time at Daddy's?'

'Yes.' He seemed to be thinking about it. 'But why doesn't he have a swimming pool?'

'Well, not everyone has one. We don't, do we?'

'Daniel does.'

'Yes.'

296

'When can we go to his house?'

'Next weekend. Another ten days.'

'Ten?' His eyes were wide. It sounded a very long time to him.

'That's all right, isn't it?'

'But why can't I play with his dog? I want to play with his dog.'

'Daniel's dog doesn't really like children.'

'Will he bite me?'

'I don't think so,' she said, though she wasn't very sure, 'just he's a guard dog and guard dogs are meant to frighten people.'

'Why?'

'To protect your home.'

'Is it in case the burglars come?'

'Yes.'

'Only bad people steal things, don't they, Mummy? I'm not bad, I'm a good boy.'

'Of course you are, you're Mummy's treasure.'

'And Matthew.'

'And Matthew too.'

The child cheered up. 'Will you play sword fighting with me?'

'Not right now, I'm busy.'

'Please?'

'Why don't you play with Matthew? Where is he, up in the bedroom?'

'He's playing pirates, but I don't want to play pirates, I want to play armours.'

'Well, why don't you go up and ask if he'll sword fight with you? Knights in armour and pirates both fought with swords, you know.'

'But he won't play properly. He'll cry.'

'Don't be too rough, then.'

Jonathan trailed off towards the kitchen door. 'Mummy?'

'Yes.'

'Will I be big and strong when I grow up?'

'Of course you will.'

'Will I be like Daddy?'

'Well, yes, I suppose.'

'Will I be like Daniel?' His voice had an excited tone that Sally thought puzzling.

'Why? Would you like to be like him?'

'I want big muscles.'

She laughed. 'You have to do lots of exercises to get those.'

'*Then* will I be strong?'

'Yes.'

He started to trail off again. 'Mummy?'

'What now?'

'Can I really go in his 'plane?'

'Daniel's 'plane?'

'He said I could.'

'Did he?'

'He said I could go in the one with four wings, this one.' He pulled a miniature yellow biplane out of his trouser pocket.

'Where did you get that?'

'Daniel gave it to me.'

'Are you sure?' She remembered, now, having seen the toy on the kitchen windowsill and imagined it was a keepsake.

'He said I could have it, really.'

'That was nice of him.' Sally smiled, thinking how sweet it was of Daniel to have given the child something of his own.

'When I grow up, I want to be a pilot.'

'You might change your mind about that.'

He'd become absorbed in the toy and wasn't listening.

Sally was beginning to get exasperated. 'Look, darling, why don't you go and play with your 'plane or something? I've got a lot to do.'

298

He finally found his way out of the kitchen door and she could hear him playing at the foot of the stairs.

'Curse you, Red Baron,' he was saying in one voice. And: 'I haf you, now, Englander,' in another, between appropriate dive-bombing noises.

Sally started to laugh. Whoever did he get that off? she wondered. Then she realised that it had to be Daniel. The thought made her feel warm inside.

You are a silly so-and-so, she said to herself. And suddenly the cares of the day paled into insignificance.

19

The saleroom at Christie's was full of Austrians and Germans showing solidarity for treasures of their national art. Ken had been leaning against the wall giving minimal attention to the bidding. Most of his interest was taken up by the quality and range of canvases on view. It was the best display of German pictures that he'd seen at auction in a very long time. An impressive number of Expressionist masters were arranged tastefully alongside some fine examples of nineteenth-century Romanticism. His eye settled on a small but beautifully executed painting of a fishing boat at night. It was by Caspar David Friedrich, one of Ken's all-time favourites, and a theme typical of the artist, who was particularly known for his nocturnal settings and wistful imagery. He went over to admire the detail, becoming so entranced by the picture that he didn't notice that the man who was standing a few paces away was one of his oldest friends.

'Wonderful, isn't it?' Tony's voice was so familiar that Ken didn't have to shift his gaze to make a reply.

'An absolute gift at four to five hundred thousand,' he said. 'Got your eye on it?'

'I think I'll bid but from what I hear, I'm up against some

stiff opposition.' Tony moved closer. 'Haven't seen you in a while. How's it going?'

'Pretty well, thanks. You?'

'Can't complain.'

'Jon okay?'

'Fine. Whiling away what's left of the long holiday planning his new philosophy course. Absolutely cock-a-hoop he is, thanks to the Pope's new book. Given him acres of material to go at.'

'I can imagine. Had to smile at the "Descartes killed God" part of His Holiness's theory.'

'Yes, that really got Jon going. Still, the discovery of consciousness did upset the apple cart as far as the church was concerned.'

'Very inconvenient, I'm sure. Don't want your believers going around thinking for themselves.'

Tony had moved along to view a study of a woman in an off-the-shoulder gown. 'This is the one I'd really like,' he said. 'Look at her, you can almost feel her anticipating who's going to ask for the next Strauss waltz.'

Ken glanced at the picture, then at the catalogue in his hand. 'Menzel . . . Mmm, gorgeous. You might be able to pick that up at a good price.'

'What do you think it'll go to? Forty, fifty grand?'

'Probably. Everything's been bid to saleroom records so far.'

'Nevertheless, they're going cheap by comparison to their French contemporaries. I couldn't believe that Max Liebermann selling for six hundred thousand. If that had been a Renoir or a Monet . . .'

'Ah, but you know how obsessed the market is with Paris as the home of all modern life at the turn of the century.'

'Well, I'm definitely going to push the boat out for that Menzel. I think it'll be a good investment.'

'You just here for yourself?'

'No, I've got a couple of commissions. You?'

'Same.' Ken nodded towards a canvas a couple of feet away. 'I had a particularly urgent demand for that Spitzweg from one of my London clients. Bit of a nuisance, really. I'd got something else lined up for today.'

'Another auction?'

'No, a view around an important house.'

'Anywhere I should know?'

'Don't think so, unless the name Kirkby Mote means anything to you.'

'It seems familiar . . . hang on, it's not somewhere near the Shropshire border, is it?'

'Yes, it is.'

'But I thought the owner was something of a recluse?'

'You could say that.'

'You must have good contacts to have got in there.'

'It took a year of gentle persuasion, but I made it eventually.'

'I'm impressed.' Tony seemed to think about it for a moment. 'It's a shame that you've had to put off your appointment because of today.'

'It was too big an opportunity to put off so I ended up sending someone to make a recce on my behalf.'

'Someone you trust, obviously?'

'Yes,' Ken said, though he'd been worrying about it all day. 'I trust her.'

'Her?'

'Sally. You know, Sally Blythe.'

'Oh, yes, I remember now. The one you've got business connections with.' Tony's stress on the word 'business' was intentionally arch.

'And that's all, before you start jumping to the same conclusions as everyone else,' said Ken, quickly.

'I'm glad, for your sake.'

302

'Why?' there was something in his friend's tone that Ken didn't like.

'Not for me to tell tales out of school.'

'Well, you've started now, so you may as well go the whole hog.'

Tony looked at him seriously. 'You're really not involved with her on a physical level?'

'No. How many times do I have to say it to make myself clear?'

'Do you know much about her private life?'

'I assume she has one, but I don't inquire.'

'So you don't know who she's going out with?'

'Of course not. Does it matter?' Actually, it mattered to Ken quite a lot, but he'd tried to push the thought to the back of his mind.

'Ever heard of a Daniel Wiseman?'

'Not that I can recall.'

'He deals in classic cars and 'planes.'

'So?'

'He dabbles in antiques, too.'

'That's not so surprising. What's your point?'

'From what I've been told, it's a pretty sure fact that he's got links with racketeers.'

'What sort of links?'

'The sort that keep just one step ahead of the law.'

Ken frowned. 'Where did you hear this?'

'Picked it up on the gay network.'

'The connection being?'

'A rather nasty incident involving a friend of a friend.'

'You wouldn't care to be more precise, would you?'

'We'll have to talk somewhere more private.'

The two men moved away from the paintings to a position at the back of the saleroom that allowed them to keep tabs on the proceedings whilst conducting a low-key conversation.

'You know Sandy, our artist friend, don't you?' Tony started.

'Only by association with you and Jon.'

'Yes, well, we only got to know him through Suzanne. They have a sort of "safe date" arrangement.'

'He's safely gay, you mean.'

'Exactly. What we didn't know, at first, was what he was in to.'

'Drugs?'

'No, under-agers. And my feelings on that are about as strong as they are on drugs, as you know.'

'Yes.'

'You see, late last year, he got himself involved with a delicate young thing of seventeen, a proper little prima donna type apparently. Anyway, Sandy fell in love with this boy but the boy kept giving him the run-around.'Course, the next thing, Sandy started to give him treats and shower him with gifts to try to keep a hold on him. The usual old garbage. Finally, in absolute desperation, he even offered to buy him the flashy car he wanted . . .'

'Which is where our friend Wiseman comes in?'

Tony nodded. 'He's the top man in that field. The arrangement was that Wiseman would find a car in time for the boy's eighteenth birthday, some six months ahead. So Sandy thinks that all's quiet on the Western Front for a while and more or less forgets about it. Things settled down, or so he believed, but then one day he suddenly got an urgent call from the hospital. It turned out that his boyfriend had been very badly got at during a fling with one of Wiseman's mates.'

Ken was puzzled. 'Is this Wiseman bisexual or something?'

'No, anything but. His list of female conquests is pretty awesome, by all accounts.'

'Then I don't get it.'

'One of Wiseman's friends is a closet queer. As something of a favour, apropos of what we still don't know, he got in touch with Sandy's friend on the pretext of meeting someone who had the car of his dreams. Anyhow, it transpires that the boy sneaked off to some rendezvous or other at The Grand Hotel. Several bottles of champagne later, the suggestion was made that the Sandy situation could be bypassed entirely if the boy showed himself willing to offer certain services to Wiseman's friend.'

Ken drew in a breath through his teeth. 'And the boy agreed?'

'Naturally. He was greedy and he was bored with Sandy. I suppose he thought that all it would take was one quick trick to land the jackpot.'

'In what sense?'

'This friend of Wiseman's is a very wealthy man – at least that was the impression he gave. He did a lot of boasting about his lifestyle and brought out what looked like evidence of it. One of the things – don't laugh – was a cloak clasp. It shows you how naïve the boy was when I tell you that he believed it when the man claimed it had belonged to Napoleon.'

'What?'

'I know, ridiculous, isn't it? Everyone knows the real thing is in a private collection.'

'Not since March.'

'Pardon?'

'It was stolen with a lot of other things from Floors Castle.'

'You mean it actually *might* have been Napoleon's cloak clasp?'

'Who knows?' Ken's mind was racing. The cloak clasp was neither here nor there, but the thought that Sally might have got herself involved with a man on the fringes of the criminal fraternity was appalling.

'Still might have been a cod,' Tony reasoned. 'If the real

305

thing had gone missing, the market for fakes would be wide open.'

'Mmm . . . so what happened with this kid?'

'Oh, he did his turn, but it started to get a bit brutal. He said he objected, but that made no impression on Wiseman's friend. He's a big bloke, powerfully built. The more the boy begged him to stop, the rougher he got. Ended up slapping him around as well as causing physical damage in areas I needn't elaborate on.'

'Christ!' Ken felt nauseated. He knew these things happened but he didn't want to hear the details.

'They don't realise what they're letting themselves in for, these little tarts,' Tony continued. 'I'm not saying that he deserved what he got, exactly, but he was rather asking for trouble.'

'So I take it that was the end of the relationship with Sandy?'

'Not straight away. He took the boy home after he came out of hospital and nursed him back to health. But he was an ungrateful wretch. True to form, as soon as he was back on his feet he was off gadding about again.'

'So much for learning from experience.'

'If anyone learned anything, it was Sandy. He's got himself a real relationship now, with someone more his own age.'

Ken's thoughts had wandered back to Sally. What he'd heard had left him with an uncomfortable dilemma. As difficult as it was for him to accept that she was entangled with another man, he'd always known, as a matter of logic, that she would take that step eventually. Beyond what he felt about it personally, his primary concern was how to warn her about this Wiseman character. It wasn't for him to interfere with her life, and he was unwilling to do so, unless he could be of some help. The trouble was that, knowing what he now knew, he couldn't say nothing. On the other hand, he also knew that anything he might say was likely to be misconstrued as self-serving. He pondered the predicament for a while.

'What else do you know?'

'Nothing. I'm telling you the story as I heard it, that's all.'

'You don't know Wiseman or his friend, then?'

'I know *of* Wiseman. Who the friend is is anybody's guess.'

'Have you any way of finding out?'

'I could ask around, I suppose, but I'm not sure what I'd come up with. There's so much chat and back-chat, you never know what to believe.'

'Anything would be a help.'

'You're worried about her, aren't you?' Tony's look was so candid that Ken couldn't pretend otherwise.

'Wouldn't you be?'

'I have to admit that I would.'

'Do me a favour, will you? Put a few feelers out without too much fuss and pass back whatever you can.'

'You might have to wait a few weeks.'

'No matter.'

'Ken?'

'Yes?'

Tony suddenly thought better of what he was going to ask. 'It doesn't matter.'

'It's all right, we've known each other long enough to talk straight.' For once he had decided to abandon his reserve. 'Yes, I do care for Sally over and above what's strictly business. That's not to say there's anything going on between us, but I feel responsible for her in many ways. There are two issues here. One is that I can't stand the thought of her going down the tubes emotionally. The other is that I won't see her stitched up professionally. They're not totally separate issues, because of what I feel, but it would be best if I tried to treat them as such.'

'I understand.'

307

'Thanks.'

'I admire you, you know? It takes a certain kind of strength to do what you're doing.'

'No,' Ken replied, 'it takes a certain kind of weakness.' What he didn't add, although it had been a thought he'd had frequently ever since he'd known her, was, And maybe, just maybe, I've finally found a way of giving back to one woman what I took from so many for all those years.

Kirkby Mote stood at the edge of one of the prettiest villages that Sally had ever seen. Two rows of neat, white-washed houses stood either side of a road that wound itself, like a cart track, in a long, lazy bend from one side to the other, leading from and to stretches of countryside that were different enough to mark the border of England and Wales. It was the height of autumn, and the trees were splendid in their final display of browns and golds, the sky so blue and cloudless that it was difficult to believe that winter was less than a month away.

Sally brought the car to a halt and just sat and looked at it all for a while. She would have liked to have bottled what she felt and saved it for a rainy day. Autumn, like spring, had such a glorious richness about it, a sense of fullness that made the spirits rise. If only it didn't have to end; if only it could be caught in some way and savoured over and over again, she thought. She took a deep breath and tried to imprint the moment on her subconscious. It would escape her, she knew, but for now she was content to soak it up and imagine that she would always remember it.

She exhaled slowly, letting her mind adjust to the challenge that lay ahead. Her instructions were clear enough. Concentrate, really concentrate. Take a good hard look, seem interested but remain aloof. It had been easy for Ken to say, he was a past master at such things. But for her, the prospect of checking out a house of this quality was very daunting.

Kirkby Mote could not be compared with anything that Sally had experienced in her travels around Sussex. There would not be the one or maybe two good pieces that she might have been lucky enough to find in the average home. This place was going to be stacked to the walls with antiques of every variety. Getting an overview that was worthy of the name was going to be a Herculean task.

Sally glanced from the car window. The hall looked perfectly charming, sitting daintily on its own little island surrounded by a moat on which two swans floated picking idly at clumps of weed. It was as if someone had drawn it as an example of the Elizabethan rural style. The half-timbered walls, the higgledy-piggledy roof tops ... all in all it had the appearance of an out-sized dolls' house or an exhibit depicting life down the ages.

What can she be like, this Mrs Lyall-Bourke? Sally wondered, thinking the name of the owner as removed from any reality that she understood as the house seemed to be. Fancy living here all on her own, with no one but a butler for company. Her mind conjured a picture of a Miss Havisham figure, distracted and dishevelled, forever sitting waiting in a cobweb-filled room. The picture swiftly dissolved and reformed itself into the more lifelike shapes and features of other elderly ladies that she'd visited. She remembered the immaculately permed hair, the dusty look of old-fashioned face powder, the faint smell of eau de cologne. It had struck her as odd that they'd all clung to their vanity, though there was no one there to see. Age had not withered their pride, as it had their fortunes. There had to be a lesson in that.

Sally dwelt on the thought for a while then began to concentrate again on the job in hand. Well, this old lady certainly isn't living in reduced circumstances, she reminded herself, so there's no danger of my feeling sorry for her. The humiliation of having been conned, albeit mildly, by the woman in Rye still nettled her. She thought of Ken's telling off, then of the faith that he was showing in her now. 'Right,' she said, straightening herself up and getting out of the car, 'let's have at it, then.' She headed off across the low stone bridge that led to the entrance of the hall, summoning up every ounce of confidence as she walked. By the time the big wooden door on the other side swung open to greet her, she felt she was ready.

'Good morning.' The butler's face was as grey as his waistcoat. It wasn't the most cheery of welcomes. 'This way, please.' He crossed the terracotta-tiled floor of the entrance lobby and Sally followed.

'Miss Blythe, madam,' he announced as they reached the room where the mistress of the house was evidently waiting. Sally went forward a few steps and saw a rather beautiful, if delicate, old woman smiling at her from a high-backed armchair.

'How good of you to come,' she said, pleasantly. 'I'm so glad to be doing this with another woman. It's very personal, you know.'

'Yes,' Sally replied, unsure whether she should stay at a distance or go further into the room.

'Do come and sit down.' The old lady indicated a Georgian sofa, covered in pale yellow double damask. 'Would you care for some coffee?'

'Thank you.'

'Some coffee, Miles,' she said, not bothering to look at the butler. He disappeared, silent as a ghost. 'Now,' she continued, 'how would you like to go about this?'

'If I could just have a general look around,' Sally began, 'I'd like to get an idea of what there is and relay it to my colleague. After he's heard my assessment, he'll be in touch with you as soon as possible to make suggestions as to what you might consider selling.'

'Your colleague.' she echoed. 'Mr Rees, isn't it?'

'Yes.'

'I hear he's something of an authority.'

'He's very highly respected in his field.'

'Mmm. And I take it that you are in a similar line of business?'

'Yes, I have my own shop in Brighton.'

'Dealing in furnishings?'

'Mostly, but I also deal in ceramics.'

'Fascinating.'

Sally had an idea that Mrs Lyall-Bourke found it anything but fascinating, but she smiled anyhow.

'Of course, you know, I have been persuaded that this is by far the best thing, although I have to admit that I was against it at first . . .' She paused to reconsider what she really thought about the matter. 'And I couldn't possibly have you going around the entire house. I'll have Miles show you the gallery, the great chamber and the parlour. I'm sure that will be adequate.'

The voice had an edge of frostiness about it, and Sally realised that she would have to tread carefully.

'I'm obliged,' she said, hoping to sound courteous enough to engender some trust.

The coffee arrived and was taken with some stiffness and formality. Sally searched for some means of breaking the ice as she poured some milk into her cup.

'I'd love to know something of the history of the house,' she said, at last. 'It really is most unusual.'

'It is something of a curiosity today, I suppose,' Mrs Lyall-Bourke replied, 'although the general plan of the building is exactly what you would expect for Tudor times. Household arrangements had not changed very much in a hundred years, so the sort of rooms that you find here and their lay-out within the larger context is virtually mediaeval.'

'With large halls for everyday use and chambers such as this one for anything private?'

'Yes. There are two halls here, upper and lower, with the more important one on the first floor, naturally.'

Sally wondered why it was natural, but didn't interrupt.

'The design of the building depended a lot on the nature of your position in society and the size of your household, of course,' Mrs Lyall-Bourke went on, 'but even the minor gentry kept a significant number of retainers. Apart from members of his immediate family, the gentleman who established Kirkby Mote probably had as many as eighty servants of one kind and another in his charge. It wasn't thought necessary to provide special accommodation for them, most would have eaten and slept in one of the halls, although more personal servants would have slept on straw pallets in the master or mistress's own chamber.'

'Who built the Hall?'

'A man called Fox. He was a senior member of the Earl of Derby's household in the mid-sixteenth century.'

'Is that his device in the window?' Sally pointed to a portion of stained glass in the oriel window which was the focus of the room.

'That is the coat of arms that his family later adopted. Fox's own device, or the one he most commonly used in any case, was this.' Mrs Lyall-Bourke unpinned an enamelled brooch which she'd been wearing at the throat of her high-necked blouse. Sally took it from her and held it carefully in her palm.

'It's exquisite,' she said, studying the tiny image of a cupid firing arrows at a unicorn, 'but what does it mean?'

Mrs Lyall-Bourke began to look marginally amused. 'They were extremely fond of allegory in those days, as you probably know. In fact, it was considered far more important to be witty than learned. What you have encapsulated, there, in the cupid and unicorn, is Fox's personal comment on life in general. It signifies chastity under attack by carnal desire.'

312

'How subtle.'

'He was a moral man but not above the humour of his age.' She took the brooch back. 'He used other devices, of course, some more mysterious than others. The idea was to stimulate the minds of your contemporaries and generally be admired for your ingenuity. There are hieroglyphs and so forth all over the house if you look.'

'I will have to keep my eyes open for them.'

'Yes, indeed.' Mrs Lyall-Bourke glanced at her watch. 'Well, time is getting on, you know, so perhaps you would like to look around now?'

'Very much so.'

There was a gracious but firm goodbye from Mrs Lyall-Bourke as soon as the butler appeared and Sally went out of the room with him feeling very meek. It was as if she had spent the morning in the headmistress's study of a school for well-bred young ladies. The sight of the butler in his sombre grey reinforced the feeling and she became intensely aware of the frigid silence he maintained as they walked back towards the entrance lobby. Their footsteps echoed up the bare stone staircase that led to the first floor.

'The gallery,' he proclaimed, in the manner of a tour guide, as they reached a door at the top. Sally stepped through it into a burst of sunlight that made her blink her eyes. When she refocused, she saw a long, broad hall entirely panelled in carved oak and a ceiling patterned with plasterwork that looked rather like an enlarged piece of lace.

'If you will start at this end.' The butler indicated towards their left, where the largest of the windows provided an uninterrupted view over the moat and out into the sur-rounding countryside. Sally paused to admire it, thinking how many feet had stood in just this position before her, how many moments of peace or anxiety had been passed, gazing through the cross-hatched diamonds of glass in front of her. She stared out over the fields for as long as she dared before

313

taking a deep breath and turning to begin her work. The butler looked impatient as he hovered a discreet distance away, but she was determined not to rush. Remembering Ken's instructions, she assumed an air of detachment and took a good look up and down the room.

One of the first things to attract her attention was a set of tall-backed chairs, six in all, which were set out at intervals on either side of the gallery. The attraction was caused less by the chairs themselves than the covers that had been put over them. These were superbly embroidered in crewel work, and although the colours had faded over the years, the riot of flowers, strapwork, shells and birds, so typical of High Baroque was as full of life as it had ever been. Sally took a notebook from her handbag and started to scribble and sketch. Before long, she was completely absorbed in what she was doing and rather enjoying herself. She passed down the gallery taking in as much detail as she could. Each chair and table, each of the marble busts on plinths, even the silver candle sconces that were fixed to the panelling at regular intervals, were carefully drawn and described before she took the hint from the butler that it was time to move on.

From the gallery, Sally was taken into the great chamber. Again, the walls were clad in a wealth of carved panelling but the ceiling here dripped stalactites of plaster which gave the room a ponderous air. She looked around, surprised to find the chamber so sparsely furnished. The feel of the room was more sober because of it and she imagined that it must always have been the intention of the original owner to give the impression of grandeur and austerity in one visual statement. It worked very well. The vast stone fireplace with its blackened back plates seemed to echo the theme: welcome, but know in whose presence you stand. Sally thought of the master at the head of a long refectory table, surrounded by his honoured guests. A fine Restoration table stood in its place now, with matching chairs, but it was

314

no less noble than the first occupant would have been. She made a note of it and a couple of paintings which were the only relief in an otherwise dark and oppressive setting, and passed on, hoping that there would be more of consequence, from her point of view, in the next room.

She was not disappointed, for the last destination on her route turned out to be a much less imposing affair. Leading directly off the great chamber by way of a short hall, the parlour had immediate warmth. Plainer oak panelling stretched up to a wooden ceiling that had been decorated with Tudor motifs and designs. Sally smiled as she noticed the cupid and unicorn that Mrs Lyall-Bourke had told her about, picked out in the light that streamed in through the high mullioned windows. It seemed that the wry sense of fun that had inspired the device had left its imprint in the fabric of the room, making it homely and cheerful. She relaxed with the change of atmosphere. To her delight, there was plenty to fill her notebook here. A fabulous suite of Louis XV furniture, a sofa and six armchairs, was the main focal point. But there were many more pieces of interest. In particular, she lingered over an unusual bureau in burr veneer, which had been coloured to imitate tortoiseshell. It was so distinctive that she was convinced it must have been commissioned by someone of great rank.

'Do you know anything about this bureau?' she said towards the ever-hovering butler.

'I'm sorry, madam?'

'This bureau,' she repeated, 'have you any idea where it came from or who it was made for?'

Not a hint of interest crossed the impassive face. 'I'm afraid I can't help you with that inquiry, madam.'

Fair enough, Sally thought, though she couldn't believe that anyone whose daily task it was to clean such a beautiful thing could be left unaffected by it. She was tempted to scribble *misery guts* beside the more relevant note she had made describing the kingwood cross bandings and pewter stringing that adorned the piece.

Another long silence filled the minutes that passed while Sally went slowly around the room. A wooden coffer, a pair of pole screens, a Queen Anne semi-circular card table, all were recorded in her neatest hand. Eventually, when she'd forgotten again that he was even there, the butler cleared his throat and she guessed that her visit had come to an end. She made a last, quick note about a pair of Japanese Imari vases that she had been inspecting then snapped her notebook shut.

'Right, that's it,' she said. He simply turned and led the way back down to the entrance lobby, where he showed her out with the same lack of warmth as he had displayed on showing her in.

Well, that was an experience and a half, Sally thought as she walked away. Her head was hurting with the effort of concentration and she wasn't much relishing the long drive home. Still, there was the dinner that Daniel had promised to cook to look forward to. And there was going to be so much to tell him that she hardly knew where she would begin.

20

'Stick the kettle on, I'm spitting feathers.' Sally backed in through the shop door, loaded down with carrier bags. Heather glanced up from the water colour she was working on.

'Good Lord, what have you been doing? Buying half of Brighton?'

'Well, I had to get enough to give him a decent do.'

'It's a children's party, not the feeding of the five thousand.'

'There will be twelve of them and they've all got monstrous appetites. Hey, what do you think of the cake?' Sally pulled a box out of one of the bags and held it under Heather's nose. Inside was a friendly-looking green dinosaur.

'Oh, isn't it great? The things they can do with icing these days.'

'Brilliant, isn't he?' Sally agreed. 'I thought he was too good to miss. Mind you, I don't know where you're meant to put the candles.'

'You'll have to line them up on his back between the big scales.'

'Do you think Jonathan'll like it?'

'Of course. Children these days love anything dinosaur-related. *Jurassic Park* has a lot to answer for.'

'Yes, they all seem to know these great long Latin names for all the different types.'

'Did you get him the castle he was after?'

'I did, but I had to go to three toy shops before I could track one down.'

'Must be popular.'

'Even so, I was surprised I couldn't get one straight away. I think people must be buying early for Christmas. In fact, I noticed that some of the stores have got their Christmas departments set up now, and there's almost two months to go yet.'

'They'll do anything to induce you to spend.'

'Well, they're not getting me involved in the mass hysteria at this point.'

'Me neither.'

Sally put the cake back into its bag and started to peer into the others to see if there was anything she had forgotten. 'Did you get him that pirate ship in the end?'

'No, I found something that I liked better. It's a jousting set, complete with knights, horses, tents for arming up in, and a king and queen with their own little dais to sit on whilst they watch the sport.'

Sally laughed. 'How sweet! Oh, he'll be thrilled. He's practically obsessed with knights in armour. In fact, I've bought him the video of *Henry V* as an extra present.'

'The Olivier version, I hope?'

'Naturally. It wouldn't be the same without his rendition of that speech he does before the battle.'

'Gosh, yes. Marvellous. They played it at his funeral, you know.'

'Whose?'

'Lawrence Olivier's, of course. I remember they showed a bit of footage from it on the box and you could see pew after pew of famous actors all going misty-eyed when that amazing voice of his hit top pitch.' Heather launched into a

318

fair imitation: ' "... And gentlemen in England now a-bed shall think themselves accursed they were not here, and hold their manhoods cheap whiles any speaks that fought with us upon Saint Crispin's daaaay!" '

They both started to giggle.

'Should have been on the stage,' said Sally, 'you've got the intonation down to a tee.'

'It used to be something of a party piece, when I was young. That and takeoffs of his Richard III.'

'Philip used to do one of those, do you remember?'

'How could I forget? I wouldn't have minded if he hadn't been so eager to repeat it at every given opportunity.'

'I think clowning around was his way of letting off steam.'

'I think it was more to do with being an attention seeker. He never stopped looking for accolades. A sure sign of insecurity, if you ask me.'

'But he should have been secure enough. He had a steady job, a house, me . . .'

'Even material things and the love of a good woman aren't enough for some people. Security comes from within not without.'

'Do you think he was that way? I mean, he always gave the impression of being steady, at work at least. I know he relied a lot on me privately, but I thought that that was just his soft side coming out.'

'It's always a dangerous sign when a man wants you to mother him too much. Being loving and caring is all very well and good, but there's no reason why you should have to do things for him that any independent adult should be capable of themselves. As I recall, you were always trailing around after him, finding his keys, finding his glasses, finding this or that bill, book or whatever. He'd just scatter things around the place haphazardly and instantly forget all about them. Then, when he suddenly needed them again, he'd

319

make you feel responsible for finding them by creating a song and dance.'

'I know,' Sally reflected, sadly. 'At first, I used to think it was sweet that he was so daffy. But as time wore on . . .'

'Your dad used to say that you had three kids to look after and it was the one who was nearly forty that was the most demanding.'

'He didn't tell me that.'

'What good would it have done?'

'It might have made me think twice.'

'I doubt it. You were so accustomed to being held respons-ible for everybody's everything that . . . heavens, here comes Jack and I'm still covered in paint.'

Sally turned to see a tall figure in a sober suit approaching the door. 'You going out for lunch?' she asked, but Heather had already dashed off to the cubby-hole at the back of the shop to wash her hands. Sally leaned over the desk and pressed the buzzer to let him in.

'Hello, how are you?'

'Cold and hungry.'

'Has gone a bit chilly, hasn't it?' They exchanged a kiss on the cheek.

'Been doing a bit of shopping, I see.'

'Preparations for the big bash this afternoon.'

'Ah, lots of jelly and ice-cream, then?'

'Crisps, biscuits and fruit, actually. Jonathan doesn't like jelly.'

'Pity, I was hoping that there might be a little left over for me.'

'You're not a jelly freak, are you?'

'Any sort of nursery pudding does me.'

Sally found the idea faintly bizarre. Despite his gentle manner, Jack Preston had all the gravitas and dignity of a man who could pass the death sentence without a hint of compassion.

'Yes, he's a sucker for my spotted dick,' said Heather, as she came back through the shop, 'it's a wonder he keeps so slim.'

'It's all the exercise I get,' he remarked. It was done in the most casual of ways – a way, Sally had learned, that was typical of his taciturn nature – but she fancied that there was a *double entendre* behind it, nevertheless. She watched the way the pair touched hands and smiled at each other. It was rather charming, youthful almost. She shuffled a bag with her foot, awkwardly.

'How long have you got?' Heather asked him, softly.

'Couple of hours. Be all right so long as I'm back in the office by three.'

'Oh, good, I'm glad it won't be a rush.' She turned to Sally. 'You don't mind my disappearing for the afternoon?'

'Not at all. I've got to be here in any case. There's a bit of business to catch up on.' She began to move her bags towards the desk. There was a curious piece of wood sticking out of one of them and she lifted it out and started to study it.

'I'll be at the cottage for four, then.'

'Hmm?'

'I'll be round at four,' Heather repeated.

'Fine.'

'Have you been at it again?'

'Pardon?'

'Honestly, can't send you out for a stamp without your coming back with something.' Heather had guessed that Sally had been unable to resist a quick rummage around the junk shops while she was shopping. 'What is that?'

'Search me. I just bought it because I liked it.'

'Liked it? It's the ugliest thing I've seen in years.'

Sally shrugged and continued to stroke the carved figure at the top of the stick. 'I don't know, it's got the feel of something special . . . something really special.'

'Well, I think it's ghastly. What do you think, Jack?'

He took the stick from Sally's hand for a second then handed it back, without comment.

'There,' sniffed Heather, 'he'd say it was revolting too, if he wasn't so polite.'

'I wouldn't say anything of the sort,' Jack protested, mildly. 'Leave the girl alone. If she thinks it's got some merit, it's got some merit.'

'Oh, well, *chacun à son goût,* as they say.' Heather started to tidy her painting gear off Sally's desk. 'Oh, by the way, Ken 'phoned for you this morning.'

'What did he say?'

'Just that he needed to talk to you.' It was a gross misrepresentation of the facts, but Heather wanted time to think through what he had told her.

'Better give him a buzz back, then.'

'Yes.' Heather wondered how much he'd say as she loaded the last of her things into her big raffia bag. 'Okay, that's me out of your way. See you later.'

Heather gave Sally a kiss and left the shop arm-in-arm with Jack. She waited until they had walked through The Lanes for a couple of minutes before asking him for his opinion.

'What do you do,' she began, 'if you think someone you know may be receiving stolen goods?'

'Are you asking me as a citizen or a lawyer?'

'Both.'

'As a citizen, I'd say drop the person as a friend and inform the police of your suspicions. As a lawyer, I'd say that as long as you haven't involved yourself in any way with the goods you think might have been stolen, there's nothing to worry about.'

'What if the person concerned has been giving you things but you don't know that they have been stolen?'

'That's a more complex matter.'

'Why?'

'Well, it depends on how innocent you are of the facts and whether you can prove your innocence.'

'But surely if you weren't aware that you'd taken something stolen, you are completely innocent?'

'How aware is aware? The issue turns on whether, at any stage, you could reasonably have been expected to be suspicious. And the word "reasonable" is open to a wide interpretation, under the law.'

'What is reasonable, in legal terms, then?'

'Oh, we could discuss that for hours. It depends on the details of your case, really. Why are you asking, anyway?'

'I think Sally may be in trouble.'

'Oh?'

'It's all a bit complicated. You remember me telling you about Ken Rees?'

'The chap who got Sally the shop?'

'Yes, that's the one. He has his own business close by in Union Street.'

'That's right, you pointed it out to me one time.'

'Well, he 'phoned this morning, more to talk to me than to Sally. He's been given a certain amount of information about someone Daniel's friendly with. It would seem that this friend could be dealing in stolen goods.'

'It all sounds rather third-hand.'

'I said it was complicated.'

'Let me just get this straight. Ken's heard something suspicious about a friend of Daniel's, right?'

'Right.'

'But he doesn't know anything concrete. I mean, he hasn't seen these supposed stolen goods himself?'

'No.'

'Then this is purely hearsay.'

'Yes, but it's no less disturbing for that.'

'You're saying that if Daniel is connected with someone

who might be handling stolen goods, the shadow of suspicion falls on him too?'

'Exactly.'

'I can see your argument, but you would never secure a conviction on that basis.'

'I'm not looking to convict anybody. Oh, why do you have to be so damned *logical*? I couldn't care less whether Daniel Wiseman is involved in anything illegal or not, I'm just worried about what might happen to my Sally if he is.'

'Look, darling, I know that's what you're worried about.' Jack stopped walking and turned to her, calmly. 'But look at the facts. What you've been told so far is gossip. So far as I can judge, there is nothing to implicate Daniel in anything untoward, *per se*. If he were the one you thought was handling stolen goods, it would be a different matter.'

'But that's what I *do* think.'

'Oh, Heather, you've got no proof.'

'Not as such, but I've got good reason for saying what I say. For one thing, he's always giving Sally things to put in the shop.'

'I thought he was in the car business?'

'He is. But often he'll pick up the odd small antique on the back of some other deal. At least, that's what he tells her.'

'It could be true.'

'Yes, it could. On the other hand . . .' She thought for a second. 'And there's something else that bothers me. He's forever hopping over to the continent.'

'Why's that a problem?'

'It was something Ken said, something about Daniel's suspicious friend having a piece that most likely was bound for a private sale abroad.'

'I don't understand what you're getting at.'

'Ken thinks that the stolen goods that his informant said he'd seen came from a burglary at a stately home earlier this

324

year. The piece in question, if it's the genuine article, is far too well-known for anyone to try and sell in this country.'

'I still don't . . .'

'Don't you see? Daniel's the perfect person to know if you happen to have some hot property hanging around that you need taking over the water. After all, he flies abroad practically every other week.'

'Good God, you've got a better imagination than Walter Mitty! That's the best two-and-two-makes-a-hundred-and-thirty-five I've heard in a long time.'

'I'm serious, Jack, really serious. You may think that I'm jumping to conclusions, but what if I'm right?'

'My dear love,' he said, kissing her affectionately on the forehead, 'you are getting yourself into a pickle over something and nothing. I know that you're bothered about Daniel perhaps having shady connections that might damage Sally in some way, but I don't see that there's much that you can do about it at this stage. Unless or until some real evidence comes your way, the best you can do is keep your eyes open and your mouth shut. She's a big girl, after all, and you don't want her to think that you're interfering. Anyway, she's got a good sensible head on her shoulders. I'm sure that if she had anything to be alarmed about, she'd have told you by now.'

'Oh, Jack, I do hope that I'm just being silly.' Heather hugged him to reassure herself.

'The last thing you are is silly,' he replied, 'and you've got every right to be concerned. Parenthood is a job for life, but there are times when the hands off approach is more prudent than hands on.'

It was the week-end following Jonathan's birthday. The children had gone with their father, leaving Sally two clear days to herself. On the Saturday morning she woke to the sound of the shower running in the en-suite bathroom. She turned lazily over in Daniel's bed and squinted at the clock.

'Seven-fifteen,' she groaned, 'bang on schedule, as always.'

She had become accustomed to his habits in the months she had known him. He rose promptly at seven, spent half-an-hour in the bathroom, another in the gym then, after yet another shower, he would finally make it to breakfast. Most days, this was a ten-minute affair to him. If it was one of 'her' week-ends, though, he'd settle down gratefully to a spectacular fry up. He said it tasted different when she made it, and in any case, he was too much of a fitness fanatic to indulge himself on a more regular basis.

Sally lay staring at the ceiling, trying to straighten her thoughts for the day. She'd planned to spend a full eight hours in the shop. Lord knows she needed to, if only to do something more restful than dash from pillar to post buying things to put in it. The rate of turnover that she'd managed to achieve was way above her expectations. Between the auctions and the private sales, she'd pulled off some neat deals with other traders, although they'd made it hard work for her. Gradually, though, she'd gained ground. The solid knowledge that she'd built up over hours and hours of looking at and handling the various pieces that had come her way, had begun to make a bigger impression than the eye-lash fluttering had. Using feminine charm was a great way of getting an intro, but once people started to see it as a blind, you were in deep trouble.

She thought of how far she'd come from the harassed days of the post-divorce period of her life, when money was a constant problem and her energy had been continually sapped by the struggle to survive. That she'd got on her feet again, despite all odds, was nothing short of a major coup and it made her feel good to indulge, just a little, in self-congratulation.

But happy as she was with the way that things had turned out, Sally was never one for resting on her laurels. Also, she knew that her fortunes could change for the worse as easily as for the better, if she didn't keep her wits about her. From idle musing, she began to turn her thoughts to making plans. Ideally, she felt, the thing to do would be to establish better links with the London trade, not because the Sussex circuit wasn't providing her with the right kind of business, but because she thought it would be a good idea to broaden her horizons. Anyway, the London trade had access to a better class of client, generally speaking, and she quite fancied having some fun seeking out top-quality pieces which she could then sell on at better mark-ups than she was currently able to get. She was considering ways in which she could make the type of contacts she needed when Daniel emerged from the shower.

'Good morning, tousle-top,' he grinned, going over to give her a kiss. 'How's your head?'

'Fine, considering. Red wine nearly always knocks me out.'

'Seemed pretty lively to me, last night.'

'Yes, I think I was a bit over enthusiastic.' She grimaced as she pulled herself up into a sitting position and he laughed.

'What have you got lined up for today, then?'

'Not a lot. Thought I'd potter about the shop for a change. You up to much?'

'Going over to Shoreham. The bloke I sold the Comanche to is dropping in.'

'Something wrong with it?'

'The electrics are playing up. I don't think it's anything major but I'll have the mechanic check it over to make sure.'

'Oh.'

'Shall we go out for dinner tonight? There's this new place in Little Western Street that people keep telling me is good.'

'Okay, it'd be nice for a change.'

'Do you want to meet up here or at the restaurant?'

'Depends what time you want to eat.'

'Around eight would suit me. I've got to drive out to Seaford this afternoon and it might take a while to get back. You know how the coast road is on a Saturday.'

'Mmm. Might as well meet at the restaurant, then. I'll just stay in the shop. I've got some research to catch up on, anyway.'

Daniel walked away from the bed giving his hair another rub with the towel that he'd brought out of the bathroom. Sally watched him go, getting a little thrill out of the sight of his naked body.

'Breakfast in half-an-hour, then?'

'Yes,' she said, stirring herself. 'Do you want the full blow-out, as usual?'

'Absolutely. Part of my conjugal rights.'

'Non-conjugal rights, you mean.'

'If you insist.'

Sally began to wonder whether he'd made a Freudian slip; he often talked as if their relationship had the permanence of a marriage but she hadn't taken what he'd said too seriously until now. Thoughts that had been lingering at the back of her mind started to form into a new vision of the future. What if he were serious? What if they did decide to get together on a more formal basis? The idea was pleasant but startling. She didn't think that she was ready for that type of commitment yet. In fact, she wasn't sure exactly how she expected the relationship to turn out at all, although she already knew that it was less of an emotional free-wheel than she'd thought it would be. Mixed feelings brought on by trying to work out why he'd said what he had kept bothering her until she finally got out of bed and decided that doing something domestic would take her mind off the issue. She threw on a dressing gown and wandered down to the kitchen. Daniel had already let the dog in on his way to the gym.

'Morning, Nero,' she said, merrily. 'Eaten any good Christians lately?'

The dog's muzzle remained in its food bowl but its eyes followed her as she crossed the room. The implied menace sent a shiver down her spine and she wished, for the umpteenth time, that Daniel would feed the animal outside.

All I need is his ugly mush first thing in the morning, she thought, it's enough to put anyone off their breakfast.

She opened the fridge and took out the eggs, bacon and mushrooms, and soon the mundane routine of preparation and cooking helped her mind wander to other things. She began to think about the court cupboard she'd bought. This piece of furniture was often commissioned in the seventeenth century when a girl was born into a well-off family. She would be given it at fifteen or sixteen when she married. Sally was wondering where she might find the information that she needed to establish where her cupboard had been made. She knew that the naive flower design that decorated the front panels of the cupboard was the clue, but so often tiny variations in the style of carving made all the difference in the world. The detective work involved in translating finer detail of this sort really appealed to her. Of course, if she got stuck with something, she could always ask Ken, but on the whole, she preferred to test her own powers of observation and do her own research. Sometimes, though, she would come to a complete full stop. Sometimes, even Ken would be lost for an answer.

That was certainly the case as far as the funny-looking stick that she'd picked up whilst doing Jonathan's birthday shopping was concerned. She remembered how he'd scoffed when she'd shown it to him. Yet, for her, the stick had a quality that went beyond the usual. For a start, there had been something like it in the collection of nicknacks that she'd taken away when she'd cleared the old seaman's house in Hastings. In amongst the souvenirs of voyages long past had been a red-brown club that had turned out to be a good example of Fijian tribal art. It had been quite a surprise when she'd managed to find a collector who paid seven hundred pounds for it. Until that stage, she'd considered it pretty unremarkable.

She wondered if she shouldn't just recontact the same collector and offer it to him. But then she thought that if she'd known more about the Fijian club, she might have been able to strike a better bargain. The best thing, she decided, would be to spend some time getting a grasp of what the stick might be before selling it on. Anything that would help her get the best possible price would be worthwhile, and since she'd only paid three pounds for it, there was no hurry to get a return on her investment.

Sally began to hum as her thoughts continued to hover around how she would fill her day at the shop. She cut the woody stumps off the mushrooms, chopped them, and tossed them into a frying pan with some butter and garlic. The distinctive smell that rose up cheered her as she gathered the discarded bits and went to throw them into the bin.

Huh, typical! she thought, flipping it open to find it stuffed to the top with rubbish. She lifted the bin liner out with some distaste and gave it a little shake to make space for the remainder of the mushrooms. As she did so, a slip of paper fell sideways up. The writing on it was distinctly feminine.

Sally stood for a moment debating whether to fish it out from the debris or not. It seemed dishonest to pry. On the other hand, the lure of maybe discovering something that she ought to know about was barely resistible. She looked around, nervously. Daniel was sure to finish in the gym soon. Still, she could make as if she were in the act of tying the bin liner up if he suddenly walked in. She tugged at the paper, disgusted with herself as much as with the left-over food that was congealed on to its surface. She had just enough time to make out three words: 'James Joyce, *Ulysses*'. As words went, they were hardly incriminating. Yet there was something about the way they were written that made her linger over them, something about the J's. This handwriting had a vaguely familiar turn about it.

'How's breakfast doing?'

Sally scrunched up the bin liner rather too hastily as she looked up. 'Fine,' she said, 'ready in a few minutes.'

'You okay?'

'Yes, of course. Why?'

'Look a bit pale.'

'I'm just hung over.'

'Never mind. You'll be all right once you've got some food inside you.' He came over and put his arms around her and it was all she could do to try and respond naturally.

'Hang on, my hands are messy.'

'You don't need your hands to give me a kiss.'

She gave him a peck and struggled free. 'Don't want the bacon to burn.'

'Rejected again,' he said, in mock anguish.

'I feel sorry for you.'

'So you should. I'm a sensitive flower, aren't I, Nero?'

The dog bounded across the kitchen, almost knocking Sally over.

'Honestly,' she protested, 'I don't know how I'm meant to cook breakfast properly with that damned animal under my feet.'

'I'll stick him in the yard,' said Daniel, apologetically, and she was immediately sorry that she'd sounded so irritable. She waited until the dog was out then wiped her hands on a tea towel and walked over to give him a hug.

'Can I have some sympathy, please? I'm feeling a bit crabby.'

'You can have whatever you like, my angel,' he said,

gathering her up in an embrace. She snuggled against him whilst he stroked her hair.

'Oh, why are you so wonderful?' Sally had already started to forget the note.

'Me?' he laughed.

'Yes, you.'

'You're as daft as a brush, you are.'

'Why do you say that?'

'Because you're the only person in the world who thinks I'm wonderful.'

'Go on.'

'Well, apart from my mum, and she's biased.'

'I'm biased too.'

'Good,' he said, and kissed her softly, 'you just stay that way.'

'I think I'm stuck with it, whether I like it or not.'

'What's not to like?'

Sally shrugged. 'I don't know.'

'Yes, you do. You're scared of getting hurt, aren't you?'

'A bit.'

'Well, don't be. I said I'd look after you, and I'm a man of my word.'

'It's not that I don't believe you . . .'

'What, then?'

'Just, I know how I feel about you but I'm not always certain how you feel about me.'

'You mean you can't tell how I feel by now?' He looked surprised.

'Some of the time . . . oh, it's all so complicated.'

'What's complicated about it? I may not be very expressive in terms of words, but surely the way I act shows how deeply I care about you?'

'Of course it does.'

'But ideally you'd like me to swear undying love and bombard you with poetry, too?'

Sally laughed. 'I suppose there's an element of truth in that.'

'Women! I don't know.'

'I can't help it.'

'What do you want? "I love you" on a fifty-foot banner that's kept in constant view?'

'Don't be silly.'

'Well, it beats me.'

'I know it sounds pathetic, but there's nothing like hearing the odd encouraging word to keep a girl happy.'

'Then you'd better tell me what you'd like me to say, and I'll say it.'

'It doesn't work like that. We like these things to be unprompted.'

'Oh, I give up.'

'Don't do that,' she said, giving him a quick kiss on the cheek, 'you're doing fine.'

'Sally?'

'Yes?'

'There's blue smoke coming out of the grill.'

'Oh, bugger!' She shot across the room and grabbed the grill pan. ''fraid it's what we technically call a bit on the crispy side.'

'Don't worry. I don't mind it like that.'

'I do.'

'Just cook a bit more. There's plenty of it.'

'You know, you amaze me. You're always so calm about things.'

'It's only a few scraps of bacon.'

'I don't just mean things like this.'

'I can get angry enough, if I've got good reason to.'

'What do you call a good reason?'

'Depends. But you'd know soon enough if I found one.'

There was an edge in his voice that was chilling and she reminded herself that what she'd seen of him so far was the

333

good side. The more forceful side of his nature, the one she felt was purposely subdued in his dealings with her, had long been forgotten.

'I hope you never get angry with me.' She hadn't meant to say that, but it slipped out.

'I can't imagine why I should,' he replied, 'although, I suppose, in the long-term we won't be able to avoid the odd argument.'

'In the long-term?'

'Yes.'

'Oh.'

'What do you mean, "Oh".'

'I didn't know you were planning on a long-term arrangement.'

'Why? Aren't you?'

'I hadn't thought about it.'

'You're fibbing.'

She coloured.

'There. I thought so.' He came across the kitchen and got hold of her again. 'There's something I've been meaning to ask you.'

'There is?'

'Uh huh.' There was a glint of devilment in his eyes. Sally giggled, nervously.

'Nothing too momentous, I hope?'

He started kissing her and she began to panic.

'Will you . . .?' he murmured. 'Will you . . .?'

Oh, God, she thought, not now! I wouldn't trust myself now.

'Sally, sweetheart, will you . . .?'

'For heaven's sake. Will I what?'

'Will you finish the breakfast? I'm starving.'

'Ooh, you beast!' she said, and clouted him ineffectually with the tea towel.

'Just testing,' he laughed. She started laughing too, and

any concern that she might have had about the meaning of the note was dispersed in that instant.

21

The bar at The Old Ship Hotel was a welcome haven from the driving rain that was lashing Brighton's seafront. A fair amount of it gusted through the door as Ken stepped in from the pavement and shook himself, rather pointlessly. To his annoyance, his glasses steamed up, so he took them off and rubbed them on his jumper. He gazed myopically into the room for the few seconds it took to get them defogged. When he replaced them, he could more or less see that the bar was empty, as he'd expected.

'Morning, Linda,' he ventured to the barmaid. 'Or should I say afternoon?'

She smiled a smile devoid of warmth as she finished pulling a pint of froth from one of the pumps.

'Any chance of a half of mild?'

'You'll have to wait a minute, they've just changed the barrel over.'

'Give us a packet of nuts, then.'

She handed them over, coldly.

'That's what I like to see,' Ken said, by way of a joke, 'a person who gets real satisfaction out of their job.'

'Huh! You want to try doing a job like this before you

pass comment. I wouldn't wish it on a dog,' the barmaid continued, draining the pump, sullenly,

'What's wrong with you, today, eh? Got out of bed the wrong side?'

'None of your business.'

'Come on now, I can see that you're not your usual cheery self.' The comment was totally fatuous. Linda always had a face like frost.

'I've got 'flu, haven't I?' she replied, huffily. 'Not that anyone cares, oh no. I come in coughing and sneezing my head off, don't I, but does it make any difference? Not to His Royal Highness, it don't.'

Ken took the snotty reference as being aimed at the bar manager.

'You should have taken the day off.'

'Can't, can I? Steve won't let me. We've got the first of the office parties starting and he says he can't spare the staff.'

'What? Christmas parties in November?'

'That's how it is, these days. There's such a lot of them that it takes a month to fit them all in.'

'Never mind. Look on the bright side. It's the waitresses who'll be doing most of the work.'

'I still have to do the pre-lunch drinks and the after-lunch drinks, don't I? Plus any spirit orders that are taken during. Anyway, at least the waitresses get tips.' She sniffed a deep, coarse sniff that accentuated her condition. 'I don't get better money, 'flu or no 'flu.'

'Have a stiff whisky, that'll make you feel better.'

'I suppose you're buying it?' she sneered.

'Okay.'

She looked surprised, then warmed, slightly. 'Do you mean it?'

'Yes. Tell you what, here's a fiver. You take out the price of a drink and my half of mild and bring me it and the change when you've finished what you're doing.'

'You're a gent.'

'So they tell me. I'll be over in that corner, out of the draft.'

He turned in time to see Jim Foley come through the door, followed by another gust of rain.

'Hello, Ken, haven't seen you in ages.' He stuck out a hand that Ken failed to shake. 'What's wrong?'

'I've got a bone to pick with you.'

'Oh? Why's that then?'

'I would have thought you could have guessed.'

Foley frowned. 'Why? Haven't done any business with you in the last year that I can remember.'

'Keep thinking.'

'You're not still mad at me over the time in Wales, are you? You know I didn't really mean to give you hassle.'

'Could have fooled me.'

'It was George and Derek putting the pressure on, honest. Anyhow, I've finished with them now.'

'Don't give me that old line.'

'No, it's true. I've had enough.' He looked serious. 'Can I buy you a drink?'

'I've got one coming, thanks.'

'Mind if I join you, then?'

'Suppose not.'

'Look, what's your gripe? I've obviously stood on your toes in some way, not that I know how.'

'Get your drink and I'll tell you.' Ken settled in his chosen corner and had a brief look at a newspaper that was lying there while he was waiting for Jim.

'Here, I made your half up to a pint,' he said, pushing a glass and some change towards Ken, 'but not before laughing Linda had given me a tongue lashing. God, she's a misery that woman. Wish little Babs still worked here.'

'Yes. Still, our loss is the casino's gain.'

'Is that where she went?'

'So I'm told.'

'I've never seen her there.'

'Didn't know you were a customer.'

'I'm not a regular, by any means, but I like to have the odd flutter.'

'As if your life wasn't risky enough.'

'What do you mean?'

'One of these days you're going to stitch somebody up who's going to come back looking for you, that's what I mean.'

Jim put his drink down, crossly. 'All right, let's have it,' he said. 'What have I done this time to get you going?'

'Just passed off a complete strop on someone I consider a very close friend.'

'Who?'

'Sally Blythe, that's who.'

'Ah . . .' Jim started to look sheepish. 'Well, I didn't know at the time, did I?'

'Didn't know what?'

'That you were . . . er . . .'

'Well?'

'That you were a kind of partner,' he said hastily. He'd heard the rumours, but didn't want to get Ken angrier than he already was by alluding to them. 'Oh, come on, you know I wouldn't have done it if I'd realised you had anything to do with her. In fact, I didn't even know that she was one of our crowd. I mean, she didn't act like it.'

'Some excuse. You're damned lucky I didn't come round and tie your neck in a knot.'

'Well, I'm sorry, but if a person behaves like an idiot, I can't be blamed for treating them like one.'

'I hope I didn't hear that correctly.'

'You know what I mean.'

'Yes. You mean that it's okay to take advantage of the weak and the innocent.'

'I'm not without scruples, whatever you may think.'

'I don't know how you can say that with a straight face.'

'At least I don't go turning over little old ladies or anything, like the knocker boys do. Anyway, what am I supposed to do if someone wants to buy something from me? Put them off? It's not for me to tell them whether a piece is right or not, it's for them to use their own judgement.'

'Even if you're the one who faked it up?' Ken scoffed. 'Funny sort of morality, if you ask me.'

'We've all got to make a living.'

'Yes, well, if I were you I'd clean up my act before someone either sticks one on you or files a complaint with Mr Plod.'

'The police can't touch me for anything, and you know it,' said Jim, defensively. 'Anyway I don't know what you're getting so steamed up about, she got shot of that chest-of-drawers afterwards, in any case.'

'Found it on the tip when you were picking around, did you?'

'I came across it in Leeds, if you must know.'

'You certain.'

"Course I'm certain. Blooming well should be.'

Ken fell silent. He'd never bothered to ask Sally what she'd done with the chest-of-drawers. He hoped it wasn't anything silly, though he couldn't seriously see her being dishonest.

'Look,' said Jim. 'I'm really sorry about putting one over on your lady friend. Let me buy you another drink to make up for it, eh?'

'No, thanks. One's enough for me at lunchtime.'

'Maybe there's something else I can do for you?'

'Shouldn't think so.'

Jim thought for a while. 'There's a nice table and chairs I've seen that you might be interested in.'

'Oh, yeah?'

'Genuine Restoration. Very good nick.'

'Really.'

'You don't sound very taken.'

Ken shrugged. 'Where did you see them?'

'Over at Derek's.'

'Thought you said you'd finished with him?'

'I have.'

'So why are you doing business with him?'

'I'm not, just couldn't help noticing this table and chairs when I was over there the last time.'

'Did you ask him about them?'

'No.'

'Why not?'

'We'd just had a major ding-dong. Didn't seem like a good time.'

'May I ask what the row was about?'

'Usual thing.'

'What? The ring?'

'Keep your voice down.' Jim looked nervously about. The bar was beginning to fill up.

'Well, was it?'

'Yes. Tried to strong arm me once too often. I'm fed up with being the patsy.'

'Glad to hear it.'

'He wanted to bring some other bloke in on the deal, too. Someone from outside. Got very nasty when I said I wasn't having any.'

'Why not?'

'There's little enough when the money's divi'd up without bringing in another player. Anyway, I didn't like the feel of him.'

'Any particular reason?'

'Just something I overheard.'

'Which you're not going to pass on?'

'Not likely. But it was beyond the pale, so far as I'm concerned.'

'I think I get your drift.' Whatever it was that Jim had

overheard, it obviously went against even his unprincipled principles, which would have to make it something highly illegal. Ken wondered again what Derek was up to on the quiet.

'Tell me something,' he said, 'what's Tom Appleton's connection with Derek?'

'Same thing as I won't get involved in.'

'Oh?'

'Can't say any more than that, except that I hope you haven't taken anything off him recently.'

'I see.' Another piece of the jigsaw fell into place. 'This whole business wouldn't also involve a bloke from the Midlands, would it?'

Jim looked stunned. 'How do you know?'

'I keep my ear to the ground.'

'Crikey, haven't heard anything about me, I hope?'

'No.'

'Thank God for that.'

'Who is he, this outsider?'

Jim's nervousness seemed to increase.

'Somebody with a predilection for violence, by the looks of things.'

'Certain threats have been made.'

'Must be big league stuff, then?'

Jim didn't answer.

'Come on, you can trust me.'

'Look, I'm sorry, it's just not worth it.'

'The threats must've been pretty good.'

'I believed them.'

'You can't give me a name, I suppose?'

'No.' He got up suddenly. 'Well, must be going . . .'

'All right, no names,' said Ken, quickly, 'but just confirm one thing. This new pal of Derek's, he's a big bloke, isn't he? Kind of hard-looking, too?'

Jim nodded.

'And he buys to order, if you know what I mean?'

Jim glanced around the room before nodding again as he hastily buttoned up his coat. 'You didn't hear anything from me, though, okay?'

'Okay.'

'Be seeing you.'

Ken didn't bother to watch him go. Already, he was weighing this new information against what he'd observed for himself. That Derek was in cahoots in some way with the man from the Midlands was now beyond doubt. But what exactly their game was Ken still didn't know. The reference that he'd made about buying to order was intended to imply that the hard-faced man was a conduit for pieces that had come from burglaries. It didn't necessarily mean that Derek was one too, although it would seem highly likely, given the circumstances.

He thought again of the hand-over he'd witnessed at the house sale in Wales, of the clandestine way in which Derek had got in and out of the same Daimler Sovereign that he'd seen outside the warehouse in Frederick Street during the summer. If Derek had got himself involved in illegal trading, it was obviously something big. Too big for the likes of Jim Foley, anyhow.

I wonder if I might not find out more by going round there for a casual chat? thought Ken. Though I doubt he'd have the nerve to offer me anything shady. The idea struck him as a good one, nevertheless. There might be some clue he could pick up, after all. And he had the excuse of the Restoration pieces that Jim had mentioned to act as a reason for his visit. He put on his mac and absent-mindedly folded the newspaper which he'd found on his seat into his pocket. 'Ah, well,' he said, as he opened the pub door and was hit in the face by an icy blast of rain, 'once more unto the breach.'

Ken hurried, head down, through the busy shopping streets, dodging puddles as he went. To his relief, the crush

343

thinned out towards the northern end of the town. He began to walk at a more measured speed, giving himself time to think through how he could get Derek to fill in the missing gaps in his information. When he reached the warehouse in Frederick Street, he found that all the mental toing and froing he'd put himself through on the way had been a waste of energy. Derek was nowhere in evidence and there was a nerd with an attitude problem minding the shop.

'The boss around?' Ken tried, tentatively.

'Gone out.'

'Any idea where?'

'Dunno.'

'Will he be back later?'

'Maybe.'

'What time, do you think?'

The nerd shrugged and slowly lit the cigarette that had been dangling from his lips for some minutes. 'You got something for him?'

'Might have.'

'What?'

'I'd rather discuss it with him.'

'Please yourself.'

Ken glanced around. He couldn't see the table and chairs that Jim had told him about but the warehouse was arranged on two floors and he thought it might be upstairs. He took what was meant to look like a vague interest in a mahogany tallboy and one or two other pieces that had been left standing around in no particular attempt at display.

'Mind if I go up?'

The nerd gave a grunt which Ken took to mean he didn't. Ken went up the rough wooden steps and into the gloom above. There was a jumble of furniture of all types, none of it anything to write home about. He picked around for a while and then went back downstairs.

Perhaps he's got rid of them already, Ken concluded.

There again they might be somewhere at the back. He wandered deeper into the warehouse, undisturbed by the man who was meant to be minding the shop. He was standing in the doorway, looking out into the yard. Ken glanced towards him. The office door had been left open and he was in two minds as to whether to have a nosy. He was about to chance it when he noticed the table and chairs, shoved up against one wall. Strange place to keep the prize exhibit, he thought, walking over. But then he saw a red 'Sold' sticker on the back of one of the chairs. So I've had a totally wasted journey after all, he thought.

He turned the chair towards the light, anyway. It was more force of habit than anything else, although there was also the slightest inkling that he'd seen something very similar to it somewhere else. Immediately, he could see that it was a very fine piece indeed. The one chair, with its graceful carved back and barley-twist uprights, by far outshone anything he'd come across in the warehouse so far. He eyed it for a moment before tipping it forward to inspect the underside. As he'd suspected, there was a mark cut into the wood, some sort of cypher that indicated who the piece had been made for. He crouched down to get a better look.

'Oi, what do you think you're up to? Can't you read?'

Ken ignored the nerd's agitated outburst and went on staring at the intertwined initials that he'd found.

'Just keep your hands off,' the nerd continued, coming up close behind. 'That set's bought and paid for.'

Ken felt the hair rising on the back of his neck, but calmly set the chair upright. 'Button it, sunshine,' he said, 'before I button you.'

The man stepped back. He wasn't up for anything physical.

There were a number of questions that Ken thought of asking as he stood there, holding the man in a menacing gaze. In the end, he thought better of saying anything that might alert Derek that he was on to him. He brushed past, brusquely, and went on his way.

There was no reply again from Kirkby Mote, and again Ken checked the telephone number and redialled, just to make sure. He drummed his fingers on the desk top, irritably. For days he'd been fuming over the loss of that table and chairs. That they'd turned up at Derek's was an even bigger snub. Just what was Mrs Lyall-Bourke playing at? It was inconceivable that after all the trouble he'd taken in going up to see her, agreeing the pieces that should be sold, reassuring her about the arrangements for their collection, she should have reneged on her side of the bargain. He stared angrily at the 'phone for several minutes before picking it up again and calling his Cheshire contact.

'Frank!' he said. 'At last. Where've you been?'

'Down in Devon. Bit of a family crisis. How are you?'

'Furious.'

'What about?'

'Mrs Lyall-Bourke.'

'Oh, you've heard, then?'

'I haven't heard anything yet, but I've seen enough to get me hopping mad.'

'Dreadful, isn't it? Saw the newspapers, I suppose?'

'Eh?'

'I've just seen them myself, my wife kept them while I was away.'

'I think we're talking at cross purposes.'

'Are we?'

'What's all this about newspapers?'

'The report of the break in, of course. It was all over the front page here.'

'You're saying there's been a break in?'

'Yes, a fortnight ago. Do you mean you didn't know?'

'Of course I didn't know.'

'I'd have thought there'd have been something in the nationals about it. It was a pretty major story.'

'Well, I didn't see anything. What happened?'

'Nobody knows for sure, although it looks like the work of a professional gang. Old Miles the butler tried to tackle them apparently, and got very badly beaten for his trouble. He's still in intensive care, so they haven't been able to find out very much more.'

'What about Mrs Lyall-Bourke?'

'She's had a stroke. Must have been the shock. They left her bound and gagged, you see, poor lady.'

'So she's in a bad way too?'

'Paralysed down one side and lost her power of speech. If she has another stroke of that magnitude, it'll probably kill her.'

'God! I thought that something strange must have happened but I had no idea that it was something as terrible as this.'

'What made you 'phone, then? You sounded pretty hacked off.'

'I'll get round to that in a minute. Tell me something. What went in this break in?'

'Almost everything that was valuable, according to the press, but they don't give exact details.'

'Is there a police contact number? They must have set up an incident room or something.'

'I did see a number somewhere. Hang on while I just find the relevant newspaper . . . here it is.'

Ken took the number down. 'Listen, one more thing. You don't know if Mrs Lyall-Bourke parted with any furniture before the burglary happened do you?'

'I very much doubt it, but to be honest I haven't a clue. I've been away for almost three weeks and haven't really had a chance to catch up with things yet.'

'All right. Well, look thanks for your help. I think I ought to give the police a ring straight away. There's something I've seen locally that might give them a lead.'

'What's that?'

'A table and set of chairs that I'd arranged to buy off Mrs Lyall-Bourke.'

'Good Lord! Are you sure?'

'Positive. They had one of the family cyphers carved on them.'

'Perhaps the gang came from your end then, though I can't see how they'd have known what there was at Kirkby Mote, unless they were going on guesswork. Nobody had been in there for the best part of twenty years – except for you, that is.'

'Yes. And that being the case I'd better talk to the police before they come round looking for me.'

'Absolutely. Let me know what happens, won't you?'

'Sure. See you.' Ken dialled the number he'd been given without bothering to replace the handset.

'Incident room.'

'Can I speak to somebody concerning the break in at Kirkby Mote, please?'

'You're already doing so. Detective Sergeant Alwyn Hughes speaking.'

'Hello, D. S. Hughes. My name's Ken Rees and I'm calling you from Brighton.'

'Oh, yes? How can I help you?'

'I think that I can help you, actually. I've come across a set of furniture locally which I'm certain came from Kirkby Mote. You see, I'm an antiques dealer and I visited the house last month at Mrs Lyall-Bourke's request.'

'What date, exactly?'

'October the fourteenth.'

'And what was the nature of your visit?'

'I went to look at a variety of pieces that she wanted to

sell. In fact, I was due to take delivery of several of them quite soon, although that's obviously out of the question now.'

'Can you tell me what those pieces were?'

'I've got a list somewhere, if only I could put my hand on it . . .' He opened his desk drawer and shuffled the papers inside it around. 'Anyway, one of them was a Restoration period table and chairs and that's what I've seen at another dealer's warehouse here.'

'Whereabouts?'

'A place in Frederick Street that's run by a chap called Derek Jones.'

'Do you know this Mr Jones?'

'Yes. Known him for years . . . ah, here's the list.'

'The table and chairs, how do you know that they are from Kirkby Mote?'

'Because they have a particular set of initials inscribed on the underside in the form of a crest. There is no doubt in my mind whatsoever that it's the same one that I saw not only on an identical table and chairs at the house but other items of furniture as well. It even appeared as a device in part of the ceiling decoration in one of the rooms, as I recall.'

'How much of the house did you see when you went there?'

'The gallery, the great chamber and the parlour. Nothing else.'

'And did you take a note of any of the things that you saw there or did you just keep a mental record?'

'I was going on . . .' Ken suddenly remembered the notes that Sally had taken on her visit and realised that she might become implicated if he mentioned them. 'Yes, I did take some notes but I don't have them with me at the moment.'

'Do you know where they are?'

'At home somewhere.' That part, at least, was true. He'd never got round to giving her the notebook back.

'Well, Mr Rees, I'd like you to find them, if you will. They could be enormously helpful to our enquiries.'

'What would you like me to do, exactly?'

'I'd like you to give us a full description of everything you remember. I'll arrange for an officer to come over to you from Brighton Central, if you don't mind, to take a statement.'

'I don't mind at all. Only too pleased to help.'

'I'm very grateful. Now, going back to the table and chairs. Are they still at this warehouse in . . . er . . . Frederick Street, is it?'

'Yes, that's right. I don't know that they're there as I speak but they certainly were four days ago.'

'Had you gone to the premises for anything in particular?'

'Yes. I went over to talk to Derek Jones about something. He wasn't in but I had a look round anyway. That's when I saw the table and chairs.'

'I see. Well, I'll have it looked into. I take it you could identify the furniture for us if it's still there?'

'Certainly.'

'Good. Can you give me your address and telephone number, please?'

Ken rattled them off.

'Thank you. Oh, just one more thing. I'm very glad that you have got in touch with us, but can I ask why you didn't do so as soon as you'd seen the table and chairs?'

'At the point when I saw them I didn't know about the burglary. In fact I only heard about it today. I was told by one of my colleagues.'

'I see. Well, thanks again. We'll be back in contact with you shortly.'

As the 'phone went down, Ken was starting to wonder whether Sally had told anyone other than Heather and him about what she'd seen at Kirkby Mote. It occurred to him immediately that the one person whom she would most probably have spoken to about it was her boyfriend. His misgivings about Daniel Wiseman surfaced again.

The trouble is, all I know about the bloke is that he might have a crook for a friend, he reasoned. There just isn't enough solid information to pin him down for a crook too.

He thought through the information that Tony had given him at the Christie's auction. There was nothing, apart from the reference to Napoleon's cloak clasp, to point a finger squarely at Wiseman's friend. And that in itself was hardly evidence, given, as Tony had said, that it might have been a fake. Another argument, of course, could be that the man had just made the whole thing up in order to impress the little gay.

But what if it was the real thing? he debated. That would mean that Wiseman's friend was involved in some way with the stately home robberies earlier this year. If not personally, then by association. That still doesn't put Wiseman himself in the frame, but it's a good enough reason to get suspicious about him. Now, if he does have shady contacts who are taking possession of antiques that have been stolen to order, what's his place in the game?

He cast around for ideas. The simple answer was that Wiseman provided another outlet for the goods that had been stolen by the professional gangs. But what if it was more complicated than that? What other uses might he have? Ken turned what he knew round every which way before coming back to Wiseman's connection with Sally. It was then that a possible link with the Kirkby Mote burglary sprang to mind.

What if he's an informant of some kind? he asked himself. Nobody had a clue what was in Kirkby Mote except for me and Sally, and I'm sure that she would have told him something about going there.

The link was a tenuous one, but when it was taken together with the cloak clasp business, it provided an interesting theory. If Wiseman's friend had others who were interested in finding places that were worth robbing, they'd need a good informant. What if Wiseman was that man? After all, his line of business would be bringing him into close contact with the fabulously wealthy often enough. He'd be well placed to know where the goodies were likely to be.

And now he's got an extra string to his bow, hasn't he? Ken thought. What could be more convenient than a girl-friend who's in the antiques trade? One who would never guess that what she was telling him was getting passed down the line?

The whole hypothesis was built on pure conjecture and he knew it. But it didn't stop him getting good and angry about it, nevertheless. As much as he could argue with himself that there was no proof of Wiseman's guilt, his gut feeling on the matter told him differently, even taking into account his natural jealousy over Sally.

Well, there's no point in saying anything to her at this stage, he decided, once he'd cooled down, but I think it might be a wise move for both of us if I were to keep a closer watch on her in future.

22

The knock on the window shook Sally from her thoughts. She'd been staring at the same blank piece of paper for a full fifteen minutes without knowing where to start. The knock came at a point where she was either going to write something or run screaming from the building. She got up to unlock the door, relieved that the choice was going to be delayed for some time.

'Where were you? Dreamland?' Julia breezed through the door in the latest of latest Chanel suits.

'Is it . . .?' Sally began, giving the coat an astonished stare.

'The real thing?' Julia finished. 'Yes. Christmas present from Oliver. What do you think?'

'It's fabulous. You lucky blighter.'

'Yeah, I am, aren't I?' she grinned, preening herself, rather, to get the most value out of her friend's envy.

'I suppose this means that you spent most of the holiday at his place?'

'*Places*.' Julia couldn't resist inching the competition stakes up another notch. 'A week in his London apartment and a week at the house in Kent.'

'Well, well. If it goes on like this you'll be walking in flashing a big diamond ring some day soon.'

'I've a feeling that he is working himself up to asking The Ultimate Question,' said Julia, smugly. 'In fact, I'd have sworn he was going to get his act together on New Year's Eve. He was looking very nervous and shifty until the champagne kicked in.'

'Don't tell me! I bet it was right on the tip of his tongue and then he started to feel a bit warm and content and decided to enjoy himself instead.'

'I wouldn't be surprised. I remember the same thing happening with Rupert – you know, the one I was engaged to for a brief but beautiful moment in Australia.'

'I'd forgotten about him.'

'Well, it is five years ago. Lot of water under the bridge since then.'

'Yes.'

'He had to have two stabs at proposing. Silly boy had wanted to on my birthday, but we were at this incredible restaurant in Sydney and the food was so good that he ate too much and went promptly into "comfortable and comatose" mode. I remember thinking how hilarious it was, when he told me all about it later. Of course, that was when he was feeling all secure because I'd just accepted him at the second attempt.'

'Did he get dead romantic and go down on one knee?'

'No, it was one of those horribly obvious moments, the kind when they happen to be on both knees at the time.'

'Eh?'

'Mid-bonk, silly.'

'I suppose doing it *in flagrante* is the guaranteed way of getting a "yes".'

'Cheapest shot in the book if you ask me,' Julia replied. 'Anyway, how's a guy to know what you're saying "yes" to if he asks you something like that at the crucial moment? I mean, it could be "yes, go on a bit more", "yes, I think I'm

354

almost there" or "yes for heaven's sake, now before it's too late!" '

Sally was glad to find she could still laugh. 'Thank God you came by. I was thinking of getting that ceremonial sword down off the wall and committing *hara-kiri* with it.'

'Why? What's the problem? Something happened between you and Daniel?'

'Not quite as bad as that, but damn near almost.'

'What?' Julia had turned a little pale, but Sally took it for friendly sympathy.

'I had an impromptu call from the neighbourhood VAT man this morning. He's not very pleased with me.'

'Oh, dear.'

'It's worse than "oh dear", I'm afraid. He asked to see my stockbook but I hadn't been keeping one properly. I had meant to, of course, but what with batting between here, the auctions and the private sales . . . then there was Christmas.'

'I know what you mean. We were frantic before the holiday too, all those interminable meetings . . .'

'Makes me glad that I work on my own and for myself,' said Sally. 'Mind you, I'm a bit bothered about Ken. I do owe him for finding me the shop and all that. Mustn't go letting him down by flunking it.'

'You're not in danger of that, are you?'

'Not really, at least I don't think so. The business has been going very well. In fact, if it hadn't done so blooming well, I wouldn't have had to register for VAT in the first place. Seems bizarre. If you do badly, you're in trouble; if you do well, you're in trouble. Just trouble of a different kind, that's all.'

'So what's the problem, exactly?'

'The problem is that you're required to keep a stockbook by law. If you don't and the VAT man decides to get mean about it, he can ask you to cough up the tax on the full selling price of your goods. Normally, you see, you only get taxed on the profit margin. So you can imagine how ruinous it would be if you were made to pay tax on the whole sale price of every piece that's been through your hands.'

'It'd run to thousands and thousands of pounds.'

Sally ran her forefinger across her throat, like a knife, 'You're talking instant death. Especially for someone like me. The smaller your mark-up the bigger the difference between what you *would* have paid in VAT, had you been smart and kept your stockbook up-to-date, and what you *will* pay now that you've been an idiot.'

'Oh hell! What are you going to do about it?'

'I'd say that unless I succumb to the alternate temptations of using the ceremonial sword or fleeing the country first, I'm going to sit right down and recreate a stockbook.'

'Is it legal?'

'Must be, the VAT man told me to do it. He was very nice, considering. He said that as long as I had a new stockbook to put in front of him when he comes back in a couple of weeks' time, he'd be prepared to overlook the incident.'

'What a relief. You had my heart in my mouth for a moment there.'

'Well, mine's still between my molars and it's unlikely to slide back down into my chest for a good long time yet,' Sally gestured over to her table. 'Look at this. This pad of A4 has been sitting here ever since the VAT man went, waiting for me to make a list. Honestly, I've been flogging myself to death trying to remember exactly what I've had in here over the past few months, but it's just impossible. Half of it went out again so fast that it hardly had time to gather dust.'

'Don't you keep a diary? You must have something to remind you of appointments.'

'Well, yes, but it's rather scrappy. Just times and vague references to destinations. I can't always remember what the references are after a few weeks have passed.'

'Then I suppose it's down to good old-fashioned brain wracking.'

'I suppose so.' Sally looked around the shop. 'I've got some of the receipts. And the old catalogue will help. If I take it calmly and slowly, I guess I'll get there in the end.'

'So what have you been up to recently, then?'

'Nothing much. Just settling myself back into the routine after the holiday, really.' She should have enjoyed Christmas. Daniel had certainly taken her to enough parties. But the lingering sense of unease that she had about some of his dealings had been made worse by meeting his friends. Some had been a little too flashy for her liking.

'The thing to do, I always think, is to plan something interesting for mid-January. That way, you've got something both to look forward to and that'll give you a lift when it arrives.'

'That's a good idea. I suppose you've already got something lined up?'

'Of course.' Julia gave a tight little smile. 'We're flying to Le Touquet for a long week-end.'

'But won't the weather be just as bad as it is here?'

'I've no intention of going further than the hotel, if I can help it, so I don't think we'll be bothered by the weather. Unless we get ice on the undercarriage going over, that is. The last time it happened we had to plonk down on a private landing strip.'

'You mean you're flying yourselves?'

'Oliver's flying, yes. Didn't I tell you that he has a 'plane?'

'No.'

'Oh. Well, he does, just a small one. Piper something or other.'

'Cherokee? Arrow?' Sally tried, using the names she'd picked up from Daniel's dealings.

'No idea. All I know is it's got wings.' Julia gave the impression of being completely uninterested but Sally knew

357

her friend better than that. She was materialistic in the extreme.

'Anyhow,' Julia continued, 'I'm looking forward to a nice luxuriate. We'll probably just stay in bed the whole time and have our meals brought up by room service.'

'Very decadent.'

'Mmm, that's what I like about it best.'

'I prefer to be out and about doing things, myself.'

'You always were one for running around. You should try relaxing once in a while.'

'Oh, I do – well, week-ends anyway, if Daniel's around.'

'Still spoiling you, is he?'

'Yes.' Sally smiled. 'Sometimes I think he's too good to be true.'

'It's a funny thing that, isn't it?' Julia mused. 'We hate it if a man mistreats us, and yet if he's kind we think that there's got to be a catch.'

'It's not entirely unreasonable, though, is it? I mean, how many times have you been well treated as opposed to mis-treated? A lot fewer, I bet.'

'Well, if they start to act badly I don't usually give them much of a chance to get worse. It's just a waste of my life. I don't know what possesses a woman to stay with a man who's giving her a hard time.'

'You stay because you love them.'

Julia snorted. 'Honestly, Sal, you're such an incurable romantic. It's not like it is in the fairy stories, you know. Men do not come along and sweep you off your feet then devote the rest of their lives to loving and cherishing you. In fact, from what I've observed, that bit normally goes out of the church window about half-an-hour after you've exchanged vows.'

'You're such a cynic,' Sally retorted. 'Anyway, I'm not saying that I expect things to be perfect. Wherever you stick

358

two human beings together in the same small building, there'll always be hiccups.'

'I still maintain that the pragmatic approach is best.'

'Then you've never been completely in love.'

'Oh, don't you think so?' Julia looked a bit surprised.

'Well, not in terms that I understand.'

'Do you think that's why I've never settled down?'

'Maybe.'

'Or maybe I just wasn't ready.'

'Could be that. Who knows?'

'I think I'm ready now, though. I mean, if Oliver did pop the question, I'm sure I'd say yes.'

'Is that because you're ready or because he's the right man?'

Julia thought about it but was obviously unsure.

'I think your silence proves the point,' said Sally. 'Tell me something. Are you faithful to him?'

'Mostly.'

'What's that meant to mean?'

'It means mostly. I don't have a secret supply of lovers hidden away or anything, but I don't see why I shouldn't hedge my bets a bit. If someone wants to flirt, I flirt. I don't necessarily fall into bed with them. In fact, I never was particularly promiscuous, no matter what you might have thought in the past. But every now and then I feel "What the hell?" and give in to an indecent urge. After all, I might just get dumped instead of proposed to and I don't much like the idea of being left feeling like a fool.'

'So at what point exactly, do you think you might be prepared to give your all to one man alone?'

'The point at which the ink's dry on the marriage certificate.'

Sally was shocked. 'Well, I'm sorry to say that I think that moment will be a long time in coming,' she warned. 'Your attitude is far too mercenary.'

'Look, I'm a lawyer and that means that there has to be a good body of established evidence in front of me before I decide that a case is worth taking on.'

'A very laudable sentiment, I'm sure, professionally speaking, but it's nonsense when you apply it to personal matters.'

'I don't think so.'

'Then we'll have to agree to differ.'

The atmosphere between the two women had soured somewhat and neither was feeling comfortable about it.

'Oh, well,' said Julia, at length, 'I guess I'll take my risks my way and you'll take yours yours.'

'I suppose so.'

'You coming out for lunch today, at all?'

'Don't think so. Speaking of risks reminds me that I'd better get on with my list for the VAT man.' Sally nodded towards the still-empty pad on her desk.

'Okay.'

'Maybe we can do something next week? Have a girls' night out or something. I really need to get this thing out of my hair now.' Sally had meant to be conciliatory, but hadn't sounded very convincing.

'Fine. Be seeing you, then.'

'Yes. See you.'

They parted with an embrace that had lost its warmth in the heat of discussion, and Sally was saddened by it. Nevertheless, she knew she could not have agreed with Julia's approach to men and relationships. It surprised her that her friend could be so hard, even though they'd known each other for so many years. But then, she thought, perhaps she had always been a romantic whereas Julia hadn't. The difference between their characters didn't matter all that much. It was the friendship that counted.

'Hello, stranger.' Sally quickly turned over the papers on her desk as Ken came in. 'To what do we owe the pleasure of your company?'

'I need some professional advice,' he said, with something of a sheepish grin.

'Good Lord! Things must be looking up if you need advice from me.'

'Not on a business matter.'

'Ah.' She'd thought it most unlikely, anyway.

'Something personal.'

Sally gave him a quizzical look.

'I've been into Boots but it's all a bit embarrassing, really. I haven't got a clue what to buy.'

'Curiouser and curiouser. Don't tell me that you keep coming out with bottles of Lucozade.'

'There's no need to get cheeky.'

She laughed, 'Well, what *are* you alluding to?'

'Baby equipment, of course. You know, clothes, toys, things for the nursery . . .'

'Baby equipment?'

'Yes,' he said, with evident delight. 'I've just found out that my line has been increased.'

Sally moved uncomfortably in her seat. The smile dissolved and her mouth became taut.

'Am I right in assuming that congratulations are in order here?'

'You are.'

'Well, well.' She started to colour. 'I had no idea.'

'Wonderful, isn't it? A six-pound baby girl to be called Emily, after my mother.' Ken had seen immediately that she'd got the wrong end of the stick but couldn't resist winding her up a bit further. After holding himself back for so long, it was gratifying to get a reaction out of her.

'You okay?'

'Me? Of course.'

'Aren't you pleased for me?'

'Thrilled.' She was anything but.

'Good. So what do you send the mother of a new-born child?'

There was a pause whilst Sally tried to come to terms with what she was feeling. She hadn't seriously considered having a physical relationship with Ken for some time, but it might have gone that way if Daniel hadn't come along. She was annoyed to think that he'd started to get intimate with her when he'd already been heavily involved with someone else.

'Well, I'm shocked,' she said, finally.

'I do believe you are.' Fancy that, he thought. So she does care?

'How can you stand there looking so smug? Really it's disgusting. A man of your age, too. Honestly, Ken, I would have thought you'd have more decency.'

He started to laugh.

'What's so funny?'

'You on your high horse. The gift is intended for my granddaughter, silly.'

'Granddaughter?' Sally was offended as well as surprised. 'This story gets better by the minute. How can you have a granddaughter? You'd have to have your own son or daughter first.'

'Quite correct.'

'But you've never even been married.'

'Since when was a ring necessary on voyage?' He could tell that the joke had fallen flat and was sorry that he'd started it, now.

'Then somebody somewhere must have had your illegitimate child.'

'Yes.'

'I can hardly believe it.'

'Why not? What's so awful?'

362

'Just I find it hard to imagine that a man of your . . . your calibre could allow such a thing to happen.'

'What's my calibre got to do with it?' He hadn't intended to start justifying himself, but it was obvious that some explanation was necessary. 'All that was nearly thirty years ago. A lot's changed since then.'

'Huh!'

'What do you mean, huh? And what are you getting so huffy about, anyway? You're not exactly Miss Morality yourself, are you?'

'I beg your pardon?'

'Well, you have sex with people you're not married to, don't you?'

'What? How dare you?'

'I'm just pointing out that people in glass houses shouldn't throw stones.'

'You've got a bloody nerve!'

'I don't think so. It's no use your playing the paragon of virtue to my supposed knave. I've heard about your private life.'

'My private life is none of your concern.'

'No more is mine yours. Anyway, you're wrong.'

'How am I wrong?'

'What you do *is* my concern.'

'Oh, is it? And what makes you think you have a right to push your nose into my affairs?'

'Without me, you wouldn't be here, for a start.'

'I see. Time to hang the dirty washing out, is it?' Sally was utterly furious. She'd always felt beholden to Ken and the feeling irked her. All she needed was to be reminded now, especially since she was feeling guilty about the VAT problem and how its consequences might rebound on him.

'I'm sorry,' he said, realising that he'd allowed himself to get drawn into a fight needlessly, 'I didn't mean that.'

'Why say it, then? This is what I get for letting you help

me, I suppose. "No strings attached," you said. Not much! More like a dirty great rope.'

'I apologise. I made a mistake.'

'Stuff your apology. I'm here today because of what I'm capable of. Not because of you.'

'You are bloody ungracious.' Ken knew that he'd teed himself up for Sally's remark, but his feelings were hurt. 'It'll serve you right when you fall flat on your face.'

'Thanks a lot. With friends like you, who needs enemies?'

'I'm not your enemy,' he said, coldly. 'It's the people who you choose to acquaint yourself with that you've got to look out for.'

'Oh? Anyone in particular?'

'Daniel Wiseman, for a start.'

Sally was stunned. She'd never mentioned Daniel in front of Ken, as a matter of delicacy.

'Have you been spying on me?'

'Don't be ridiculous.'

'Of all the cheap . . .'

'Look, everyone in The Lanes knows who you're going with. I can't go anywhere without being told some new and lurid tale.'

'*Lurid*?'

'Didn't you know that your boyfriend's reputation goes before him? A real lady killer, they say. And supposedly something of a stud.'

'Dear me, I may swoon away!' She heaped on the irony. 'I'm so glad you told me before I succumbed to his wicked wiles.'

'Be sarcastic, then. You'll find out that his dubious assets extend beyond the physical soon enough.'

'What are you on about?'

'Never mind.' Ken already hated himself for letting his envy show. Going one step further had not been a great move either. He still had no more to condemn Daniel on than what Tony had told him.

'You can't come in here making accusations without explaining them. Come on, spit it out.'

'It's just that he moves in some pretty sleazy circles.'

'Don't we all?' Sally shuffled her papers irritably. 'Is this all it's about or is there another juicy titbit that you can't wait to pass on?'

'That's all I have to say. Just watch him. If he's connected with the type of people I believe he's connected with, you could end up being tarred with the same brush.'

'Ooh, I just love the air of mystery,' she scoffed. 'Get to the point, if you have one. I haven't got the whole day to waste.'

'You can never listen to anybody else, can you? I wouldn't be saying all this if there wasn't something serious behind it.'

'Seems what you're saying is a load of old tosh to me. "He moves in some sleazy circles", indeed. Not exactly the news of the century, is it?'

'You think you're so smart, don't you? Well, if you're not interested in watching your own back, I'm damned if I'm going to watch it for you.'

'It's nice to know that you still take me for a complete dimwit. You're not my sole protector, you know. I can look after myself quite adequately.'

'Fine. Do so.' He turned.

'What's this really about, Ken? I don't understand. Why go wittering on about Daniel's connections if you don't intend to follow up what you say? Or is it the other stuff that's bugging you, truthfully? The stuff about his reputation in the past? What are you trying to do, make me jealous? If so, it's a pretty pathetic attempt.'

'I've had enough of this argument.'

'I haven't. I think I'm beginning to get it, now. You're trying to spoil things for me, aren't you? Trying to spoil what I've got with Daniel. Just because you helped me set up the business you think you own me. You probably even thought that because of that I'd come across one day.'

She shoved her chair back. 'That's it, isn't it? Don't try to deny it. You're no better than the others after all. You hate the idea of my being with Daniel because whilst I'm with him you haven't got a chance yourself. Well, forget it. I'm not giving him up, whatever bit of nastiness you care to come in here spreading about him. And I'll tell you something else. Even if I finished with him tomorrow, you'd be last on my list of replacements.'

He'd had his hand on the door latch, but now he let his arm drop. He paused for a moment to control his emotions.

'You'll cut yourself dead with that tongue of yours one of these days,' he said, barely concealing his rage. 'You know, at the beginning I admired you for what I thought was guts and determination. But I can see now, that I was wrong. What I took for courage was arrogance. What I took for drive, sheer obstinacy. That I misjudged you is one thing. Others, less well-intentioned, won't. Don't call for me when the vultures close in. You're on your own from here on in.'

'Good,' she said, more angry at herself than at him. She hadn't meant to be so vicious and she regretted it violently but her injured pride was smarting too much for her to back off.

'Goodbye.'

'Ken, I . . .' she started, but the door had slammed behind him. 'Oh, God. Now look what I've gone and done.'

She thought of running after him and trying to make it up, but the feeling of being all alone overwhelmed her. It was a less attractive prospect than she'd imagined.

23

He was tall and slim, probably about forty, and it was the second time that he'd come into the shop that day. At first, Sally had paid little attention to him. When he'd come in at around ten in the morning, she'd been too excited by the letter she had received from the British Museum to notice that he was taking a peculiar interest in a vase that formed part of the display in the cabinet which stood in a central position against the wall facing her desk. At that time, he had appeared to be browsing. Now, though, he asked if she would unlock the cabinet so that he could view the vase. The request did not strike her as out of the ordinary. In fact, she rather thought that it might mean she was about to make a sale. Yet the man's attitude was so offhand that she wondered if he was another dealer up to the usual trick of trying to look as disinterested as possible. He remained aloof and serious whilst she got the keys from the drawer of her desk. It was only as she crossed the room that she began to feel that there was something in his demeanour that had the quality of officialdom.

'It is a very attractive piece,' said Sally, lightly, as she took the vase from the shelf. 'Do you collect Oriental art?'

'May I handle it?' The deliberate evasion of her question

led Sally to believe that he was a dealer, after all. She immediately sharpened her wits for the bout of bargaining she was sure would follow, if he decided that the vase was for him. The rich colours of the cloisonné decoration came to life under the light, making the contrast between the delicate pink of the chrysanthemums and teal green of the pheasant that were pictured there all the more striking against the black background.

'Meiji period, is it?' the man asked.

'Yes. Although the wooden stand is later.'

'But the two are of a piece, so to speak?'

'They go together, yes.'

'That's how they came to you?'

'Yes.'

'And where did the vase come from?'

'It's precise provenance is obscure,' she'd entirely missed his meaning, and thought the question related to the vase's origins, 'but with a piece like this, proof of age is more important than proof of where it came from. There would have been many Japanese workshops producing vases of this type, so it's hard to say exactly where it would have been made. There was no individual imprint, as such, although occasionally you might find a piece that is signed. Normally, there's just a mark to indicate the reign that it was produced in. You can see the stamp on the underside, that confirms that the vase is Meiji. Apart from that, there are no clues.'

He tipped the vase, glanced at the red seal mark on the bottom and seemed satisfied.

'I take it that you bought this vase from another dealer?'

'It was a private sale,' she said, coldly.

'Somebody local?'

By now, Sally was becoming irritated with the line he was taking. She considered that how she had come by the vase was no business of his. It was time to close the conversation down.

'Are you interested in the piece or not?' she asked, hoping to make it clear that she had no intention of wasting any more breath on the subject.

'What are you looking for on it?'

Ah, that's more like it, she thought. 'Perhaps you'd like to make me an offer?'

'I'll think about it,' he replied, abruptly. And with that he left the shop.

'Bloody hell!' Sally muttered after the door had clicked shut behind him. 'The nerve of some people.' She replaced the vase in the display cabinet and locked the door. Just then, the 'phone rang.

'Hi, darling, how's your day going?' Daniel's voice was bright and cheery.

'Just had some twerp in looking at that vase you gave me,' she said, grumpily. 'Don't know who the devil he was but he didn't half ask some cheeky questions.'

'Oh? Like what?'

'Where it had come from, stuff like that.'

'In what sense?'

'In the normal sense, I presume. I mean, had it been a Deco figure, I could have understood someone wanting to know whether it was by a famous maker or not, but you know that there's virtually no way of placing Oriental ceramics. Well, not down to the actual workshop, anyway. You might be able to say what area it might have come from . . .'

'What else did he ask?'

'Oh, all sorts. But what really got me going was that he obviously thought that I would tell him who I'd bought it from. Just-as-if department!'

'So you didn't tell him?'

'Certainly not.'

'Must've been a bit of a crank.'

'Who knows? He didn't look like one, although there was something odd about him.'

369

'Odd?'

'Yes, something in his bearing. He seemed faintly military, in some way. You know, not expensively dressed but impeccably. That usually means that a man's been in the services, especially if he's younger than mid-fifties. He was very tidy and proper, very precise, right down to the neatly clipped moustache.'

'Oh?'

She didn't register the sudden change in his voice as anything remarkable. 'Anyway, he went away in the end, thank heavens. I was having a nice day until he walked in.'

'Found something good?' Daniel had regained his normal poise.

'Looks like it. You know that funny stick that I picked up?'

'No.'

'Yes, you do, the carved one that I kept behind the desk and everybody kept telling me was the worst piece of rubbish in history.'

'Oh, that thing.'

'Yes, well, that thing is a very rare and valuable thing, as it turns out.'

'Go on.'

'That's what it says here,' she said, triumphantly lifting up the letter that had arrived that morning. 'According to the British Museum, it's a nineteenth-century Hawaiian God stick. They say that they're extremely rare, particularly this one, but that their expert confirms that that's what it is.'

'Blimey. Well done you.'

'There you go, you see, I'm not such an idiot, after all.'

'What do you think you'll do with it, then?'

'Put it up for auction, of course. I'll have to contact the London houses and see when and where the next sale of tribal art is.'

'So it's been a good day so far, really?'

'Yes. That bloke took the edge off it a bit, but I'm over it, now.'

'Good. Look, the reason I 'phoned, apart from to say hello, was that there's been a change of plans for tonight.'

'Oh, so we're not going to the cinema after all?'

'Or anything else, I'm afraid. Sorry, sweetheart, but something urgent's come up so I shan't be able to see you.'

'What? Not at all?'

'No, sorry.'

'Oh, well. Guess I'll just have to make do with a lonely little supper, then.'

'Don't put it like that. It's not deliberate, you know.'

'I know.' She smiled gently to herself. 'What is it? Problem with one of your deals?'

'Er . . . yeah. Have to go abroad. May be away for a few days.'

'Gosh, that sounds serious.'

'It'll be okay. Just a bit of a hiccup, that's all.'

'You're sure?'

'Yes. Nothing that can't be sorted.'

'Will you ring me?'

'If I can.'

'Oh.' Sally's disappointment was clear from the flatness of her tone.

'I mean, of course I'll ring you. I just don't know when I'll have time to get near a 'phone.'

'All right.'

'Lots of love, then, and I'll speak to you soon.'

'Yes. Bye, darling.'

Sally was still feeling fed up as she put down the 'phone. She shuffled the papers on her desk for a moment, then got up and went to the cubby-hole at the back of the shop. She filled the kettle and flicked down the switch on the socket it was connected to. As she did so, a bright tongue of electricity flashed through the gap around the switch.

'Blasted thing!' She'd moved her hand away in time to avoid getting a shock. 'Must get Daniel to have a look at it.'

She brooded about him as she waited for the kettle to boil, not much liking the idea of not seeing him for a few days. But why? she asked herself. Why does it matter so much? It's not as if I haven't got other things to do with my time. She dwelt on the thought for a while and came to the conclusion that she had begun to centre her life around him, or the idea of them as a couple as any rate. That was the trouble with any emotional involvement. You'd start by thinking you could keep it at arms' length but gradually it'd begin to get more and more important. Finally, there'd hardly be a free-thinking moment that wasn't occupied in some way by what you felt about him, what he felt about you, what the latest exchange between you meant. It was a minefield, the whole thing, and to think that she'd been cocky enough to believe she'd be able to walk through it unscathed!

Sally took the mug of tea she had made and wandered back into the shop. She'd just remembered what Heather had said about not getting too attached to one man too soon. She'd been right, of course, but it was a bit late to do much about it now. She hadn't intended for things to turn out the way they had. It had just sort of happened on its own. Sally sighed and looked up at the portrait of her father hanging on the wall.

'Oh, Dad,' she said, wishing that she still had him to talk to. He'd always been so sensitive and caring when she'd gone to him with emotional problems. Not that there was a problem that she could exactly identify today, but there was some feeling deep down that told her things were not quite as they should be. It had been building up over the months in small, almost negligible ways. Little niggles that had made her wonder whether she knew less about Daniel than perhaps she should. The way he would slough off references to where he'd been and who he'd been seeing was one of the things that bothered her. She couldn't pin-point why. And perhaps the feel of some of the friends of his that she'd met over the Christmas period had influenced her. Two or three had certainly fallen into the 'wide boy' category. And then there were Ken's insinuations.

Her gaze passed from her father's picture to the display cabinet beneath. The vase that Daniel had given her glinted innocently in the light. She bent to look at it, and again received the uncomfortable feeling that she'd seen it some-where before. It had occurred to her several times in the past, but she'd always thought that her mind had been playing tricks on her. After all, she'd seen so many photographs of similar pieces during the course of her research into Oriental art, to say nothing of all the pieces that she'd actually handled.

Oh, I must be getting stupid about it because of that man, she thought. But then, an image of the serious-looking face with its perfectly trimmed moustache re-formed in her mind. What had it been about him that had given the impression of authority? What was there to fear from anyone in authority, anyway? She moved away from the cabinet and went back to her desk. Part of the stockbook that she'd been trying to recreate for the VAT inspector lay under the letter that she'd received from the British Museum.

Maybe it was somebody from the VAT office, she reasoned. Perhaps they're trying to get a lead on who I've been doing business with so that they've got a secondary check on what kind of money I've been making. She already knew that they'd be able to trace anything that she'd bought at the sales, all they had to do was go through the books of the auction house concerned. Yes, that's probably it, she decided. Either that or they're just keeping an eye on me to make sure I don't forget to put absolutely everything on the list. She remembered how Ken had warned her that once the VAT people became interested in you, they'd be watching every move. He'd even told her a horror story about some trader who'd denied doing a certain deal in cash because he'd frankly plain forgotten about it, only to have the VAT man produce a photograph of the money changing hands. No one had any idea how and by whom the photograph had been taken, given that everyone concerned in the deal knew each other and would hardly have snitched. However, the event had passed into the folk history of the antiques world as a cautionary tale.

That's obviously what it's all about, Sally told herself. Well, I'll spoil their fun by making sure that there's nothing to find.

The tedious business of itemising every piece that had been bought and sold since she'd started her business had knocked a lot of time out of her schedule over the previous week. Resent it though she did, Sally realised that the best thing to do was not to keep picking at it, but to get the job over with once and for all. She set to with her usual determination, hardly noticing the hours as they passed. By the end of the afternoon, she was most of the way to having a completed record. She stretched and yawned and decided to award herself five minutes off. Somewhere outside a siren was blaring. She glanced through the window but there was nothing to suggest that there was anything exciting going on nearby.

'He's probably late for his tea,' she said, using the joke that had been her father's favourite whenever any vehicle with a blue flashing light would go dashing by. 'Speaking of which . . .'

She took the biro she'd been using to write into the cubbyhole with her while she went to brew a new pot of tea.

'You're not going to get me, this time,' she scolded the electric socket as she plugged the kettle in, and flipped her biro round in her hand so that the end with the plastic stopper came into contact with the switch. Again, a bright flash sparked out. 'See, fooled you.' She started to hum a little tune as she waited for the water to heat. It was then that it occurred to her that it must have gone pretty dark. She could see a strobe light playing on the back wall of the shop that could only be coming from outside, though for the second or two that passed before the door buzzer went she couldn't understand what the meaning of it was. As soon as she looked round the entrance to the cubby-hole to see who was there, the penny dropped. There were two men in dark overcoats waiting. One had a small moustache.

Sally's heart missed a beat as she went to answer the door. When she opened it, she noticed that behind the two men there was a policewoman. The man with the moustache flashed an identity card in her direction as the three stepped inside the shop.

'Miss Sally Blythe?' he asked. She nodded, limply. 'I am arresting you on suspicion of handling stolen goods, Miss Blythe. You are not obliged to say anything, but it is my duty to inform you that anything you do say may be taken down and used in evidence against you.'

The words hit her like a bombshell.

'I don't understand!' she exclaimed. 'What's this about?'

'If you'll just come along with me, miss,' said the policewoman, taking her firmly by the elbow.

'But you can't. I have children to pick up from school.'

'If you'll just come along, your rights will be explained to you at the station.'

Sally was out in the street before she remembered her handbag.

'My bag,' she pleaded, 'can't I bring my bag?'

The policewoman followed her back into the shop to get it. The two other officers had already taken the drawers out of her desk and were sifting through the contents.

'What are you doing?' Sally's voice was strangled. 'You have no right to go through my things.'

'A search warrant is not necessary under the circumstances,' replied one of them, indifferently.

'Come along, miss,' said the policewoman, more kindly, 'it will all be explained at the station.'

The drive to the police station was the most miserable journey Sally could remember taking since she'd been called to Steyning after hearing that her father had died. She thought of him now, of Heather, of a time before Heather. Suddenly the sight of the chequered band around the policewoman's hat unlatched a long-forgotten memory, and she recalled a room that smelt of chalk dust, the sense of fear, the solemn face of her old headmaster as he mouthed the words that had destroyed her childhood: 'There has been a terrible accident . . .'

Sally covered her face with her hands and let the tears come. The horror of that moment pierced her to the heart, the pain as fresh as if it had happened yesterday. The pain increased as she struggled to bring back an image of her mother and realised that there was only the haziest impression of her left. Photographs had taken her place for so long that there was no substance in any vision that Sally could conjure. The greatest grief was in this total loss.

By the time they arrived at the police station, she was in a state of deep shock, her senses so dull that she barely took in the droning monologue of the Custody Sergeant as he booked her in.

'You have the right to a solicitor . . . you have the right to have a relative or friend contacted . . .'

She nodded, vaguely, unsure that it wasn't just part of some grotesque fantasy.

'Didn't you say that you had children to collect from school?' prompted the policewoman.

'Children . . . yes.'

'Is there anyone who can pick them up for you?'

'I . . .'

The Custody Sergeant saw Sally sway slightly and thought her legs were going to go. 'You all right, miss?'

'All right? Yes, I think so.'

'Perhaps you'd better sit down for a while.'

'No, I . . . Heather. Must 'phone Heather.'

'A friend?' asked the policewoman.

'My step-mother.'

'What's her telephone number?'

For a moment, Sally couldn't remember. Then, she pulled herself together and told them.

'Very well. I'll let her know you're here,' said the Custody Sergeant. 'Do you have a solicitor, or shall we get one for you?'

Sally thought briefly of Julia, but then shook her head.

'This way then, please.' The policewoman took Sally away to a room which had no windows. She searched her briefly and then went through her handbag.

'Why do you have to do that?'

'Just making sure that there's nothing that you could do yourself or anyone else any harm with,' said the policewoman, briskly. She took out her notebook and made a list of every item that had come out of the bag.

'How long will you keep me here?' Sally asked, at last.

'Hard to say, miss. Could be up to twenty-four hours, in the first instance.'

'Twenty-four hours?'

'Or up to thirty-six, if necessary.'

'What?' Alarm recharged her dulled senses.

'Those are the rules.'

'But I don't even know what I'm meant to have done yet.'

'It will all be explained to you. This way, please.' The policewoman escorted her down a corridor and into another room where a man was waiting behind a bare desk.

'Thank you, WPC Haines,' he said, then to Sally, 'Sit there, please.'

She took the seat opposite him and watched while he broke open two new tape cassettes and put them into a machine that was built into the top of the table.

'This interview will be recorded,' he told her, 'and you have a right to a copy of the tape afterwards.'

He clicked a switch and cogs started to turn. 'You are not obliged to say anything,' he intoned, 'but anything you might say may be used in evidence. This is an interview between Miss Sally Blythe of Jacob's Cottage, Fulking, and Detective Sergeant Thomas Hendry of Brighton Central. It is being recorded at Brighton Central station and the time is now seventeen thirty-three.'

He raised his eyes to Sally. 'You have been arrested on suspicion of receiving stolen goods. Do you understand the charge?'

'No,' she replied. 'I've no idea what you're talking about.'

'Do you understand the meaning of the charge?'

'It means you think that I have got something that has been stolen, I suppose.'

'That is correct. And do you know what that item or items may be?'

'No.'

He sat back. 'Let's just have some personal details. Are you single, married or divorced?'

'Divorced.'

'And do you live alone?'

'Yes.'

'No children?'

'Two. Two boys.'

'Do they live with you?'

'Yes, of course.'

'And who is their father?'

'My ex-husband,' she said, beginning to flush.

'Could you give me his name and address?'

'Philip Whitehead, flat five, 121 Marine Parade, Brighton.'

'And you're divorced?'

'Yes.'

'How long have you been divorced?'

'Almost three years.'

'And you've lived on your own since then?'

'Yes.'

'Do you have any relatives, apart from the children that is?'

'A step-mother.'

'Does she live in the district?'

'Yes, in Steyning, she has a shop and a studio there.'

'What kind of studio?'

'An art studio. She's an artist.'

'Do you see her very often?'

'All the time.'

'So you would describe your relationship as close.'

'Yes. Look, is this really necessary?'

'If you'd just answer the questions, Miss Blythe.'

'But you still haven't told me what I'm supposed to have done.'

'You are here on suspicion of receiving stolen goods.'

'I *know* that. But what goods?'

'If you'd just answer the questions, it'd save a lot of time.'

Sally glared at him, to no effect.

'Is your step-mother your only living relative?'

'I've got an aunt in Dumfries, but I haven't seen her in years.'

'Do you have any boyfriends?'

'I have a man that I'm seeing, yes.'

'His name?'

'Daniel Wiseman.'

'Address?'

'The Willows, Black Lion Lane, Henfield.'

'You have a relationship with this Mr Wiseman?'

'Yes.'

'How long have you known him?'

'About seven or eight months.'

'What does he do?'

'He deals in aeroplanes and classic cars.'

'Do you know much about his business?'

'Not much, no. He has an office at his house and an office at Shoreham airport, but so far as I know, most of his business is conducted elsewhere.'

'Around and about locally?'

'Well, yes. Although he travels around the country quite a lot too.'

'Where to?'

'I don't know, all over the place. He doesn't tell me the details.'

'Do you spend much time in each other's company?'

'We see each other two or three nights a week and most week-ends.'

'And he never discusses his business with you?'

'He tells me the odd thing.'

'What sort of odd thing?'

'Well, occasionally he'll tell me about this or that car or 'plane that he's selling.'

'Anything else?'

'He generally tells me if he has to take a special trip to collect something.'

'Such as?'

'Car spares, or something like that. Especially if it means going abroad.'

'Does he travel abroad much?'

'Every couple of weeks or so.'

'How does he travel?'

'He flies himself, usually, although sometimes he drives.'

'What route does he take when he drives?'

'Newhaven–Dieppe, normally. Sometimes Dover–Calais.'

'And what does he tell you he's doing?'

'I've told you, collecting car spares or some such.'

'Have you ever been on one of these trips with him?'

'No.'

'So you don't know where he goes?'

'I know that it's Belgium or France or wherever, but not the exact place, no.'

'Does he ever bring anything back apart from car spares?'

'Not normally, although he might bring the odd small thing.' Sally suddenly remembered the two Dutch paintings that Daniel had given her to sell some months before and wondered whether she ought to have mentioned them.

'Gifts for you?'

'Yes, sometimes.'

'What sort of gifts would they be?'

'Anything from a bottle of perfume to a piece of salami.'

'Nothing more valuable?'

She was beginning to feel guilty and thought he might notice. 'Once in a while he might bring me something for the shop.'

'Your antique shop.'

'Yes.'

'So he might bring you back an antique?'

'Yes.'

'Could you give me more details?'

'Well, once he brought a couple of paintings, other times he's given me a ceramic or a decorated box . . .'

'Have you ever asked where these things came from?'

'Not specifically, no. As far as I know, he just buys things that he comes across when he's doing other deals. That's quite normal, in this business.'

'But he's not an antiques dealer.'

'No, but the sort of people he does business with generally have a high standard of living. You would expect them to own the odd antique.'

'Have you ever met any of these people?'

'His customers? No. I've only met his friends.'

'Is this one of them?' He produced a black-and-white photograph and slid it across the table. Sally looked at it.

'I don't think so.'

'Are you sure?'

There was something familiar about the features of the man in the photograph, but she couldn't quite place him.

'I think so.'

'I'd like you to be sure.'

She looked at the blunt, almost brutish face more closely. 'I really can't be certain, but I don't think I've ever met him.'

The officer took the photograph back. 'Now, when Mr Wiseman brings you something for your shop, does he just give it to you or does he ask you to pay for it?'

'I don't pay him on the spot. We have a kind of private arrangement. I try to find out what the piece is worth, then I put it in the shop. If and when I sell it, we split the profits.'

'You say that you find out what the piece is worth?'

'That's right.'

'He doesn't tell you what he thinks it's worth.'

'No.'

'Doesn't he say what he paid for it himself?'

'No. Usually, you see, he'll have picked it up as part of another deal.'

'Could you explain what you mean?'

'I mean that he might agree to buy something part cash and part something else. The something else might be anything, a box of spares, some special equipment . . .'

'Or an antique?'

'Well, sometimes, yes.' Sally felt as she was explaining it that she was digging herself into a hole. 'It may sound unorthodox, but it's quite common for dealers to say, "I'll give you two grand and that sofa for X," or "I'll take that cabinet off you for fifteen hundred, if you throw in Y as well." '

'I see. So you're quite happy that this is the way in which Mr Wiseman buys the things which he later gives you to sell in your shop?'

'Yes . . . why?'

'I think that'll do for the moment, miss,' said the officer. 'This interview concluded at eighteen-fifteen,' he added towards the tape recorder, before clicking it off.

'What happens now?' asked Sally.

'You'll be taken to the cells so that you can have a rest.'

'You mean I'm going to be locked up?'

'Just for a short while. I'll get somebody to bring you refreshments.'

'But what are you keeping me for?'

'We may need to question you again later. If you'll come with me, please.'

The hour in the cell seemed to tick by in leaden seconds. Between bouts of awful upset and anger, Sally went over and over the interview she'd just given, hoping that she hadn't made replies that would get her into any more trouble than she was already in. She gave up pacing around the room after a while and sat on the bed. It was hard, and the rough blanket that had been thrown over it irritated the backs of her thighs. She fidgeted uncomfortably as she tried to collect her thoughts.

It's obviously that ruddy vase, she told herself, why else would the one with the moustache have taken such an interest in it? Why else would he have tried to find out who I bought it from?

The questions she'd taken as impertinent in the shop began to make sense in the context of the events that had overtaken her.

Okay, so it's the vase and they think it's stolen . . . well, I suppose it must be stolen, if they've gone as far as charging me with receiving. But I didn't know it was stolen, and clearly Daniel didn't know it was stolen, so I guess that as soon as they've established that to their satisfaction, everything should be all right.

She wondered briefly whether taking something that you didn't know had been stolen made you just as guilty as if you did know. Wasn't there a line that went: 'No knowledge of the law is no excuse'?

I don't believe that a British judge would send you down for theft on that basis. She had just managed to console herself with that thought when she suddenly realised that if she'd been arrested on suspicion, they might by now have gone off to arrest Daniel on the same charge.

Hang on a minute, though, they haven't asked about the vase yet. She went over the interview that she'd given again, just to make certain. Thank heavens for that. I might have dropped Daniel right in it. She felt relieved that he was out of it. Her own predicament was bad enough, without him being dragged into it. Anyhow, they couldn't arrest him even if I did tell them about the vase, could they? He's gone away. She wondered what would happen when he came back. Probably all be sorted out by that time, she thought. Least, I hope so . . .

She could hear the sound of feet approaching. They stopped outside the cell door and there was the rattle of keys.

The Custody Sergeant led her back to the interview room where a different plain-clothes policeman was waiting. She was about to take her position in the chair facing him when he looked up.

'Will you take her fingerprints, please, Sergeant?'

Sally felt her scalp prickle with fear. Before she had come to terms with the implications of the request, the Sergeant had already pressed her hand on to an ink pad, then on to some paper and offered her a cloth to clean herself with.

'What's this in aid of?' Sally asked, crossly.

'You are not obliged to say anything . . .' The plainclothes

384

man calmly recited the formal caution as he produced two new tape cassettes and put them into the machine.

'This is a second interview with Miss Sally Blythe at Brighton Central,' he said. 'I am Detective Inspector Graham Davies. The time is now nineteen-forty-five. Miss Blythe, you have been arrested on suspicion of receiving stolen goods. Your rights were explained to you when you arrived at the station. Did you understand those rights?'

'Yes.'

'Have you asked for a solicitor?'

'No.'

'Do you want one now?'

'I want to know exactly what I'm supposed to have done, first. I mean, why do you need my fingerprints?'

'Answer the question, please.'

'No, I don't want a solicitor.' She folded her arms, irritably.

'Do you have a job or profession, Miss Blythe?'

'You know very well I do.'

'If you'll just co-operate . . .'

'Very well, I am an antiques dealer with a shop in Middle Street presently occupied by two of your officers.'

He ignored the jibe. 'How does your business operate?'

'I buy and sell antiques, sometimes at auctions, sometimes privately, sometimes at the shop.'

'If you buy privately, what do you do?'

'I go to people's houses.'

'Do you know what they want to sell beforehand?'

'Yes, they'll have given me a description of sorts over the 'phone. If it sounds okay, I go over and take a look.'

'And sometimes buy.'

'If whatever it is is good enough.'

'Do you ever go anywhere without knowing what you might find there to buy?'

'No . . . well, that is, not any more. I used to do house

385

clearances. You never knew for certain what you'd turn up on one of these.'

'But you don't do that any more?'

'No.'

'Any particular reason?'

'I don't need to. I have enough business with auctions and private deals.'

'So you never go to somebody's house purely speculatively?'

'No.'

'Have you ever been to this house?' He pushed a photograph of a pretty Tudor building in front of her. She saw at once that it was Kirkby Mote.

'Yes,' she said, the astonishment showing on her face.

'Can you tell me when?'

'Some months ago . . . October, no, September, I think.'

'How many visits did you make?'

'Just the one. I spent a couple of hours looking around.'

'What did you go there for?'

'I went to take a note of items of interest.'

'Not to buy something specific?'

'No, just to look.'

'Speculatively, then?'

Sally blushed. She'd walked right into that one. 'It wasn't something that I'd set up for myself. I was asked to go there by a friend of mine.'

'And who might that friend be?'

'Another dealer. His name's Ken Rees and he's got a shop in Union Street.'

'You're saying that it was Ken Rees who arranged the visit?'

'Yes. He had intended to do the view himself, of course, but the date had been made in advance and when the time came, he found that it clashed with something else he had to go to.'

'So you went on his behalf.'

'Yes.'

'And did you find anything of interest?'

'There was a very good collection of antiques in the house. I made a note of the various items and reported back to Ken.'

'What kind of note?'

'A written note.'

'Where is that written note now?'

'Ken's still got it, I think.'

'What happened after that?'

'I left him to do whatever he was going to do about it and forgot about it.'

'You forgot about it?'

'Yes. I've told you. The visit wasn't something that I'd set up for myself, I was simply doing a friend a favour.'

'What did your friend do after you'd reported back to him, as you describe it?'

'He decided on the things that he might like to buy and then recontacted the owner of the house to talk over the possibilities.'

'Did Ken Rees go to Kirkby Mote subsequent to your visit?'

'Yes.'

'What happened there?'

'As far as I know, he arranged to buy certain pieces and to have them collected at a later date.'

'When was he due to have them collected.'

'I don't know. Some time this month, I think.'

'How often do you see Mr Rees?'

'Two or three times a week. It depends, really.'

'On what?'

'How busy he is and how busy I am.'

'What is the nature of your friendship?'

'We are colleagues.'

'That's all?'

387

'Yes. Look, I don't see the point . . .'

'When you see Ken Rees, what do you discuss?'

'Business, mostly. General trade chat.'

'Did you discuss what he was going to buy from Kirkby Mote?'

'He mentioned one or two items of furniture but he didn't go into detail. He hardly needed my opinion, after all.'

'What do you mean?'

'I mean he's been in the business for years. I'm a novice by comparison.'

'I see. Do you know of anyone who might have gone to Kirkby Mote besides you and Ken Rees?'

'Of course not. Why would I?'

There was a knock at the door. The Custody Sergeant came in with a piece of paper and put it in front of Detective Inspector Davies. He looked it over and nodded.

'Miss Blythe, there is a certain Japanese vase in your shop, black with a flower and bird motif. Can you tell me where it came from?'

'It was given to me by my boyfriend. I explained how he sometimes gives me things to the other officer.'

'It was given to you by Daniel Wiseman?'

'That's right.'

'Did he tell you where he got it from?'

'No.'

'And you didn't ask him?'

'I've already explained that he often comes across things that he thinks I might be able to sell during the course of his business.'

'Do you know Mr Wiseman's whereabouts.'

'Where he is now, you mean? No.'

'You're sure.'

'Yes, I'm sure. He 'phoned me earlier to say he was going abroad for a few days but he didn't say where to.'

'Didn't you want to know?'

'I don't need to know. If he says he has to go away on business, I take it that he has to go away on business.' Sally tried to look unruffled but even as she said it, she realised how crazy it sounded. *Why* hadn't she been more inquisitive? Why had she been so trusting?

'I see. I'd like to ask you again about the vase. Are you absolutely positive that it was Mr Wiseman who gave it to you?'

'Completely positive.'

'When did he give it to you?'

'I can't remember precisely. Sometime before Christmas.'

'A week? A month?'

'I've really no idea. It was very busy in the run up to Christmas and I didn't take particular note.'

'What did you do with the vase after Mr Wiseman gave it to you?'

'I put it in my safe whilst I did some research on it and afterwards I put it into my display cabinet.'

'What did you find out about the vase during your research?'

'That it was a good example from the Meiji period.'

'Nothing else?'

'There was nothing else to know. I just wanted to value it properly so that I didn't ask for the wrong price on it.'

'Was the vase in any way familiar to you?'

Sally wondered what he was driving at, and decided to answer cautiously, 'Only in as much as it was like other Oriental vases that I'd seen.'

'Where?'

'In books on the subject and, of course, houses that I've visited in the past year.'

'Did you see anything like it at Kirkby Mote?'

'There was a pair of Oriental vases there, but I seem to remember that they were Imari. A different style of thing

389

completely.' She was beginning to get the picture. 'Why? Has something happened?'

'Were you aware that there has been a burglary at Kirkby Mote?'

'Good God, no! When?'

'You didn't know?'

'Of course not.'

'One more thing. Did you ever discuss with anyone other than Ken Rees what you saw in Kirkby Mote?'

'Not discuss, exactly . . . I might have mentioned something about it to friends or family.'

'Did you mention it to Daniel Wiseman?'

'Yes, I think so.'

'In what sort of detail?'

'I can't remember.'

'Did you show him the notes you made on the day of your visit?'

'No, of course not. If I talked to him about it at all it would have been in general terms.'

'Are you in the habit of telling him about what you've been looking at in various places?'

'Yes, it's quite normal for us to talk over our day's work. It's just what any couple would do.'

'Very well. We'll finish the interview now. I will remind you that you have been arrested on suspicion of handling stolen goods. The charge still stands, but for the moment you will be released on police bail in your own recognisance. The Custody Sergeant will bring you a document to sign to that effect.'

'You mean I can go home?'

'Yes, but you must remember that you will be on police bail.'

'What does that mean?'

'It means that you will be asked to come back to the station in about a week, unless there are any further charges to be made in the meantime.'

'What further charges?'

'That depends on the results of our enquiries.'

Sally's initial elation suddenly went very flat. 'I wish I knew what this was all about.'

'You'll be released, now,' Davies reiterated calmly. 'The Sergeant will explain the terms and conditions but I must warn you that if you do not return here on the given date, you will be arrested forthwith and taken to court.'

24

'So that's the story, in all its gory detail.' Sally stared into the mug of cocoa in her hand. It was past midnight and she was groggy with exhaustion. Heather patted her knee, reassuringly.

'You poor darling, you must feel like you've just done five rounds with Frank Bruno.'

'I think five rounds with Frank Bruno would have been infinitely preferable, actually.'

'But the charge, as it stands, is "suspicion of handling stolen goods",' said Jack, who was pacing the floor, with his hands behind his back, 'so it looks as though the police have nothing more concrete to go on than the fact that they found the vase in your shop. On the other hand, they might know quite a lot more and just be biding their time.'

'That's enough, Jack, can't you see that she's beyond it?' Heather objected.

'I just want to get the issues clear,' he replied. 'Now, Sally, the vase was given to you by Daniel, but you're not sure when and you don't know where it came from originally?'

'No.'

'But there would seem to be a connection between it and

Kirkby Mote, going on the line the Detective Inspector was taking in his questioning.'

'Yes. I told him I didn't know there'd been a burglary there, but I don't think he believed me.'

'Do you think the vase might have come from Kirkby Mote?'

'It could have, I suppose, although I don't remember seeing it there. The place went on for ever and I only saw three of the rooms.'

'What about Ken? Might he have seen it when he was there?'

'Possibly, but I think he would have mentioned it. Anyway, as far as I know, he only went into the same part of the house as I did.'

'You're sure it wasn't in any of the rooms that you visited?'

'Yes . . . well, no, not completely. Oh, I don't know.'

'Jack, please!'

'It's important, Heather. The next time the police come calling, we want to be prepared for them.'

'I can't face the thought of going through that lot again,' Sally groaned. 'Oh, Jack, do you really think you can help me?'

'I'm sure I can. But I need to know what's likely to be thrown at you. Who knows what evidence might come up in court?'

'They haven't said they will be taking her to court yet,' said Heather.

'The point of making a formal charge is to give notice of the intention of bringing a case to court. Of course, the charge may yet be dropped for one reason or another. But we have to act on the assumption that it won't be. Tell me honestly, Sally, has there been anything in Daniel's behaviour to lead you to believe that he may be involved in anything that isn't entirely above board?'

'I can think of something,' put in Heather, darkly.

'What?' Sally recoiled.

'I wish you wouldn't interfere.' Jack's voice was suddenly sharp. 'Just think about it carefully,' he added more gently, towards Sally. 'Anything at all? Even the smallest thing?'

'Well, not really,' she answered, at length. 'He never tells me much about what he's doing.'

'Is there anything that you might have heard that has given you cause for concern? From his friends, for instance?'

'Nothing in particular. I don't like some of them, though.'

'Why not?'

'Don't know, really. Something in their attitude. Too smart by half.'

'In what way?'

'Well, a lot of them are kind of pushy and over-inquisitive. Seem to think that it's okay to want to know everything about me but get very guarded when I ask them about what they do. Then there's the other kind, City-slicker types who do nothing but bang on about corporate structure or this or that deal at Lloyd's.'

'I see. Not much to go on there.'

'But what about that friend of his that Ken told us about?' Heather asked, determined to stick her oar in whether Jack liked it or not.

'That's not relevant.

'Well, I think it is.'

'What are you on about?' Sally broke in. 'Ken hasn't said anything to me about a friend of Daniel's.'

'That's because he's got more sense,' said Jack. 'Really, Heather, rumour mongering won't get us anywhere.'

'You don't know. Look, Sal, there's something Ken told me that he hasn't told you, for whatever reason and that is that Daniel has connections with somebody Ken believes could be dealing in stolen antiques.'

'What?'

'He didn't say exactly what the connections were but he

was very worried that if what he'd heard was true, it might backfire on you some day. And if you ask me, that day's come.'

'Hang on, Heather. You're jumping to conclusions again,' Jack started, but Sally cut across him.

'When did he tell you this?'

'Months ago.'

'Well, why didn't somebody say something? I mean, here's me going around all wide-eyed and innocent while you lot are conducting what amounts to a conspiracy of silence. Terrific!'

'It's nothing of the sort. The only reason I didn't mention it before was because what Ken said was, well . . .'

'Inconclusive,' finished Jack, 'supposition based on supposition.' He shook his head. 'You're wasting everybody's time by bringing it up.'

'Ken must have thought there was something in it.' Sally had been feeling sorry about the row they'd had for some time. She could see now why he'd been so cagey. If only she hadn't been so quick off the mark. If only she hadn't let her sensitivity over being a woman in a man's world get the better of her. She let out a moan and covered her face with her hands.

'Oh, darling, don't upset yourself any more.' Heather put her arm around Sally's shoulders. 'We're all worn out, I think.' She looked towards Jack and noticed the dark rings under his eyes. 'Let's let it rest for the moment, shall we? Things will look different in the morning.'

When morning dawned, things had started to look very different to Sally. But not in a positive way. Her head had been spinning all night with dreams that brought back the full drama of her arrest, leaving her feeling as drained as if she had had no sleep at all. Depression settled over her like a shroud and all attempts to fight it off proved futile. She wondered how she would get through the week ahead with the threat of re-arrest hanging over her. It seemed as if the situation was hopeless, as if there was nothing that she could do to influence events that had now been set in motion. The old spirit languished under the weight of this depression and for a long time she lay immobile, staring at a fixed point on the ceiling. The only sound she was aware of was the dull thud of her own heart.

Gradually, the mass of unresolved worries settled into some sort of shape, with the one she had been the most unwilling to face at the top of the pile: Daniel. Sally struggled to summon up all the courage she could and finally exposed her greatest fear. What if Daniel was really involved with people who were handling stolen antiques? What if he had involved her in the process of passing them on? She thought of all the things that he'd given her to sell over the months, of the casual way in which he would shrug off any reference to where they had come from, the way that he would act as if he had no knowledge of their value, despite having a name as one of the shrewdest operators around in his own business. It struck her at once that if any other dealer with his reputation had presented something to her in that way, her suspicions would have been aroused immediately. Yet for him, because of him, or more truthfully because of the way she felt about him, she'd ignored her instincts.

I've got to know, she told herself. I've got to find out whether I've been had or not. No matter how painful the revelation might be.

She turned over and picked up her watch. As she did so, she saw the note that Heather had left on the bedside table saying that she'd taken the children to school and would be back around midday.

The children! thought Sally, kicking herself for getting so bound up with feeling sorry for herself that she'd forgotten about the possible knock-on effects of her predicament. And what'll happen to them if I get thrown in the slammer?

396

What'll they tell the other kids about what's happened to Mummy? How will they feel when I've been branded a criminal?

She flung herself out of bed and started to dress, not caring that there were no fresh clothes or that the ones she was putting back on still carried the distinctive smell of the disinfectant that had been used to clean the police cells.

If I'm going down I'm going to take a few people with me, she decided. And if Daniel Wiseman has to be one of them, so be it.

The journey to Henfield was accomplished at remarkable speed. Sally's jaw set solid in an attitude of cold determination as she drove along. The idea of picking through Daniel's belongings whilst he was away would normally have offended her sense of decency. As things stood, though, it was a necessary evil. The sight of his house gave her an empty thrill today. Where so often she had turned up the driveway full of excitement at the thought of being in his arms, this time there was only a bleak indifference. She brought the car to a halt in the courtyard and sat brooding for a few moments, trying to work out the most efficient plan of action. There would be no trouble getting in. She had a key and knew how to disable the burglar alarm. The one glaring problem would be how to placate Nero. She'd never had to get past him on her own before and it was touch and go as to whether he'd lick her hand or lunge at her throat. The gamble struck her as one that she had no option but to risk. She swallowed hard against the fear of what he might do to her if he once got wind of her anxiety. There was only one point in her favour. Both she and the vehicle had been familiar enough to stop him from barking.

I either chance it or I go away, she thought, as she watched the dog pacing around the car with mounting unease. So what's it to be? Death or dishonour?

Sally held her breath and stepped out. To her immense

relief, she was still walking upright when she reached the kitchen door. Nevertheless, her hands were shaking so much that she had difficulty getting the key in the latch.

'Come on, boy,' she called, as cheerily as she could. And she went in and switched off the alarm.

Calmer, now, Sally opened a tin of dog food and scraped it out. Nero sat watching her patiently, waiting for his command.

'Here you are,' she said, 'a nice bowl of chow to keep you occupied.' But she was cautious enough to let him get well stuck in before she turned and headed off into the living room.

It's all very tidy for somewhere left in a hurry, she thought, lingering a while to see if anything was noticeably different. The Sunday papers stood neatly stacked in their usual place, to one side of the settee. The coffee table books, glossy and impressive, were turned at their usual angle. Sally glanced around and began to wonder whether the stress of the previous day hadn't addled her brains. There was nothing odd about what she saw at all, except that she would have expected the room to look a little more lived in. That it wasn't was hardly a sin. She went out into the hall. Her original intention had been to see what she could find in Daniel's office. Now, though, she felt inclined to go upstairs to his bedroom first. There was no explanation as to why she felt that way, and for a moment she hovered at the foot of the stairs, telling herself she was being silly. Finally, she went up, hating herself with every step she took.

The bedroom, at least, was a fair scene of devastation. Sally was comforted, for once, by the sight of towels littering the floor. Daniel had the habit of dropping them where he stood just as soon as he'd finished rubbing himself down. She looked at them and allowed herself a knowing smile. For all the times this practice had irritated her in the past, there was some consolation in it, now. It reminded her of happier mornings, of the intimacy that had built up between them. Surely that was more important than some half-baked notion that she'd cooked up in a fit of trauma?

Sally felt a pang of remorse for what she was doing. The breach of trust seemed the more unforgiveable to her in this, the room where all their secrets had been shared. She glanced towards the bed, thinking of the passion that had so often left it looking as it did at this moment. The pillows disordered. The linen thrown back into a crumpled heap. She walked up and stroked the sheet on his side, thought-fully. What had he done to deserve her anger, after all? Nothing. It was all a stupid mix up over some stupid vase.

'Oh, darling,' she whispered, wishing she could hold him, wishing that he could be there to tell her that everything would be okay. She pressed her face against one of the pillows, in the way that she would after he'd just left her side, hoping to catch a trace of his scent on the cotton slip. But instead of his smell, there was another. A hint of perfume that was different to any that she wore.

The feeling of dread which possessed Sally in that instant was worse than anything that she had been prepared for. Incredulous, she lifted her head. It couldn't be! She had slept in this place herself the night before last. There hadn't been the opportunity for anything else to happen between that and his leaving the country. Unless he had stayed on after he was meant to have gone.

In a sudden frenzy, she started opening and closing drawers. The cabinets that stood at either side of the bed, the chest-of-drawers, the cupboards in the en-suite bathroom, all were searched for clues, but clues of a different kind to the ones she'd been looking for before. She had arrived with one quest, only to find herself on a different mission entirely. The absurdity of the situation was mostly lost on her as she gave way to the worst excesses of jealousy.

The bedroom search proved fruitless. Panting and

399

frustrated, Sally went back downstairs and into the living room. She looked round again. There had to be something. But still nothing offered itself to help confirm her fears. She stalked off towards the office and pushed open the door. There had been a very significant change, here. The piles of paper that Daniel always filed on the floor had been cleared away. The boxes that were normally lying around were missing. She tried the filing cabinet. It was locked.

For a minute or so, Sally stood there fuming. Then she noticed the digital display on the answerphone that stood in the centre of Daniel's newly neatened desk. There were four messages. She toyed with the idea of playing them back.

If only the blasted things didn't wind back to the start after you've collected the messages, she thought, if anyone else rings, these'll just get recorded over. And he's bound to find out about the missing messages when he gets back.

She cursed the technology that wouldn't allow her to pry any further. Then she thought of another way.

Could always take the tape out and play it on the stereo. She slid the cover back. Damn, it's a micro cassette. Just as she was about to abandon hope, she realised that there was yet another possibility. Above the tape was a plastic sticker giving two different security codes. There was nothing to indicate which one had been selected.

'Must be some way of telling,' Sally murmured. She turned the telephone from one side to the other. 'Ah ha!' There was a switch marked 'Remote Code 2/Code 1/voice'. She clicked it carefully between the three positions to check which one it had been set to.

'Code two.' She put the 'phone down, grabbed a pen and wrote the number given for that code on the back of her hand. There's more than one way of skinning a cat, she thought, smugly, as she slid the cover back over the tape cassette.

The feeling of having made some progress gave Sally a

fresh idea. She knew that if Daniel was going to fly any-where, he'd have had to fax a flight plan to the Civil Aviation Authority first. She clicked up the cover of the fax machine and punched a button. Slowly, a sheet of flimsy paper emerged with twenty lines of print: the dates, transmission times and telephone numbers of the last bunch of messages sent.

'How very handy,' she said to herself as she quickly scan-ned the information, 'and here's what we needed to know . . .'

The final transmission, to the number she recognised as the CAA, had been sent at 7.30 that very morning.

So he was here all the time. The realisation settled the issue of whether she'd been right about smelling perfume in the bedroom or not. He had lied to her. Simple as that. She wondered how long the floosie who he'd spent the night with had been around.

'Bastard!' She stormed out of the office. It was even more vital that she knew what messages were on the answering machine now. Back in the kitchen, she made straight for her handbag. When she'd first come in, she'd just plonked it down on the nearest available work surface. What she hadn't noticed, in her haste, was that there was a paperback book lying close by. It was James Joyce's *Ulysses*.

The note! Suddenly, she remembered the scrap of paper that she'd found in the bin some weeks before. She extended a hand and gingerly opened the front cover. There, in the same strikingly familiar writing, was the legend: 'To darling Daniel. As always, it has to be the last page. Julia'.

'What?' The exclamation came out of Sally's mouth with such force that it set Nero barking.

'Shut up!' she yelled. Then added to herself in lower tones, 'No . . . no . . . let's not get silly here. There must be hundreds of Julias in Brighton.'

She flipped the book over and glanced at the last page.

The famous sex scene came back to her within a couple of lines, but the rhythm and metre, the play on the word 'yes', that had given her her first naughty thrill when she'd read it surreptitiously at the age of fifteen, palled with this reading. She closed the book sadly and pushed it away.

'Oh, my God.' Suddenly, she felt sick and giddy. She gripped the work surface to steady herself. How much more pain? As if it wasn't enough to have lost one man to another woman. But this!

The wounds that she'd suffered in the divorce opened again and a rage against all those hurts rose out of her distress. She wanted to smash something, to scream, to cry, but the same awful numbness that had gripped her after her arrest settled over her again. All she could do was stare bleakly at the book that Julia had given him.

'You were my best friend. My best bloody friend.' Her voice cracked as she thought of all the things they'd shared over the years. They'd been inseparable since the day they'd started school! How could she have double-crossed Sally like this? How could he?

'It's such a waste.' She'd started shaking. 'Such a fucking, bloody waste.'

She grabbed up her bag violently and headed for the door. The sudden movement put Nero on his guard. He jumped into her path and started growling, meanly.

Jesus, I'd forgotten about you. Sally eyed the dog and tried to calculate whether he'd really go for her. Judging by the curl of his lip, she decided he definitely would. Daniel always said that once he'd let you in, he'd never let you out again. What do I do now?

She stood frozen to the spot while she attempted to think up a plan. There had to be some trick. Some command that would get the dog to move. Daniel obviously had no trouble with him.

Sally tried to remember the house-quitting routine that Daniel used. She stepped forward.

'Out!' she cried, raising an arm and pointing. But that didn't work. The dog snarled and shifted his stance, in readiness to pounce.

'Get out!' she shouted, panicking rather. That didn't work either.

The alarm, she remembered, now. Daniel always did that first. Offering a silent prayer, she walked purposefully across the room and pressed the code number on to the key pad. The alarm started bleeping its warning that it was about to set. As soon as he heard the pips, Nero let his shoulders relax.

'Come on,' said Sally and opened the door. The dog skipped out into the yard ahead of her. She stepped out after him quickly and turned the key in the latch.

'Wherever you are, God, I owe you one,' Sally muttered. And she got out of there. Fast.

Jacob's Cottage seemed different, somehow. Sally looked at the pretty patchwork of its half-timbered walls and wondered why. She had the most curious sensation of having been away for a very long time, yet no more than forty-eight hours had gone by since she'd left it. The sensation stayed with her until she got indoors. Then, the kind of tearful relief that welled up inside her jogged her memory. The last time she'd felt this way was when she'd brought Jonathan home as a newborn baby. She'd realised then that the trauma of the birth coupled with being shut up in a strange room at the hospital for so long had altered her picture of the world. Everything had looked familiar and unfamiliar at the same time. Her harrowing experience at the police station, was reproducing the same effect.

It feels tarnished now, she thought, my lovely little house, my sanctuary spoiled by his having been here.

Resentment at Daniel's betrayal flared up again. Sally took a remote control from her handbag and walked towards the 'phone. She dialled Daniel's number and held the control over the mouthpiece. When the recorded message had run through, she tapped out the two-digit code number she had written on her hand then pressed 'Play'. Her heartbeat increased as she heard the tape wind back.

'Hello, mate. Nigel here. Found an Aston Martin DB23 convertible you'll be interested in. Give us a ring.' *Beep!* The end-of-message signal was so loud that Sally had to move her ear away from the 'phone for a second.

'Daniel, darling. Away again? Naughty boy. Harry and I are having a little supper party on the eighteenth. Do call back and say that you can come.' *Beep!* Sally moved the receiver quick enough that time. She waited for the next message.

'Hello, it's me.' The voice of her best friend was all too recognisable. A sickening cramp gripped Sally's stomach as the message played on. 'Just so stunned with the brooch that I had to say thanks again. See you when you're back.'

The signal went once more but Sally was so shocked that she hardly noticed it. The last call on the tape began.

'Daniel? Oliver Mason. Look, I'm still having trouble with the Comanche. It's the electrics, as usual. Meant to be taking Julia to France next weekend so really need to have it looked at pronto. Call me at home, can you? The Kent number.'

Sally slowly lowered the 'phone. So that was the connection. She could see now that it must have been all too easy for Julia and Daniel. They would have met often enough when her boyfriend was buying the 'plane.

Suddenly, everything that Julia had said about hedging her bets by having the odd fling fell into place. You two-faced cow, Sally thought, livid that she'd been played for a fool for so long, all that time you were asking me about how things were going with Daniel, you were doing your best to drive us apart!

Sally slammed out of the house in a fit of fury. Driving up to Brighton, all she could think about was how she was going to decimate the woman who had been her best friend. It didn't occur to her that Julia might not be around to be decimated. She was determined to get her, come what may.

Half-an-hour circling around for a parking spot did not improve Sally's temper. Finally finding a place near the sea front, she stalked off through The Lanes towards her shop. As she crossed Ship Street and turned into Dukes Lane, she saw that there was a crowd ahead of her. The closer she got to it, the more aware she became of the smell of smoke.

'Don't go any further. There's nothing you can do.' A kindly hand came to rest on her shoulder and she knew at once that it was Ken's. Sally turned and then gasped. The fresh stitches that had been put into his face made his mouth look twisted.

'Don't worry,' he said, 'you should see the other fella.'

'What happened?'

'I'll tell you later. I think you'd better come and have a drink.'

'I don't want a drink . . .' Sally looked back towards the crowd. 'What's going on up there?'

'Drink first. Explanation after.'

It was a short walk to the shop in Union Street. Ken led her inside and made her sit down.

'Here,' he said, producing a brandy bottle from the drawer of his desk and pouring out a large glass, 'get some Dutch courage inside you.'

Sally took a sip.

'No. Have a good slug.'

'Why?'

'Because you're going to need it.'

'Oh, come on.'

'Will you do as I ask, for once?'

She flushed. She knew that she deserved a damned good lecture for what she'd done. 'There . . . look, I'm really sorry about the other day. I had no right to tear in to you like that. I was mortified afterwards. Please say you'll forgive me? I can't bear there to be bad feelings between us.'

'I forgive you,' he said, though he was still hurt. 'But don't let it happen again.'

'I won't. I promise.'

'Okay. Now hold tight and don't faint on me . . . it's the shop. Your shop. There's been a blaze.'

'What?' Sally leapt up and rushed to the door.

'There's no point in that,' said Ken, going up and pulling her away, 'they'll let us know the worst when it's over.'

'How? I mean . . . oh!' Her knees started to give and she had to cling to his arm.

'Here.' Ken manoeuvred her back into the chair. 'I don't know how it started. Went up at about six this morning. The fire brigade couldn't trace you so they got on to me, being a key holder and all that.'

'Is it . . . very bad?'

'Looks like it. They had a terrific struggle getting the flames under control. These old buildings go up like a tinder box.'

'Oh my God.' Sally sank down in the chair.

'I'm sorry, love. After all you've been through, too.' He gripped her hand. 'I heard the news.'

'Did you?'

'Heather told me. She 'phoned at lunchtime to ask if I'd seen you.'

'She must have wondered where I'd gone.'

'Well, she was a bit concerned. Where were you?'

'Out snooping.'

'Oh?'

406

'I think you were right about Daniel. I went to his place this morning. Found out more than I'd bargained for.'

'What?'

'That he's been having an affair with my best friend, for one thing.'

Ken was truly shocked. 'The miserable . . .'

'Bastard,' Sally cut in. 'Yeah, great, isn't it? Never rains but it pours.'

'Have another brandy.' Her hands were shaking and he had to hold her glass still.

'Look, what was it you heard about Daniel exactly? Heather said something about shady contacts but she didn't seem to know much more.'

'I was most of the way to finding out more myself when this happened,' Ken pointed to the gash on his face, 'obviously got too close for comfort.'

'Who was it?'

'Couple of charmers who leapt out on me when I was going home last night. Thought I was being mugged at first. Later, I figured it had to be a warning.'

'Why? I mean, what do you know?'

'The name of one of the main movers in an antiques smuggling ring.'

'Who?'

'Nice fellow, he is. Got a sideline in hurting little boys for sexual kicks.'

Sally grimaced.

'I'm not sure yet what your friend Daniel's involvement is, but I do know that he set up a date for the pervert. You remember Sandy, the artist who was at Tony and Jon's party?'

'The one who wanted to paint me?'

'That's him. He had this boyfriend, see, a teenager, and the kid wanted a flashy car. Sandy introduced him to Daniel, who later introduced him to a friend. The friend turned out to be our smuggler.'

'Wait a minute. You're saying that Daniel set up the introduction?'

''Fraid so.'

'Jesus.'

'It's okay. He's not a closet gay. Like I said, his reputation is impressively heterosexual.'

'I've learned that to my cost,' Sally gulped. She could feel her control slipping again. 'But how did you find out about all this?'

'Tony told me. He got the dish from Sandy. Later on, I came up with another part of the story and had him track the boy down for me so that I could ask him some questions.'

'So what's going on?'

'The only thing I know for sure is that the smuggler, a man called Grimsditch, aptly enough, had hold of some property that came from a burglary at a stately home. I'm pretty certain that he was connected with the appearance of a table and chairs from Kirkby Mote at Derek Jones's warehouse too.'

'What? Which table and chairs?'

'The ones that were in the great chamber. It was definitely them. I recognised them from the cypher on the underside.'

'Yes, I remember. I did a drawing in my notes.'

'Of course, the furniture'd disappeared again by the time the police went round there,' Ken continued, 'so they haven't been able to stick anything on anybody yet.'

'Except me.' Sally's eyes narrowed. 'Ken, that table and chairs aren't the only things from Kirkby Mote to turn up in Brighton.'

'They aren't?'

'No. When the police picked me up on suspicion of handling stolen goods, it was because of a vase that was in my shop.'

'Ah, yes, Heather did say something vague about a vase.'

'It was a vase that was given to me by Daniel. I didn't realise before because it wasn't something that I wrote down at the time, but I'm certain now that it was in Kirkby Mote. Not in one of the rooms that I was shown formally but the room that Mrs Lyall-Bourke was in when I met her.'

'You're sure?'

'Yes. I thought it was a bit familiar when I was given it but you know how it is. You see so much stuff in a week you can't remember all of it.'

'Have you told the police?'

'I told them about Daniel but not about remembering seeing the vase. It was their linking the vase and Kirkby Mote that got me thinking about it.'

Ken looked at her seriously. 'You know that Mrs Lyall-Bourke and her butler were beaten up during the raid? That the old girl had a stroke and might even die?'

Sally shook her head. 'That's terrible.'

'It gets worse. You realise what'll happen if she does die, don't you?'

'No.'

'This'll turn into a murder investigation, that's what.'

'But . . . oh, Ken, you don't think that Daniel might have been involved in the actual burglary, do you?'

'I've no idea. But if he was, I hope they bang him up for a good long time.'

'What shall we do?'

'I vote that we pool our resources and go and tell the police everything that we know. Unless you've got any better ideas.'

'No. But there's one thing I've got to do first.'

'What's that?'

'Deal with some unfinished business.'

It was easy to find out where she'd gone to lunch. There was a temp on the reception desk and she was too busy filing her nails to worry about whether she should have divulged the information or not.

'They're all at that Italian place near the theatre. *Il Duomo*, I think it's called.' She gave a loud tut as the 'phone started to ring. 'Good afternoon, Backhouse, Fry? No, I'm afraid he's out at the moment . . .'

Sally left Julia's office and headed off towards the Theatre Royal. She had no idea how she was going to handle the confrontation that she had in mind. All she knew was that it was going to be pretty spectacular. She crossed North Street and turned into New Road. When she reached the restaurant, she could see that there was a drinks party in full swing. The sign on the door read 'Closed', but she walked straight in anyway. A bossy-looking maître d' came forward.

'Hello,' she smiled confidently, 'Sally Blythe of Backhouse, Fry. Hope I haven't missed much? Been stuck in court all morning.'

His frown was readily converted into an understanding beam. 'Welcome, *Signorina*. Franco, a glass of wine for the lady.'

Sally picked up a glass from the tray that was hastily offered and moved into the crowd. Before long, she spied Julia, dressed formally for a change, deep in animated conversation with two of her colleagues. Sally watched her for a moment, her anger so intense that she had trouble keeping the wine from spilling from her shaking glass. She moved forward, every swear word in her vocabulary on the tip of her tongue. Julia looked up as she came closer. Her face was a picture to behold.

'What are you . . .?'

Sally had stopped suddenly. There was a brooch pinned to Julia's jacket. A most unusual brooch.

'Well, well,' she said coldly, 'I see that you've been handling stolen goods in more ways than one.'

410

'I say!' blustered one of the men, and stepped sideways.

'She's talking nonsense. Someone get her out of here. Waiter!'

'A present from your lover, no doubt?' Sally continued, and jerked forward Julia's lapel. 'Cupid and a unicorn. How sweet.'

'Leave me alone . . .'

'Gladly.' Sally let go. 'Gentlemen, you are my witnesses. Have a good look at that brooch. You'll need to be able to describe it later.'

'Who is this woman? What's this about, Julia?' A senior partner had heard the raised voices and moved up to find out what was going on.

'It's nothing . . . just a mistake.'

'No,' said Sally, 'there's no mistake.' She rounded on Julia. 'Did he tell you where he got that brooch? Did he? Or were you too busy fucking each other's brains out to care that an old lady might just die because of it?'

'Look here . . .' started the senior partner.

'No, *you* look here. The brooch that your friend there is wearing was part of the loot taken in a robbery. A very violent robbery. Two people are in hospital as a result. You're a lawyer. I don't need to tell you about the Theft Act. Do you seriously want somebody in your firm who may be connected with aggravated burglary?'

'Is this true, Julia?'

'She's utterly mad,' she replied, calmly. 'The brooch was a gift. There's no more to it than that.'

'Try telling that to the judge,' sneered Sally.

'Young lady, I'm afraid I have to ask you to leave.' The maître d' had arrived to investigate the commotion. Now he came up and took Sally by the arm.

'It's all right. I'm going.' Sally began to turn, then looked back. 'Oh, by the way . . .' she said, and tossed the contents of her glass into Julia's face. 'That's for old times' sake.'

25

'Well, this just about puts the tin lid on it.' Sally threw the letter down on the kitchen table. 'Might as well jump off the pier whilst the going's good.'

'What is it now?' Heather shooed the children upstairs and shut the interconnecting door. 'More problems with the insurers?'

'The insurance problems are nothing compared to this. Look.' She shoved the letter under her step-mother's nose. 'Wipe out. Finish. Good night Vienna.'

Heather gasped. 'But they can't. Surely not? Don't they know that there's been a fire?'

'Oh, they know all right. Told them about it within a couple of days. Didn't make any difference.' She put on the funny nasal voice that she equated with officialdom: ' "I'm very sorry, Miss Blythe, but without your stockbook, we will have to make an assessment." '

'But you did do a new stockbook.'

'Yeah, but it went up in flames, along with everything else. And there's no such thing as a third chance with the VAT man.'

'Twenty-two thousand pounds . . . oh, sweetheart!'

Sally had wandered over to the cork notice board that

hung near the door. 'About time you came down,' she said, unpinning the old cartoon that she'd stuck there. 'I'm suffering from serious sense of humour failure.' She looked at the cartoon one last time then screwed it up and threw it in the bin. 'Used to make jokes about that. "God's finger's on the SMITE button," I used to say. Huh! Don't think it's been anywhere else for the past two years.'

'How long have you known about this?'

'Quite a while. That is, I knew they were going to make an assessment. I didn't know how much for.'

'Why didn't you say something?'

'What was there to say? Anyway, there was enough going on at the time, what with Jack down at the police station trying to get the charge against me dropped, and you, me and Ken trying to salvage what we could from the wreckage of the shop. The grand catalogue of disasters was long enough, without adding another to the list.'

Heather put an arm around her and gave her a hug. 'Wish there was something that I could say to make things better.'

'So do I. I don't know, I'm so numb from all this that I can't even have a good cry. There isn't a tear left in me.' Sally went to the sink and started to fill the kettle. 'You wouldn't think that something as innocent as this could be the cause of a major catastrophe, would you?' she said, holding the kettle up in front of herself for a moment. Daniel always said that the electrical wiring was dangerous, she thought. The sudden reminder of him made her stiff. 'Of course, I would never have left it plugged in normally,' she added, hastily, 'but what with the police coming and taking me away . . . ah, well. It's no use saying "if only" now.'

'I know it's too late for recriminations, but I do wish that you'd been properly insured. At least you'd have had something to build back up on.'

'Don't you think I've been kicking myself black-and-blue over that ever since the fire?' Sally slammed the kettle down.

'I'm sorry, darling.' Heather reached out and touched her arm. 'Didn't mean to rub it in.'

'Oh, it's all right.' Sally shrugged. 'It's just that the broker's given me enough speeches on the subject already. He says that I'm jolly lucky to be getting any money off the insurance company at all. There's something written into the contract to say that they don't have to cough up a penny if you've been underinsured.'

'What will you get back?'

'Sweet Fanny Adams. Apparently, the formula is that you only get a percentage of the sum you insured for anyway. They take the view that if your goods were insured for, let's say, half of what they were worth, you have taken the responsibility for the other half. In other words, you've effectively had two insurers, the company and yourself. So if a disaster occurs, they're only liable for fifty per cent of the original sum insured. You have to cover for the other fifty per cent yourself.'

'Talk about a "heads I win, tails you lose" situation,' said Heather. 'They really make sure they hang on to their money, don't they?'

'Oh, it's marvellous what they hide in the small print. They've got you every which way. I think if people really knew the ins and outs, they'd never bother to insure anything.' Sally poured the tea, morosely. 'Do you remember when we were cleaning up the shop all that time back and we sat on the floor and toasted the good ship Sally Blythe? It all looked so promising, then. Who would have guessed that it'd all go wrong so soon? I hadn't even been in there a year . . .'

'But you did so well,' said Heather, searching around for something encouraging to say. 'You could do it all again, you know. You really could.'

'What? Go back and start all over again? You have to be

414

kidding. No, I've had it, I'm finished. Chucking the towel in.'

'You can't just give up.'

'Can't I?' Sally cut in. 'Just watch me.'

'But how will you live? What about the children?'

'I don't know. I'm all out of bright ideas. Guess we'll muddle through somehow.' Sally took her mug over to the table and picked up the letter from the VAT again, 'Twenty-two thousand pounds. Where the hell do you think I'll find that?' She laughed, suddenly. 'And there was me worrying about ending up in jail for handling stolen goods. I'll probably end up there anyway for non-payment of taxes. Do you think I'll go down for long?'

'Don't talk like that,' Heather hissed, 'you can't let things go that far. You've got to do something about it. For Pete's sake, Sally, don't just lie there bleeding and wounded. Get up and fight!'

'What with? The fight's been knocked out of me.' She stared into her mug, pessimistically. 'I've lost the lot. My shop, my livelihood, my best friend . . .' She wanted to add Daniel to the list, but she was still too hurt and disgusted by what had happened even to say his name.

'You've still got us. Me, Jack, the children . . . and Ken. He's been such a brick.'

'You've all been wonderful. Nobody could have had more support.'

'Well, then. Come on, cheer up. I'm sure that between us we can come up with some way of getting you back on your feet.'

'Heather, you're a sweetheart. But even you can't work miracles.' Sally managed a resigned sort of smile, 'Come here a minute and give me another hug . . . that's better.' She buried her head in Heather's waist. 'You know, there's only one good thing to have come out of this and that is that I've finally realised how much I love you. I think I always did,

415

but I haven't been very good at expressing it. I spent a lot of the time in the police cell thinking of my mother. And you know what? I couldn't bring an image of her to mind that wasn't somehow connected with you. You're her. You've been her for as long as I can remember and I was trying to push you away all the while, trying to make it not so. I'm sorry. I'm sorry for all the times I must have hurt you. I just wanted to tell you that.'

They were both close to tears.

'You're a bloody saint, do you know that?' said Sally, wiping a knuckle along the edge of her eye. 'The best Mum in the world.'

'You don't know how long I've waited to hear you say that.' Heather's voice was croaky with emotion. She clung on to Sally for a few moments, then added, 'I never had my own. But I'm glad I had you.'

'Glad I had you, too.' Sally glanced up, at last. 'Look at us. What a pair, eh? Sobbing away like a couple of schoolgirls.'

Heather laughed. 'What the hell? Having people who care about you is all that matters. The rest is just things.'

'You're right. Houses, shops, possessions. What's it all for, anyway?' Sally replied, but then her eye fell on the VAT letter again, and she stopped feeling quite so philosophical. 'Paying the bills, that's what,' she added, gloomily. 'Oh, let's take the kids out and forget about it for a while. I know, let's go to the fun fair. I could do with a good scream.'

'But it's so expensive.'

'So what? Order me a taxi to the bankruptcy court. If I'm going to go, I might as well go in style.'

She'd been hanging over the 'phone since late-morning waiting for it to ring. When it did, she grabbed so fast at the receiver that she almost pulled the thing off the table.

'Well, they've got him.' It was Jack's voice.

'Who have got whom?'

416

'The police. Daniel. He just calmly walked into Brighton Central and gave himself up.'

'Typical. Smooth sod,' snorted Sally. 'I hope they lock him up and throw the key away.'

'Ah, there's good news and not so good news on that front.'

'Go on.'

'The good news is that he did the decent thing and told them that you were completely innocent.'

'That was big of him.'

'Don't knock it.'

'So what's the not so good news?'

'He'll probably get off very lightly, if not altogether.'

'What?'

'You've got to admire his nerve, but from what I'm told, he's trying to make a deal to save his neck by turning Queen's Evidence.'

'I don't believe it! He's as guilty as hell.'

'Not quite. In fact, he's hardly more guilty than you were.'

'What do you mean?'

'I mean that there's still no evidence to prove that he did anything more than receive stolen goods.'

'Yes, but he did it knowingly, didn't he? I thought you said that everything turned on that.'

'What's to say that he did know?'

'He must have, mustn't he? I mean, he was obviously a big chum of the smuggler bloke, you know, what's his name? Grim . . .'

'Grimsditch. Yes. But being friends with a crook isn't enough. Unless there's concrete proof that he helped to plan or actually took part in the burglaries, there's not a lot the police can charge him with.'

'Can't they get him for being an accessory to the crime? Surely the fact that the vase that he passed off on me came from Kirkby Mote proves the connection? And what about the brooch he gave to Julia?'

'It's still not enough. Oh, she's been asked to leave the firm, by the way. It'll be tough for her to find another practice to take her on, too. Locally, anyway.'

'Good. Hope it hurts. But I still don't understand. How can there not be enough evidence? With what I knew and Ken knew, you'd have thought the case was watertight.'

'It's not as simple as that. If Daniel claims, which I'm sure he will, that his connection with Grimsditch was purely friendship and that anything he took from him was taken in good faith, he doesn't have a lot to fear.'

'But what about the information he was obviously passing on? It could only have been he who told Grimsditch and his mates what was in Kirkby Mote. Courtesy of me, I might add.'

'He could have given him the information unwittingly, couldn't he?'

'We both know that's ridiculous.'

'I'm quite serious. There wasn't a tape recorder in the room at the time, so we'll never know for sure what he told Grimsditch, will we? Nor yet, indeed, whether he told him anything at all.'

'God, it's bloody exasperating! Too frustrating for words. So what happens now?'

'The police will continue with their inquiries. I expect that whatever Daniel can tell them about Grimsditch will help them no end. But they still have to nail him with something specific. Once they track him down, that is.'

'I suppose the chances of that are pretty remote. Must be well out of the country by now.'

'Who knows? Anyway, all we can do is watch and wait. At least your name's completely cleared. That's the main thing.'

'I feel so sorry for Mrs Lyall-Bourke and her butler,

though. It doesn't seem fair that innocent people are lying in hospital after being mugged and burgled while the crooks who did it walk free.'

'I know, I know.' Jack sighed. 'It's at times like this that I always think about the Al Capone case, you know.'

'Why Capone?'

'Well, it's always amazed me that despite everything they knew, the police could never touch him. And yet there was stacks of evidence that he had people murdered by the dozen.'

'Wait a minute, though. Didn't he die in jail?'

'Quite right. But he wasn't in there for homicide.'

'What did they get him on, then?'

'Tax evasion. It's a hoot, isn't it?'

Sally groaned, 'Uh . . . thanks for reminding me.'

'Pardon?'

'Well, I'm the next one in clink for tax offence, aren't I?'

'Don't be silly. I've told you, the VAT people will give you time to pay.'

'It's going to take the rest of my life to pay that lot off. Twenty-two thousand, Jack. That's a lot of dough.'

'Better keep at it, then. How are things going, by the way? Making much progress?'

'I'm trying, but I hate going into the shop. I know that the damage could have been worse, but somehow I can't face it. I keep thinking about everything that was lost.'

'Chin up. It can all be replaced.'

'With what, may I ask?'

'Other things, of course.'

'But there isn't going to be enough capital. No, Jack. It's a nice idea but I can't work up any enthusiasm, given the circumstances.'

There was a pause. 'Listen, Sally. I didn't really want to get into this over the 'phone, but I've been thinking. There's a little nest egg I've got tucked away that I've been meaning to invest in a new venture. It'd have to be done properly, of course, but . . .'

'Oh, Jack, please don't. I can't bear the thought of taking money off family.'

'I'm not family, am I? And anyway, it wouldn't be taking, just borrowing.'

'You know what I mean.'

'Well, look. I know you're still upset about everything, but think it over, eh? The offer stands if ever you want to take it up.'

'Thanks.'

'I've got the greatest confidence in you, Sally. We all have. I know you're feeling battered and bruised right now, but you'll be okay once things have settled down a bit. Really you will.'

'I guess you're right,' she said. But she didn't believe it. For a long time she just sat there staring at her hands while she picked over the events of the previous few weeks. Of all the trials and traumas that she had suffered, the one that she couldn't get over was Daniel's betrayal. She couldn't understand why he'd done it, although she felt that Julia must have thrown herself at him. And there were very few men who could resist an offer like that.

Why am I still making excuses for him? she wondered, suddenly feeling angry at herself. He's responsible for his own actions, after all. But she had not learned to control the softer emotions that she felt for him, yet, and she knew it.

Oh, why did he have to come back now? she thought, allowing a proper picture of Daniel to form in her mind. Why did he have to come back at all? Why couldn't he just drop off the edge of the earth and leave me to grieve in peace?

'Because real life is not convenient.' The sound of her own voice echoed around the empty kitchen, startling her, rather. She shook her head. That's what Heather would say at a moment like this, and she'd be right. Real life was messy. Neat solutions were few and far between.

Another hour passed with Sally waiting by the 'phone, dejected and anxious by turns. When she couldn't stand the agony any longer, she picked it up and dialled Ken's in-car number. There was no reply.

'Oh, come on,' she grumbled, 'you must know by now.' She began pacing up and down the kitchen. I should have gone myself, she thought, why didn't I go myself? It can't have been worse than waiting around like this. She'd known all along that not going to the auction was an act of cowardice. For all the excuses she'd come up with, not one held much water. The simple truth was that she couldn't face another defeat.

She glanced at her watch. Damn. Going to have to go and pick the children up, soon. Oh, come on, Ken!

The silence was beginning to drive her crackers. She wondered whether she shouldn't just ring Phillips' and ask them what the lot number had sold for. But then she chickened out of that too.

What's wrong with me? she asked herself, crossly, though she knew perfectly well that she'd lost her nerve. Perhaps, as Ken had said, she should have plunged straight back into it, she should have been more sportsman-like and got back on to the horse that had just thrown her, despite almost breaking her neck. That's all very well, but I'm not feeling very sporting, she thought, looking at her watch again. Well, I can't hang around any longer.

She set off on the school run and completed the drive in a mechanical fashion. The first thing she did on her return was to check her 'phone for messages. In a way, she was more relieved than disappointed to find that there were none.

'Can we play outside, Mummy?' Jonathan tugged on the back of her coat that she hadn't got around to taking off.

421

'It's a bit cold and wet,' she said, 'why don't you watch the telly instead? The cartoons will be on now.'

'But we want to play football.'

'It's getting dark.'

'Please.'

'Oh, okay. But you'll have to put your wellingtons on.'

The children bounced off while Sally continued to shuffle aimlessly about the kitchen. She was still unsettled and found it difficult even to get her mind around the tea menu.

'Ring, blast you!' she shouted at the 'phone, as she looked towards it for the umpteenth time. It refused to obey. She snatched it up, angrily, and dialled Ken's number again.

'Hello?'

'Ken! Where are you?'

'Just coming down the lane.'

'Why didn't you ring?'

'Thought you'd prefer to hear it in person.'

'What happened?'

'Er . . . I'll be there in a second. Tell you then.'

The moment's hesitation set her panicking. It was obviously bad news. She dashed to the door. The headlights of Ken's car cast a bright beam up the drive. She watched them move slowly towards her with a rising sense of dread.

'Hooray, it's Ken!' The boys leapt on to him as he stepped out of the car. 'Did you bring us some sweeties?'

'Jonathan! Matthew!' Sally scolded, but she knew that the tradition was too well established for disapproval to have much impact. Ken pulled two packets out of his coat pocket and patted each child on the head.

'You'll ruin their tea,' she added, half-heartedly.

'They'll be all right. How are *you*?' he asked, gently.

'You tell me,' she said, accepting his chaste kiss.

'Got anything to drink?'

'There's half a bottle of wine in the fridge.'

'Crack it open, then.'

422

They moved into the kitchen.

'So what happened?' Sally hardly dared ask, but she had to face it some time.

'It was much as I thought, really.'

'Oh?' she took out two glasses as stoically as she could and prepared herself for the worst.

'Mmm. Pretty brisk trade, though a couple of the pieces were taken off for lack of bids.'

'Not my God stick?' Sally's eyes were wide with apprehension. 'They didn't pull the God stick, did they?'

'No,' Ken replied, and took the bottle of wine from her hand and poured it out.

'Oh, tell me. Tell me, I can't stand it any longer!'

'Well, you got more than you paid for it. What was it again? Three quid?'

'Yes . . . but . . . I know, they set the reserve too high, was that it? But I don't understand. The museum said that it was very, very rare.'

'Still only worth what someone's willing to pay for it.'

Sally nodded, sadly.

'Never mind.' He put an arm around her. 'You'll still be able to pay off a few debts.'

'Great. In one door and out the other.'

'It'll get the VAT man off your back.'

'Oh,' she brightened, 'so we got more than the eighteen grand, then?'

'Just a little.'

'How much? Twenty? Twenty-two?'

A grin was starting to spread over Ken's face.

'Are you teasing me?'

'*Moi*?' he said, in the way he did when he definitely was.

'Ken . . .'

'Just a moment.' He put down his wine and took off his glasses. 'Right, ready now?'

'Come on, you blighter, stop messing about.'

'Have another guess.'

'No.'

'Go on. If I'm going to get a sock in the jaw, it might as well be worth it.'

'I refuse to play,' she said, but the look on his face made it irresistible. 'Oh, all right then, one more. Twenty-five, and that's my best offer.'

'Nowhere near.'

'What then? What? What?'

He took a deep breath. 'Double.'

Sally dropped her glass.

'In fact, more than double. Fifty-one thousand to be exact. Minus one pound fifty for the glass, of course.'

There was silence, then an ear-splitting scream. When the children raced in from the garden, they found the two adults locked in a bear hug, laughing and sobbing at the same time.

'Ugh! They're kissing,' said Jonathan, and turned to his brother with a knowing frown. 'They'll have to get married now.'

Matthew looked puzzled. 'Then will we get sweeties every night?' he asked.

'Hope so. Come on, last one to the barn's a cissy.'